J.D. BARKER

SOMETHING
I KEEP
UPSTAIRS

A CHILLER

ALSO BY J.D. BARKER

Forsaken

She Has A Broken Thing Where Her Heart Should Be

A Caller's Game

Behind A Closed Door

4MK THRILLER SERIES

The Fourth Monkey

The Fifth To Die

The Sixth Wicked Child

WITH JAMES PATTERSON

The Coast to Coast Murders

The Noise

Death of the Black Widow

Confessions of the Dead

The Writer

WITH OTHERS

Dracul

Heavy Are The Stones

We Don't Talk About Emma

For Sam Reid.

The history you made is only surpassed by the history you preserved.

Something I Keep Upstairs
Published by:
Hampton Creek Press
P.O. Box 177
New Castle, NH 03854
Worldwide Print, Sales, and Distribution by Simon & Schuster

Copyright © 2025 by Jonathan Dylan Barker
Registration: 1-14115722171

Hampton Creek Press is a registered Trademark of Hampton Creek Publishing, LLC
For information about special discounts for bulk purchases, please contact Simon & Schuster Special Sales at 1-866-506-1949 or business@simonandschuster.com
Cover Design by Domanza
Book design and formatting by Domanza
Author photograph by Bill Peterson of Peterson Gallery
Manufactured in the United States of America
ISBN: 9798989265480 (HARDCOVER 6x9)
ISBN: 9798989265497 (PAPERBACK 5.25x8)
ISBN: 9798990746114 (EBOOK)

For a haunted house to be born, somebody has to die.

–Unknown

Names have been changed to protect the...

MY NAME IS Billy Hasler.

When I was a kid, my best friend's name was David Spivey. I haven't said that name aloud in nearly eleven years. It had been at least nine since I'd last written it down, and I have mixed feelings about putting it on paper here. I've been told I should, though, so there's that. They tell me it will be good for me, but I can't help but wonder if they really mean it will be good for them.

A lot of people want some kind of closure from me. Honestly, that's a big ask. I'm still waiting for my own closure to come.

I've been told that if I continue to keep all this to myself, bottled up inside, the pressure will build and one of these days I might just…

Kablooey.

Okay, that's silly, but that's what the doctors tell me.

That's what my mom tells me.

That's what my remaining friends tell me.

Most certainly the police. Their visits aren't as frequent as they used to be, but they still come around. Mundie gave up. Sandy Lomax has long since retired, but that's never stopped the latest fresh-faced officers on our small force from knocking on my door.

Hey, I read the file and I was wondering if you could spare a few minutes to talk about Chief Whaley, those kids…

I tell them enough to make them go away.

Just enough to understand that the sponge has been squeezed dry by many hands before them, and I have nothing left to give.

Even that little bit—a few words here, a few words there—it always feels like a betrayal. A betrayal to Matty, Izzie, Chloe, Kira, even Alesia, the pact we all made—but most of all, a betrayal to Spivey (everyone called him Spivey, even his mom, which I always found odd), because we'd been together the longest and that bond had been the toughest. It held out when the others began to snap.

I'd known Spivey since we were four years old. The two of us grew up on New Castle, a small island off the coast of Portsmouth in New Hampshire. There's a playground on the island commons, and if my mother is to be believed, she spotted another four-year-old boy out there one morning with his mother, and the two adults quickly paired us up. When you grow up on an island with a population of less than nine hundred, friend pickings are slim. We attended Maude H. Trefethen Elementary together—there were only eight others in our class and thirty-seven total students in the entire school. Our world expanded when we went on to Rye Middle and Portsmouth High. The latter two were over the bridge on the mainland; the first was about three hundred feet from my front door, and on warm days my mother would let me walk by myself, although I suspect she followed me in those earlier years.

Like many small coastal towns in New England, New Castle has a sordid history. Our house went up in 1923 and was considered one of the "new" homes. Most around us were built in the sixteen and seventeen hundreds, some earlier than that. Our local tourist draw, Fort Stark, saw its first of many remodels way back in 1808. The New Castle Inn has been sheltering visitors since 1698, and our local post office opened its doors on Main Street in the summer of 1864. The island started as a colony and served as a military stronghold during history's more turbulent times. In the quiet years between, it was a fishing village. Paul Revere once rode through here at the start of the American Revolution; there's a plaque about a mile from my house.

This place is older than dirt.

When you're a kid surrounded by history and nostalgia, you don't much appreciate it. Not really. No more than you realize what a blessing it is to have the ocean a stone's throw away or neighbors who know you by name, neighbors who wave every day rather than shirk their eyes to the ground and live in a bubble—I found those people on the streets of New York during the year I tried to leave this place after the horror of that particular summer. I suppose that's why I came back. Away from New Castle, I found myself in my own bubble, and I quickly learned I wasn't the best company. Not then. I needed people I knew, even if they all came at me with questions.

If Spivey and I had grown up anywhere else, I'm sure we wouldn't have been friends. I was good at sports (made the varsity football team at sixteen), never had trouble making friends, had a girlfriend by fifteen. Spivey spent a lot of time alone, comfortable in his own head. His favorite place was out on the rocks to the east of the Coast Guard jetty, just sitting out there facing the water, what we locals called the reach. Most days, he'd have his guitar with him—a beat-up Rickenbacker he'd found out in his shed when we were nine; nobody knew how it got there—and that was all the company he really needed. I'm not gonna pretend to know anything about music. I don't know a G chord from an F, but I know what sounds good, and Spivey always sounded good. He was one of those people who could hear a song once and pluck it out on his guitar as if he'd been playing the tune his entire life. He'd sing too, but not when anyone was around; you'd have to sneak up on him to catch any of that, but I'll be damned if he couldn't hold his own with those on the radio. My folks (my dad a real estate investor and mom a teacher) got along well enough. Spivey's dad was an alcoholic who worked on a local fishing boat, and his mother had a thing for pills. That might be the other reason he spent so much time out on those rocks. Spivey had a bubble, too.

You could see the house from those rocks.

White and black with a red roof on a little island about a quarter-mile off the coast of our bigger island, but I never gave it much thought. No more than I did the lighthouses further out or the edge of the Coast Guard station peeking out from the bend. I don't know if Spivey did, sitting out on those rocks. I guess he might have, but he didn't talk about it. He never once mentioned his grandmother lived out there. Not until the day our lives changed.

I wish to God he hadn't.

There are a lot of things I'd like to take back.

06/22/2010 - TUESDAY

1

I COULDN'T TELL you today's date without looking at a calendar, but Tuesday, June 22, 2010 might as well be tattooed on the back of my hand. Spivey and I were sitting in Mr. Hurley's algebra class, staring at the second hand on the clock above Hurley's blackboard. We had less than a week left in our junior year; finals were behind us (Spivey aced most of his, and I was fairly confident I'd pulled a B minus average for the quarter). Nobody wanted to be here, including Mr. Hurley, who had his feet up on his desk as he thumbed through an old edition of *Car and Driver*. Spivey was scribbling away in a notebook, and I was passing notes with my girlfriend, Kira Woodward—*I love you. I love you more, Billy Hasler. No, I love*—at the time, I had no idea if I really loved her, but I did enjoy getting laid, and that particular day she'd worn these cut-off jean shorts and a white tank top I had no trouble picturing on the floor of my Volvo— a 2004 hand-me-down from my mom when dad surprised her with a new BMW last Christmas.

Two rows behind me, Rory Moir was busy making paper footballs. About every minute or so, one would sail through the air in Spivey's general direction but come up short. Some days it was paper clips, others it was rubber bands. Spivey had perfected the art of ignoring the projectiles just as he had learned to shrug off the occasional trip in the hallway or the choice words Rory scratched into his locker any time the custodial staff decided to give them a fresh coat of paint. Rory had no particular reason not to like Spivey other than a personal desire to be a deft asshat, but he had zeroed in on him way back in middle school and had spent the last five years perfecting numerous methods of torture and torment.

Rory knew better than to actually hurt him. I had twenty pounds on Rory. Football practice kept me in shape, and he knew I'd step in if he crossed the imaginary boundary we'd established. That didn't mean he wouldn't test that boundary. I suppose I let him only because I was hoping for the day Spivey would step up and defend himself. After five years, that day had yet to materialize, so the three of us just assumed our usual roles.

Part of me felt bad for Rory; I guess I gave him a little slack, too. His mother had run off when he was only seven, leaving his father alone to raise him, and daddy was no prize. During his younger years, his father had spent just as much time inside Concord Correction as he had outside, and while he'd managed to stay on this side of the bars since taking custody of Rory, it wasn't for lack of trying. He'd been picked up numerous times for DUI and suspected of several B&E's, but none of them ever stuck. Part of that was luck, and the other part came from having three cousins on the Portsmouth police force willing to turn an eye or make a call or two whenever his name came up on the blotter. *Doing his best*, they'd say. *Single father. Tough to find work—fewer fishing boats around every year. Do you know anyone looking for a good deckhand? He can keep it together when he's got steady work. Particularly when that work takes him offshore, away from the Lobster Tail Tavern in town. Cut him a break. You know, for the kid.*

Rory launched another football, and this one hit Spivey's left foot. Dick.

He knew Spivey had leukemia (in remission now), and even that wasn't enough to get him to dial it back. I wanted to bean him with one of my textbooks. Spivey would be the first to tell you he didn't want anyone to treat him different because of that bullshit, but it still bothered me.

The knock at the door startled all of us, including Mr. Hurley, who damn near fell out of his chair getting his feet back on the ground. He straightened up when the door opened, and Principal Wilson gestured for him to step out into the hall. The rest of us straightened up when we spotted Chief Whaley standing behind him.

A police officer in school was never a good thing. For those of us who lived out on New Castle, seeing Whaley was a double whammy because he wouldn't make the trip into Portsmouth unless he was on island business.

When the door closed behind Hurley, I took quick stock of the faces in the classroom. Only five of us were from New Castle, and Mateo Fernandez (Matty to us) was looking particularly nervous. Chloe Kittle, too. Kira was staring at me, and if Spivey had bothered to look up at all, he'd quickly lost interest because he was busy with his notebook again, lost in what looked like an intricate drawing of a sock.

I turned back to Matty and raised my eyebrows. He gave me a shrug, flicked me off for good measure, and returned to watching the door.

It opened about a minute later, and Hurley looked back into the room. "Mr. Spivey? Go ahead and gather your things—step out here, please."

Twenty-seven pairs of eyes swiveled in unison and landed on my friend, followed by various *oohs* and *ahhs*. Someone started humming "Bad Boys" from that old cop show.

"You been diddling cats again, Spivey?" Rory asked.

This brought on several obligatory laughs, but wasn't the ballbuster he'd hoped for.

Spivey looked up from whatever he was drawing. "Am I coming back? Billy's my ride."

"Bet he is," Rory muttered.

The look I shot Rory's way shut him down before he could build on that particular dig.

Chief Whaley stepped into view again and found me in the room. "You too then, Mr. Hasler. Let's go now."

I felt a lump grow in my gut and started ticking off the various infractions I'd committed in recent memory. There were plenty, but nothing I could think of that would call for a show like this. In my seventeen years on the planet, I couldn't think of a single instance where a kid got pulled from class by the police. Whaley had stopped by my house once about a year ago after he'd heard a couple of us had been smoking pot up at the fort, but even then, he hadn't spoken to my parents, just gave me a quick scolding out in the driveway before heading back out on patrol.

I reminded myself this wasn't about me; this was about Spivey. Spivey never did anything wrong, and that meant something bad had happened.

As I gathered my backpack and followed after him, Kira held her thumb and forefinger up to her ear. *Call me.* The corner of her mouth curled up in a mischievous grin and this warmth rolled over me. I couldn't help but smile back. Yeah, maybe I did love her.

2

WITH A WARY look at Spivey, Mr. Hurley stepped back into the classroom, pulling the door closed behind him. Principal Wilson sidestepped and blocked the door's window so those inside could no longer see out, a move he'd perfected over the years.

Chief Whaley placed a hand on Spivey's shoulder. The chief had been the chief for as long as I could remember, an elected position he had no trouble securing year after year. He was a large man, about six-two, probably two-ten or so. He'd played football right here at Portsmouth High back in the eighties; several of the MVP trophies in the cabinet near the gym had his name on them. Wide receiver. He still held the record for most yards in a single season. He got a full ride to Plymouth State, I knew that much, but I don't know why or when he stopped playing. He'd gone a little soft over the years, but most of him was still muscle, not fat. His brown hair was gray at the temples and clipped short, but he didn't look much different from some of the old photos I'd seen.

Spivey tried to put up a strong front, but his lower lip was quivering. "Did something happen to my mom?" He blurted this out before the chief could speak.

Not two years ago, Spivey's mother had overdosed on fentanyl. He'd been the one to find her, slouched over in a recliner in their living room, soaking in her own piss, some talk show blaring on the television. Nine more pills were laid out in a neat row on the table beside her—on deck, ready to go—but the three she'd already swallowed had been enough since she'd chased them with Jack Daniels. He'd called 911, held her hand in the ambulance, and they'd pumped her stomach at the hospital, gave her a few shots and an IV with some magic mix of who-knows-what—she was talking as if nothing happened only a few hours later. His dad had been out at sea on a lobster boat, and when he got back, he seemed more concerned about the Jack missing from his bottle than he was about her. It hadn't been her first trip to the hospital. Spivey had found more pills hidden in the freezer, tossed those, scrubbed the recliner as best he could, and reset the room for the next time. Nobody was under any illusion there wouldn't be a next time.

I looked down at my shoes. If this was the conversation Spivey had been expecting, I really didn't want to witness it.

Chief Whaley lowered his voice. "Your folks aren't home, son. I stopped by your place before driving out here. Do you know where they are?"

Spivey shook his head.

"Your dad's around, though?"

"He's been going out on Milligan's boat the last few runs. They got back two days ago. I don't think they're going out again until Monday."

The chief and I exchanged a quick glance. We both knew what that meant for Spivey's dad. Most likely he was sleeping off last night on someone's couch. I could rattle off several contenders. I'm sure Whaley could too. If I had to guess, he probably checked a couple before heading to the school.

The chief shifted his large frame. "When was the last time you talked to your grandmother?"

"My grandmother?"

He nodded. "Geraldine Rote."

I thought I knew all there was to know about Spivey, but I'd never heard that name before.

"Who?"

"Geraldine Rote," he repeated. "Your mom's mom."

A puzzled look washed over Spivey's face. Then something clicked. "Oh geez, I was maybe eight the last time she came around. Thanksgiving. She stayed for like an hour, and it was all kinds of awkward. Nobody talked. I think she brought the food, though, because mom isn't a very good cook, and I still remember that turkey." He looked up at the chief. "That's her name? Geraldine?"

Chief Whaley considered this, seemed to choose his next words carefully. "Would you recognize her?"

Spivey looked over at me as if I held the answer. I just shrugged. Then he told the chief, "I don't know. Maybe. It's been a long time."

Principal Wilson, who had been silent through all this, decided it was time to weigh in. "What's going on, Chief?"

Whaley let out a shallow breath. "We got a woman dead over at Henry's Market. Came in at the tail end of lunch, ordered a cup of coffee and a bagel, and passed away at the table. The ME thinks it was a blood clot. Won't know for sure until the autopsy. Whatever it was, it was sudden. Looking out the window one moment, dead the next. No wallet or ID on her. Ralph Peck was in there when she passed and he thought it might be Geraldine, but wasn't sure. He hadn't seen her in a long time. Thinks so, though."

He reached for the phone in his back pocket and clicked through several screens. "If I show you a photo, can you tell me if you think it's her?"

Principal Wilson stiffened, and his lips went thin. "He's a minor, Chief. Maybe you should wait until you locate his mother."

Chief Whaley kept his eyes on Spivey. "If you don't want to, son, I understand."

Spivey gave him a nervous nod. "I'll be eighteen next month. It's okay, show me."

Principal Wilson looked like he might object again, but he said nothing.

The chief brought up his phone and held it between us.

I leaned in to get a better look.

The woman's eyes were thin slits behind silver wire-framed glasses. Her gray hair was long for an older woman, pulled back in a ponytail. And she was wearing a beige sweater. At the sight of her, two thoughts went through my head: First, I was looking at a real dead person. The second thought was probably similar to what Spivey was thinking—the drugs his mother had done, the harsh way she treated her body, had been hard on her and aged her prematurely. She looked far older than her thirty-seven years. The woman on the chief's phone must've led an opposite life, because she looked younger than she probably was. Swap out the gray hair for brown and take away the lines around her eyes and mouth, and the two of them could have been sisters. I had no doubt this was Spivey's grandmother, and judging by the way his mouth fell open, he didn't either.

Chief Whaley saw it too. He fumbled his phone back into his pocket and asked me, "Can you give him a ride back out to his place and call me when his mom turns up?"

I was about to respond when my own phone rang.

My dad.

I held up a finger and answered. "Hey, Pop, I—"

"I need you to come down to my office, right now. Put your teacher on the line if he gives you trouble about leaving early. Right now."

"Chief Whaley is here, and he asked me to—"

"Now. It's important."

Before I could reply, he was gone. And everyone was staring at me.

3

MY DAD'S REAL estate office was on the fourth floor of the Leland Building in downtown Portsmouth off Bow Street overlooking the Piscataqua River. I parked in the garage and took the elevator up. When the door slid open to the lobby, Ms. Atkinson looked up from her desk and smiled. "Hey, Billy."

Early forties, slim, dressed in a white blouse and gray pantsuit, she'd worked for my father for as long as I could remember. First in a little two-room hole off South Street, then the more spacious office across from Citizens Bank. They'd moved into Leland three years ago, after my father became more active in commercial properties.

"I've been summoned."

"He told me." She bobbed her head toward his open door behind her. "Go on in. He's waiting for you."

I found my dad standing at the large window at the back of his office, facing the water, phone pressed to his ear. I closed the door and eased into one of the leather chairs in front of his large mahogany desk as quietly as I could.

"… Do I need to speak with the building inspector? If the foundation meets code, I don't see how he can increase the load requirements on us. That's the reason there's a building code. Last I checked, we're not required to follow The Book of Chuck; we follow the code. If we need to drag Stew in and put a motion out to the zoning board, we could lose a couple weeks. Does he have any idea what that will cost us? There'd be layoffs. No way around that."

I could see his smiling reflection in the glass. He'd told me once, always smile on the phone. It didn't matter if the person you were speaking to couldn't see you, always smile and it would come across in your voice. That was clearly bullshit, because he sounded pissed.

"Try to talk to him yourself. He likes you. We can play nice for twenty-four hours. That's it. If you can't work this out by tomorrow, we need to move on a Plan B. We've got all our subcontractors lined up and ready to go. We've got maybe three days of wiggle room before the rest of the schedule starts to fall like dominoes. I don't know about you, but I don't want to clean that up. We might as well burn our profit. Call me back after you talk to him."

The hand holding the phone receiver went slack, and he looked out the window a moment longer before turning and returning it to the cradle. He took a deep breath and settled into his chair across from me, the smile never leaving his face. "And I thought today was going to be a quiet one. How are you holding up?"

I was about to tell him Spivey's estranged grandmother had passed away when I realized he already knew. I had no idea how he knew, but he did. Of course he did. His next words confirmed it.

"How's Spivey doing?"

"I… I don't know. He just heard right before you called me. Whaley gave him a ride home. How did you…?"

He waved a hand through the air. "I've got an ear to the ground, always. You know that. What about his folks? His mother?"

My dad grew up out on New Castle and went to school with Spivey's mother. Rumor was they'd dated their junior year, but he never talked about that. I'd also heard he blamed Spivey's father for her drug problem (she'd met him her senior year), but he never talked about that, either. I did know she passed on a full-boat scholarship to UNH at graduation, and I imagined the blame for that landed on Spivey's father's shoulders, too. Pops wasn't the only one with an ear to the ground.

He opened a desk drawer, took out one of his business cards, slid it across to me.

I looked at the card. "I know how to reach you, Dad."

"It's not for you, it's for Spivey."

"Spivey? Why?"

He didn't answer that, only looked at me with that smile on his face. I made no motion to pick up the card. "What do you know?"

He settled back in his chair. "I know Pamela and her husband are in no position to deal with what is coming. Do you know they took out a second mortgage on their house the last time Spivey got sick? They're scraping to get by every month. It's unfortunate, but it is what it is. What little money Keith pulls in on the fishing boats barely covers their taxes, medical bills, and utilities, and he drinks away the rest. The second mortgage put them underwater. The bank owns more than they do at this point. When winter rolls around and oil prices go up... no money coming in... they'll be in a rough patch looking for a lifeline."

Oh, this again. My father had made a run at their property a few years ago and Spivey's dad shot him down. Refused to sell. Years back, New Castle had been nothing but a fishing village with a few small farms. Local wealth had been in Portsmouth and a few of the surrounding towns, not on the island. That changed when taxes out in California began to skyrocket and residents started seeking out waterfront properties in other states. With no state income tax, New Hampshire became a hotbed. Buyers homed in on our little island in droves. Prices jumped. Spivey's family had owned their place out on Murdock for generations, and his dad had siphoned funds from the equity every chance he could, first to buy a fishing boat of his own (which hadn't left the dock since the motor crapped out in '03), then to help keep Milligan's 72-footer alive. Not as a loan with collateral, maybe some interest, but some handshake deal Harry Milligan would never repay. A little more for bills, utilities, and who knew what else... this was the kind of thing my family talked about around the dinner table.

The Spiveys could have sat back, done nothing, and cashed out. Instead, Keith Spivey had squeezed the property dry, and Pamela let him. Although my father had no business knowing, I'm sure he had all the details on a spreadsheet somewhere, probably knew the Spivey family finances better than they did. He'd swoop in, pay off the bank, put a little more cash in the Spiveys' coffers, then build and flip some McMansion on the land. The Spiveys wouldn't get much out of it, maybe enough to live another year, but he'd make a nice profit. That's all he really cared about. I knew how Pop paid our bills, but I didn't have to like it.

"Why don't you call them?" I said. "I don't want to get in the middle of this."

He reached across the desk and slid his card closer. "I'm only trying to help."

I eyed him for another second, then took the card and shoved it in my pocket. I had no intention of giving the business card to anyone, but I knew if I didn't take it, this conversation would go on until I agreed.

I wanted to get over to Spivey's house.

"That's my boy."

I stood. "Can I go now?"

"Give David my best. Pamela and Keith, too."

None of that mattered. By the time I got there, Spivey's house was deserted; his dad's truck was gone. I wouldn't see Spivey again for three days, and when he finally did reappear, he had the worst timing.

06/25/2010 - FRIDAY

1

SITTING BEHIND THE desk in his cramped office at New Castle PD, Chief Whaley took the manila folder from Sandy Lomax and tested the weight. Light, for sure. "This is all you could find?"

Sandy shrugged. "Geraldine Rote never set foot off that rock, not since she was a kid. I asked around, and most folks on the island never knew her name. Only a couple of the old-timers, and none were too eager to talk about her. Best I can figure, she was some kind of hermit, living out there all by her lonesome. Not much about her in records, just a couple mentions years back." She nodded at the folder and brushed a loose strand of hair back from her face, tucked it behind her ear. "You gonna need me for anything else tonight?"

Whaley dropped the folder on his desk. "Big date?"

"A TV dinner, the finals on *American Idol*, and my neighbor's coming over so I can dye her gray roots away. Biggest night of my life."

Whaley glanced across his office at the clock hanging out in the hall, but couldn't make it out.

"Half past seven," Sandy said. "You best be getting home soon, or Mary will have you eating TV dinners too."

His wife's face stared up at him from the framed photo he kept in the corner of his desk. He could almost picture her impatiently tapping her foot, telling him that Sandy Lomax might be on to something. A framed photo of his brother sat next to Mary. Same goofy look on his face he'd always had. He died when they were kids, cystic fibrosis. Not a day went by he didn't think of him.

"I'm leaving in a few minutes," Whaley told both photographs more than Sandy, then flipped the folder right-side up and opened the flap. "Right after I run through this."

"Uh-huh," Sandy scoffed. "See you tomorrow, Chief."

He waited for the door at the end of the hall leading out to the small lobby to clack closed behind her before looking down at what Sandy found.

There was a marriage certificate—Geraldine Louise Walton married Lester Herbert Rote, signed by Judge Bloomfield and witnessed by Lucinda Marchant. Lucinda had worked in town hall back when most of the roads around town were still dirt. She'd passed nearly twenty years ago in a nursing home out in Exeter. Whaley had never known her, but her name came up on a lot of documents. Courthouse wedding. Not uncommon back then. He flipped the page, looked at the next one.

A missing persons report filed by Geraldine Rote on her daughter, Pamela Rote, dated twenty years ago. Pamela Spivey now. Whaley checked Pam's date of birth and did the math; she would have been seventeen at the time. Geraldine had called New Castle PD and reported her daughter missing at 1:34 in the morning. Scribbled down near the bottom of the page was a note that simply said:

Found with Keith Spivey near bridge at 1B. Bags packed. Potential runaway? Picked up by GR at station: 3:27 a.m. Closed.

That wasn't exactly breaking news. For better or worse, she went on to marry the guy.

Worse, his mind muttered. *That one went on to be worse.*

No doubt about that.

The third and final page might have been the start of all that. It was a copy of a restraining order filed by Geraldine against her own daughter and several others, signed by a judge in Rockingham County, dated about three years after the missing persons report. It prohibited Pam Spivey from coming within five hundred feet of her own mother, specifically the family home. The restraining order also listed Keith Spivey, Ted Hasler, and someone named Laura Dubin.

Whaley knew Pam and Keith married right out of high school, and at first he thought that's what this was about—Geraldine unhappy with her daughter's choice in husband, but no, the dates didn't work out. Pam was twenty when her mother filed the restraining order, married at least two years. Again, Whaley worked the math in his head and it clicked—Geraldine didn't take out the order when her daughter married; she took it out when her daughter gave birth.

Whaley considered that for a moment, tried to come up with a reason a woman wouldn't want to see her own grandchild, but his tired brain offered up nothing. Certainly nothing that explained why Ted Hasler and that other woman were listed.

His gaze fell on the name of the attorney who had drafted the order. He tapped it with the tip of his pen, then circled it—Lockwood Marston, Esquire. This was the second time in three days he'd encountered that name. The first had been at Henry's when Geraldine died.

2

KIRA DID THIS thing with her hands. I'm not exactly sure where she learned it. (I told myself probably cheerleading camp—several girls in a dark cabin dressed in next to nothing, comparing tips, tricks, and notes. The same place they practiced kissing and generally got comfortable with female sexuality between pillow fights and long showers together.) Most likely it was something her previous boyfriend asked her to do, something he'd seen in a porn. Either way, she was damn good at it, and I sunk a little deeper into the back seat of my car.

The sun had gone down about an hour earlier, and a half moon stood out in the sky. We were parked down at the end of Ocean Street in the fire lane directly next to the no parking sign. Just above the rocky bluff, next to the path leading down to the beach. Same place we usually parked. I'd spent the last twenty minutes strategically working my hand up the front of Kira's shirt and under her bra, while she did the hand thing. Her heart was thumping nearly as hard as mine as we kissed. We'd worked up enough steam to turn all the windows white. It was shaping up to be a good night.

Kira drew her lips across my neck to my ear and whispered, "Do you want to go for a swim?"

I cupped her breast and felt her nipple against my palm. "I'm fine right here."

She gave me a gentle squeeze and kissed my earlobe. "I think I want to go in the water."

"It's probably cold." I reached for the snap on her jeans, unfastened them, and slipped my hand down the front. She was wearing some lacy something-or-other. Further investigation might be in order.

"There's nobody out there," she breathed, moving to that little spot behind my ear, her hand picking up speed. "We've got the whole beach to ourselves. We could do it on the rocks. Ocean air. Waves crashing around us..."

That wasn't fair. She knew how much I liked the rocks.

Before I could reply, Kira had the car door open and was outside. She gave the empty road behind us a quick glance, grinned mischievously, then lifted her shirt up over her head and dropped it to the ground while walking backward toward the path to the beach. She tugged off her jeans next and stood there in the moonlight just long enough to watch me practically fall out of my car and start after her, then she vanished down the hill with a laugh, her dark hair ruffling in the wind.

Here's the thing—as beautiful as she was, I think it was her laugh that got me. Her voice felt like a snuggly blanket, something I wanted to wrap myself in. Her sense of humor. She listened when I needed to get something off my chest and always seemed to know exactly what to say to make me feel right. With other girls I'd dated, spending time together sometimes felt like a chore. I had to work at it. With Kira, it was effortless. It was the time apart that hurt.

I found her bra and panties on the sand, and by the time I spotted her again, she was in the water up to her waist, her arms wrapped around her chest. "Oh, it is cold!"

I didn't much care at that point. I would have clawed through ice to get to her. I shrugged out of my clothes in a series of awkward hops and steps, reached the water's edge, and splashed her.

"You jerk!" Kira shuffled back several more feet—the water reached her shoulders—pushed backward off the sandy bottom, popped up for a moment, then landed on her back with a big splash. She scissored her legs in several quick motions and sent a flurry of freezing water at me before disappearing completely beneath the surface.

Swimming in the New Hampshire ocean could best be described as survival. At its warmest, the water might reach sixty degrees, maybe sixty-five. If you remained still, breathing grew difficult and your limbs became these heavy numb things that only weighed you down. The water basically killed you slowly. I knew better than to stand still—I worked my way out to where Kira vanished, willed my legs out from under me, and dropped like a rock beneath the surface. Like ripping off a Band-Aid—let the chilled water engulf me—the world went quiet, muffled. I popped back up a moment later, in time to get smacked in the face by a wave of frothy water. I inhaled saltwater, coughed, and blinked it away, scanning the surface for Kira. I didn't see her, but that didn't scare me. She led the varsity swim team to numerous regional championships, JV before that. She held the county record for the two hundred meter.

I don't know how she got behind me, but I felt her warmth press against my back, then her hands on my shoulders. When I turned, her lips were on mine and her legs twisted around me, pulling me tight against her. I hobbled toward our favorite rock, one of several large boulders worn smooth, the surface glistening and black. I raised her up out of the water, sat her on it, and couldn't help but stare. She might have been the most beautiful creature to ever walk this planet, every curve perfectly sculpted. Her skin prickled with gooseflesh as water rolled off her shoulders, dripped from her hair, caressed every inch of her as she returned my gaze with those mocha eyes of hers. I slipped my hands up her legs and leaned in closer.

Kira gasped.

"I know," I muttered, nuzzling her neck.

"Shh." Her body stiffened. "That's not what I mean. There's somebody out there."

At first I didn't move. I hoped I heard her wrong, then she said, "Near the path by your car."

I craned my neck, but didn't see anyone. "Are you sure?"

"I saw someone walk down from the road."

The moon had dropped behind some clouds, and what little I could see of the beach was thick with shadows. The dark moved through the tall seagrass and trees like oil; even the sand looked black.

"Don't move," I told her. "Maybe he'll go away."

"It's freezing."

It was. The moment we stopped moving, the icy ocean reminded us just how cold the water was. Each wave seemed to drop another degree as they rolled in behind us and crashed against my back. I tried to shield her as best I could, but I wouldn't be able to take much before we'd have to get out.

"There!" she said into my ear. "On the bluff, up near the end of the drain pipe."

The drain pipe was this ancient metal fiasco partially buried under the sand. It ran up the length of the beach, disappeared in the dunes at the back, and helped keep the wetlands up in the Commons from flooding. Horribly rusted, water spurted from holes and created little rivers in the sand. I found the end of the pipe and followed it up the beach toward the back. At first, I didn't see anything; then I did. This tall, dark shadow, unmoving, hidden in the darker shadows up top.

"Do something," Kira whispered.

"Like what?"

Our clothes were on the beach; we hadn't even thought to grab a towel from the trunk of my car.

"We need to get out," she told me.

She was right. We were both shivering and I couldn't feel my legs anymore. Whatever heat the moment had generated was gone—if we stayed in the water much longer, we'd be in trouble.

"I'll go," I said with chattering teeth. "I'll get rid of whoever it is, then you can come out."

She nodded. "Hurry."

My body didn't want to move, and when I finally did, my muscles screamed. As I rounded the rocks, Kira pulled her legs up out of the water, brought her knees up to her chest, and shrunk into herself. Naked or not, I didn't really care who saw me lurch out of the surf or what they saw; I was too damn cold to worry about that. With one eye on that shadow, I made a beeline for my underwear and jeans, shucked into them, and lumbered up the sand.

Whoever it was didn't move, not at first. It wasn't until I got close that I realized who was standing there.

Spivey.

His guitar was resting in the sand, propped up against his leg. His hands were in his pockets, and the look on his face was something between embarrassment and worry. "You know there's sharks out there, right?"

I wanted to punch him. Haul off and beat him senseless. Instead, I said, "Turn around."

He did. He twisted around and faced the bluff. When his back was to me, I shouted over my shoulder. "Kira, it's okay now!"

"I've seen them from the jetty," Spivey went on. "Blue, sandbar, tiger. We've got great whites, too."

"You're lucky I don't beat the shit out of you," I mumbled, scooping my shirt from the sand and pulling it over my head.

He looked sheepishly down at his guitar. "I'm sorry, man, I came out here to clear my head. Didn't know you'd be here."

Behind us, Kira splashed up out of the water.

"Dude, she gave me wood."

That time I did punch him. A hard knuckle to the shoulder. "That's my girlfriend, douchebag!"

"Ow!" Spivey stumbled a few feet and rubbed his shoulder. "No, not Kira. My grandmother!"

I almost hit him again. "That might be worse."

He let out a sigh. "Can I turn around now?"

I looked back over my shoulder. Kira was dressed, sort of. She had gotten her jeans back on, her bra too, and was reaching into the seagrass near the path for her shirt.

"Yeah, okay. Eyes front, though."

As he turned, he stole a glance at Kira anyway. I honestly couldn't blame him; I would have too. She didn't seem to care because, cold or not, she stomped up to him in only her bra and jeans and kicked him in the shin before putting on her shirt. "You're an ass."

"Okay. How about everyone stop hitting me, please?"

Kira nuzzled under my arm and glared at him. "This is why you don't have a girlfriend."

"I may not have a girlfriend, but I own my own island."

I pulled Kira closer, the two of us stealing warmth from each other. "What are you talking about?"

A grin returned to his face. The kind a cat might have after swallowing a mouse whole. "My grandmother owned Wood Island, and she left it to me in her will."

Kira twisted and looked out over the water at the small island positioned between two lighthouses about a quarter-mile from the shore. "*That* Wood Island?"

He nodded.

There wasn't much to see. There was a house out there, one or two outbuildings, but it was dark. I vaguely remembered it being lit up every once in a while, but I figured those lights were on timers. "I thought the Coast Guard owned that place?"

He shrugged. "Apparently, my great-grandfather bought it from the Coast Guard back in the forties for a dollar." With each word, he sped up, like he'd been holding this in and couldn't keep it from getting out once he started. "It was falling apart and wasn't any good for fishing—the bigger boats couldn't get to it because of all the rocks, so nobody wanted it. He bought it, fixed it up, and my grandmother inherited it when her parents died. She left it to me. I had no idea she lived out there. My folks never said anything. They never talked about her. Mr. Marston told me—"

I held up a hand and cut him off. "Whoa, slow down. Who is Mr. Marston?"

"Her attorney," he replied. "That's where I've been, in Boston. When Chief Whaley took me home the other day, my parents were already packing. Marston had called to tell them Geraldine passed, gave us his address, and told us he was under instructions to read her will as soon as we arrived. I think my parents thought she'd leave everything to them, so they were in a hurry to get down there... boy, were they pissed."

"Geraldine?" Kira said softly.

"Geraldine Rote," Spivey told her. "That was her name. My mom gets mad if I call her grandma, so Geraldine."

I was still looking out over the water, trying to wrap my head around this. *Your grandmother gave you an island?*

The grin on Spivey's face widened. "The island. The house. Everything on it. And a fat bank account in some kind of trust to maintain everything. Dude, serious nik nok."

When we were around five, I had a book called *Tick Tock, Time to Rock*. For some reason, Spivey had trouble pronouncing *tick tock;* it came out as *nik nok.* It became our thing—some phrase we worked into so many conversations over the years it just came out now without much thought.

Spivey owned an island.

Kira and I exchanged a look.

Homes on New Castle with just a sliver of a water view sold in the millions. I could only imagine what that place was worth. Even if the house was falling down—which it most likely was—the land alone… a private island… I thought of the business card my father had given me. I'd left it on my dresser back in my room. He knew. Within hours of that woman dying, he not only knew she died, but he knew what was in her will. For that matter, who told Marston she'd died? Chief Whaley didn't know who the dead woman was until Spivey ID'd her at school, then he took Spivey straight home. Marston had called his parents before that, so who told her attorney? Wait, that wasn't exactly right. Ralph Peck had told the chief he thought it might be Geraldine Rote, but wasn't sure. Did Ralph Peck know my dad? Maybe. But how would he know her attorney?

"Can we go out there?" Kira lit up. "I mean, if it's yours, we can, right?"

Spivey drummed his fingers over the strings on his guitar. To this day, I couldn't tell you what notes he played, but I still remember them. Those three notes were the start of something. He looked at both of us, his brain clearly reeling. "We're gonna need a boat."

Kira squeezed my arm. "Matty's got one."

Nik nok.

3

I TOLERATED MATTY Fernandez, but I never considered him a friend. He was an arrogant, self-centered jerk who'd sell you out for a warm beer and half a Snickers bar before he'd do you a favor, but like I mentioned earlier, someplace this small, you worked with what you had—and Matty had a boat.

His parents owned a small fleet of lobster boats that they docked at the marina near BG's Boat House off 1B South just beyond the inlet for Sagamore Creek. Their house was down the street on Harbor View. By the time we got out there, it was nearly ten. Matty worked for his dad on weekends, which meant an early morning start; he'd be home.

Kira texted him while I drove. He told us to meet him at the end of his driveway so we wouldn't wake his folks.

Spivey rode in back and didn't say much. Every time I looked at him in the rearview, he was staring out the window, lost in thought. I could only imagine what was going through his head. A week ago, he'd been wondering how he would pay for college. If he'd even be able to go to college. Now all that had changed.

Although he'd grown up with us on the island, he'd always been a bit of an outsider. Sure, we played together in the park when we were kids, and he was at many of the birthday parties over the years, but as I got older, I realized this was our parents attempting to include him. His folks became somewhat of a cautionary tale they leaked out to the rest of us in little pieces as we got older. When Spivey's mother overdosed, nearly died, my dad sat me on my bed and told me every single person was three decisions away from achieving all they could possibly want from life. He also said we were always three decisions away from absolute failure. Circumstances may dictate the obstacles we face along the way, but the solutions could be found within ourselves if we took the time to look.

Here's the thing—my dad felt the need to tell me that. I'm pretty sure on some basic level, Spivey already knew it. His home life was no secret, but he'd never let it hold him down any more than he did the leukemia. If anything, the problems he faced only pushed him harder. The night his mom almost died, a wall had gone up. An intensity had come over him I'd never seen before. He harnessed the pain and channeled it. Every time his father came home drunk or confessed another of his financial blunders, that wall hardened and the intensity grew. When assholes like Rory Moir picked on him, that wall hardened and the intensity grew. Even the leukemia he beat into submission.

So I understood how he reacted to adversity, but I couldn't think of a single instance where someone threw something good his way. Some big windfall? I had no idea how he would handle something like this, and that frightened me a little.

We found Matty standing at the edge of the street with a cigarette glowing between his fingers. He'd thrown a jacket over his pajamas. As I pulled to a stop, he stomped out the cigarette and motioned for Kira to roll down her window. He ran over and stuck his head in the car, eyed Kira and me, then grinned at Spivey. "You lucky son of a whore."

Spivey leaned forward. "Can you get us out there?"

"What do I get out of it?"

Matty's eyes flashed back on Kira as he said this. It was brief, but there it was. They'd gone out a few times during our freshman year, long before she and I got together. I knew it was over, but that did nothing to stifle the pang of jealousy in my gut whenever he looked at her like that.

"You get our undying gratitude," she told him flatly.

"Not good enough. I take you out there, you hook me up with Alesia."

"From cheerleading?"

He nodded.

"I don't think she likes boys."

"Even better. She can bring a friend."

Kira rolled her eyes. "I'll see what I can do."

He looked back at Spivey. "Hey, Detective Dillweed, if your grams died at Henry's, she must have a boat of her own somewhere. She sure as shit didn't swim to and from the island."

I hadn't thought of that. It was a good point.

Spivey shrugged. "Her attorney said she owned a 22-foot skiff called *Annabelle*, but he had no idea where she docked when she came to town."

Matty's eyes narrowed. "I'll ask around. It'll turn up. Abandoned boats tend to draw attention. If nobody's looking for it, maybe I'll strip it for scrap."

Spivey wasn't about to take the bait. He was a man on a mission. "Will you take us out there?"

"Now?" Kira pushed.

This got her another one of those looks, then he shook his head. "Tomorrow. Wood Island is surrounded by rocks. I'm not taking a run at it in the dark. No way. Meet me at the docks at six. It'll have to be a quick trip, though. I gotta be home by nine to help my dad. Figure fifteen minutes to get there, fifteen to get back. That leaves about two and a half hours to look around." He shot me a sullen look. "I suppose you can go too."

"Blow me, dickhead."

He winked at Kira, tapped the roof of my car twice, and started back up his driveway toward his house. Over his shoulder, he called, "Six. And bring Alesia!"

My parents were asleep by the time I dropped off Kira, Spivey, and got home. I showered and closed myself in my room as quietly as I could. My father's business card—which I knew I'd left on my dresser—was sitting in the center of my bed. I tossed it to the floor and climbed under the sheets. I fell asleep thinking of Kira, but I dreamt of bad things.

"We'll never make it," she said in my ear, her voice broken by another wave crashing over our heads. "We're too far from shore!"

I pulled her tighter against me, held her as close as I dared while still pumping my legs to keep us afloat. My muscles didn't want to work anymore. The burn I'd felt only moments earlier had been replaced by pins and needles and this numbness creeping through my limbs. The icy water sapped the strength from me. "Do you see it? Where did it go? Where the hell did it go!?"

Kira didn't answer; she only buried her face deeper into my shoulder and sobbed.

"You should go," I told her. "You're faster than me." A deep pain roiled the small of my back. "I'm not sure I can swim at all."

She didn't answer, only shook her head and gripped me tighter.

"Maybe we should try to get back."

We were too far, though; we wouldn't make it.

We sank beneath the water for a second—my mouth filled with saltwater. I coughed it back out. I had stopped kicking, only for a second. Didn't want to, just did. I couldn't keep this up. I couldn't swim for both of us. "We gotta move, Kira. Gotta—"

"Oh, God, there!" Her body went stiff, and she pointed to our left.

I followed her finger, but only caught a glimpse of the fin before it vanished beneath the dark surface about thirty feet away.

06/26/2010 - SATURDAY

1

THE NEXT MORNING when I picked up Spivey, his father was standing on their porch, the front door open behind him, his face twisted with anger. Spivey hustled into my car and slammed the door.

"What's going on?"

He tugged at the seat belt, missing the latch twice before clicking it into place. "Just drive."

So I did.

He didn't speak, but I knew that wall of his had grown a little thicker. Whatever happened, his blood was boiling.

By the time we got to the dock, Kira was already there. Matty was busy loading a cooler and life jackets into his boat. Matty's sister, Izzie, was standing behind him, and so was Chloe Kittle, Izzie's best friend. Those two were sophomores, a year behind the rest of us. Kira was wearing cut-off jean shorts, a white bikini top, and had her hair pulled back in a long ponytail. Dark sunglasses were perched precariously on top of her head. My heart thumped.

"Why are all these people here?" Spivey groaned, jumping out of my car and heading toward them before I even shut the engine off.

Spivey shouted something, I couldn't make out exactly what, but

Kira moved quickly between him and Matty with her arms outstretched, keeping them apart as I ran up.

Whatever Spivey said, Matty wasn't happy about it. "Look, man, I'm doing you a favor. You want to be a dick about it, find some other way to get out there."

I eased between them and wrapped an arm around Kira. "Whoa, what's going on?"

Matty jerked a thumb toward Spivey. "Your buddy here wants to put a cap on the number of people for our little excursion. My dad said we can take the boat as long as we take Izzie. Izzie wants to take Chloe." He waved a hand around. "Might I add, there's no Alesia here, so we're only up by one person. I don't see what the big deal is."

I didn't either. Matty's boat was a 25-footer with plenty of room.

Spivey's face was beet red, worse than when I picked him up. Most likely he was running on a short fuse after whatever that was with his dad. At least that's what I told myself.

I walked Spivey back several paces and lowered my voice. "Why exactly can't they come?"

Something flashed behind Spivey's eyes, and for a brief second I thought he might haul off and hit me—he looked *that* angry. Which was silly, because Spivey had never hit me—or anyone else, for that matter. I'd never seen him get violent. It vanished as quickly as it came, replaced by something more akin to frustration.

"They're too young," he finally said.

"We're not kids," Izzie shot back. "We're both fifteen. Why are you being a jerk?"

The redness rushed back into Spivey's face. I quickly held out my hand toward Izzie, silenced her before she could say something that would make things worse, and looked at him. "Tell me what's going on."

Spivey licked his lips and sighed. "Remember how I said Marston told me everything was held in a trust?"

I nodded.

"The island. The house. The money… all of it is in this trust managed by him and his office. I've got a copy of it back at the house, and the damn thing is this thick." Spivey spread his thumb and pointer finger out about two inches.

"You're a minor," I told him. "Trusts are normal when property is willed to someone under eighteen."

I'd seen enough of them helping my dad around his office. When I was around fourteen, he'd even given me a "dad lesson" on trusts and tax shelters, transfer of property, that sort of thing. He got frustrated when he learned they didn't teach us that stuff in school. "It's basic money management," he groaned. "I'm guessing they don't tell you credit is evil either, do they? No problem teaching you revisionist history, old news, but they don't bother giving you the tools you need to succeed in life." All that had set him off, and he made it a point to drop these little bits of wisdom on me whenever he had the opportunity.

"I called it a trust," Spivey told me, "but that's not exactly right. Marston said it was something called a conservatorship and he was the executor. Ownership doesn't transfer to me when I become legal; it stays with him indefinitely. It's mine, all of it, but he manages everything, oversees it. And there are these... rules..."

"Rules? Like what?"

"All bills are to be paid by the conservatorship, never by me personally. If I need something, I've got to go through Marston. I'm not even allowed to buy something and submit a receipt—he needs to arrange purchases on his end for anything beyond things like groceries. Repairs, supplies, anything like that, I've got to go through him. Aside from general maintenance, I'm not allowed to make any changes to the house or property, and I'm not allowed to sell. He specifically said my folks are never permitted to set foot on the island. I guess that's some sort of grudge thing, but Grams put it in there—she also said nobody below the age of sixteen can go out there, either." He looked down at his feet, then back at me. "There were more, a bunch more, but the kicker was at the end. If I violate *any* of the rules—stipulations, he called them—I violate just one, and ownership of the property and all remaining assets transfers immediately to the town of Kittery, Maine." He looked out over the water dismissively. "The state line is out there in the middle of the reach, so technically Wood Island is in Maine, not New Hampshire, so it wouldn't even go to New Castle if I screw things up."

"I don't know that she can do that," I told him. "I can have my dad look into…"

I cut myself off. I didn't want my dad involved in this any more than he already was. He wouldn't be looking out for Spivey; he had his own agenda. He'd made that very clear.

Although we had stepped away from the group, we were still within earshot. Izzie chimed in, "I'll be sixteen in two weeks and Chloe's birthday is right after mine. Who's gonna know, anyway?"

When Chloe was twelve, she got into the whole goth thing. Witchcraft. The macabre. Marilyn Manson. New Castle had several cemeteries, and she was no stranger to any of them. Some of the tombstones dated back to the sixteen hundreds, and she made it a point to learn who was buried where and when. She'd spent countless hours combing through the historical society records, digging up ancient ghost stories (any New England town worth its salt has its share) and scribbling them all down in her journals. Her favorite had been something called "The Stone-Throwing Devil"—hundreds of stones rained down on George Walton's tavern, and the devil had to be vanquished by some preacher out of Boston named Increase Mather back in 1682, around the same time the people of Salem, Massachusetts realized they had themselves a witch problem.

George Walton's tavern was now somebody's home, and one time, Chloe talked the owner into letting her spend an hour in their crawlspace. Her parents were less than thrilled when they found out. Now Chloe no longer wore the makeup, her wardrobe contained colors other than black again, and her taste in music had shifted to the boy bands Izzie blared. A phase, everyone said, because that was what they were supposed to say. She was Izzie's best friend, and her brother hung with us, so I tried to look beyond all that. She still creeped me out, though.

Kira said, "A lot of people see that place as a historical site. That's probably what your grandmother meant with all this stuff. She doesn't want you to paint it purple or damage the place. Can't trust children to be respectful." She said the next part in her best old woman's voice. "Best to keep them from setting foot on the lawn, young troublemakers. The whole lot of them."

None of us wanted to see Spivey lose everything. Even Matty's eyes had softened. "My dad said we can't take the boat unless we take them, so how about they stay in the boat?"

"I don't want to stay in the boat!" Chloe groaned. The first time she'd spoken at all. "I want to look around. I hear that place is haunted. Nobody's gonna see us."

"It's not…" Spivey rolled his eyes and took several more steps down the dock. He ran his hand through his hair, then turned back around. "Okay, they stay on the boat."

"Helllooo," Izzie said, raising her voice. "We're right here."

Spivey turned and looked her dead in the eye. "You can go, but I need you to stay on the boat. Just this once, until we can figure things out. Once I get a better handle on what all this means, you can come back out. Can you do that?"

"There may be cameras or something out there," I added. "Give us a chance to check things out."

I didn't really think Marston had cameras. Kira was probably right. Grandma just wanted to keep the riffraff away. But I knew how sensitive Chloe was after finding a hidden camera in the girls' locker room about a month back. That had freaked everyone out, but her in particular, since it was in the smoke detector right above her locker. Her hand shot over to Izzie's and grabbed it, then she nodded.

From a cooler at his feet, Matty tossed everyone a bottle of water. "Sun's out. Stay hydrated or you'll get a nasty headache."

I chugged about a third and dropped the bottle into the built-in cupholder to my left.

Five minutes later, we were pulling away from the dock.

2

"EVERYONE WATCH FOR rocks," Matty said, easing back on the throttle and slowing the boat to a crawl. "We're a few hours away from high tide, so it should be okay, but we don't want to get stuck."

"I can't even see the bottom," Kira said, leaning over the side.

Matty craned his neck and looked out over the bow. "When this was a life-saving station for the Coast Guard, they dredged it out. The main channel used to be about forty feet deep. The problem is, nobody has maintained it for about a hundred years, so the ground can come up on you fast, like right over there—"

He pointed about twenty feet ahead and to the left at several jagged black granite peaks sticking out from the water like the old, rotten teeth of some long-forgotten prehistoric monster.

Izzie shielded her eyes from the sun and looked ahead. "It's not as big as I thought it would be."

I had to admit, after spending a lifetime glimpsing Wood Island from the beach a quarter-mile away, it was strange seeing the place up close. It wasn't as big as I thought it would be either, but it was big enough. If I had to guess, the island itself was maybe an acre, but that probably changed drastically with the tides, because even at the highest point, it was only a few feet above sea level. A large stone wall surrounded most of the island's outer edge, with enormous rocks creating a natural barrier on the rest. The main house stood at the island's center. It was two stories with a tall square tower reaching up even higher—a 360-degree view of the ocean that must have been spectacular. A widow's walk broke off from that and followed the high roofline. The house had several chimneys, white siding, and a red shingle roof that looked to be in good repair. The water was fairly calm this time of year, but during the winter we had some nasty storms, and I could easily picture a large wave rolling over the top, swallowing the place whole.

Spivey was in my head. He said, "Marston told me the entire island is granite. When they built everything, they had to blast out the basement. See how Kittery juts out on the far side, creating an inlet? It's a natural barrier from harsh weather and nasty waves. Back in the day, large ships would anchor here instead of the port because the water stayed calmer. Wood Island has never flooded. Not once."

"What are those big black doors?" Kira asked.

"That's the boathouse. See those tracks coming out the front? How they disappear in the water? They're rails. The boats go on ramps inside and the Coast Guard would launch them out for rescues, then haul them back in on a winch."

"Are the Coast Guard boats still in there?"

Spivey shrugged. "Marston didn't say."

"There's your grandmother's boat," Matty said, pointing ahead at the dock. "Geez, it's made of wood. Probably worth a small fortune."

All our heads swiveled at once. The 22-foot skiff was bobbing in the water, tied to the dock. White and red like the house, with *Annabelle* stenciled in black letters on the side.

"If the boat's here, how did she get to New Castle?" I asked. "Who brought it back?"

Nobody had an answer to that one.

The dock was long, at least a hundred feet. Matty maneuvered his boat behind *Annabelle* and expertly throttled back as he twisted the wheel, easing us up next to the dock. "Somebody jump out and grab a line."

I figured Spivey would go, but when he didn't move, I did. The dock was several feet above us, but there were ladders every ten feet. I scrambled up the nearest and turned. With one hand on the wheel, Matty tossed a rope up to me. I twisted it around one of the cleats, pulled the boat close, and tied it down. We did the same at the back. Not my first rodeo. Half of my friends owned boats before they got cars. Back in elementary school, they taught us to sail sunfish.

When the boat was secure, Matty switched off the motor, crossed over to the ladder, and pulled us a little closer. "Who's first?"

When Kira stepped over, he put his hands on both sides of her waist and helped her up. I wasn't too thrilled about that, even less thrilled about the way he eyed her ass as she ascended. She must have known what I was thinking because she grinned and gave me a peck on the cheek when she reached the top.

Spivey was next, then Matty.

Chloe and Izzie were left eyeing the ladder. I suppose they were hoping someone had changed their mind, but the look Spivey gave them put an end to that real fast. "Not a single foot out of this boat. Understand?"

"Whatever." Izzie huffed. She pulled her t-shirt up over her head and shrugged out of her shorts, revealing a red bathing suit. Dropping back into one of the bench seats, she squirted sunscreen into her palm, slathered it on, then handed the bottle to Chloe. "Get my back and I'll get yours." She rolled over and stretched out.

Chloe only half heard her. She was busy studying the house. "I can't believe your grandmother lived out here all by herself. What did she do for power and water?"

Spivey pointed at a small outbuilding off to the left. "There's a generator in there, and you can't see them from here, but Marston said there are solar panels on the other side of the roof. There's a cistern down in the basement for water. She captured rainwater. This place is completely off the grid." His eyes lingered on Izzie for a second, half-naked and sprawled out under the sun, then went back to Chloe. "I'm serious, you two need to stay on that boat."

I could only imagine what Chloe was thinking. She probably knew this place better than anyone and was itching to poke around. I expected her to argue, but she nodded softly and settled into the seat next to Izzie, kicking off her shoes.

She may have moved on from the goth thing last year, but she was still the palest person I knew, and part of me wanted to get out of there before she stripped down to her skivvies and blinded us all. I shuffled several feet down the dock, away from the boat, and tried to scrub that thought from my head.

Kira had her phone out, taking pictures. She held it up above her head and turned in a slow circle. "There's no service out here. That's weird."

That was a little strange. New Castle was directly to our west, Portsmouth too, and Kittery wasn't far either. Although we were surrounded by water, there were cell towers on at least three sides.

Spivey didn't seem to care much about that; he was halfway to the house.

3

THE CONDITION OF the dock surprised me. I had no idea when it had been built, but it looked new. Matty paused to get a better look at *Annabelle* bobbing in the water. "Who brought her back?"

"Does it matter?"

"Guess not. It's just weird. Dad was right, though—it's a nice boat. This is hand-built. You can see the tool marks. Not some factory mass-produced garbage." He ran his hand over the side. The wood was polished to a glossy finish. Even near the waterline, I didn't see any barnacles or growth. No scratches from bumping up against the dock.

"Somebody's got boat envy," Kira said in a sing-song voice, walking by. She grabbed my hand again. "Come on, I want to see what's inside."

"Go ahead," Matty told us, jumping onto *Annabelle*'s deck. "I'll catch up."

I was interested in the boat too, but Kira dragged me along, off the edge of the dock to the house's small porch. The door was open.

"It's got a full tank of gas and the key is in the ignition!" Matty called out from behind us. A second later, I heard the deep rumble of *Annabelle*'s motor. He might just try to keep it.

The porch was as well-maintained as the dock, not a single creak. The support beams had some of the same tool marks as the boat. I didn't see how that was possible, though; the lumber looked new. There was no way it was original to the house. Maybe whoever Spivey's grandmother hired to handle maintenance used some kind of old-world technique to tie into the historical aspect of this place. That might explain some of the weird stipulations in her will.

"Helllooo?" Kira called out as the two of us stepped over the threshold, into the house.

I'd been in my share of old houses, and I suppose I expected this one to be like those—crooked floors, cracked plaster walls, faded and peeling paint, spiders pissed about the intrusion staring back at us from every corner. There was none of that. Despite all the windows being closed, the air didn't even smell stale or musty. We were standing in a large mudroom with a kitchen through an open door off to our left. The walls were pale yellow and freshly painted. Although ancient, the hardwood floor had been waxed and buffed to a shine with not a speck of dirt other than the scruffy tracks left by Spivey. Kira was barefoot, and I also felt the need to take off my shoes, like someone would yell at me if I didn't. I left them at the door as we stepped into the kitchen.

The countertops were a rich, polished mahogany, same as the cabinets, and all the appliances were stainless steel, a few years old at most. Damn if I didn't smell fresh bread, although I didn't see any on the counter.

Kira noticed it too. She went straight to the oven and opened the door. There was nothing inside. The refrigerator was stocked, though. "There's like a dozen meals pre-cooked in here. Look at this..." She reached inside and plucked a note from a bowl covered in aluminum foil. "Meatloaf. She left reheating instructions. There's soufflés, soup... oh my God, look at this homemade mac and cheese!"

There was an entire pan, complete with crusted breadcrumbs on top.

"You think it's still good?" She was beaming. She dipped her finger in the side and licked off the cheese.

"She's been dead for less than a week. I guess so. But I don't know if we should eat any of this stuff. Feels kinda weird with her funeral tomorrow."

"So don't." Kira shrugged. "But I'm hungry."

I looked at all the notes. Everything in the refrigerator was tagged and labeled with reheating instructions. If she lived alone, why would she do that?

Kira moved the pan to the counter and scooped a mound of mac and cheese onto a plate she found in a rack above the sink. She loaded it into the microwave, tapped out one minute, and hit start. "If you think I'm gonna pass on grandma's home cooking, you're crazy."

There was a large cookie jar next to the breadbox.

I plucked off the lid and looked inside. The scent of fresh chocolate chip cookies wafted out, and my mouth began to water.

I took one out and tentatively bit into it.

My mother was a pretty good baker, but holy hell, she couldn't hold a candle to Spivey's new found Grams. I ate three before the microwave dinged on Kira's snack and a fourth while she was busy shoveling spoonfuls into her mouth as if she hadn't eaten in a month. Neither of us spoke, but I'm pretty sure our faces told Matty all he needed to know when he came through the door holding his cooler.

His eyes jumped from the cookie in my hand to Kira's plate. "That's what I'm talking about!"

He set the cooler down on the floor and opened the refrigerator, whistled at all the food, then shuffled some things around to make room. He began unloading beer, a bottle of rum, a few two-liters of soda, and more water.

"Are you planning a party?" I asked, my mouth full with another cookie.

He shoved a large bottle of vodka into the freezer next to a half dozen wrapped and tagged steaks—NY strip, rib eye, filets. "I've been floating most of this stuff in a cooler under one of our docks for a month so my dad wouldn't find it. Figured I better move it to Spivey's bachelor pad before my luck ran out. What's with all the notes?"

I shrugged.

There were more on the refrigerator door. He plucked one off and handed it to me. "Might want to get on this one."

It said, *Please feed Emerson for me.*

"Who's Emerson?" Kira asked, puzzled.

I looked around the floor, expecting to find food and water for a cat, maybe a dog, but there was nothing.

Matty held the note between two fingers. "That's a little creepy. Like she knew she was going to die or something."

"Maybe Spivey should ask that Marston guy if she had a pet?" Kira suggested. "It might be hiding."

Matty finished with the cooler, grabbed a cookie, and looked around. "Where the hell is Spivey?"

I tilted my head back and shouted out his name.

A moment later, he called back, "I'm upstairs! You gotta see this!"

4

"... YOU'VE REACHED the law offices of Lockwood Marston, Esquire. I'm afraid no one is available to take your call, but if you—"

Whaley hung up.

Fourth time he'd tried the number in as many days.

Fourth time he got voice mail.

He was about to try another number when Jolene Peterson set his large coffee down on the counter next to the bag with his morning Danish. "Anything else for you today, Chief?"

Henry's Market was busy, standing room only, yet the table where Geraldine Rote passed away four days earlier was empty. Nothing marked it, no sign or photo of remembrance or anything, but everyone stepped around it, giving the small table a wide berth.

"Folks talk," Jolene said quietly, following his gaze.

"That they do." He scooped up the bag and coffee and started for the door. "Give my best to Perrie."

He was about to cross Main to the police station when he spotted

Ted Hasler leaning in the window of a Red Audi, arguing with the woman in the driver's seat. He barely got out before she stomped the gas and sped off, leaving a dark streak in the asphalt.

"Everything all right, Ted?"

Ted Hasler spun around. His face was beet red, so filled with emotion that he looked almost as if he didn't recognize Whaley. Ted turned back in the direction the Audi had gone, clenched both fists, then slowly stretched his fingers out. Clenched and stretched again. When he turned back around, the anger had turned to red blotches and a boyish smile tinted with nerves. "Cliff. Sorry you had to see that."

Whaley took a sip of his coffee but said nothing.

Ted's face went red again, this time with embarrassment. "It's not what you think."

"I'm sure it's not."

"I wouldn't cheat on my wife."

"Didn't say you were." Whaley took another sip of his coffee. He learned a long time ago that the best way to get a person to talk was simply to keep his mouth shut. Ted didn't take the bait, though. The two men faced each other for the longest moment, then Ted blew out a breath and started for his car. "I need to get to the office."

"Have a wonderful day, Ted."

Ted raised a hand, flopped it around in the air, but didn't look back. He climbed into his car and drove off toward Portsmouth. When he vanished around the bend, Whaley pressed the transmit button on the microphone clipped to his shoulder. *"Hey, Sandy?"*

"Yeah, boss."

"Can you run a plate for me?" He rattled off the license plate number from the red Audi.

Sandy replied a few moments later. *"Registered to a Laura Dubin in Portsmouth."* His phone dinged, then she added, *"I sent you her address."* A few seconds later, she asked, *"Where do I know that name?"*

He was wondering the same thing, then it clicked. "It was on the restraining order you printed for me last night," Whaley told her. "Geraldine Rote banned her from that island years back, along with Pam and Keith Spivey, and Ted Hasler."

5

WE FOLLOWED SPIVEY'S voice past a large pantry (fully stocked), a living room (comfortable, but no television), and a library overflowing with books to the staircase at the back of the house. Not a speck of dust anywhere. If someone had told me this house was new construction and it had never been occupied, I would have believed them. Although the walls and ceiling were plaster, there were no cracks. The paint appeared fresh. Even in those places where dirt loved to accumulate, like on top of the baseboards, it was spotless. Spivey's grandmother must have spent every waking moment cleaning.

Kira rushed ahead but stopped at the first landing, studying the walls. "I thought she didn't speak to Spivey's family? Where did she get all these?"

The walls were covered in framed photographs of Spivey— dozens, at ages ranging from newborn up until recent. A few shots couldn't be more than a couple months old.

"I don't think these are from his folks," I said softly. "They're not school pictures. He's not even looking at the camera."

"They look like surveillance shots," Matty pointed out. "Grainy, like she used a long lens. Grandma went and got her spy on."

"It's kinda sad." Kira ran her finger along one of the wood frames. "They cut her out of the family and she was out here all alone, but she still wanted to be a part of their lives. Maybe this was the only way she could."

"Any idea why they had a problem with her?" Matty asked, studying a picture of Spivey when he was maybe eight years old, sitting on his butt in the middle of the ice-skating rink at the elementary school, a big shit-eating grin on his face.

I shook my head. "These are all pictures of Spivey; none of his mom, her own daughter. That says something, I suppose."

"Are you guys coming up or not?" Spivey shouted from above.

We took the steps to the second floor and found something I don't think any of us expected.

Lockers.

Floor-to-ceiling wooden lockers lined the hallway.

"Oh, that's cool," Matty said. "These must be left over from when the Coast Guard owned the place."

"This one still has a coat in it!" Kira beamed. She reached inside and took out a full-length black peacoat, draped it over her shoulders, then gave us a salute. "Private Woodward reporting for duty, sir!"

Standing there in her short-shorts, bikini top, and the coat, she made for one sexy private. She cocked her long leg, then gave us a quick twirl, the coat fluttering around her.

We found hats, boots, uniforms. Old photographs hung in some of the lockers, loved ones long passed. Girlfriends, wives. Several pin-ups from ancient magazines. Scantily-clad women smiling provocatively at the camera rendered in faded shades of black and white, sepia, and dull colors. Upper shelves held everything from old toothbrushes and razors to journals and balled-up socks.

"It's like someone froze this place in a time capsule." I ran my finger over the glossy stained wood, knowing I wouldn't find dust there either.

Kira shrugged out of the coat and ticked off several points on her fingers. "Grandma Spivey was one hell of a cook, an even better house-keeper, a budding photographer, *and* a historian. Who knew?"

"If you had any doubt this place was designed to be party central, I think this room seals the deal," Matty said, standing at a wide door on our left.

I walked over and looked inside.

The room was huge and every wall was lined with bunk beds. Eight in total—blankets, pillows, and sheets neatly folded and sitting at the foot of each one, as if their occupants could return at any time for a quick nap between shifts.

"I feel like there should be a red rope here at the door and a little plaque that says CREW QUARTERS with some description. Like we're on a school field trip or something," Kira said, peering in from beside me. "I get that Spivey's family bought this place from the Coast Guard, but why leave it like this? Shouldn't it be a bedroom or something?"

"Grams lived alone, remember?" Spivey called out from the room across the hall. "She probably didn't need all the space, so she just preserved it instead. She didn't preserve everything. You're missing the best part. Get in here!"

We crossed the hall and my mouth dropped open.

The master bedroom.

Spivey was sprawled out on a king-size bed, his hands crossed behind his head, resting on a mound of pillows. The smile on his face was so wide, it practically reached his ears. "Welcome to my love nest. Be sure to drink plenty of fluids and leave your inhibitions at the door. Once this train leaves the station, it stops for no one. Nik nok."

"You're a tool," Matty mumbled.

"I'm a tool with my own freaking house," Spivey corrected him.

The room was huge, nearly half the second floor. Fully furnished with immaculately maintained antiques. With my dad being in realty, we had bought and sold our share of estates over the years, and he had taught me what to look for. The end tables next to Spivey's newfound four-poster bed were mahogany and satinwood with Hepplewhite fan inlays. If I had to guess, they were worth anywhere from two thousand to ten thousand dollars each. The bench at the foot of the bed, the dressers, the two chairs surrounding the table with a marble chess board near the window—those things were worth even more.

Kira went to the bed, turned, and fell back on the mattress beside Spivey. "I'm fully prepared to be a kept woman if I get to live here."

"Hey, Billy," Matty said softly. "If your girlfriend is ready to dump you over the bedroom, you don't want her to see this bathroom."

He was right about that.

The bathroom was about ten feet deep and nearly twice as long, all marble with two hand-carved vanities, a separate room for the toilet, and a shower large enough to park a car in it. All of it sparkled and smelled of bleach. A basket containing soaps, shampoo, conditioner, and body wash sat on a small table near the center of the room. Fresh towels were stacked beneath it.

Kira had gotten up, and I heard her gasp behind me. I grabbed her around the waist before she could slip by and get inside. "He's right, time for you to go," I teased, tugging her back.

"This is incredible. What did your grandmother do for a living?" she asked Spivey without turning around.

"No clue. Other than that one Thanksgiving dinner, I don't think I ever met her." Spivey tilted his head. "There are two closets. If you're gonna be my sex slave, I guess you can pick one."

She turned and started back toward him. I pulled her close before she could get too far. "You're gonna leave me, just like that?"

Kira batted her eyes. "He *is* giving me a closet."

There were two very large walk-in closets in the bedroom, and both were empty. Nothing but bare hangers.

"Marston must have sent someone ahead to clear things out," Spivey said. "All the dressers are empty too. Same with the drawers and cabinets in the bathroom."

"Well, that was thoughtful," Kira said, wandering slowly through each space.

"I think that's who left the notes, too. Apparently, whoever it was, they have a sense of humor. I found this one on the phone by the bed."

He held it out so we could all read it.

Don't answer the phone.

"That's not weird at all," I said in my most sarcastic voice. "Maybe that's Emerson's job."

"Emerson? Who's Emerson?" Spivey asked.

Matty showed him the note from the fridge.

Please feed Emerson for me.

"Oh man, I really hope we don't find a dead cat around here like a month from now," Spivey said. "I'll ask Marston when we get back. He'd know if she had any pets." He pulled several small sheets of paper from his pocket. "I found more. I've been picking them up as I go. This one was on the basement door."

Watch the pilot light. It's been known to go out.

"That one seems pretty ordinary to me." Kira shrugged. "Ours goes out all the time. My dad's always bitching about it."

"Sure," Spivey agreed. "But what do you make of this one?" He held up another.

Never lock the doors.

"Probably don't need to, right?" Matty said without missing a beat. "You're on a damn island."

Spivey shrugged. "Marston told me she didn't have keys for any of the doors, so I asked him if I should get them rekeyed and he said, 'I wouldn't.' Not, 'Sure, great idea, kid. Protect your newfound shit.' Or, 'Maybe they'll turn up.' Just, 'I wouldn't.'"

"Lawyers love to talk in circles," Matty said. "My dad says they get paid by creating confusion and charging everyone to unravel the mess."

"I don't know, it kinda makes sense, right?" I reasoned. "You don't want to lock the doors if you don't have keys. Someone's just looking out."

"Sure," Spivey agreed. "Maybe with that note, I guess, but what about this?"

He showed us another and all four of us went quiet.

Anyone here at sunset must stay until sunrise.

"Okay, that's freaky," Kira finally said.

Matty clucked his tongue. "Naw. That one makes sense too. Remember what I said about the rocks? Getting in and out of here can be dangerous if you can't see where you're going. That's all that is. At some point, you should try calling the harbormaster. Maybe they can put markers for the channel out there. Better yet, have your new buddy

Marston call. Attorneys have superpowers when it comes to things like that. Get him to stop writing notes and do something useful."

Kira's hand slipped into mine and led me back toward the stairs. "I want to check out the tower before we go."

"The view's insane—I was already up there," Spivey told us, heading back down. "I haven't been in the basement yet."

"I'll go with you." Matty followed after him, two steps at a time. "I want to see the cistern. And the boathouse. Can't forget that."

Kira and I climbed the steps to the next landing and found a single door, locked with a heavy dead bolt that didn't look very old.

"Somebody clearly didn't read the note," she said, testing the knob.

I was pretty good at visualizing floor plans, and based on the windows we saw outside, this house only had two full levels—the first floor and the second below us. Whatever was behind this door was under the peaked roof. "There's not much room up here. It's probably storage or something."

"Maybe Spivey will let us turn it into another bedroom. We wouldn't need much, just a couple blankets. Someplace private all to ourselves," she purred and pecked me on the cheek before turning to the final set of stairs, which were far narrower and steeper than the rest— more of a ladder than actual steps. I followed her up through a hatch in the tower floor and crawled out.

I'd always had a problem with heights. I'm not sure why. I'd never taken a big fall or tumbled out of a tree or anything like that, but the moment I got to my feet, my legs felt shaky and I wanted to turn back around. If Kira hadn't already been up there, I probably would have. I didn't, though. I swallowed the lump in my throat and wrapped my arm around her shoulders—if we were going down, we'd go down together.

Scary height or not, the view was incredible.

The tower was maybe eight feet square with two windows on each of the four walls. Ocean views on one side, the reach and views of Kittery and New Castle on the others. There was also a narrow door leading to an even narrower widow's walk outside, and I was grateful that door was secured with another padlock, because Kira would have certainly gone out there. Instead, she turned to me, put her arms around my waist, and pulled me close. "I want you to do naughty things to me up here."

"Now?"

The word slipped out before I could stop it, and the mischievous look on her face turned into a frown. "You don't want to?"

Let me be clear—there was never a time I didn't want to. At seventeen years old, a shift in the wind was enough to get me started. But as I held her there in the tower, as I tried not to look out the windows and to focus only on her, I felt sweat bead on the back of my neck and forehead. My heart was racing for all the wrong reasons.

"Oh, fuck," she said softly.

"I want to, but—"

Kira smacked my chest. "That's not what I mean, look—" She pointed out one of the windows.

I followed her finger down the dock to Matty's boat and understood.

Izzie and Chloe were no longer in the boat. Instead, they'd spread towels out on the dock.

Kira went to the window and eased it open. "Hey!"

Izzie twisted her head and looked up.

Without a word, Kira pointed a definitive finger at the boat.

Both girls got up sluggishly, taking their time.

Spivey never saw them. We figured that was a good thing.

We'd later learn it made no difference.

06/27/2010 - SUNDAY

1

I'D NEVER BEEN to a funeral and didn't want to go, but Spivey said he'd been up half the night fighting with his folks and didn't want to ride with them, so that was that. I agreed to pick him up at the end of his street and we rode to Oceanside Cemetery in relative silence, both dressed in our Sunday best, tugging at ties neither of us felt like wearing.

"A few of us are going back out to the house later, if you want to go," Spivey said in this absent-minded voice as he looked out the windows. He had dark circles under his eyes and looked half asleep, like he should just crawl back in bed, but I didn't press it.

"Oh, yeah?"

"Just Matty, his sister, Chloe… you and Kira, if you want. Like a housewarming, but I want to keep it small."

"What about the rules? Izzie and Chloe are both too young, aren't they?"

Spivey shrugged. "I asked Marston about that and he said it didn't matter anymore."

I wanted to ask what exactly that meant, but we turned off the main road and pulled into the parking lot at the Commons before I got the chance.

Oceanside Cemetery was near the front of the Commons, across from the library. I found an empty space and we walked toward the small crowd of mourners.

The cemetery wasn't large, only about two acres, but it was one of the few on the island that still had vacancies. Many of the properties had family cemeteries, little burial grounds tucked away in the back corners of yards. Our house had one of those, and we had no idea who was actually buried there. The stones were so old the text had worn away a long time ago.

Spivey's grandmother was being laid to rest close to the stone wall and black gate at the entrance of the cemetery, in a part I thought had reached capacity years back. Most likely, that meant she had purchased the plot a long time ago.

As we approached, an older man in a dark gray suit turned and gave Spivey a soft nod.

"That's Marston," Spivey told me in a low voice.

I spotted Spivey's mother sitting in a chair near the front, but his dad wasn't there. Chief Whaley and Officer Mundie stood off to the side, back near the trees, both in full uniform. The Chief watched us as we walked up. In all, there were ten people along with the minister from New Castle Congregational, our only church.

When the casket came into view, I froze. The sight of that glossy black box suspended over an open grave, the mound of dirt next to it concealed under a green tarp… I didn't want to get any closer.

In a tentative voice, Spivey said, "I should probably…"

"Go ahead," I told him. "I think I'll hang back here."

I expected him to sit next to his mother. Fighting or not, that seemed right. He didn't. Spivey rounded the outer edge of the mourners and stood beside Marston. The minister started speaking a few minutes later, reading passages from a worn Bible he'd marked with strips of red felt. Talk of dust to dust and ashes to ashes, verses he most likely recited as often as marriage vows. I'd be lying if I said I knew his name; my family had never been big on church. We attended midnight Mass on Christmas a couple times and even went on Easter once, but nobody would consider us regulars. We had our own Sunday tradition at the Hasler house, and that involved sleeping late, eating a large breakfast, and parking ourselves in front of the television for the rest of the day to catch whatever game was catchable. My dad preferred baseball over football, but he'd watch the latter with me. Even made a point of turning off his phone on most Sundays. He wasn't the perfect father, but he tried.

A throat cleared to my left, and I turned to find Mr. Peck standing a few feet behind me in a wrinkled black suit and faded burgundy tie, his gray hair sloppily slicked back. He was holding an old fedora in his hands. He didn't seem to recognize me at first, and when he did, his jaw tightened and he gave me a subtle nod. "Billy."

My father had helped him sell the lot next to his house a few years back, and I occasionally saw him around town, but aside from that, I didn't know him very well. There were dark bags under his eyes and he hadn't shaved in several days; the deep wrinkles of his face were lined with gray stubble. He probably wasn't sleeping. I know I wouldn't be after identifying a dead body.

"Chief Whaley told us you recognized her at Henry's?"

He scanned the backs of the heads in front of us, seemed to linger for a moment on Spivey and Marston, then nodded softly. "I did. It's been a while, but I knew her and her husband from way back." He gave me a sidelong glance. "When I was about your age, I suppose."

"Any chance her husband's name was Emerson?" I asked.

"Emerson? No." His eyes flashed and his gaze narrowed. "Where did you hear that name?"

"We found a note. Spivey thinks it might be her cat."

He swallowed. "Don't know about no cat. Her husband's name was Lester. Lester Rote. They got themselves married young on account of the war. I think he wanted to put a claim on her before he shipped out. It was… a different time then."

"Was she already living out there? On Wood Island?"

Mr. Peck looked across the crowd again, then toward the cars.

I don't think he wanted to be there any more than I did. Again, he nodded. "Never made much sense to me. I suppose she considered it home, there's something to that, but it's so damned isolated. No place to grow up. Certainly not the kind of place to raise a family. Kids need room to breathe. Place like that does nothing but smother you."

"You were friends, right? You've been out there?"

"I've been out there." His voice dropped lower and his gaze fell to the ground, as if he'd just confessed to some sort of crime. "Couple times back when we were kids. Her folks had a thing about children on the island, so we snuck by 'em. Lots of ways to get hurt when you live on a rock surrounded by water. You get caught standing in the wrong place when the tide comes in and it can mean trouble. I mostly saw Geraldine in school and at church. Her family came in on Sundays, stayed the day. Back then, service was more of a whole day experience, more social—picnics, music in the Commons—not so much of that anymore. Different time," he said again. "We were close when we were younger, but time has a way of separating people as much as all that water does. Lester wasn't much of a church-goer. He went early on for her, but then they attended less and less. Eventually, not at all. Over the years, we all drifted apart. I went about my life and they went about theirs. Probably been twenty years or more since I saw her last." He nodded toward the plot to the right of Geraldine's casket. "I think the last time was when Lester passed. That's the last time I remember for sure."

I couldn't help but look at the tombstone next to the casket. Black granite with moss growing on one side. "How... did he die?"

Mr. Peck glanced down at his feet and shuffled his shiny black shoes in the dirt. "Drowned. Took a boat out for a little deep-sea fishing and got caught up in a storm. Stupid to have gone out on his own like that, but it gets back to what I was just saying. When you live out there, all isolated, it grows on you. Got to enjoy his own company probably more than others. He went out one Saturday and just never came back. The grave there next to Geraldine's is empty, nothing but a marker for Lester."

"Is that how he made a living out there? Fishing?"

He shrugged. "Not sure, to tell you the truth. Often thought on that one myself. I don't know what they did. Family money would be my guess. Don't know that I recall anyone who lived out there actually working a real job, so they musta had something stashed away."

I wondered if maybe that's what caused the rift between Spivey's grandmother and his parents. Made sense. They were drowning in debt. If she had the means to bail them out and didn't, I could see that causing all kinds of problems.

"Ask me, I think the loneliness eats away at you," Mr. Peck went on. "Don't know exactly what happened to her folks, but at some point, Geraldine lost them, then she lost Lester, and she was out there all on her own after that. All them years. A person can only take so much of that. Loneliness grows in a person like a cancer. Eats away at the good and replaces it with this empty void 'til there ain't nothing left. Can't blame her for what she done."

"What do you mean?"

"Ending things, like she did."

He must have seen the surprise in my face as he said this, because he pursed his lips, cursed softly, and glanced across the way at Chief Whaley. "Oh, hell. I thought you knew. Figured your friend told you."

"The chief said it was a blood clot or something."

Mr. Peck shook his head and his voice dropped so low I had trouble hearing him. "I guess they're keeping things quiet out of respect. Geraldine put something in her coffee, not sure exactly what. They got a camera up in the corner at Henry's, and Jolene Peterson told me you can see her plain as day, dumping some powder into the mug, stirring it up, and taking a nice, long drink. All calm-like. Then she just sat there and waited." He went back to shuffling his feet. "Look, this ain't my business, and I probably shouldn't be telling you. Maybe it's best you talk to your friend."

Spivey was still standing next to Marston, his fingers laced together and his head bowed. I wondered if he knew, and if he did, why he didn't tell me.

Mr. Peck placed a hand on my shoulder. "You know how you might do best by your friend? Getting him to sell that place. Start his life free of the burden and with a little money in his pocket. He doesn't want to live out there. I don't think Geraldine and Lester were ever happy. Her folks, neither. He's standing at the start of a road others have already traveled. There is something to be said about hindsight."

Marston turned to me then, and for the first time, his gaze met mine. He couldn't have heard what we were talking about, he was too far away, but something in his face told me he knew. He had these cold eyes. A grayish-blue color. I'd never heard the man speak, but somehow I knew his voice. I heard it plain as day telling me, "The rules, Mr. Hasler. Be mindful of the rules."

2

"NOT THAT ONE." Whaley pointed. "The one next to it, marked 93-04A71."

From the wobbly wooden ladder, Officer Mundie turned back to the shelf, eyed the boxes up top, and promptly sneezed four times in quick succession. That only stirred up more dust and he sneezed again. When he finally got it under control, he sniffled and wiped his nose on his sneeze. "We're looking for what, exactly?"

Whaley wasn't exactly sure what to tell him. He didn't know himself. He was scratching an inch, one he was sure wouldn't go away on its own. Mundie was a good kid, but the ink on his criminal justice degree from State was still wet, and he'd only been with New Castle PD for six months. He was also a townie, grew up less than a half-mile away, which meant anything Whaley told him would certainly find its way into the local gossip the next time Mundie visited the Lobster Tail and played a game of pool or two with his friends. Whaley didn't want to fuel the rumor mill. The truth was, Geraldine Rote's death had spooked him. He wasn't about to admit that aloud, but it had. He'd encountered his share of dead bodies over the years, four other suicides, but nothing like that. The woman had appeared so calm on the video, even relieved. Her hands weren't even shaking as she drank.

… Then there was the letter.

The phone call that followed.

He hadn't told those kids any of that, no reason to.

"Little hand here?" Mundie muttered, holding out the box at an awkward angle, his legs shaking nearly as much as the ladder.

Whaley reached up, took the box from him, and set it on an old metal desk in the corner of the sub-basement. He used the tip of his fingernail to cut the yellowed tape and removed the lid as Mundie came down the ladder and stepped up behind him.

"What the hell is *Brigadoon?*" Mundie asked, pointing at the book sitting on top of various files and documents.

Whaley reached in and took it out. It was a paperback from the New Castle Library. The card in front said it had been checked out by Whaley's predecessor, Chief Nelson, in January 1993.

Mundie whistled. "Seventeen years of late fees. If Nelson hadn't died, the library might have put a lien on his house to collect. That's a Broadway play, right?"

The colorful cover was fairly worn, the binding heavily creased. A number of pages had been dog-eared, and when Whaley flipped through, he saw numerous highlights, too. "Mary and I saw it years back in New York. It's about a village in the Scottish Highlands that's cursed and only appears to the outside world for a single day every hundred years. The rest of the time it just blinks out."

"Well, I hope it was better than *Cats*. I sat through that two years ago and I still have nightmares. Those fuckers are already trying to take over the world. Cats would enslave us if they were six feet tall— they sure as shit don't need to sing and dance while they do it. Creepy as hell."

Whaley flipped to one of the dog-eared pages near the back. A single paragraph was highlighted in yellow and underlined with black ballpoint to emphasize:

Jeff stood dumbfounded and stared at the spot his friend had been. The shape of Tommy hung in the mist for only a moment, his hand outstretched in a wave, the village at his back and Mr. Lundie at his side, then all of it vanished. Nothing but trees older than God with trunks the thickness of houses along the bank of the river. Brigadoon *gone as if it had never been.*

As weird as that was, it was the words written in the margin that really grabbed Whaley. Scrawled in a neat script:

Not every hundred years, but how often? What the hell is the trigger?

"Someone takes his Broadway very seriously," Mundie said, reading over Whaley's shoulder.

"Do you remember Chief Nelson at all?"

Mundie huffed. "Sure, he used to run us off the beach nearly every Friday night. Nice enough guy. Never married, lived alone. Rumor was he was gay, but nobody ever saw anything to back that up."

"That's not what I meant. Was he a good cop?"

Mundie shrugged. "Hell if I know, I was just a kid. I guess so, they kept him on for something like thirty years."

Beneath the book was a thick folder labeled *L. Dubin*. Clipped to the inside cover was a photograph of a girl, maybe fifteen or sixteen. A distant shot taken with a telephoto lens. Whaley had no trouble matching her to the woman he'd seen Ted Hasler arguing with yesterday. She might have been nearly two decades older, but there was no mistaking those emerald green eyes of hers, or the auburn hair. Atop several loose-leaf pages of notes was a brochure titled "Witches of Salem." There was also a thin stack of printed pages clipped together, which looked like a printout from an old microfiche machine. The top page said "Haunted Portsmouth and the History of New England." Scribbled on the inside flap of the folder were two names with question marks—one he recognized, one he did not.

Marston?

Emerson?

Deeper in the box he found folders for Ted Hasler, Pam Rote, and her future husband, Keith Spivey—all contained similar photos from back when they were kids. There were also folders on Ralph Peck, Geraldine and Lester Rote, and another labeled Whidden. Whaley quickly flipped through them before putting everything back inside and replacing the lid. He hefted up the box and started for the stairs. "Thanks for the help, Mundie. Lock up and get back on patrol."

Mundie eyed him curiously. "Are you going to tell me what this is all about?"

"Nope."

3

THAT NIGHT AS we approached the island, a chill came over me, one of those shivers that rolls through you from head to toe. There was no particular reason for it. At a quarter to eight, the sun was still out but dipping low, and the temperature was holding in the mid-seventies. It was warm enough, but Kira must have noticed me shivering because she nuzzled a little closer and looked out over the side of Matty's boat at the water rushing by. "Thinking about your dream?"

I had told her about the nightmare with the shark.

I wasn't going to at first, but I was terrible at hiding things from her, and she saw something in my face when we were waiting on Matty's dock for him to return with his boat—he'd run Spivey and the girls out to the island and left a note saying he was getting gas and would be right back for us.

I wasn't thinking about sharks now, and I almost thanked her for bringing that particular happy thought back to the forefront, but instead, I said yeah, that's exactly what was on my mind, because that was better than telling her what I was really thinking about, and that was what Mr. Peck had said.

My mind's eye kept conjuring up images of Spivey in his seventies trudging around that little island all by himself. Some forgotten hermit

the local kids told stories about. I had no trouble picturing him climbing into *Annabelle* one day, sailing off to the middle of nowhere and
pulling the drain plug, then sitting on the bow and watching the water
come in. Maybe he'd raise a glass to Lester. Maybe he'd pour some white
powder into that glass first, a little something to take the edge off like
good ol' Grams at Henry's. Seemed the long-term residents of Wood
Island had a knack for creative departures.

Every time I forced these images out of my head, they crept back
in. And while I had no trouble sharing nightmares about sharks, I saw
no reason to bring Kira down with thoughts of suicide, loneliness, and
general blah. She was excited about Spivey's newfound love shack—we
all were—and I reminded myself of that.

New Castle was a small place, and there were very few spots where
we could get away from the watchful eyes of our parents and their net-
work of friends. Even the secluded road near the beach where Kira and
I liked to park was no real secret. Most likely, our parents had parked in
the same spot. Maybe their parents before them. Everyone knew exactly
what time Chief Whaley rolled down that way on patrol, just like we
knew what time he passed through the Commons or any number of
other secluded hidey-holes. You could set a watch by him. I don't think
that was an accident. There was this unspoken rule between the adults
and the teenagers—we'll give you a little privacy to do what teenagers
do, as long as you do it in these designated places.

Wood Island was a game-changer when it came to privacy. It was
Privacy 2.0. Not only was it impossible for the adults to check up on
us, but Chief Whaley had no jurisdiction out there. I suppose Kittery
Police could send a boat if they wanted to, maybe the harbor patrol
or the Coast Guard, but we'd see them coming, and I'm pretty sure
they couldn't set foot on the island without permission. We weren't
bad kids, don't get me wrong. Aside from a little pot, none of us had
ever done drugs. We drank a little bit, but all teenagers did that. And
honestly, wasn't this better than a bunch of us getting together behind
one of the grocery stores in Portsmouth or down by the old fort? Under

the bleachers at the high school? At the tail end, nobody would be getting behind the wheel of a car. Whatever minor mayhem we created would be contained and more-or-less isolated from civilization. We were tucked away nice and safe. I'm fairly certain even the most narrow-minded adult would see that.

And Spivey wouldn't be alone.

There was that, too.

None of us were going home tonight.

We were all staying on the island.

Kira had told her folks she was spending the night at Alesia's, and although she wasn't here, Alesia agreed to cover. My parents thought I was staying at Matty's. He told his parents he was staying at my house. Chloe and Izzie had done the same. Spivey just left. His dad went out on Milligan's boat a day early, and his mother didn't much care what he did.

We'd done this same little dance last summer and spent the night in tents out in the mountains near Conway. Our parents had no clue we'd even left town.

Matty motored up to the dock, tied down, and the three of us went inside.

The house must have been well-insulated, because I didn't hear the music until we were standing on the porch. In the kitchen, Matty went straight to the refrigerator and plucked out three beers. He pointed proudly at a sign on the door as he produced a bottle opener and shouted over the music, "I made a rule of my own!"

Scrawled in blocky letters, he'd written:

If you start a drink, you must finish the drink.

Seemed perfectly sensible to me.

Christ, the music was loud. Maroon 5 with "Moves Like Jagger." Not a personal favorite, but it would do.

Matty popped the tops, handed out the bottles, and raised his high. "To tonight, hopefully the first of many!"

Kira clinked her bottle against mine, then Matty's. "To tonight."

Her free hand was in mine as she said this, and she gave me a gentle squeeze.

I raised the bottle to my lips and took a nice, long, cold drink, wondering how many more it would take before Mr. Peck's persistent voice was vanquished.

The music dropped off and Spivey shouted from the living room, "Get in here!"

We found him sitting on the floor between a coffee table and the largest stereo I'd ever seen. With Klipsch speakers and a Marantz receiver, the setup dominated the corner of the room. Chloe and Izzie were on the couch, both holding beers of their own and making that special face a person made when they weren't used to the taste. It had been about two years since I made that face.

None of the lights were on, but a number of candles were burning on random shelves around the room. Flickering light battled the growing shadows as the sun dipped beneath the horizon.

Matty dropped down on the couch next to Chloe and eyed the stereo. "Where did *that* come from?"

"I found it in the closet." Spivey beamed. "It was still in the packaging like Grams bought it and packed it away, then forgot about it."

I went over and got a better look at the receiver. "This probably cost a couple thousand bucks."

"Nothing but the best for Geraldine. Found that too. "

He pointed at a 55-inch television leaning up against the far wall, still in the box. Another box with a wall mount was lying on the floor beside it.

"Seriously? Which closet?"

"The one up on the third floor landing off the tower."

"You found the key?" Kira asked, dropping down on the floor next to him. "I call dibs."

She winked at me. This was the room she wanted to turn into our own private sanctuary.

Spivey shrugged. "Wasn't locked."

"No locking the doors!" Chloe and Izzie said in unison before clinking their beer bottles together and taking a drink.

Apparently, someone had shared the new rules.

I saw Kira try that door, but I hadn't tried it myself. "Maybe it was just stuck," I offered. "It's an old house."

"Either way, it's mine. You said I could have a closet," Kira said. "I want that one."

"You don't want that closet. It's a cluttered mess. Full of all kinds of grandma crap."

"And high-end electronics," Matty added.

"… And spiders and rats and mice."

"Ew." Izzie groaned.

"Okay, maybe not, but there's a lot of stuff in there." Spivey looked up at me, still standing. "Pull up some rug. We're gonna play a game."

I settled down on the floor next to Kira. "What game?"

Spivey chugged the rest of his beer, set the bottle down on the coffee table on its side, and gave it a quick flick of the wrist. "Spin the bottle."

"Dude." Matty frowned. "I'm not playing spin the bottle with my sister and her little friend."

Chloe elbowed him in the gut.

"You'd play if Alesia were here," Kira pointed out.

"Yeah, well, she isn't. Whose fault is that?"

"I asked her. She said maybe next time."

"Uh-huh. Guess you'll have to wait a little longer to see me naked." He tugged up the corner of his shirt.

Kira was wearing a thin green sweater over a white t -shirt, jean shorts, white socks, and sneakers. Tack on lacy under-things and we had a final tally of nine items. Ten, if you counted the headband holding her hair back. That was enough to probably keep her at least partially clothed in a solid game of spin the bottle, but I was fairly certain I didn't want my girlfriend getting naked in front of anyone but me, so I nixed that real quick. "How about quarters?" I said.

Spivey looked around the room. "Anyone have a quarter?"

Nobody did.

Izzie chimed in with, "Truth or dare?"

Kira said, "Never have I ever."

"How about we combine them?" I suggested. "You have to pick truth, dare, or tell a never have I ever, and nobody is allowed to repeat, so we have to run through all three before we can start over."

Kira kissed me on the cheek. "This is why I love you. Always thinking."

"All right, I'll go first." Matty leaned forward. "Truth."

"Oh, nice. Take the easiest one off the table, why don't you?" Spivey said.

Matty snapped his fingers three times. "Gotta move quick when you play with me."

"Okay, Mr. Speedy," Kira said. "Here's your truth… have you ever gotten laid?"

His face went red and he eased back into the couch. "Whoa, coming out of the gate like that, are we?"

"Yep. Just like that."

He took a sip of his beer, but said nothing.

"Does that mean no?"

"I thought if we don't want to answer, we drink. Isn't that how it works?"

"No, you have to answer."

"I think he's right," Chloe said. "That's how it works."

"You're fifteen," Kira replied. "I'm pretty sure you don't know how either of those things work."

"I know how to play the game *and* I've gotten laid."

"Oh yeah? By a boy?" Kira fired back.

It was Chloe's turn to redden. She took a sip from her own beer and seemed to shrink into the couch.

"That's what I thought."

Matty said, "The answer is no. I have not. I'm saving myself for you."

Kira cocked her head. "Guess I'll tell Alesia not to waste her time then."

"All right," I interrupted before *that* could continue. "Who's next?"

"I'll go," Spivey said. "But I'm getting something stronger. If we're going to have any fun, beer just won't do."

He got up, went to the kitchen, and came back with the bottle of vodka from the freezer and a shot glass. "New rule. If it's your turn and you don't want to do whatever, you gotta do a shot. All else, we stick with beer. Fair?" When nobody objected, he added, "Also, I'd like to point out that the sun just set and Rule Number Five is in effect. Everyone is stuck here until sunup."

He filled the shot glass, set it in the middle of the table, and settled back into his spot. He studied everyone's faces, then said, "I think I want to expand on a working theory. A follow-up, if you will, to something Ms. Kira here said." He cleared his throat. "Never have I ever… kissed a girl."

"Just so we're clear," Matty said. "Anyone who has kissed a girl needs to drink?"

"Yep," Kira replied and took a drink.

I smiled at her. "Really?"

"If you're a good boy, maybe I'll tell you all about it."

Everyone else drank too, including Izzie and Chloe, and none of us missed the look that passed between them before they did.

Spivey's eyes narrowed and he grinned. "I knew it!"

Izzie's face grew red. "It's not exactly a secret."

"I dare you to kiss her now," he fired back.

"It's not your turn. You just went."

"Then I dare you," Kira said.

Matty covered his eyes. "I don't want to see my sister—"

"Oh jeez, give it a rest." Chloe groaned. She reached across the table, took the glass of vodka, and swallowed it in one gulp, then she turned to Izzie and kissed her full on the lips. This long, lingering kiss that went on for nearly half a minute. When she was done, she slammed the glass down on the coffee table and grinned. "I find it best to get that sort of thing out of the way early."

Izzie, still blushing, wiped her mouth with the back of her hand. "For the record, we both just did that vodka shot."

All of us just stared.

His face still covered, Matty finally said, "Is it safe to look now?"

When nobody answered, he took his hand away. "Izzie's room is next to mine, and with all the slumber parties lately, I gotta wear noise-canceling headphones just to get any sleep. Bad 'tings been hap-nen in 'dat room."

Spivey refilled the shot glass. "Your sister just became a whole lot more interesting, Matty. Nik nok."

"Whatever, dickhead."

Kira rolled her eyes. "Whose turn is it?"

"Mine," Chloe said. "We're back to truth, right?"

"We've done them all, so you can pick whatever you want."

She took another sip of her beer and leaned across the table toward Spivey. "Do you think this house is haunted?"

4

"THAT'S NOT HOW it works," I said. "You don't get to ask him a question."

Chloe ignored me and pressed Spivey. "Do you know the history of this place?"

"Goth Girl can't go anywhere without looking for spooks," Matty complained.

"She's not goth," Izzie mumbled under her breath.

"Why, because you talked her into wearing a color other than black?" he fired back. "You can paint her nails pink and dress your little play-toy however you want—she's still a death rock-listening vampire wannabe. Probably got her nipples pierced and a tattoo of barbed wire somewhere where her mom can't see."

Chloe stuck out her tongue. "Wouldn't you like to know."

Spivey reached for the shot of vodka, drank it, and set the glass back down on the table. "Why would it be haunted? Because it's old?"

"Because of what this place used to be."

"And what was that?"

Chloe motioned toward the shot glass. "I want another first."

Spivey refilled the glass and slid it over to her.

She drank that one down like a seasoned pro, and I tried to remember how many she had had. Was that number three? Her eyes had gone all glossy. If she wasn't drunk, she was well on her way. Apparently, she wanted company, because she said, "*Everyone* needs to do a shot, then I'll tell you."

Spivey gave her a sly smile. "I like where your head's at, Thursday."

I think we all looked at him a little odd; then he explained.

"Wednesday is the goth girl from the Addams family. Since Chloe has moved beyond goth, I hereby dub her *Thursday*."

"That's dumb," Izzie said.

"It's an official house rule. Moving forward, I will refer to her as nothing but *Thursday*. So it has been said, so it shall be." Spivey refilled the shot glass and slid it toward Kira.

Kira weighed a buck nothing, but I knew from experience she could drink any one of us under the table, myself included. She credited this to her lack of body fat and fast metabolism. I think it had more to do with the four slices of bread she ate prior to consuming alcohol and the glass of water she had been busily chugging when I picked her up. Either way, she made quick work of the shot, held it out for Spivey to refill, then gave it to me.

The vodka burned as it went down my throat. I tried not to make a face, but did anyway. The others laughed, and the glass worked its way around the table.

Intent on getting her drunk, Spivey not-so-subtly tried to slip Chloe another, but Izzie snatched it up before she could drink it and placed the shot in the center of the table. "Let's save this one. I want to hear this."

Spivey grinned and let it go.

It was good to see him happy. After all the bullshit he'd been through over the years, he deserved it more than anyone.

The sun was gone now, the only light coming from the candles. The room was awash in dim yellows, oranges, and wakening shadows. The walls seemed to draw a little closer. Like the house wanted to hear what Chloe had to say as much as the rest of us.

Izzie's hand in hers, Chloe moved to the edge of the couch. "In 1869, the Coast Guard used this entire island as a yellow fever quarantine facility. Any ship that came into Portsmouth with sick people on board had to drop them here. Some of them even had to dock. They made them stay until they either died or got better. There was no real treatment. Little food and water; hardly anyone recovered. A lot of sailors back then were criminals. Not much better than pirates. Between the fevers, lack of food, no place to sleep or take shelter, there were a lot of murders. You could hear the screaming all the way at the Commons."

Kira smirked. "You're making that up."

Chloe slowly shook her head. "It's in the records at the historical society. They even have a log of all the people who died."

Spivey said, "The Coast Guard built this house *way* after all that. Nobody ever died inside."

"How can you be sure?" Chloe replied.

"Wait," Kira said. "Are you saying they really put all those sick people out here?"

Spivey picked the corner of the label on his beer bottle, got ahold of it, and tore it off. "Marston gave me the full history. He told me they made the ships tie off on the rocks and dock, but that was the extent of it. They brought temporary housing over from the base for the Coast Guard doctors, but they made the sick people stay on the ships to keep it contained and out of their own camp. Anyone who died died onboard the ships, not on the island itself."

"Oh, so we're surrounded by dead bodies instead of on top of them," Matty muttered. "That makes me feel much, much better. How many?"

"Hundreds," Chloe said before Spivey could respond.

The weight of that word hung heavy in the air.

Spivey finished his beer. I expected him to say she was lying, but he didn't. Instead, he said, "It's not like they just threw the bodies overboard and let them rot in the water. They're not out there. Not anymore."

He got up, went to the kitchen, and came back with six more beers. He handed them out along with the bottle opener. Being a gentleman, I opened Kira's, Izzie's, and Chloe's before tossing the opener in Matty's general direction.

Matty let out an epic belch.

Kira took a small drink and inched closer to the table. She wanted to hear more. "So what *did* they do with the bodies?"

"Burned them," Chloe said. "They had these huge fires you could smell for miles around. Rumor was the soot and ash made it all the way to Rye and Exeter."

All of us fell silent. Kira's eyes drifted to the window, the rocky shore just beyond the house.

Spivey didn't respond, not at first. I think he wanted this to sink in. Then he finally laughed. "Oh, man. She's really got you guys going." He shoved the shot glass toward Chloe. "Why don't you tell them *where* they burned the bodies, Miss Thursday?"

Chloe let the question hang for a moment before sighing. "At the docks in Portsmouth, where they keep the salt mounds now."

"*Not* out here," Spivey said.

"Not out here," she replied. And she actually sounded sad about it.

He slid the shot closer to her. "Drink."

She swallowed the vodka before Izzie could stop her, and although she did her best to make it appear painless, I had a pretty good handle on who would be first to puke.

Spivey refilled the shot glass and set it in the center of the table again. "The truth is, there is no record of anyone ever dying out here on the island. The island's been used for a million things over the years, but a burial ground is not one of them."

"We're in New England," I said. "There are graves *everywhere*."

"Not here," Spivey insisted. "Marston said even when this was a life-saving station, the Coast Guard stationed men here in the house and deployed from here for storm rescues and shipwrecks, but they never brought survivors back to the island. They weren't equipped for that. They took them to one of the hospitals on the mainland, either Portsmouth or the Coast Guard base. Sometimes Rye. Never here."

I thought of Marston watching me at the funeral. Those cold eyes of his. "Do you think he'd tell the truth about something like that?"

"Why would he lie?"

"Nobody wants to live where someone has died," Kira said. "It's bad juju."

She was right. My dad used to talk about that back when he sold residential real estate. Whenever someone toured a house, that was usually one of the first questions they asked. He was also quick to point out New Hampshire law does not consider any death in a home to be a "material fact," therefore it is not required to be disclosed. If a buyer asks, and the seller knows, they should answer truthfully, but no legal action could be brought against the seller or agent if they don't. I'm fairly certain my father would have sold the Amityville house as a quaint fixer-upper and not said a word.

The shot glass made another round, and I took another drink when it was my turn. It went down easier, and wasn't that always the case with alcohol? It snuck up on you like that. Harsh at first, then warm and comforting, like an old friend. *Here, have another!* Then you tried to stand and realized you couldn't, walking was out of the question, and only two choices remained—expulsion or pass out. The warmth in my belly and haziness in my head told me I was trudging along somewhere in that middle ground.

I thought of Spivey's grandfather, Lester Rote, motoring away from Wood Island in some fishing boat. Geraldine somehow finding her way back to New Castle before committing suicide. Maybe that was another one of the rules—no dying on the island. Because that made sense, right? If some places invited death, maybe others repelled it. But no, that was drunk-thought. Places didn't do either of those things. Then I vaguely remembered a story about a field in Africa where elephants went to die. They walked hundreds of miles to get there, to die where their ancestors had. Dinosaur bones found in clusters. Indian burial grounds, cemeteries—weren't those the same thing, really? Places where the dead found each other. A reunion of sorts. So if a place could draw death, why not push it away?

"Half the houses on New Castle are haunted," Chloe said. "Portsmouth is even worse. Have you guys ever heard of the Chase House?"

When nobody answered, she went on.

"It's on Middle Road. It got built in the late eighteen hundreds as an orphanage. Not long after it opened, a girl hung herself in her room on the second floor and died. People have seen her wandering the hallways, standing in the window looking out at the street. Doors lock for no reason. Lights turn on and off by themselves. *It's all her.* If you try to get close, she runs away and disappears. If you stand out on the sidewalk, real quiet, sometimes you can hear her screaming inside the house."

"That's just something they tell the tourists," Matty mumbled.

Chloe shook her head. "I've heard her."

"I have too," Izzie said in a quiet voice.

Matty narrowed his eyes and glared at his sister. "When?"

"Last summer. I thought Chloe was making it all up, so she brought me out there. It was really creepy. We heard a scream inside the house, from upstairs somewhere, then a few minutes later, some woman came out of the house and picked up the newspaper from the stoop and acted like nothing happened. Chloe asked her if she heard it, and the woman told us it happens all the time, but you can only hear it outside."

Matty took a drink of his beer, then stated flatly, "Local tourist bullshit."

"I heard the John Paul Jones house is haunted," Kira offered, and I realized she was getting into this. Actually getting into it. Kira was great at feigning interest in a topic—she could put on a polite smile and nod at the perfect moment and make whoever was speaking feel like the center of the universe. It was one of her superpowers. When someone spoke to Kira, she *always* appeared interested, even when her mind was somewhere else. Even when she didn't give two shits about what they were talking about. Now, though, there was a spark in her eyes I rarely saw. A childlike glint. Like seeing presents under a Christmas tree for the first time.

Chloe nodded at her; she felt it too. "*Everybody* knows about that place. It's run by the Portsmouth Historical Society, and they have records of people seeing someone coming out of the attic dressed in old-fashioned clothes, walking into one of the rooms, and vanishing. Happens all the time there. The people who have seen it say it plays out like a video—a man—middle-aged—he does the same thing every time. Doesn't matter who's standing there watching, and he doesn't seem to notice them."

Izzie nudged her. "Tell them about the music hall downtown."

Chloe's eyes lit up. "Oh, that place is really creepy. A bunch of those paranormal research television shows have done stories about it. It's filled with hot and cold spots. Weird lights that blink on and off in parts of the theater that aren't wired for power. The cleaning crew has reported hearing music coming from the piano on the stage when nobody is there. Actors have reported seeing people out in the audience dressed in costumes—they're in a seat one second, gone the next—even during rehearsals when nobody is supposed to be there."

"Bullshit." Matty coughed into his elbow. "Do you think that place would still be around if they didn't have some kind of angle to bring in the tourists? Without the ghost stories, that building would be a Whole Foods right now. Or a CVS."

"You're an ass," Kira told him.

He twisted on the couch. "You wanna see my whaaat?"

For a second, I thought she might throw her empty beer bottle at him. Spivey must have had the same thought, because he plucked it from her hand and went to the kitchen to get more.

She seemed to forget about Matty and turned toward me. "You're awfully quiet. What do you think?"

"I don't know, I think Matty might be right."

Her elbow jabbed into my gut.

"Ow!"

"So what do you think happens when we die? Do you think we just blink out and that's it? We're gone?"

I almost answered that, then I remembered that Kira's aunt died in a car accident last winter and they'd been very close. I wasn't about to go down that rabbit hole. Instead, I said, "Nobody knows. Not for sure."

"People, living things, are energy," Chloe said. "Nothing ends, the energy just gets redistributed. Sometimes it gets trapped. I think that's what happens." She looked over at me. "Like you said, we're surrounded by graves. If all the dead bodies around New England stood up at once, they'd probably outnumber the living ten to one."

Matty smirked. "So now zombies are real too?"

She shook her head. "That's not what I mean. Think of all those people as energy. Where is it supposed to go? It just builds and builds, looks for ways to get out. It's everywhere. Sometimes it gets strong enough for us to see, bleeds over into our world. Other times, it simmers. When people die in a horrible or violent way, the energy gets trapped, embedded. The dead get stuck in a house. Sort of like when someone smokes inside—you can paint, scrub, even replace all the carpet, but that smell is still there. Other times, I think the dead get confused. They don't understand that they're dead. They're lost. Some of them go back to places that are the most familiar to them, like the music hall. But no matter what, that energy *has* to go somewhere. It doesn't vanish."

"That's horseshit," Matty replied. "Horseshit, horseshit, horseshit."

"Come on, you've never seen a ghost?" Kira asked him. "Not once?"

"Have you?"

She edged the shot glass toward him. "You wanna hear, you gotta drink."

"Everybody's *got* to drink," Spivey said.

And just like that, the shot glass made another round.

5

"I WAS WITH Alesia," Kira said. "Two summers ago. We snuck out of my house and went to Point of Graves Cemetery at like one in the morning. Annie McCormick dared us and said we had to get a time-stamped picture at the Vaughn family tomb. It's that big one, all the way in the back."

Chloe beamed. "Oh, I know that one, it's—"

"Shh." Kira silenced her. "My story."

My stomach wasn't very happy about the latest influx of alcohol, and I felt a soft rumble, followed by a gurgle. In an effort to cover that up, I raised my beer bottle and drank the little bit that remained. I hadn't seen Spivey get up and retrieve more, but he replaced the empty in my hand with a fresh one, clinked his own bottle against it, and looked back at Kira all in one fluid motion that blurred together as I watched it play out. I told myself to slow down, then drank a little more beer. There was clearly a disconnect between my mouth and my brain. I'd have to rectify that. Maybe give them both a stern talking-to.

Kira reached for one of the candles and held it close to her face for a moment, let the light dance over her skin as she studied the flame, then set it on the table between us, next to the shot glass (full again). "So, the Vaughn tomb. The Vaughn family emigrated from England in the sixteen hundreds, but I don't think anyone really knows much about them other than they were one of the first families to settle in this area. Their tomb looks sorta like a stone coffin, but it's deceptive. It's actually a door. Back in the eighteen hundreds, some guy opened it up. I think he was hired to help maintain it or rebuild it or something, but he found stairs inside. The stairs led down to a giant brick room, and in there he found twenty-eight bodies. None of them were in coffins; they were just scattered around the room surrounded by pottery and other personal possessions. Twenty-one adults, four teenagers, two young children, and one baby."

"What, like a mass suicide?" Matty asked.

Kira shrugged. "Nobody knows. Not for sure. But a lot of people have seen their ghosts. They come up the stairs at night and wander around the cemetery. The whole family."

Chloe's mouth was hanging open. "Did you see them?"

Kira stared at the candle flame for a moment, then she shook her head before answering. "No, but we could feel them. The hair on our arms stood up and there was this electricity in the air, kinda like it feels after lightning strikes close by. There was no wind, none at all, but when we were standing next to the tomb, we both felt someone breathing right behind us. Like a really tall person was right there, and Alesia swears she heard someone whisper her name, an old man with a heavy English accent. We ran out of there so fast we never got the picture."

Chloe's eyes settled on the flame too. "I've got a book at home with all the haunted places around here, and there are a bunch of stories just like that. Not just from people who believe, but skeptics too. It's real."

Spivey, who had been quiet through most of this, finally spoke up. "Nobody actually dies *in* a cemetery. So why exactly would it be haunted?"

"Same reason the music hall is haunted. The spirits are drawn there."

"Like the elephants," I muttered.

Kira looked at me. "Huh?"

"Nothing."

Matty shoved the shot glass toward me. "Say something stupid, you gotta drink."

That made very little sense, but I swallowed the vodka anyway and made a show of setting the glass back on the table upside down. I almost knocked the candle over, but Kira caught it before it could tumble all the way. I'm pretty sure nobody saw that. Okay, maybe everyone saw it.

Spivey's guitar was sitting off to the side of the couch. He picked it up and plucked at several of the strings. "So even though nobody has ever died here, this place could be haunted?"

Chloe considered this. "It's possible."

"How do we… ? " H is voice trailed off as he thought this over. Several more notes came from the guitar.

"We'll need a Ouija board."

"Do you have one?"

Chloe nodded. "I can bring it next time." I saw Izzie lean toward her, whisper something in her ear, but I couldn't make out the words.

Beside me, Kira said, "Whoa, someone's gonna pass out!"

I looked around the table, wondering who she was talking about, then I realized everyone was staring at me. She was talking about me.

"I'm not gonna pass out," I told her.

But the words came out more like, *Immma nota psssss ut,* and I realized my recent assessment of my personal state of drunkenness might have been slightly off. I said this last part aloud, and that just brought a laugh from everyone, including Chloe—Miss Thursday—who easily should have gotten here first, but if she was as drunk as me, I didn't see it in her face. She seemed too busy thinking about what Spivey had just said. Or maybe she was thinking about Spivey's great-grandparents, because for some reason, I was, even though we hadn't talked about them. I was wondering how *they* died. More specifically, I was wondering *where* they died. I was wondering if Spivey had asked Marston *that.* Because he should ask him *that.*

I know I wanted to ask about them, but my mouth was no longer cooperating. I also realized I was lying down on the opposite end of the room from the others. Not sure when exactly I moved. Someone (most likely Kira) had set me up nice with a pillow and quilt, even a glass of water a few inches from my head.

They were playing the game again.

I heard someone (I think it was Spivey) dare Izzie to go down in the basement all alone. She had to stand down there in the dark for one full minute before she could come back up. Kira told her to check the pilot light in the furnace while she was down there—it'd been known to go out, you know.

I decided to sleep then, just for a little while. I drifted off wondering if anyone had bothered to feed Emerson.

When I woke, the room was dark, and I was alone. The lights were out, the candles were dead, and all was silent. Twenty after four in the morning, according to my watch. I drank the water Kira left for me and got to my feet. I needed to use the bathroom, but instead of going that way, I found myself at the window. That's when I saw them. Kira and Matty. Sitting out there in the moonlight on a big rock (not unlike *our* rock) facing the ocean. A blanket draped over their shoulders. Gentle waves were rolling in. I didn't much care about the ambiance—heat rose in my gut, and I wanted to put a knife through the back of Matty's head.

Going outside was a blur, and so was my lumbering approach across the narrow beach to the rocks. I didn't have a knife, so I picked up one of those rocks instead, felt the weight of it in my hand, the heft. Found a nice, sharp corner. It would do nicely.

When I reached them, though, there was no *them*. Kira was alone.

There was no rock in my hand either, and I was thankful for that, because she turned when she saw me and smiled. "There's my sleepy head. Did you get sick?"

I opened my mouth to tell her no and vomited in the sand.

06/28/2010 - MONDAY

1

WHALEY HAD RELOCATED to the small conference room across from his office. His cluttered desk was simply no place for additional clutter, and the moment he started unloading the box from storage, he knew he'd need more room.

He'd never been much of a reader, so rather than slog through the copy of *Brigadoon*, he'd stopped at Video Zone on his way home last night and rented a copy of the 1954 film starring Gene Kelly and Cyd Charisse. Mary had eyed him curiously when he'd put that one in the VCR, but after a few minutes, she made a bowl of popcorn and settled in beside him.

"It's for work," he'd told her.

"Uh-huh."

And that had been that.

He enjoyed it a little more than he'd ever admit publicly, and Mary had nodded off about an hour in. To her credit, she usually only lasted about twenty minutes on movie nights before giving in to sleep.

About the same time she started snoring, he took the book out and flipped through the dog-eared pages and highlights, keeping pace with the film. He kept going back to the two sentences Chief Nelson had left in the margin:

Not every hundred years, but how often? What the hell is the trigger?

In the book and the film, the village only appeared once every hundred years. The film made no mention of a "trigger" or reason. It wasn't explained; it just was. Whaley supposed that might frustrate some people, but he didn't think it took away from the story. He had no idea why his predecessor would focus on it.

Then there was the first half of that comment—*Not every hundred years, but how often?*—both the film and the book (he found the first mention on page 138) specifically pointed out it *only* happened every hundred years. So what the hell was he talking about?

When the film ended at half past eleven and Whaley found himself sitting there in the dark with his wife passed-out on her half of the couch, a thought popped into his head—am I *seriously looking at some old musical as if it were part of an investigation? Actually treating it like evidence?*

Christ, if anyone got wind of that…

He set the book down on the end table, rose and stretched, and took his wife to bed.

His head would be clear in the morning.

Then it wasn't.

He spent the night tossing and turning with images of Geraldine Rote behind his eyelids, and finally went in to work about an hour before sunup, where he unpacked the box.

There were eight files in total:

Laura Dubin

Ted Hasler

Pam Rote

Keith Spivey

Ralph Peck

Lester Rote

Geraldine Rote

... And one simply labeled *Whidden*.

The first four had far more detail than the others. The Whidden file only contained a single sheet of paper, while the information on Ted Hasler was nearly an inch thick—everything from school transcripts and traffic citations to a full background check courtesy of the FBI's NICS database. It was the financial data that really jumped out, riddled with underlines and notes by Chief Nelson. He'd chronicled everything from Hasler's first few real estate transactions and loans back in the eighties and nineties to activities up until Nelson had retired. With the very first, he'd still been in high school—only sixteen years old when he purchased an acre of land in Rye with a private loan arranged by—

Whaley stared at the name for several seconds, as if expecting it to change when he blinked, but it didn't. There it was—*Lockwood Marston, Esquire*—in typed print, circled several times in blue ink, no doubt by Nelson.

Marston's name appeared on several of the other transactions, each one larger than the last. Whaley found similar dealings in the folders for Laura Dubin, Geraldine and Lester Rote, and even Ralph Peck, although those dated much further back. Geraldine inherited a sizable estate when her parents passed (including Wood Island), and Lester married in. As for Peck, although you'd never know it if you spoke to him, he owned several commercial properties, including a strip mall in Exeter. Dozens of transactions with Marston involved in one way or another.

If those particular folders detailed the creation of wealth over time, the data on Pam and Keith Spivey told a very different story. There were several arrest reports, delinquent credit card and loan statements, a copy of the restraining order. Arranged and cataloged in date order were two lives coming apart. Failure followed by failure. Other than the restraining order, Marston's name only appeared once—he'd attempted to post bail for Keith Spivey after a bar brawl in 2004. Keith had refused and opted to spend the weekend in jail.

Finally, Whaley held up the single page from the Whidden folder, a handwritten note predating Chief Nelson. He'd seen that one before—Nelson had actually told Whaley all about it when he took over for him years back. An old case, kind of a rite of passage. Whaley had no idea what it meant or how it played into all this.

"Chief?"

Sandy was standing at the door, frowning.

Whaley set the page down. "What is it?"

"Pam Spivey called in, damn near hysterical. Something about her son. I think you need to get over there."

2

I'M NOT SURE exactly what time I got home from Wood Island. We'd all piled into Matty's boat a little after sunrise and motored back to New Castle in relative silence. I had a nasty hangover, and I wasn't alone in that. There was little talk. We all communicated in grunts and nods, settled into our seats, and stared forward until we finally reached the shoreline. Kira and I thanked Matty for the ride, said a half-assed goodbye to Izzie and Chloe, got in my car, and that was that. I dropped Kira off at home, then drove on autopilot back to my house and my bed, which I fell into without bothering to take off my clothes.

Of all of us, Spivey had been the only cheerful one, not hungover at all. He'd offered to cook breakfast, said there was plenty of food, but we all bowed out on that.

Home.

Bed.

Yeah.

He'd stayed out on the island, said he'd take *Annabelle* home later.

Like I said, I wasn't sure what time I got home, but I know exactly what time I woke for the second time, because my father's heavy-handed knock on my door scared the shit out of me. I smacked my alarm clock off the dresser when I jerked awake in bed—thirty-five after eleven. Midday.

"Billy? You up?"

Two thoughts entered my head at the sound of his voice.

First, I was in trouble. Because it was summer vacation and I couldn't remember the last time my father had gotten me out of bed unless I was late for school or practice or something, and I had none of those things today. Second, it was Monday, and my father shouldn't be home— he should be at the office. Nobody should be home. Classes at University of NH had one week left. Mom would be at school, Dad should be at the office, and I should be sleeping off—

"Billy," he knocked again. "You have a visitor."

He tried the doorknob and tentatively opened my door.

I managed to get the sheets up around my neck as his head poked inside. I don't think he realized I was still dressed. If he did, he didn't say anything. He gave me a quick glance, then looked over at my desk in the corner of the room like he was slightly embarrassed as he spoke and wanted to offer me a little privacy. "Hurry up, son. It's important."

He was gone then, the door closed, and I sat up.

I had no idea if he remembered what I had been wearing the day before, but I shrugged out of my jeans and sweatshirt just in case and quickly threw on an old t-shirt and pair of shorts. I ran a brush through my matted hair, which did nothing but turn it into this disheveled poof that I then spent another minute trying to flatten before finally giving up. He knew I just got out of bed. Hopefully he shared that bit of news, because I was not prepared to impress anyone.

On my way out the door, I scooped up a container of Tic Tacs from my dresser, poured about half of them into my mouth, and crunched down—minty fresh, ready for the day.

I'm not sure who I expected to be out there waiting on me, but I can tell you who I didn't expect, and that was Spivey's father. Yet there he was, sitting on the couch in our living room, his hands folded in his lap, his gaze on Mom's Oriental rug under the coffee table. Dad was standing at the kitchen door, leaning slightly on the jamb. For the first time, I got a good look at him and realized he was dressed in a suit, which means he had either gone to the office and come back home or hadn't left yet. He never wore a suit on his days off.

He nodded over at the couch. "Billy, you know Mr. Spivey, right? David's father."

It was odd to hear Spivey's first name. Almost as odd as hearing his father called *Mr. Spivey*, because I'd always known him as Keith. Spivey was Spivey and Keith was Keith, and Christ, did my head hurt. I knew I smelled like beer, but that was probably okay since Keith *always* smelled like beer, and he was far better at it than I was.

My eyes briefly met my dad's, and I guess I hoped for some kind signal, a code word or something, but that never came. Instead, he nodded back at the man on our couch as if just the fact that he was sitting there explained all that needed to be explained.

Spivey's father looked up at me and twisted his fingers together. He was most definitely more of a mess than I was. His face was red and puffy. I wasn't sure if that was from the drinking, lack of sleep, or both. He had a fresh cut on his left cheek and his knuckles were bruised. Two buttons were missing from his flannel shirt, and I got the impression he'd just been in a fight. Like he literally just wrapped up some brawl, hopped in his car, and drove here. Turns out I was wrong about that, sort of.

"Mr. Spivey here came to my office for a visit this morning," my dad said. "He's worried about his son."

That set off my bullshit detector and brought me a little closer to awake. I couldn't remember a single day *Mr. Spivey* had been worried about his son any more than I could remember him being worried about his wife, the never-ending soap opera at their house, or anything other than where his next drink would come from. I didn't like the fact that my head went there first, but it did. I'd grown up alongside Spivey and heard all the stories. I'd watched their family come unglued and knew the man sitting in our living room was the least likely to care where those pieces fell. I wasn't a dumb kid; this was about money. That's why he went to my dad.

I swallowed what was left of the Tic Tacs and cleared my throat. "I thought you went out on the Milligan boat?"

"I did. Was. I had him bring me back. I probably should have gone home first and cleaned up, but this couldn't wait. I thought... I thought Pam had things under control, but she called me and..." His voice trailed off for a moment and he fidgeted with one of the scrapes on his left hand, his eyes looking left and right and back again like a tennis match was playing out on the floor. I'm not exactly sure how much time went by, but when he looked back up at me, his eyes were damp. "You know David is... Spivey... you know he's sick, right? He talks to you about it? I know you guys are close. I'm just not sure what he shares. He doesn't tell me."

My father was watching us, but he said nothing. He looked at me the way fathers were prone to do. Like they could see through you and read everything in between.

"I know he's in remission," I told Keith. "He seems to be doing much better than the last time. Stronger. Happier. He hasn't brought it up in close to a year."

The last time.

The last time he'd gone into remission, we were thirteen, and it lasted for nearly a year. The time before that, we were ten. Eight, I think, the third time. I didn't remember much about the first. It was his hair that always seemed to stick out from those earlier times in my memory. They'd shaved his head to stay ahead of the chemo, and when he was in remission, he rarely cut it at all. Some rebellious act of defiance. All our lives, he was either bald or growing it out. His hair was long now. Long enough for a ponytail.

Keith had said *is* sick. Not *was*. That wasn't lost on me.

Leukemia has symptoms, and when you grow up with someone fighting the disease, you become intimately familiar with all of them. With Spivey, it always seemed to start with these red spots on his skin. Sort of like a rash, but not. He'd get tired and drop weight. Didn't want to eat. When it got worse, there were fevers, swelling around his neck and under his arms. He'd bruise easily. His skin grew pale and became this patchwork of white, red, purples, pinks, and blue. Then the chemo would start and all that would get way worse.

I thought of Spivey last night, laughing and drinking with us. I thought of the last few weeks, the last few months, and I couldn't recall any of these symptoms. I suppose Spivey might have hidden it from me, but he never had before. I might have been the only person he actually talked to about it. The last time the symptoms started to come back, he told me first. He told me before anyone.

"He was supposed to start treatment again this morning at Portsmouth Regional," Keith said. "He promised Pam and me he would go, but he missed his appointment and he's not answering his phone. I know he's out there at that... that house. I called the attorney..."

"Marston."

He nodded. "Right, Marston. I hoped maybe he'd go out there and talk some sense into him, but all he did was remind me that if I go out there, or if Pam goes out there, Spivey forfeits ownership. He rattled off Geraldine's bullshit rules for the tenth time. He doesn't give a shit about the boy's health. I almost had Milligan run me out there anyway. Figured who would know, right? But I can't do it. My boy hates me enough. I can't take away the one thing that's making him happy. Not right now. At least, I don't want to, but I will if I have no other choice. I'll drag him off that island screaming, if that's what it takes."

"Billy," my father spoke for the first time in a while. "Mr. Spivey and his wife both agree it's in their son's best interest to sell the property and use the funds to help with his care."

"There's a treatment center in Texas," Keith cut in. "Anderson Oncology. It's one of the best in the country. Our healthcare only covers a fraction of the cost, but if he sells that place, we'll be able to afford it. They're doing some cutting-edge stuff there, procedures you can't get anywhere else. They might be his only opportunity to beat this thing."

His voice cracked as he said all this. He was good, damn good, but I didn't believe him. I wanted to. I seriously wanted to believe this was

Spivey's dad looking out for his only child, but he had seventeen years' worth of baggage in the way, and there was no getting by that. I knew my own father, too. I knew where his head was at. I wouldn't be surprised to learn that he'd found this place in Texas and dangled the idea in front of Spivey's parents like a carrot—if you sell, they'll make your boy better, and you'll have plenty of money left over to solve the rest of your problems. Your bills will go away. The cancer will go away. College will be covered. No more trudging around on the decks of old fishing boats to put food on the table. How about a drink? I know it's early, but we should celebrate—good ol' Geraldine flicked a switch, and the light at the end of your tunnel is finally burning bright.

I saw all of this in my father's face as he watched me. He tried to hide it behind that poker-faced stare of his, but it was there. After allowing about a minute for everything to sink in, he held out my cell phone and said, "Can you try calling him?"

I didn't reach for it. I let him hang out there in the air. He needed to know I knew. Instead, I said, "There's no signal out there."

Of course, there was a landline. I didn't know the number, but the little voice in the back of my head said one of these men would have it. If they didn't, my father surely could get it.

There was also a rule to consider—*Don't answer the phone.*

Spivey would never pick up.

Turns out, he didn't have to.

My cell phone began to ring in my father's hand, and the three of us saw Spivey's name on the caller ID at the same time.

3

MY FATHER PUSHED the phone toward me, and I let it ring two more times before I finally took it from him and answered the call. I could see the anger brewing behind his eyes, but he did his best to keep it in check. Unlike Spivey's father, who wore his anger on his sleeve, my dad had learned to bury his under several layers of clothing.

I raised the phone to my ear. "Hey."

"Hey."

"What's going on?"

Spivey went quiet for a moment, then said, "Is he there?"

I didn't have the call on speaker, but his voice was loud enough for the three of us to hear. I could tell by the way they were looking at me. I looked over at Keith. "Yeah. He's here."

Another beat slipped by.

I could almost see Spivey chewing on his lip as he contemplated this.

"Can you meet me at my parents' house?" he finally said.

"When?"

"Now?"

I looked over at the clock, more out of habit than anything. His house was only a few minutes away. "Yeah, sure."

Spivey's father had stood up and was halfway to the door. I'm not sure if he heard this last part.

Spivey said, "Oh, and Billy?"

"Yeah."

"Bring your own car."

I took a quick shower—a boarding school shower, my father liked to call them. Three minutes of nothing but fast-moving hands and soap. Two minutes after that, I was dressed and heading for the door. Spivey's father was already gone. My dad looked like he hadn't moved—he was still in the living room, right where I'd left him.

"We should ride together," he said, starting for the door, keys in hand. "We need to talk about this."

I shook my head. "If all this is true, that's just going to spook him. You should go back to work."

He grabbed my shoulder, not hard, but enough to slow me down. "I think you and I need to get on the same page."

"We can talk later." I shrugged him off and went out the door. "I need to help my friend."

"That's what I'm trying to do, too," he replied, adding, "they'll take the legal route if they have to. He's a minor in need of treatment. They could say he's not of sound mind. This could get really messy."

I didn't respond to any of that. I wanted to, but I'm pretty sure if I said any of the things going through my head, this would turn into a fight. Instead, I got in my car, slammed the door, and left. I expected to see his BMW in my rearview mirror, but he didn't follow me.

Spivey's dad had parked at an awkward angle in front of their house. The door to his battered pickup was hanging open.

The moment I shut off my motor, I heard yelling—Spivey's dad, his mom, and Spivey, all three shouting over each other to the point where I couldn't make out any of it.

Spivey came flying out the front door, a stuffed backpack in one hand and a crate of CDs in the other.

He started toward my car. His parents appeared behind him, his dad bounding onto the porch and his mother stopping in the door-way, clenching a bathrobe in a balled fist, looking like she'd just gotten up even though the day was half over. I didn't even get my seat belt undone before Chief Whaley pulled up behind me and rolled to a stop. He didn't switch on his lights or siren. H e didn't have to; everyone went quiet at the sight of him. Spivey paused mid-step, glared at the patrol car, then stomped to my passenger door and yanked it open. He dropped into the seat and slammed the door. "Drive. Just drive."

I couldn't, though. Whaley was blocking me in. He'd gotten out of his car and was walking up toward my window.

"Goddamn it, Billy. Go!"

"Just calm—"

"Don't tell me to— "

Whaley knocked on my window.

I forced a smile that probably looked as fake as one of my dad's and rolled the window down. "Afternoon, sir."

Christ, I sounded guilty and I didn't do anything.

Whaley looked across my car at Spivey's parents on the porch, then crouched down. He glanced past me to Spivey in my passenger seat. "What's going on, son? Where you off to?"

Spivey didn't look at him. He glared at my dashboard, red-faced. "You know exactly where I'm going."

"I heard you have someplace else you oughta be."

"Who called you?"

"Your mother. She's worried."

Spivey grunted. "Worried. Right. Worried her golden goose is getting away is more like it."

"I think she just wants what's best for you."

"They can't make me go. Neither can you."

"You're a minor."

Spivey's hand went to the pocket of his jeans and I saw Whaley tense. He actually started to reach for his gun and stopped himself, probably some instinctual cop thing he nixed after telling himself it was just Spivey, but involuntary or not, that didn't make the move any less scary.

Spivey found what he was digging for, a business card, and he reached across me and held it out to Chief Whaley. "That's the number for my attorney. I spoke to him an hour ago. He said they can't force me any more than you can. He told me I had the legal right to refuse the moment I turned sixteen. If they want to make me sit in that chair again, they have to get a court order, and with me turning eighteen in less than a month, there's no way a judge will sign off on that. I'm not going through treatment again. They can't make me. You can't make me. Nobody can make me." He looked Whaley dead in the eye. "If you try, he's ready to drop a lawsuit on my behalf against you and the town for violating my rights."

Whaley nodded at the card but didn't take it. "This that Marston fellow?"

Spivey nodded.

The radio on Whaley's shoulder squawked. Sandy Lomax's voice. *"Chief?"*

He reached up and pressed the transmit button. "This is Whaley. Go ahead."

"We just got a fax from some lawyer addressed to you. He's threatening to sue you if—"

Whaley pressed the transmit button again, cutting her off. "Just put it on my desk, Sandy. I'll take a look when I get back."

"Copy."

Whaley drew in a deep breath and looked over at Spivey. "Not much of a dawdler, is he?"

"He'll win," Spivey said flatly. "I don't want to, but I'll tell him to file if I have to. He's already working on having me emancipated retroactively and evaluated mentally so they can't try and bring in someone to say I'm crazy. They want to take this from me, and I'm not going to let them. Nobody is telling me what to do. Not anymore."

His palms resting on my door, Chief Whaley splayed out his fingers in surrender. "I'm not here to pick a fight, son. Tell me what you want to do."

"I wanna be left alone."

"The way your mother explains it, there's a window on your treatment."

"I. Want. To. Be. Left. Alone."

He enunciated each word, and if there had been room in my car, I got the impression he would have stomped his feet in time as he spat them out, sounding more like an aggravated toddler than my best friend, but it was clear to both of us there was no changing his mind.

"Okay," the chief said, rising to his feet. He gave me a look, one that said, *work on him*, and I just turned away. If they were pulled in yet another direction, my arms might tear off.

Spivey's parents remained on the porch, watching this play out. I'm not sure how much they were able to hear, but the moment Whaley started back toward his car to move it out of our way, Spivey's dad was moving. He'd grown up with Whaley, playing tee-ball together as kids—and cop or not, Keith was fuming. Whaley shouted something at him through the open window of his patrol car, something with enough teeth to stop him in his tracks, then he pulled the cruiser off to the side and motioned for us to go.

I started my car back up and put it in reverse before someone changed their mind. I didn't want to be anywhere near this anymore. "Where are we going?"

"Can you come back out to the house with me? There's something I want to give you."

I nodded. I didn't want to go back out there, not now. But I wasn't about to abandon my friend either.

"I docked *Annabelle* at the Piscataqua café." Spivey settled back in the seat and watched his parents and the chief shrink in the side mirror. "You can park around back."

4

SPIVEY DIDN'T SAY another word as we drove, and neither did I. This thing needed to simmer down. We were on the water, halfway back to Wood Island, before he finally broke the silence.

"Don't tell anyone the cancer is back, okay? I don't want them to treat me different, and they will. You know they will."

Spivey stood at the helm of *Annabelle*, one hand on the wheel, the other on the throttle, motoring us across the harbor with the skill of a lifelong sailor, not someone who'd only come into possession of the boat days earlier. The sky was slightly overcast and the air cool for July, but it felt good to be out on the water, breathing in the salt. The moment we left the dock and pulled away, it felt like the tension remained behind us on New Castle like discarded baggage. The growing rift between me and my dad seemed to shrink the farther from shore we got, and at that moment, part of me understood why Spivey wanted to run.

"Why didn't you tell me you were sick again?"

Spivey didn't look at me; his eyes remained on Wood Island, growing larger as we drew near. "If you saw the look on your face in the car when you picked me up, you'd understand why. Pity or something. Worry. I don't know, but that look wasn't there last night when we were all hanging out having fun. It was obvious someone told you. You suck at hiding that crap. I guess I just wanted one summer where everything was normal. No doctors, no worrying about bloodwork, no tests, no treatments, no hair loss, fatigue, or getting sick for no reason. I just want to be a normal teenager. Couple months. That's it. This is really our last chance for that. We graduate next summer, head off to college, start whatever comes next. This summer—cars, boats, girls, no real responsibility—it's our last chance to just be kids. You get that, right? I'm sure you feel it too."

I knew what he meant. The future felt like this big, looming void. Senior year. College. Career. Family. Adulthood. A year ago, all that seemed so far off; now it was just over the next hill. In many ways, he was right— this was our last chance to be teenagers, to enjoy the moment. But none of that changed the fact that he was dying and didn't have to. The future was scary, but I wanted him in it.

My grip on the side of the hull tightened as we bounced over a series of waves. "You can't skip treatment, though."

"I'm not skipping treatment. I'm just putting it off until the end of summer."

"Can you do that?"

"I can do whatever I want."

"That's not what I mean. What happens if you wait? Doesn't it just get worse?"

"It's *barely* back," Spivey replied. "I can read my bloodwork as good as the doctors at this point. I've seen it all my life. My white cell count is just a little high. It was way worse when we started treatment the last time. *Way worse*. If I wait a few months, it's not going to make any difference."

"What about this treatment center in Texas your dad—"

He waved a hand. "Marston found someplace way better in Vancouver. He's working on getting me in and said my trust will cover the bill. My parents' plan is bullshit. It's just their way of taking control. And even if I wanted to do all that, I can't."

"Because you can't sell."

He nodded. "I can give the property away or pass it to my heirs like Geraldine did, but I'm not allowed to sell. If I do what Marston says, I get to keep the house, I still get treatment…"

"*And* you get your summer," I added.

"We *all* get the summer of summers."

I let all of this sink in, and there was no denying that it made more sense. If my dad found the treatment center in Texas as part of some master plan to get Spivey to sell, he probably spent all of two minutes searching the Internet. No real thought, just someplace that fit the bill. I seriously doubted Spivey's parents found it. Neither of them seemed to have the skill to seek out something like that. This also meant my father wouldn't get the sales commission he was pining for, and Spivey's parents would get eaten alive by their debt. I was perfectly okay with those things happening as long as I didn't lose my friend.

"You're sure you can wait? On the treatment?"

Spivey eased the throttle and brought us up alongside his dock. "I don't know all the specifics, but Marston gets paid by my trust, and those payments end if I die. He's got his own reasons for keeping me around, and I'm okay with that. I signed a few things the other day that allow him access to all my medical records and to speak on my behalf with the doctors. Let's just say I've got a lot more faith in him than I do in Keith and Pam."

I hopped out of the boat onto the dock, caught the line, and tied down *Annabelle*. Spivey shut the motor off and got out behind me, then started toward the house at a quick pace. "Come on."

He led me around the side, to the boathouse, and stepped inside.

I hadn't been in the boathouse yet, and my jaw fell open.

The ceiling soared at least twenty feet, maybe more, held up by large wooden beams and thick poles down the center of the room. The floor was made of wide pine planks worn with so many years, they looked more like stone than lumber. Two wooden rescue boats sat on ramps pointing at large black doors as if ready to deploy. One was painted a dark green and the other maroon. The walls of the boathouse were covered in anchors, life vests, oars, and vintage signs explaining safety protocols, tide charts, and weather patterns. There were also packs with safety gear and medical equipment dating back to the last century. Like the bunkroom upstairs, it felt like someone had captured time in a bottle.

Spivey gestured proudly at the two boats. "Pick one."

I think my jaw dropped the rest of the way to the floor. "What?"

"If we're about to spend the greatest summer of all summers out here, I can't have my best friend hitching rides. You need your own boat."

"I… I can't just…"

"Oh, you can and you will." He stepped closer to the green boat. It bore the name *Mervin F. Roberts* in stenciled letters on the bow. "I had Matty look them over and he said this one was the best. It's wood, like *Annabelle*, but solid construction—clear white oak frame and cypress planking. Grams kept up the maintenance." He reached inside and ran his hand across the small helm. Opened a door and revealed a hidden steering wheel and controls. "This one's got a small inboard motor. Think of it as an aftermarket upgrade. The boat dates back to the thirties, but the motor is almost new. I think she had them hide it all like this to keep the original aesthetic." He nodded at the maroon boat next to it. "That one requires oars and about six people to operate. It's pretty, but not practical. Totally your call, though. Pick one."

I wasn't sure what to say.

I walked around *Mervin F. Roberts* in a slow circle, sliding my hand over the wood and paint. Nearly a hundred years old, and it looked like it had never been in the water. I was speechless, literally speechless—I opened my mouth and nothing came out but a thin gasp.

Spivey beamed. "*Merv* it is!"

"You can't give me a boat."

"Well, technically, you're right," Spivey replied. "Another of Grams's rules. I can't give it to you because it belongs to the island." He raised a finger. "However, I can let you borrow it indefinitely. Think of it as a loaner. It's yours to use for as long as you need it. End of summer or whatever, it comes back here. Deal?"

I couldn't say no, even if I wanted to.

07/02/2010 - FRIDAY

1

TURNS OUT IT was Chloe—a.k.a. Thursday—who eventually got Alesia Dubin to come out, not Kira. It was Friday, the 2nd of July. Four days since Spivey's defection from home.

It had only been four days, but a lot had changed. For starters, word had gotten out. Alesia Dubin wasn't the only newcomer to the house. When Kira and I motored up in *Merv*, there were six other boats tied off on Spivey's dock, and the only one I recognized was Matty's. A couple kids from Portsmouth High were standing around outside near the rocky shore, drinking and smoking cigarettes. Even more were inside. At least a dozen semi-familiar faces—people I recognized, but nobody I would consider a friend. Not a close friend, anyway. There was trash strewn around too, and I didn't like that. Spivey's grandmother had kept this place spotless, and litter felt disrespectful. In the kitchen, just inside the door, Spivey had posted a large sign with the house rules. Some were familiar, others were new.

THE RULES
Please Feed Emerson
Don't Answer the Phone
Watch Pilot Light in Basement

Anyone Here at Sunset Must Stay Until Sunrise (Unless Spivey says you can go)

Never Lock the Doors

Nothing Can Be Removed from the House

If you Start a Drink, You Must Finish the Drink

No Rap, Reggae, or Country Music Permitted

Violators will Be Shot

Second Floor and Above = Off Limits to Guests (Unless Spivey Approves)

Spivey is King

So it is written, so it shall be.

There was a black marker on the counter. Kira picked it up and added a rule of her own:

You Must Pick Up All Trash

She replaced the marker, and I kissed the top of her head. "Good call."

Some kid with moppy blond hair was stationed at the refrigerator, apparently tasked with handing out beer. He thrust a can into each of our hands as we stepped into the crowded living room. There were at least fifteen people crammed in there. The stereo was off and the room was oddly quiet. All the lights were out. Several people were sitting in a circle on the floor with others standing around. Spivey was there, Chloe and Izzie next to him. Another girl who looked familiar, I think her name was Kelly. Then Matty. And to Matty's left, Alesia Dubin.

All of them had their eyes closed and were holding hands. A coffee mug sat on the floor between them in the center of their circle, and although the room was dark, I could make out *Henry's Market* stenciled on the side. Kira squeezed my hand. "Is that…"

"Can't be."

Because it couldn't be. If Spivey's grandmother had in fact poisoned herself (and at that point, I had heard from numerous people that she had), Whaley would have logged her mug into evidence. It would be safely tucked away at the police station or maybe some county facility. There was no way it could be sitting in the middle of Spivey's inherited floor.

Alesia's dark hair was swept back over her shoulders, and she wore a silver chain around her neck with some kind of green amulet dangling between her breasts. It had an odd glow to it, either reflecting the little light in the room or phosphorescent, I wasn't sure. She tilted her head back and said in a low voice, "Geraldine Rote, we command you to appear to us one and all, show yourself and be one with us, join us from the afterlife. Your spirit is among friends. Your spirit is home. Use this vessel of death as a conduit, a tunnel. Allow it to anchor you. Follow my voice to this familiar place. Follow my voice from the dark void to this place of light. Come back to us, Geraldine Rote. Come home..." She let the words hang there for a moment, then opened one eye. "Now, Spivey."

Spivey cleared his throat and said, "I, the blood of your blood command it."

"Show us you're here," Alesia said softly. "Give us a sign."

I don't think anyone was breathing, myself included. All these people, as still as statues, their eyes fixed on the small circle on the floor, on the coffee mug at the center of them.

Bang!

Kira yelped. Half the girls in the room screamed. A couple of the boys, too. My heart cracked against my ribs with enough force to send my last breath back up. Everyone's eyes popped open and all the heads in the room turned toward the noise in one fluid jerk.

A boy I didn't recognize was standing in the doorway of the library. He wore a button-down shirt and suspenders, and a name-tag was glued to the center of his chest. It read *Hello, I am Benny*. He'd dropped his beer (the source of the bang), and it was slowly spreading around his feet in a damp, foamy pool. "Sorry!"

"Ah, Christ." Spivey groaned. "Someone get him a towel."

A towel flew in from the kitchen and smacked *Hello, I am Benny* in the head.

Spivey got to his feet. "Clean it up, then you're on pilot light duty in the basement. Nik nok."

"Yes, sir," Benny replied, dropping to his knees.

Sir?

Kira leaned into my ear. "I forgot to tell you, Alesia thinks she's a witch."

"You're kidding, right?"

She shook her head. "She used Ancestry.com to trace her family back and found out she had a great-great-great something-or-other in Salem during the witch trials, and her relatives here on New Castle were witches, too. Not the creepy, pointy-hat scary kind. They used herbs to help heal people. Blessed houses, crops. That sort of thing. That amulet she's wearing is from the sixteen hundreds. Her mom gave it to her over the winter. I guess it's been passed down through all the women in her family. They're all witches."

"Isn't her mom the manager at Costco?"

"Exactly."

Yeah, so that made perfect sense.

Spivey came over before I could ask her what she meant. He was holding a beer, and judging by his eyes, not his first. "I was supposed to cut myself and drip the blood into the mug, but I'm not sure I'm ready to go there just yet. Project Poltergeist is still very much in the planning phase."

"I'm not sure I want to know what that is."

He turned to Kira. "You didn't tell Sleeping Beauty here about Project Poltergeist?"

Kira took a sip of her beer and smiled sheepishly. "I'm sorry, I didn't realize that was a real thing. We were all just talking."

Spivey sighed. "It's the greatest idea I've ever heard. How could it not be a real thing?"

"I'm not sure I want to know," I repeated.

"Chloe came up with it last night when the Ouija board didn't work," Kira said.

I felt a lump in my gut. "You were here last night? I thought you wanted to stay home and watch a movie with your mom?"

Kira's face flushed. "Mom went to bed early, then Chloe and Izzie showed up at my window. I snuck out for a few hours. Matty brought us over."

"Why didn't you tell me?"

"It was late, I figured you were already in bed."

I looked over at Matty. He was hovering over Alesia, a big shit-eating grin on his face. He glanced over at me, raised his beer, then went back to her.

Kira put her arm around me and pulled me closer. "Oh, relax, Billy, it was just a ride."

"You should have told me."

Spivey cleared his throat. "Annnyway. We messed with the Ouija board for almost three hours and got nothing. I should have known it was bullshit when I realized it was manufactured by Hasbro. I seriously doubt the people behind Monopoly and Twister have the fast track to the afterlife." He nodded at the game box sitting up on the fireplace mantle. "I think we're gonna just burn it."

"You're not burning my Ouija board—I paid thirteen dollars for that," Chloe muttered, stepping up next to him with Izzie on her arm.

"Well, what good is it? It's broken."

"It's not broken, we just need someone to talk to." Chloe frowned. "You somehow inherited the only house in New England that isn't haunted."

Spivey raised his beer. "Well, to Project Poltergeist, then."

"Project Poltergeist!" Voices echoed all around us before drinking.

I wasn't sure I wanted the answer, but I asked anyway. "Okay, I'll bite. What is Project Poltergeist?"

Spivey's face lit up. "We're going to turn this place into a haunted house."

Chloe was grinning too. "Not like the kind that pop up around Halloween, all decorated with people in costumes jumping out at you trying for cheap scares, but a *real* haunted house."

"Why exactly would you want to do that?"

"The real question is why *wouldn't* you want to do that?" Spivey replied. "How cool would it be to own a haunted house?"

Not very, I thought, but I knew I was in the minority on all that. I knew seances were a regular part of Kira's sleepovers with her friends when they were younger, and Chloe was obviously obsessed. Probably Alesia too, and that meant Matty was on board whether he believed in that sort of thing or not. The idea clearly made Spivey happy, and considering all the nastiness with his parents hanging in the air, I wanted to see him happy. Every time his shirtsleeve rode up, I caught myself looking at his arms for those telltale red and purple spots, signs of fatigue, or any of the other symptoms, and I hated myself for that. I felt like I was spying on him, and I technically never agreed to do that. But I didn't say no either, and that may be where the guilt was coming from.

"How exactly do you make a haunted house?"

Spivey's eyebrows rose and a mischievous look spread across his face. "I'll show you."

2

WHALEY HAD ALWAYS been a light sleeper. He had no trouble dozing off in front of the television or even at the dinner table with the in-laws, but when it came to putting his head down on the pillow in his bed, closing his eyes, and shooting for an honest-to-God good night's sleep… well, his brain wasn't much into that. His wife, Mary, she had no trouble. He knew that because he spent nearly every night listening to her breathing as it quickly leveled off, then fell into that familiar, comforting rhythm after only a handful of minutes. He'd listen as he fought to keep his eyes pinched shut, reconcile the myriad of thoughts bouncing around his head, and sometimes count. Someone once told him counting was supposed to work, but it rarely did. Eventually, he did fall asleep, but he'd be up at one, again at three, five, then with the sun. All while Mary softly snored away, oblivious to all his tossing and turning.

When his phone rang at half past eleven, he knew it would be something bad—his phone only seemed to ring for the bad—and his brain muttered softly: *See, this is why I keep you up. Best to be alert and prepared like a good Boy Scout. You're welcome.*

He pressed the answer button and raised the phone to his ear, knowing Mary would sleep right through it, as always. "This is Whaley."

"Chief, it's Mundie. Sorry to bother you."

"What is it?"

"We're getting noise complaints from out at Wood."

"Did you tell them to call Kittery? Wood Island's not our jurisdiction."

"Of course. I called Kittery myself, and they told me we need to handle it since all the kids out there live here on New Castle."

"Well, that's not exactly true, is it?"

Mundie sniffed. "We've been watching the boats as best we can, and we got maybe five townies out there right now—most of the others look like they came in from Portsmouth."

Whaley sat on the edge of the bed and ruffled his hair. "Then call Portsmouth."

"Did that already. They told me to call Kittery. Not their problem."

The next time his phone rang, it would probably be one of the local selectmen. Maybe a reporter for one of the area papers. Whaley knew kids were drinking out there. Probably a handful of drugs, too. There'd be sex, maybe a scuffle or two—typical teenage stuff. If it wasn't happening out there, it would be happening somewhere else, and while most people seemed to believe his job was to prevent it, he knew the truth—his job was to contain it. As long as it was all happening out there, it wasn't happening on one of his beaches or at the dead-end of one of his roads. It wasn't happening at the Commons or some other town property. Kids would be kids, and kids needed to be kids *somewhere.* How loud could it be? That island was at least a quarter-mile out.

"Try parking at the docks," Whaley suggested. "When a boat comes in from Wood, run a search. Give whoever's at the helm a field sobriety test. Seize anything seizable. Scare the shit out of them. Word of that will travel out there faster than anything. They need to know we're watching."

"If they're drunk, want me to arrest them?"

"Just don't let anyone drive. Give 'em a ride home, wake up their folks—make them pick 'em up, put the fear of God into all of them. Tell 'em next time they're getting booked, charged, the whole deal. This time, you're cutting them loose easy, but it's a single stamp ticket."

"Yes, sir."

Whaley glanced over at the red glowing numbers on his nightstand clock. "Anything else going on?"

"We got an Amber alert out of Newington about twenty minutes ago. Sixteen-year-old female, name of Lily Dwyer went missing around midday. She was at Fox Run Mall with some friends, went off on her own, and didn't show up for the meet-and-ride home. Probably nothing."

Friday night. Probably off with her boyfriend somewhere.

"Send her photo out to everyone and keep me posted."

His phone dinged.

"There you go."

Whaley glanced at the display. White, green eyes, shoulder-length blond hair. "Is this current?"

"About a week old. Her mom said she dyed her hair pink yesterday."

"Pink?"

"Apparently, that's a thing now."

Whaley rubbed the top of his scalp. "Well, should make her easier to find. No trace on her phone?"

"Either switched off or in a dead zone somewhere," Mundie replied. "Last tower pinged at the mall at a little after two."

That wasn't uncommon. Most parents forced their kids to switch on location tracking services on their phones, and if they didn't outright tell them to do it, they planted some kind of tracking app. Some did both. In the never-ending battle of Child versus Parent, teenagers tended to hold the upper hand, wise to all those little tricks. When they didn't want their parents to know where they were, most turned location services off. Some shut their phones down completely or left it somewhere. The savvier of the bunch handed their phone off to a friend (who would remain wherever it was they were supposed to be) while they went off to do whatever was really on deck, and the career parent one-uppers kept a second cell phone their parents knew nothing about.

Any parent who actually thought they had control of their teenager was living in la-la land.

"You nab any boats at the dock coming in from Wood, ask if they've seen her out there. You get a bite and we've got an excuse to head out there and check things out up close."

"Will do."

Whaley disconnected and settled back down on his pillow, pinched his eyes shut again, and listened to his wife's steady breathing, still out cold. This time he'd try counting backward from a thousand. He'd gotten to 627 when his phone pinged with a text message. Mundie again:

Portsmouth chief called—Lily Dwyer's mother told him her daughter went to the mall with a girl who lived out here on New Castle. Thought her name was Karla. We don't have a Karla. We do have Kira Woodward. I saw her head out to Wood with Billy Hasler about an hour ago. Want me to motor out and talk to her?

Whaley held the small screen several inches from his face, closer than he would have even a year ago—his eyes were going to shit. Not quite ready for glasses, but that day would come soon enough. Beside him, his wife coughed twice, then fell back into a light snore. He forced his vision to focus and read the message again, then let out a sigh. The gears in his brain were winding up, the machinery humming, starting the early shift whether he wanted to or not. Once the machinery was warm, there was little chance of slowing things back down. If he put his head back down on his pillow, he'd spend the next four hours staring at the ceiling.

He eased his feet off the bed and thumbed out a quick reply:
I'll go.

3

SPIVEY LED US to the stairs at the back of the house and down into the basement. Unlike the rest of the house, which was in pristine condition, the basement steps were made of worn splintered wood with a rickety two-by-four railing running down the side, clinging to the wall with loose screws. Several bare bulbs dangled from the ceiling, doing their best to beat back the dark and losing. The walls were chiseled granite, lined with old tool marks, thin cracks, and larger fissures where the stone had broken away, leaving the surface scarred.

"Marston said it took almost a year to build this, longer than the house," Spivey said. "All the rock had to be blasted and hauled away by hand. No heavy equipment back in the day, and even if they did have something like that, there was no easy way to get it out to the island."

I couldn't see the floor until we were halfway down, and I don't think Kira could either; she hugged the wall, and with each step her grip on my hand tightened. The air tasted damp and moldy, and I felt a pressure in my ears that made it hard to hear. "We're underwater right now, aren't we?"

"Technically, yeah. The basement floor is fifteen feet below sea level at high tide."

We reached the bottom, and I spotted Benny sitting in a metal folding chair near the far wall facing the furnace. Several empty five-gallon plastic buckets were stacked next to him.

"How's the pilot light, Benny?" Spivey asked him, tugging at the string of another overhead bulb.

He didn't look up or face us, only said, "Burning tight and bright, sir."

I stuck a finger in my ear and prodded around, trying to lessen the pressure, but it did little good. Like being on an airplane. I couldn't hear the music or any of the people upstairs anymore.

The basement was huge, and with the exception of Benny and his chair, empty. Every few feet, large beams rose out of the dirt floor to the trusses above, supporting the house. Only the furnace looked new. Several large oil tanks stood against the wall on one side, and an ancient wood-burning stove stood on the other. Lumber stacked next to that, old logs, everything covered in thick cobwebs. Pointing at the stove, Spivey said, "That's how they used to heat the house. Marston said it still works, so Grams left it as a backup. Wood ducts run from the stove to those trusses up there, then up to the other floors. At some point, someone ran modern metal ducts inside those and installed the furnace." He pointed at the opposite corner, at what looked like a large room without a door. "That's the cistern. Rainwater gets captured on the roof and runs down to there; it holds five thousand gallons. Sinks, toilets, showers… all the water for the house comes from there."

Kira kicked at the dirt on the floor. "If they dug out the basement from rock, why is the floor dirt?"

"Potatoes."

"Potatoes?"

"They grew potatoes down here," Spivey explained. "Onions… a few other things. Whatever they could, I guess. During the winter, it was easy enough to get stuck out here… water, food, even power, everything was—is—off the grid."

I knelt down and stuck my fingers into the dirt, then looked up at the ceiling above. "That's at least ten feet. How deep is the dirt?"

Spivey cocked his head and said over his shoulder, "How deep is the dirt, Benny?"

"Unknown, sir."

"Didn't I ask you to dig a hole yesterday and figure it out?"

"You did, sir."

"And?"

"Permission to show you, sir."

"Granted."

"What's with the military jargon?" I asked.

Spivey shrugged. "He's a kid, so I told him the only way he could hang out here is if he did everything I told him. No exceptions. Matty called him Private Benny yesterday, so I guess it stuck. Isn't that right, Private Benny?"

"Sir, yes sir." Benny went to the corner of the room, switched on another overhead bulb, and pulled a tarp off a very large pile of dirt. He then slid a piece of plywood off the hole beside it. "I got about six feet before I had to leave."

The three of us went over and looked down into the large hole; a shovel with a red handle was resting at the bottom. Old roots poked out from the sides like bony fingers. I thought of the hole back at the cemetery, the coffin holding Spivey's grandmother suspended above it, and shivered.

Spivey rested a hand on Benny's shoulder. "Head back upstairs. You can work on this again tomorrow. Take those buckets up with you."

"Sir, yes, sir." He gave Spivey a salute, retrieved the empty buckets, and hauled them up the steps.

"That's kinda mean," Kira said. "Treating him like some kind of slave."

A grin crawled across Spivey's mouth. "Forget that. Did you bring something?"

Kira nodded and reached into her pocket, took out an old silver hair comb. "This belonged to my grandmother. She was wearing it when she died."

Spivey's eyes brightened. "You're sure?"

"I was there. My mom and me. She passed away three years ago from complications of pneumonia at an assisted living facility in Dover. They told us she only had a few hours left, so my mom did her hair and makeup, helped her into one of her favorite dresses. She'd had this hair comb since she was my age. Her mother had given it to her, so we put it in her hair. We planned to bury her with it, but she left it to me in her will."

"It sounds important to you. Are you sure you're okay with this?"

She considered that, then nodded. "If it works, and I can somehow talk to her, it will be worth it."

"If what works?" I cut in. "How about someone fill me in on what I missed."

"Did you ever see *Pet Sematary*?"

This came from Chloe, who was standing midway down the stairs. I hadn't heard her come down.

"Sure," I replied.

"Everyone must bury their own," Spivey said in a thick New England drawl, his best imitation of the old guy from that movie. "It was Ms. Thursday's idea. Well, Stephen King's idea. Whatever. Either way, it makes sense. At least the core principle."

"It was *Alesia's* idea," Chloe corrected him. "She came up with it almost right away after I told her what we wanted to do."

Kira twisted the comb between her fingers, the tarnished metal catching bits of the dim light. "We're taking items owned by the dead and burying them down here. In the basement."

"Not just items *owned* by the dead," Chloe interjected. "Items *haunted* by the dead. Things from haunted places. Cursed objects. Whatever we can find. We're burying it all down here and capturing the energy. Alesia thinks the energy will build, and we might be able to channel it."

I could barely see her, up there on the stairs, nothing but a faint outline in the gloom, but something told me she was smiling just like Spivey, and that worried me a little. I wasn't sure what was worse—that she believed something that silly would work, or that it might *actually* work. Worse still, Spivey and Kira were standing there telling me all this as if they were rattling off facts. Like step-by-step instructions from IKEA.

"That's just a movie," I said.

Spivey shrugged. "Well, technically it's from a book."

"That doesn't make it true."

"Doesn't mean that it's not."

I looked down at the floor, at the dirt, and that's when I noticed something I hadn't seen at first. Maybe it was the dim light, maybe I just didn't want to see it, but there was no denying it now—the dirt floor was lumpy. Dozens, maybe as many as a hundred small holes had been dug, filled, and tamped back down, all over the basement.

Spivey slowly wandered around, gesturing at the ground. "We've got seat cushions from the haunted Music Hall in Portsmouth. A floorboard from the John Paul Jones House taken from the hallway where everyone says the ghost is most often seen. An old piece of rope from the Chase Home, that orphanage where the girl killed herself. Brian Neblow broke into their shed out back and cut off a length. Mallory Tilsdale's dad owns a crematorium in Exeter. She got us all kinds of stuff, things they find in the ashes after they burn the bodies—teeth, jewelry, pacemakers. I couldn't tell you what half the crap she brought yesterday was, but she had bags of it. We've got bullets from the display case at the historical society downtown. Bullets that *killed* people. An old sword and some knives. Everything buried down here is linked to the dead."

Chloe came down the rest of the steps and stood at the bottom. "Alesia said the items connected to people who died tragically, suddenly, or as part of some rage are the strongest, but they *all* hold power. Alone, they're probably harmless, faint, like a single firefly in a field. But you put them all together and you can light up the night."

"In King's book," Spivey went on, "the ground itself is haunted. It's an old Native American burial ground belonging to the Mi'kmaq tribe. Steve didn't make that part up—those people were real. The burial grounds were real. Their tribe was huge, but mainly north of here— Canada and up in Northern Maine. I don't know if they ever made it this far south, but the point is, the burial ground was the trigger, or the catalyst, facilitator, incubator, whatever… it all depends on how you look at it."

Spivey must have caught me looking back at the stairs. I only glanced away for a second, but that was enough. He knew me my entire life, and on some level, he understood how my mind worked. He knew I was thinking about the buckets he had Benny haul off.

"We've been bringing in dirt from all the area cemeteries," he told me. "Got two buckets just from around the Vaughn tomb. One of them came from inside—from the floor of the room where they found all the bodies." There was a fire in his eyes now, an excitement I'd never seen before. His voice dropped a little lower. "I made a new rule the other night—anyone who sets foot on the island needs to bring something that belonged to someone who died, something haunted, or a bucket of dirt from a cemetery, no exceptions. Nik nok."

The hair on the back of my neck was standing, same with the hair on my arms. I didn't know if this was because of what he'd just told me or because I felt like I was standing at the center of a mass grave, and I didn't much care. I wanted to get out of that basement. I probably would have if Kira hadn't been holding my hand when she crossed to the west wall, near the cistern.

"Is this a good spot?"

"Sure," Spivey told her. "You have to dig the hole with your hands, no tools, like in King's story."

I hadn't seen *Pet Sematary* in a long time. It had been even longer since I'd read the book, but I remembered the ground being hard, like rock, nearly impossible to dig. Kira had no such problem. She scooped away the dirt with very little effort, dug her hole, and presented her grandmother's comb. The ground opened up and welcomed her gift like a hungry child. Swallowed it whole as she swept dirt back over the top and patted it down with her palms.

From the top of the stairs, someone shouted, "Spivey! Get up here!"

4

SPIVEY LOOKED UP at the ceiling as if he could see through the floor and catch a glimpse of whatever was happening upstairs, then he shot up the steps, two at a time. The rest of us followed after him.

The house was empty—everyone had gone outside.

We were in the kitchen, nearly to the door, when Kira stopped me. "Your hand is bleeding."

A nasty splinter was sticking out from my palm, probably from the basement railing. I pinched it between two fingers and plucked it out, but that didn't help matters much—it was like removing a cork from a bottle. Blood began to pool in my palm and drip down the side of my hand.

Kira grabbed a dish towel from the counter and quickly wrapped it, then looked back toward the center of the house. "We need to find you a bandage."

"Later," I told her, heading for the door. "I want to see what's going on."

With my good hand, I pulled her outside, and we found everyone standing out near the dock. The tide was in, and only a narrow sliver of the beach remained.

"Oh, crap. It's Rory Moir," Kira said, catching a glimpse through the crowd.

I saw him then, too. Not just Rory, but his two lapdogs, Zack Kirkley and Colin Booth. "What the hell are they doing out here?"

"Alesia."

"Huh?"

"She's been sorta dating him."

"Sorta?"

"They dated last summer and on and off before that," she quickly explained. "They went out a couple times over the past few weeks, and she remembered all the things she didn't like about him and broke it off yesterday. That's why she agreed to come out here and maybe give Matty a shot."

Oh shit, Matty.

That's when I heard him.

He shouted something from the opposite side of the crowd, near the water.

"Come on."

I led Kira through all the people and we made our way to Spivey.

Matty was standing to his left, Alesia behind him. Rory was on the right, between Matty and the dock, a half-empty beer bottle in his hand. Zack Kirkley and Colin Booth flanked him, their hands balled into fists, ready for a fight.

"Get in the boat, Alesia." Rory's arm flapped behind him, gesturing toward a small skiff tied loosely to the far end of the dock. His words were slurred, and it was clear this wasn't his first beer. Like Matty, Rory worked the fishing boats with his dad on weekends and during the summer, and that kept him in pretty good shape. If I had to set some kind of pecking order, I was bigger than Rory, Rory and Matty were an equal match, and Spivey was the runt of the litter.

That didn't stop Spivey from walking out between both of them.

"If she doesn't want to go, she doesn't have to. You don't have permission to be out here." Spivey took a step closer, got right up in his face. "This is private property."

I'd never seen him stand up to Rory like that.

Rory went bright red. "Shut up, dickhead. Nobody's talking to you."

Zack and Colin took several steps closer. The three of them formed an arrowhead of drunken assholes with Rory at the point.

"Get in the boat, Alesia," Rory ordered again.

Matty took a step forward, tried to get Alesia to move further behind him, but she didn't budge. Instead, she shook her head. "I'm not going anywhere."

"The three of you need to leave," Spivey insisted. "Now."

"We're not going anywhere without my girl."

"I'm not your girl," Alesia shot back, her feet firmly planted in the ground. "I'm not anybody's girl."

Rory shot her a dismissive look, the corner of his mouth curling up just a little. He was hoping for a fight and made no attempt to hide it. His eyes were glossy and held this maniacal look. They darted around the crowd from Alesia to Spivey to Matty and all the others standing around, like he was sizing up his chances and the potential audience not *if* this played out, but *when*. He looked like a wild animal backed into a corner. Although he'd come here for Alesia, it was Spivey who had his attention now, and that seemed to fit the bill just right. Rory's muscles twitched under his shirt. "I've been waiting years to kick your sorry little ass. This seems as good a spot as any," he spat out. "You're nothing but a pussy, just like your daddy."

Spivey took another step toward him, and I knew that was a mistake. Rory wanted him to make the first move.

I started toward them both, but Kira held my arm. "Don't," she said softly.

Rory could kick Spivey's ass on any given day, no doubt about that, and with the leukemia back, he had no business fighting. I hadn't told Kira, Matty, or anyone else about all that because I promised Spivey I wouldn't. But my folks knew. Spivey's parents knew. Others too. And if something happened to him, *if I let something happen to him*, I wouldn't be able to live with that. First and foremost, he was my friend.

"He needs help." I pulled away before she could say anything else and went to Spivey's side. "Get the hell out of here, Rory."

Thankfully, Matty stepped up too.

The rest of the group collectively shuffled back a step or two, clearing room for whatever came next.

Rory didn't seem the least bit worried about any of this. He chugged the rest of his beer, then cracked the bottle against a rock and reversed his grip on the neck—jagged glass, sharp end up. "Zack, what did we see in the water on the way here?"

"A shark."

"What kind of shark?"

"Great white. Right over there." Zack pointed just off shore, no more than fifty feet beyond the dock.

"Big, right?"

"At least a ten-footer. Maybe eleven. Big enough."

Some spit dripped down the corner of Rory's mouth, and he didn't bother to wipe it away. The look in his eyes had gone crazy, hungry. He twisted the broken bottle in his hand. "I bet if we carved up Spivey and his buddies nice and good and tossed them out there in the water, they'd be gone in a minute."

"Oh, a ten-footer would make quick work of them," Zack agreed. "And where there's one, there's more. Nothing draws a frenzy like chum in the water."

"Drop the bottle, Rory," Matty said. "Don't do anything stupid. You're gonna get yourself hurt."

"Alesia needs to get in the boat, or a lot of you are gonna get hurt."

A rock sailed over my head and caught Rory in the shoulder. A nice hefty one, solid granite. His body twisted with the blow, and his free hand went to the spot where he'd been struck. That crazy look in his eyes grew worse as he glared at the rock near his feet, then back at the crowd. "Who the fuck?"

Alesia was already holding another one, bigger than the last. "Leave, Rory. Nobody wants you here."

"You skanky bitch. You trying to get cut too?"

Someone threw another rock.

This one hit Colin Booth in the forearm. He yelped and shuffled back several steps. Another rock caught Zack Kirkley square in the chest.

"You're trespassing," Spivey said. "All three of you. On my property. I'm within my right to use deadly force if I have to. I'm allowed to defend myself."

Spivey's hand snaked around his back and slipped under the tail of his t-shirt. That's when I saw it.

I could get behind rocks, but not this.

I had no idea where or when he'd gotten a gun.

I didn't know what kind it was; I could only see part of the handle sticking out the back of his jeans, but a gun was a gun, and holy shit, Spivey had a gun.

I choked down the lump in my throat. "Spivey, you don't want to do that."

Growing up in New Hampshire, none of us were strangers to guns. We'd gone on hunting trips when we were younger. My parents had at least three handguns at the house and two rifles. I knew Spivey's dad had several hunting rifles and a shotgun, although it had probably been years since he'd picked one up. There were two very simple rules we'd all had drilled into our heads since we were kids—only pull a gun on another person in self-defense, and never pull a gun on another person unless you were prepared to use it. After years of torture at Rory's hand, I was willing to bet Spivey wanted nothing more than the chance to pull that trigger. New Hampshire laws gave him the right to do so, but I had no idea what the law was in Maine, and technically, that's where we were standing. I only knew if he took out that gun, there was a very good chance Rory would end up with a bullet in him.

Drunk or not, Rory sensed something had shifted. He'd seen Spivey reach behind his back, but more importantly, he'd seen the faces of all the people standing behind Spivey. "Last chance, Alesia. You either come with us, or you're one of these losers. There's no coming back."

"Oh, I think I'll be okay right here, Rory."

Spivey's grip tightened on the gun. His arm was trembling. Not much, but I could see it. Rory saw it too, and that slight sign of weakness reignited whatever fire was burning within him. His eyes narrowed and he twisted the bottle in his fingers. "What you got back there, Spivey? You planning to stick me with a knife?"

Spivey's grip tightened on the butt of the gun. He tugged it slightly out of his jeans.

"Spivey…" I said his name softly, enough to get his attention. I was about to grab the gun from him, but I didn't get a chance.

The flash of red and blue lights lit up the harbor.

That was followed by several chirps of a police siren.

5

THINGS MOVED FAST.

"Give me the gun," I quietly told Spivey. He did. A revolver. I dropped it in the sand at my feet in one quick motion, burying it with the toe of my shoe as I watched Chief Whaley and two other cops pull up to the dock and tie off. I hoped Spivey, Rory, and the others standing between us were enough to block Whaley's view.

I wasn't the only one to move. Rory tossed the broken beer bottle into the water. He didn't try to hide the move—like a drunken pitcher, he wound up and threw the busted bottle overhand. It splashed into the surf and vanished.

Between hushed whispers, other bottles and cans disappeared. None of us were old enough to drink, and hiding your alcohol when the police appeared was practically an instinctual move. Chief Whaley saw all of it as he walked down the dock toward us, Officer Sandy Lomax behind him. Officer Mundie stayed out on their boat.

"Littering out here is a five-hundred-dollar fine, Mr. Moir," he told Rory. "I should make you wade out there and find it."

Without missing a beat, Rory told him, "Lucky for me, we're standing in Maine right now and not New Hampshire, Chief. Jurisdictions and all that. I'd hate to see you overstep."

"Yeah, lucky for me." Whaley eyed him for a second, then cocked his head toward the dock. "The skiff back there is yours, right? If we search it, what are we going to find onboard? Better yet, if I hold it and call the marine patrol out here, what will they find? Being a friend of your father's, it's probably best I have them do it. Only thing worse than a jurisdictional problem is conflict of interest, and should something illegal be found on your boat, I'd hate to have some pesky detail like that get in the DA's way when he charges you. That also saves me the trouble of listening to your dad try to bail you out again. Much cleaner if I let them haul you in. Cleaner for me, anyway."

Rory waved a drunken hand toward the crowd and raised his voice. "You gonna bust everyone, Chief? I'm no lawyer, but this sure feels like harassment. Singling out me and my friends when you got this whole group out here."

"You're the only one trespassing, Rory," Spivey said.

And that got him an irritated stare from both Rory and the chief. Whaley let several seconds tick by before facing Rory and lowering his voice. "You best leave, Rory, before you say something to get yourself in real trouble. I'll give you sixty seconds to find your way back to your boat and off this island, and you'd better have the common sense to sit your ass down in the passenger seat and let someone else do the driving. You wanna give me an excuse to haul you back to the station, I'm fine with that too. We'll sort it out when you're sober. Your call."

Rory looked like he was about to say something more, dig himself a deeper hole. He even turned his bloodshot eyes back on Spivey, and for a second I thought he might mention the gun, but he hadn't gotten a look at it, didn't really know what Spivey was about to pull from behind his back, and he didn't do that either. Instead, he smiled at Whaley and started toward the dock. "Catch you soon, Spivey! Real soon."

Zack Kirkley and Colin Booth followed after him, and all three climbed down into their skiff with Officer Mundie watching closely from the patrol boat. Colin got behind the wheel, not Rory, which was a good thing. When Colin twisted the key, the engine coughed, sputtered, and died. He tried three more times, but the motor wouldn't start.

Spivey took a step toward the dock. "Dammit, I really want them gone."

Luckily, the motor fired up at that point. They untied and vanished into the harbor.

Chief Whaley turned back to the crowd and raised his voice again. "It's late, folks. Probably time the rest of you get home, too. Everyone but Kira Woodward, Izzie Fernandez, Chloe Kittle, and Alesia Dubin.

I want the four of you to stick around. I know you're here, so don't try to sneak off on me."

Nearly everyone moved toward the dock, a mass exodus. Jurisdiction or not, no one wanted to push Whaley. He'd given an out, and nobody needed to be told twice. Except maybe me and Matty, because neither of us moved. I wasn't about to leave Kira behind, and Matty wouldn't bail on his sister. I'm pretty sure the caveman in him had made some kind of claim on Alesia too, even if she wasn't quite ready to acknowledge that.

Without looking back at the dock, Whaley added loudly, "I know you're all responsible young adults and none of you would get behind the wheel while intoxicated. If anyone feels they shouldn't be motoring or driving, I suggest you form a line with Officer Mundie—he'll run you back to the beach and help you get home. I'd hate for one of the deputies I stationed back at the marina or the docks to pick you up for DUI." He glanced at Officer Lomax. "Can you give Mundie a hand? See that everyone gets home safely?"

Officer Lomax nodded and headed back toward the dock.

I shifted my weight and placed my foot on the spot where I'd buried the gun. I didn't mean to. It was one of those times where my subconscious hit the manual override on my brain and took over the machine. The last thing I wanted to do was draw attention, but that was precisely what I did. Whaley looked directly at me. I expected him to somehow see the gun under the sand, draw his own weapon, and tell me to get down, get out of the way, or maybe just shoot first, ask questions of the survivors later, but he wasn't looking at the gun, he was looking at the bloody towel in my hand.

"Do you need medical attention, Billy?"

Through all this, I'd completely forgotten about the cut in my palm, and when I looked down at the towel, I was surprised by the amount of blood. You'd think I'd lost a finger. I lifted my hand and tentatively peeled the towel away. Apparently, I'd run dry, because the bleeding had stopped. The cut was nasty, though. A thick chunk of my skin flapped there, red and angry. My hand was a sticky mess and began to throb. "I just caught a bad splinter. It will be okay. I can clean it up myself."

"You staying out here tonight?"

I nodded.

"Your folks know?"

He knew they did. I'm not sure if he said this to offer me some kind of cover or just out of habit. I nodded again anyway.

He looked over at Matty and the girls. "What about the rest of you?"

Soft nods all around, including Alesia, which surprised me.

Whaley seemed caught up by her, too. "You're Laura Dubin's daughter, right?"

"Yes."

"It's a big house," I told the chief. "Plenty of room for anyone who wants to stay."

"I'm sure there is."

I could see his mind working. Calculating whatever lies had been told to clear the way for all of us to drop off our parents' collective radar for the night. Determining ages, boy versus girl ratio. I'd always had a hard time pinning Whaley down, and I honestly didn't know if he'd keep all this to himself or get on the phone and wake up everyone's parents the moment he got back to the station. We'd inadvertently paired off—Kira with me, Alesia next to Matty, Izzie with Chloe—which wasn't lost on him either. Neither was the fact that Spivey was standing off to the side alone as the last of the partygoers worked their way down the dock.

Whaley cleared his throat and studied the faces of the girls he'd asked to stay behind, and I realized none of this was a surprise to him. He'd known they'd be here, knew before he'd even gotten out of his boat. He probably knew who was staying the night. Maybe knew who had stayed out here on previous nights. I had to wonder how closely he was watching this place. After that conversation back at my house with my folks and Spivey's dad, I also wondered who he was reporting back to.

"When was the last time you all saw Lily Dwyer?" he asked the girls.

Kira was holding my hand, and I felt her fingers tense at the mention of that name. I had no idea who Lily Dwyer was, but Kira certainly did, and if Whaley knew all that other stuff, he most likely knew the answer to the question he'd just asked. I wanted to tell Kira all that, but there was no way I could.

Kira exchanged a quick look with the other girls, then said, "She was with us at the mall earlier. Did something happen?"

"Did she come out here with you?"

Kira shook her head.

"When did you last see her?"

"At the mall, around one."

"Was she with anybody?"

Nobody answered that one, not at first, and Chief Whaley latched onto the silence, because the quiet was more telling than a shout. "She turned her phone off at twelve after one, at the mall. She didn't go home, her phone is still off, and her parents are worried sick. Who was she with?"

The silence again.

Izzie looked down at the ground. "She went to the movies."

"With a boy," Chloe added.

"What boy?"

Quiet.

Nervous glances.

"What boy?" Whaley pressed.

"She said his name was Brian," Alesia finally said.

"Brian what?"

"She didn't say."

"He's a senior at Exeter, if that helps," Izzie added.

Kira chimed in with, "She met him online."

"Why would she turn off her phone?"

"Because they went to the movies," Izzie said again.

I knew that was bullshit. Nobody turned off their phone to go to the movies. At best, they silenced it. If this girl turned off her phone at the mall, it was because she didn't want her parents to know she left the mall. The movie was bullshit too. Saying she went to the movies bought two hours, maybe a little more. Two hours away from the mall with this Brian guy, whoever this Brian guy was. If I saw through all this, I'm sure Whaley did too. That was clear by what he said next.

"Where did she *really* go?"

I half expected someone to say the movies again, and Chloe looked like she was about to, but she pinched her lips shut and said nothing.

"Look, girls," Whaley went on, growing impatient. "She's fifteen. She's been missing for more than twelve hours. It's one thing for you to cover for her so she can slip off with her boyfriend for a little while, but what we got here is something else entirely. I need to know what you know. What if it were one of you missing?"

Another look passed between the girls, and I could tell by the way Kira's gaze lingered on Alesia that there was a lot more to this. "You better just tell him," I said to her softly. "She might be in trouble."

Silence again, but not as long as before. Kira's hand grew clammy, cold. "Lily was supposed to meet us back at the food court at three, and she didn't show. We waited until four—"

"Quarter after," Chloe cut in quickly.

Kira nodded. "Quarter after. We did a few laps around the mall looking for her, but couldn't find her. At five, we had to leave. We figured this Brian guy would get her home."

"The guy she met online that none of you knew," Whaley said.

Again, Kira nodded.

"Can you describe him?"

"We didn't see him. She met up with him after she left us. Out in the parking lot, I think. She didn't really say."

"And you let her?"

"She's not exactly a friend of ours." Alesia shrugged. "We barely know her from school. She just heard we were going to the mall and asked us to cover for her, that's all. It was a last-minute thing. It's not like we're her babysitter or anything. She covered for me about a month ago, so I told her we'd cover for her. No big deal."

"No big deal," Whaley muttered. He clucked his tongue several times, considered all this, then asked, "I don't suppose any of you got a picture of her today? Something recent?"

All four reached for their cell phones.

I watched as Kira swiped through several screens and found a photograph taken earlier in the day. She was holding the camera, her arm stretched out and to the side—the image captured Alesia, Izzie, Chloe, herself, and a girl I didn't recognize with bright pink hair and a pair of round John Lennon sunglasses perched precariously on top of her head, all smiling at the camera, Toro's Tacos and part of the mall food court blurry behind them. She turned the phone toward Chief Whaley so he could see it.

He squinted and took out his own phone. "Can you send that to me?"

"You gotta use AirDrop," Spivey said. "There's no service out here."

Whaley held his phone up over his head. "No service? Why is that?"

Nobody answered. We still hadn't figured that one out ourselves.

Kira knew how to AirDrop, though, and the chief's iPhone dinged. "Just click on that to accept it."

He did, and the photo appeared on his screen. He looked back at Alesia. "No service… so if she tried to call any of you tonight, you wouldn't know?"

"She wouldn't call us." Alesia shrugged again. "Like I said, we barely know her."

"But she might." He looked back toward the dock. Mundie had run several kids back to the beach in the patrol boat and was on his way back. "I'll need you girls to come back with me so we can check."

A flash of panic ran through Izzie and Chloe's eyes. Of all of us, they'd get in the most trouble if their parents found out they'd lied and come out here.

Alesia said, "I'll go. If she tried to call anyone, it would be me. She doesn't have their numbers."

"You're all going," Whaley insisted, and before anyone could object, he started back toward the dock.

6

A MOMENT LATER, they were gone, their running lights fading into the dark.

I turned to Spivey and finally let out the breath I'd been holding for what seemed like ten minutes. "Christ, where did you get a gun!?"

"Grams had it. You think she'd live out here all by herself without some kind of protection? I found that one in the nightstand next to the bed, another on a shelf in the kitchen hidden in a jar, a third one in the couch cushions. Found two rifles up in the closet, too. There's probably more. Apparently, she was big on the Second Amendment." He looked around. "What did you do with it?"

"You could have hurt somebody!"

"Damn right. Think I'd let him come at me with a bottle? Fuck that. Marston told me under Castle Doctrine I can shoot anyone who trespasses out here. All I gotta do is ask them to leave once. If they don't, and I feel threatened..." He made a gun with his thumb and forefinger and mimicked pulling the trigger. "Boom."

"You think it's that easy?"

He grinned. "Did I miss a step? I should have plugged him."

"This isn't a fucking joke. You kill someone, and you'd have to live with that. You pull a gun on someone like Rory Moir, and you'll have to kill him. It's not like he'd walk away. Stupid idiot wouldn't back down. He'd give you a reason."

"Exactly. Nik nok."

"Just give it back to him." Matty groaned. "You don't have to get all fired up. Rory's a dick. He's always been a dick. He comes from a long line of dicks. If he's not dead by twenty-one, he'll be in prison.

Either way, nobody's gonna cry over him. Least of all, Chief Whaley. At this point, I'd be more concerned with when Rory plans to come back, because you know he will. No way he's letting *that* go. Too many people saw."

There was no point in arguing. I crouched down and dug the gun out of the sand. It was a .38, loaded with six rounds. When I handed it to Spivey, he fumbled the cylinder open, dumped the bullets into his hand, and blew the sand out of the barrel. "I'll have to clean it again."

"Marston teach you how to do that too?"

I'd meant that sarcastically, but Spivey nodded. "He did."

Matty was staring out over the water. "You think the girls are coming back?"

"Spivey almost shot someone and all you can think about is getting laid."

"Nobody got shot, and yes," Matty replied. "I'd like to get laid."

"No, Matty, I don't think the girls are coming back."

And they didn't.

Neither did I. Not for nearly a week.

07/09/2010 - FRIDAY

1

BY THE FOLLOWING morning, Lily Dwyer was all over the news. The county-wide Amber alert went state, then national. All of them showing that same picture from Kira's phone.

The image had been cropped so the other girls were no longer visible; there was only Lily Dwyer smiling up at the camera with her pink hair, dressed in a tan cardigan and jeans, last seen at Fox Run Mall in the company of an older boy named Brian initially believed to be a student at Exeter High. The police figured out pretty quick that he wasn't. Six "Brians" attended Exeter, all had alibis for the morning of July 2nd, and none had any clue who Lily Dwyer was.

I'd heard they searched Lily Dwyer's laptop and all her social media accounts and found no trace of the guy. That didn't really surprise me. We all used Tor browsers online whenever we did something we didn't want our folks to see. Tor bounced your signal all around the world and erased every trace of whatever you did. Kira actually maintained two Facebook profiles: a public one her parents could monitor and another under a bogus name only a few of us had access to. Using a program called SocialEase, she automated posts to the public profile so she didn't have to bother with it and occasionally "checked in" from public places so her parents knew where she was—or thought they did, anyway. She wasn't alone in all this; half my friends did it too. The point is, I knew whatever the police found on Lily Dwyer's computer and cloud accounts was probably fake, and her real life was hidden away somewhere no different than any other high school kid.

Someone had uncovered security footage of Lily Dwyer walking out the south entrance all on her own, and there was no footage of the parking lot. The mall's management company claimed insurance reasons prohibited the use of cameras in the parking lot. Kira and the other girls had been interviewed not only by Chief Whaley, but the state police and the FBI, and were unable to offer any more than they initially did. I'd seen that photo of Lily Dwyer so many times it was ingrained in my head. Their story never changed, and although I had no reason to doubt them, something about all of it felt off. When I told Matty, he just called me a paranoid asshole. Maybe I was.

Either way, I didn't go back. None of us did. Or at least that's what I thought.

I want to be clear about something. I didn't abandon my friend. Looking back on that night and what came later, particularly to someone looking in from the outside, it may seem that way. But if I did, it wasn't intentional. I just needed to get away for a little while and catch my breath. Regroup.

The Spivey standing on that beach about to pull a gun, the guy who seemed like he *wanted* to pull a gun, wasn't the kid I grew up with. In that moment, I didn't recognize anything about him. He'd always been the quiet guy with the odd sense of humor who liked to occasionally pick up a guitar. He'd been Rory's punching bag for a lifetime. For better or worse, that's how their particular puzzle pieces fit together. I protected Spivey when things went sideways—that's how my piece snapped in. Those were things I understood, things I could count on as being the way of the world.

Inheriting that house changed Spivey. Not just his financial situation, but *him*. I'm not sure I can explain it, even after all this time.

I've tried; believe me, I've tried. Emboldened him? Fortified? Strengthened? That might be close, but none of those words fully encompass the situation, because those are things you'd expect to happen. Transformed him? That might be closer. Whatever it was, I didn't want to be around it. The last time I saw the Spivey I knew was in the hallway at school when Chief Whaley had come to tell him his grandmother died. The guy I hung out with after that day was someone different, and the changes were still coming fast. The guy with the gun on the beach, that was a glimpse of who he was becoming. He reined it back in, and I was glad for that, but it wasn't meant to last. The guy with the gun would be back soon enough, and the next time, he'd be far more surefooted.

When I woke on Friday the 9th, a week after the business with Rory and the gun, I was home alone, both my parents at work, and I crawled out of bed at the ripe hour of eleven-thirty in the morning. Took a quick shower and headed toward the kitchen to get some breakfast, or maybe it was lunch. Whatever, I was hungry. I was supposed to pick up Kira at one for a day at the beach, so I had some time. Rye Beach (because I didn't want to look out at Wood Island off the coast of New Castle all day). Normal summer stuff. And that was exactly what I needed.

The door to my father's home office was open.

That was a rarity.

At first, I walked right by, and it didn't click in my head until I was standing in the kitchen, then I backtracked and found myself standing in the hallway looking in. Not exactly sure why.

Carrying a bowl of oatmeal, I'd wandered in there once when I was four and ate at his desk. I may have gotten some oatmeal on his chair. On the floor. On some papers he had left out. He wasn't happy about any of that and began locking the door that night. It had remained locked every time I tried the knob in the years that followed (I think I gave up checking around eight or nine). Even if he was home, he kept the door shut.

Standing there, looking in, I felt this invisible barrier at the threshold. Half of me suspected an alarm would sound if I crossed into the room. Maybe a buzzer would go off in Dad's pocket and he'd come rushing in. There might be a camera hidden away somewhere, the kind that would send him a picture of me looking all guilty creeping across the carpet. Although, that was silly. Not because he wouldn't go that far, but because he'd need my help to set up something like that. I was intimately familiar with our WiFi and everything on it, and he came to me whenever he needed the password.

I'd never once caught my parents snooping around my room. If they did, they were stealthy about it. On some level, I'm sure they knew digging around my drawers would be a violation of the trust between us. And looking in on my father's office, actually going in there, would be no different. Worse, in their eyes.

If I got caught.

His car wasn't in the driveway, I could see that much from where I stood; his office faced the driveway and the window behind his desk looked out onto the street. I'd see him coming.

I had no business in there, I knew that, but I needed some answers, and I knew he was holding back from me. The fact that he hadn't mentioned Spivey or Wood Island in more than a week told me he'd found some other source of information. His silence only meant he'd given up on getting my help. I was under no illusion he'd moved on.

Part of me actually felt justified as I stepped into his office and crossed to his desk.

There was nothing on the desktop, but I found what I was looking for in the top right drawer—a thick manila folder with *Wood Island* written across the tab in my father's neat handwriting. For the years that would follow, I don't think a single day of my life slipped by where I didn't think about the contents of that folder. The least of which was Geraldine Rote's Last Will and Testament—as disturbing as that was, the rest was worse.

2

I LATER LEARNED that wills are a matter of public record, easily obtainable by anyone willing to spend some time in the clerk's office and pay one dollar per page, but the morning I lifted the document from that folder, I had no idea how my dad had come upon it, and I suspected the worst. Shitty of me, I know, but that was the nature of our relationship.

The first page wasn't really anything special.

> *I, Geraldine Rote, resident in the City of New Castle, County of Rockingham, State of New Hampshire, being of sound mind, not acting under duress or undue influence, and fully understanding the nature and extent of all my property and of this disposition thereof, do hereby make, publish, and declare this document to be my Last Will and Testament, and hereby revoke any and all other will and codicils heretofore made by me.*

Considering Wood Island was technically in Maine, not New Hampshire, this opening seemed a little odd to me, but having never seen a will before, I figured someone much smarter than me had decided this was fine as is and left it. If I had to guess, she saw New Castle as her home and wanted to state that in some way. I wasn't alone in questioning that part. Someone (probably my father) had underlined that opening sentence and drew a big question mark off to the side.

The next section, titled *Expenses & Taxes*, stated all debts and expenses related to her death and funeral were to be paid by the estate at the discretion of her "Personal Representative" Lockwood J. Marston, Esquire, who is named in the third section.

None of this was new to me, so I flipped to the next page, which began with *Disposition of Assets* in large, bold letters at the top.

> *I devise and bequeath my property, as detailed in Schedule A, both real and personal and wherever situated, to my grandson, David Anthony Spivey, as full beneficiary to be held and maintained in*

Conservatory as detailed in the Conservatory Trust organized and administered under separate documentation by my Personal Representative or the acting Representative of my Personal Representative, should my Personal Representative become incapacitated.

That little bit made my head hurt, but I got the gist of it. Marston ran the show, and when Marston died, retired, or quit, his successor would take over, whoever that might be.

I flipped through and found Schedule A on the last few pages. It was a detailed list of everything Geraldine Rote owned, beginning with Wood Island and the house and ending with a series of bank and stock accounts, not just locally, but several in places like the Cayman Islands, Zurich, and Madrid. There were also a number of businesses listed with names like Carrington, LLC; Bridgeton Reserves Corp; and Kelemtin, Inc. I used my phone and took pictures of each page. I had no idea what any of them were, but they painted a very simple picture—Spivey was far wealthier than I thought.

I turned back to the beginning of the will, then found the section that came after *Disposition of Assets*. This next section detailed the *Stipulations*. "The rules," as Spivey had called them:

- *The entity may never be sold. Ownership may be relinquished in one of two ways:*
- *Donation to the township of Kittery, Maine*
- *Bequeath to a blood relative*
- *Should Keith or Pam Spivey return to the entity, ownership will default to the township of Kittery, Maine*
- *All items found on or within the entity are considered property of the entity and may not be sold, only borrowed, loaned, and returned under pre-established terms*
- *Tokens of less than sixteen years of age will be considered property*
- *Those present at sunset must remain until sunrise, unless permitted to leave by the Caretaker*

— Established Stipulations may only be adjusted through coordination between the Caretaker and Personal Representative

— Emerson must not famish

I had no idea what half of that meant. Entity? Caretaker? Token? And fucking Emerson again. Maybe some of it was more lawyer-speak, but that last one? Considering none of us had found Emerson yet—her cat, dog, hamster, pet snake, or whatever—it had most likely starved to death by now. When Kira had brought it up, Matty had joked and said sooner or later the smell would take us right to him, be patient.

The rest of the will seemed pretty straightforward—signatures, stamps, county recording docs, that sort of thing. I put the will off to the side. I photographed everything with my phone and moved on. I was on a fact-finding mission; I could figure out the meaning of these things later.

Beneath the will was a printout on glossy paper I recognized from the microfiche machine down at the library. With the internet, it didn't get much use these days, but there was no mistaking the crinkly thermal paper. The printout was from the *Portsmouth Herald* and dated June 19, 1972. The date was circled in red ink. It was the obituary for Spivey's grandfather:

> *Lester Herbert Rote passed doing what he loved best: fishing. He set out on Saturday and did not return. The sea claimed him as one of her own. Lester most likely fell victim to the storm of that night. While the search for his boat, Annabelle, continues, it is not expected to be found. He was much loved and survived by his wife, Geraldine, and daughter, Pamela. Services will be held at Oceanside Cemetery, New Castle, NH, on Saturday, June 25, presided by the Reverend Luston Balk.*

The mention of *Annabelle* meant one of two things—either his boat was eventually found, or this was some kind of misprint. I tried to remember my conversation with Mr. Peck at Geraldine's funeral. I was pretty sure he said Lester Rote didn't come back, but he didn't say if they ever found his boat.

Beneath the obituary was another printout from the microfiche machine, a newspaper article dated about a week earlier, also from the *Portsmouth Herald*. I got about halfway through the story before I had to sit down. I practically fell into my father's chair.

Old Bones Found on Wood Island

June 8, 1972. KITTERY - *Federal authorities were expected today to examine the skeletal remains of two bodies discovered on Wood Island, according to Perleston Pert, State Police information officer.*

A Dover, NH man picnicking on the island Sunday found a skull poking above the ground. The discovery was reported to police yesterday.

A local officer indicated the man, realizing his find to be a skull, buried it.

Pert said excavation by police found the incomplete skeletal remains of a person. He said further digging revealed more incomplete remains within a few hours, indicating a second person.

He remarked it appeared as if the bones had been there "for some time."

Pert said at this point the State Police have nothing further to do with the investigation, as federal authorities have jurisdiction.

However, the Boston office of the FBI said it is now conducting an investigation to determine if the federal agency does have jurisdiction.

Peter W. Culley, of the state attorney general's criminal investigation division, said the office was involved in the investigation up to a point.

He said, "As far as we're concerned, we've concluded it's a federal matter."

The Coast Guard is now patrolling the island to keep the curious away.

The island, which lies off of Fort Foster Park, was last used by the Coast Guard in 1946.

It was later put up for auction by the federal government, and the General Services Administration then withdrew it from sale. One month later, the auction was reinstated and the property sold for one dollar to a private buyer believed to be the current caretaker.

The article didn't say, but I knew that private buyer was Geraldine's father. Spivey's great-grandfather.

My dad had circled the date on this story too, and that wasn't lost on me—Lester Rote had died about a week after those bodies were found.

Vanished. A voice in the back of my mind pointed out.

No body found.

And his boat came back.

Did he?

I wasn't sure what any of this meant, but Spivey needed to know. He needed to know now.

3

I TOOK PHOTOGRAPHS of the microfiche printouts and left the folder open on my dad's desk along with a note that said:

We need to talk.
- Billy

I'd been docking *Merv* behind Piscataqua Cafe. Nobody told me I couldn't, and nobody bothered the boat there, so it seemed like as good a spot as any.

On my way, I called Kira and told her I might be late, giving her a bullshit excuse about a flat tire on my car. I'm not sure why I didn't tell her the truth. Something had felt off between us since this whole thing started. It got worse when Lily Dwyer disappeared, and I think part of me wanted to talk to Spivey before the rest of the group found out. I wanted to see his face when I told him.

You want to know if he already knows. And loose lips sink...

Don't get me wrong, I wanted to trust Kira. A few weeks ago, I would have trusted her to hold my worst secret, but I knew from the bits and pieces I'd gathered she'd become as obsessed with Project Poltergeist as the rest of them, and it felt like she was keeping secrets of her own.

Twenty minutes after calling Kira, I motored *Merv* away from the Piscataqua Café, and twenty minutes after that I tied off at a cleat on Spivey's dock behind *Annabelle* and hustled toward the porch.

I knocked on the back door, and when nobody answered, I let myself in and stepped into the kitchen.

"Spivey? You here?"

All the trash was gone.

I didn't know who cleaned up, but the kitchen was spotless and smelled like lemons and ammonia. Spivey's makeshift sign detailing the rules was still there. He'd erased Kira's rule— *You Must Pick Up All Trash*—and rewritten it, probably so the handwriting would match. Spivey had always been anal about things like that.

Damn, the house was quiet.

"Spivey?"

The living room was clean too, the furniture shiny with polish. Spivey had hung the large television over the fireplace, but it wasn't plugged in; the cord dangled several inches above the floor. A knitted quilt was folded and draped neatly over the back of the couch.

Nobody there either.

Still sleeping?

Maybe.

It was nearly one o'clock, but it was summer and I doubted Spivey had any place he needed to be any more than I did.

I called out his name again, and when he didn't answer, I crossed over to the stairs. I was about to head up when I noticed the photographs on the wall.

They'd changed.

The images of Spivey at various ages were all still there, but there were new ones, and they weren't pictures of Spivey. The photograph that caught my eye was a 5x7 in a gilded frame hanging on the far left side. Two girls in bathing suits lying on the dock on towels. Although I couldn't make out their faces, I knew they were Chloe and Izzie. And while my mind told me this next part was impossible, I knew the photograph had been taken the first day we all came here, the day they'd been told to stay on the boat and didn't. The image was shot from high up, from a distance, either from a window or that widow's walk Kira and I had discovered off the tower on the fourth floor behind one of the only locked doors in the house.

Was there a security camera up there?

If the house had a security system, I had never seen it. Spivey had never mentioned it. That didn't mean there wasn't one, though.

You think she'd live out here all by herself without any kind of protection?

Grams had guns, why not a security system?

Beneath the picture of Chloe and Izzie was one of Benny, and this one had been taken down in the basement, no doubt about that. He was covered in dirt, the shovel in both hands, lobbing dirt up out of that hole he'd been working on the last time I was here. He wasn't looking at the camera, didn't seem to know his picture was being taken.

There were more framed photographs. I recognized some faces, but not all. There were none of me, Kira, or Matty, which seemed strange since we were Spivey's closest friends. I was pretty sure half of these kids didn't go to Portsmouth High. Just random kids who had come out to the house over the past few weeks looking for a party.

"Holy shit!" a voice shrieked.

I looked up the steps.

Alesia Dubin was standing there, halfway down from the second floor landing wearing nothing but a pair of skimpy black underwear. She quickly covered her breasts and blushed. "What are you doing here?"

I opened my mouth to speak, but nothing came out. I felt the blood rush to my face and I'm pretty sure my jaw fell far enough to smack my shoes. Being the captain of the cheerleading squad, Alesia's body was trim and toned with not a single tan line or blemish. I knew she had long legs—I caught my share of glances during football games—but nothing like this. I'd never even seen her in a bathing suit. She had the flattest stomach I'd ever seen, lined with just a hint of ab muscles. Several freckles dotted the skin to the left of her belly button. In a millisecond, I took all this in, frozen, unable to move.

Alesia tilted her head to the side, groaned, and dropped her hands. "Get a good look, then wipe the smirk off your face, Billy. It'll be the last time you see it." As if to punctuate this, she turned on her toes in a quick circle and flashed her backside. Her hair was wet, her skin glistened, like she'd just gotten out of the shower. It was this next part that brought me back. "Does Kira know you're here?"

"Ah. Yes. I mean, no," I stammered. "I mean, I just needed to talk to Spivey, so I shot out here real quick. I'm meeting up with her after. What are you..."

I didn't finish the question, because it really wasn't any of my business. My brain wasn't working right, and I really needed to stop talking, and I most definitely needed to stop staring.

Alesia stood there for a moment, one hand on her hip, then turned and started back up the stairs. "Spivey's probably in the basement. Next time, knock."

"I did..." I started to say, but Alesia slammed the bedroom door before I could finish.

I stared up at the empty staircase for at least a minute, because *that* just happened and I needed to regroup, then I took the steps down past the photographs, into the basement.

I found Spivey sitting on the same folding chair where we had found Benny, unmoving, his face inches from the furnace door. He was dressed in a plaid shirt I didn't recognize and old jeans, no shoes or socks. Only one of the bulbs burned above, and most of the basement was dark. A haven of shadows, cobwebs, and dust.

"What are you doing down here?"

He didn't face me. At first, I wasn't sure he even heard me, then he said in a low voice barely above a whisper, "Damn pilot light. I turn my back and it's out again."

"Dude." I lowered my voice and jerked my thumb over my shoulder. "Alesia Dubin is half-naked upstairs!"

He leaned closer to the furnace; blue light danced over his face. "I've lit the stupid thing three times since I came down here."

"Did you hear me?"

"We've been kinda seeing each other."

"*You're* seeing Alesia Dubin."

I didn't mean for this to come out as harsh as it did. Or make it sound like a complete impossibility, but in all the years I had known Spivey, not once did he have a girlfriend, a date, not even a single drunken hook-up. And nobody came out of the gate with a girl like Alesia Dubin. You worked your way up to the Alesia Dubins of the world, you didn't start there.

Spivey blew gently into the furnace—the flame jumped but stayed on. "She came back the day after Whaley crashed the party and we just got to talking. I don't want to say one thing led to another, but that's sorta what happened. She spent the day out here. Just the two of us. Before I knew it, we were kissing out on the rocks, then I offered to cook her dinner, we ate that in front of the fire, then we were upstairs, doing the—"

"*You and Alesia Dubin?*"

"It would really be helpful if you didn't sound so surprised."

"What, you're not?"

He leaned back in the rickety chair and crossed his legs. "Maybe a little. I couldn't sleep that first night. I kept looking over at her, the captain of the cheerleading squad naked in my bed. I didn't want to close my eyes because I figured she'd be gone when I opened them, but nope, she was still there in the morning. The next day, the day after that." He let out a soft sigh. "This may sound silly to you, but honestly, I think I just needed someone to talk to. So much has happened in the past few weeks, it feels like I stepped on a moving train. All this business with Grams. My folks. The cancer coming back. She's a great listener and seems to understand me. I didn't realize how much I needed that until she showed up."

"I think you're going to find that's more important than—"

"The horizontal mambo? Bump and grind? Hide the snake? Batter dip the corn dog? Feed the kitty?"

I laughed. "Yeah. That."

"Probably shouldn't tell Matty."

"*Definitely* shouldn't tell Matty."

"Not yet, anyway."

I drew a finger over my lips. "I won't say a word."

"Did Benny tackle you at the dock?"

"Benny?"

"He's supposed to be on guard duty in case Rory comes back."

"I didn't see him."

"Wonderful."

My eyes fell on a purplish bruise on his right wrist. It wasn't very large, but it was there nonetheless, and my mind raced back to the last time the leukemia had returned. The bruises had started on that same wrist.

Without looking at me, Spivey tugged his shirtsleeve down and covered it up, then drew closer to the small furnace door. "Fuck me, there it goes again."

He produced a stick lighter from the dirt at his feet, fired it up, and relit the pilot light. "I don't get it. There's no breeze down here. It's not clogged or anything. Marston had someone out here yesterday to look at it and he said there's nothing wrong. This is the third furnace that's been in the house, and they all had this same problem."

I looked around the basement. "Must be air coming in from somewhere."

"Yeah, well, good luck finding it. Better men than you have tried."

The air felt horribly still down here, like a tomb that had been sealed for years. Damp, like mildew, with an underlying sweetness to it I couldn't pinpoint. I looked over at Benny's hole; it was covered with a ratty tarp.

The ground around it was lumpy, like most of the basement now—I didn't want to think about the things buried down here.

I remembered why I came and took out my phone. I loaded up the images from my dad's office and handed it to Spivey. "I found all that in my dad's office. I don't know if he pulled everything together himself, or got it all from your dad, or whatever, but I figured you should see."

Spivey flipped through the images. Pinching and zooming in order to read the text. "Marston told me Lester had his own boat. I think he said it was called *High Hopes* or something like that. He didn't use *Annabelle*. That's some kind of mistake…" His voice trailed off for a moment as he studied the other page, the one about the bodies found. "This… this is new. This could be huge. Have you shown it to anyone?"

I shook my head.

"You need to come tonight."

"What's tonight?"

He finally got up from the chair. "You haven't been here for a while, so you missed some stuff. I gotta show you something."

He returned my phone and started up the steps.

We found Alesia curled up on the couch with a tattered paperback of *The Amityville Horror*. She'd pulled on a loose tank top and a pair of shorts. Half the pages were creased with folds, and she was busily highlighting something. More to herself than anybody, she said, "The root of this story is tragedy. First, you've got Ronnie DeFeo, he kills his entire family in cold blood. Then the Lutz family comes in behind him thinking they can slap a coat of paint over the horror that happened there and make it all go away. How exactly would that work? I mean, the bloodstains were still there, right? Just because you can't see them doesn't mean they're gone. Some stains just don't come out. You can paint them whatever happy color you want, but underneath the blood, the tragedy that put the stain there has soaked into the grain, like mold or rot."

Or cancer, my mind muttered, joining the conversation. *Try all you want, you'll never get it all out. You can pretend it's not there, but that doesn't make it gone.*

"Where are the marbles?" Spivey asked her, looking around the room.

She nodded at a glass bowl on the coffee table.

Spivey plucked two large black marbles from the bowl and crossed the room to the far wall. "So this is crazy. Watch…"

He set one of the marbles down and released it. It slowly began to roll across the floor, picking up speed as it went, and vanished through the doorway leading into the kitchen.

"I don't think there's a single house in New England with a level floor. What exactly does that prove?"

A familiar grin spread across Spivey's face. "Check this out."

He moved to the opposite side of the room and crouched down near the kitchen door, placed the marble on the floor, and released it.

The marble rolled in the opposite direction, back to where the first one had started, momentum growing until it cracked against the baseboard and stopped.

That made no sense.

I had no doubt the floor was uneven, but it couldn't slope in both directions at the same time.

4

IT WAS NEARLY two o'clock by the time I motored *Merv* back to the dock behind the Piscataqua Café and tied down. The sun had climbed high, and even out on the water the air had grown warm enough to bring out a light sweat, dampening my shirt.

As soon as I had a signal, I called Kira and got her voicemail again. I shot her a quick text—*Tire fixed! Still home?* A moment later, I saw that she read the message but didn't reply.

I started to put my phone back in my pocket, then sent a text to Matty too—*u around?* I watched the message switch from *Delivered* to *Read*, but he didn't reply either. I immediately wanted to take it back, but of course I couldn't. Matty would be at the marina, helping his dad, had to be. And Kira... she was either still at home, angry with me, or maybe out with some of her friends. She wouldn't be with Matty— that had been a dream, a *bad* dream, but not real. I told myself I had no reason to be jealous. Told myself several times, but that didn't help much. The nagging little voice of my subconscious just grew more insistent.

I decided to go to her house, where I knew I'd find her sulking. I'd grovel until I made things right. I'd even worked out a speech in my head. I was on the second draft when I rounded the corner of the Piscataqua Café and found Chief Whaley's cruiser parked next to my car in the lot.

His engine was switched off, the driver-side window down, and he was looking out over the water. I was about ten feet away when he looked up, although I'm sure he spotted me long before that. "Hop in, Billy. We need to talk."

I stood there for a moment, eyeing the back door. I was about to reach for the handle when he added, "Up front is fine... today, anyway." He added a wink after this last part, but I wasn't so sure he was kidding.

Swallowing the lump in my throat, I rounded the car, got in the passenger seat, and pulled the door shut a little harder than I probably should have.

When I reached for the seat belt, he said, "No need for that, we're not going anywhere." He nodded out toward the water. "How's he doing out there?"

I didn't like that. It felt like some kind of continuation of the talk at my parents' house with Whaley and Spivey's dad. Like I had been drafted as some kind of informant. "Chief, I'm really not comfortable talking about—"

He waved a hand and cut me off. "It's fine, son. I get it. What I'm really wondering here is if Rory Moir has given him any trouble. You can tell me that much. I spoke to the chief out in Kittery, and he's more or less sworn off that island as his personal headache, and the marine patrol won't swing by unless I call them. Even then, it's a chore to get a response. Technically, Wood doesn't fall under my purview either. I t's a jurisdictional black hole out there, but somebody's got to keep an eye on things, keep the peace."

"Rory hasn't been back out to the island, if that's what you mean. Not as far as I know, anyway."

"But you haven't been spending much time out there, have you?"

I didn't answer that, and he gave me that dismissive wave again. "Rory's not one to let sleeping dogs lie. I think he might be planning something. He's smart enough to let some time go by, but dumb enough to still do something stupid when he thinks nobody's watching."

"Spivey's got people on lookout."

No way Rory would get by that crack security team.

… And guns. Of course, there's the guns.

I waited for Whaley to ask me who exactly was on lookout. Or maybe grill me on Lily Dwyer—*You sure you haven't seen her out there? Did Kira or the other girls tell you anything? Come on, you know her, right?*—that sort of thing, but instead he said something completely unexpected.

"If I share something with you, do you think you can keep it to yourself?"

My stomach tightened up. "Sure."

He rested his arm back on the open window and looked out over the water. "I'm guessing you heard Geraldine poisoned herself that day at Henry's, right? Stories like that tend to have legs, especially around here. I know how people talk."

I nodded.

"Well, she didn't. I got the autopsy report back and the medical examiner didn't find any poison."

"I thought someone saw her—"

That wave again. "Jolene Peterson saw her take a small foil packet from her bag and dump some powder into her coffee. The residue on the foil came back as brown sugar. Nothing poisonous about it. She just brought her own sweetener."

"So how did she die?"

"Intracranial aneurysm." He tapped the side of his head. "It's like a small balloon in an artery in the brain. It can sit there undetected for months, even years, then one day it pops. Can cause a stroke, sometimes just a bad headache, but in the worst cases, instant death. She probably had no idea it was there. Even if she did, she couldn't possibly know when it would go." He seemed to be working this out in his head as he spoke; his words slowed, and although his eyes were on a large tanker ship lumbering by, he didn't seem to be focused on it. "She never left that island. Never. I haven't been able to find a single person who'd seen her in years. The one day she does..."

"... is the day she died."

Whaley nodded. "I'm having trouble letting go of that."

"Maybe it was the stress," I suggested. "Anyone cooped up for so long... it's got to be stressful to go out. Maybe that triggered it."

"That's called agoraphobia. When someone is afraid to leave home. That was my first thought too, so I asked the medical examiner, and he said stress could easily trigger an aneurysm. Strong emotions raise blood pressure, and that increased pressure can lead to rupture. Makes perfect sense when you lay it all out."

I wasn't sure why he was telling me all this. I got the feeling he just needed to talk it all out. Why me, though? This was cop stuff. "So… that's probably what happened, right?"

Whaley drummed his fingers on the window frame. For a second, I thought he was going to drop it. Instead, he took his phone out from the pocket of the driver-side door, tapped through several screens, and handed it to me. "Geraldine was holding that envelope when I got to Henry's."

I stared at the small screen, then using two fingers, I pinched the image and made it larger because I thought I'd read it wrong. I hadn't, though. Across the front of the plain white envelope, in shaky hand-writing were the words:

> *Don't move me until 3 p.m.*
> *David Spivey—it's on you now*

"I don't understand," I said softly.

"That makes two of us."

"What was in the envelope?"

"A copy of her will."

I looked back over at him. "You said she couldn't know she was going to die."

"That's what the medical examiner told me, yes."

The phone was trembling in my hands. I lowered it to my knee, hoping he didn't notice. "What happened at three o'clock?"

Chief Whaley clucked his tongue. He did that sometimes when he was thinking. "The landline at Henry's rang. It was her attorney, Lockwood Marston. He asked for me specifically, like he could see me standing there, told me the copy of her will was for my records, and arrangements had been made for a local funeral home to pick up her body when I was willing to release her. I told him it might be a little while. He said he understood, 'under the circumstances, and all,' and told me to contact him when the ME was finished with her." Whaley's voice fell off for a second. "He knew where she was going to die.

He knew when. And he made arrangements. All for something most would consider an unpredictable act of God. They both did, because she clearly knew all this too."

I tried to wrap my head around what he just told me, because it was weirder than he may have realized. "The day you picked up Spivey at school, the day she died, he said his parents were already packing when you dropped him at his house. Marston had called and told them she died, said he was authorized to share the will with them as soon as they got down to his office in Boston." I looked back over at him. "Are you sure the sugar—"

He knew what I was going to say. "The local lab tested three times, then I sent it off to the feds. They agreed. Nothing but brown sugar. They even ID'd the brand. Nothing out of the ordinary found in her blood."

The two of us sat there in silence for a long time. I didn't know what to say to all this any more than he did. Finally, he lowered his voice. "I'm sharing this with you because nothing about it feels right, and Spivey is smack in the middle. I've got no crime here. Nobody did anything wrong, from what I can tell. But nothing about it… fits… and when you do what I do, things need to fit." He turned to me. "*It's on you now*, what do you think she meant by that?"

"I have no idea."

Again, we went quiet. Something about the chief telling me all this felt wrong. Like he was giving me a peek behind a curtain into a room I had no business seeing. What came next only made things worse.

"Got a lot of people making a grab for that island, including your father. Things are about to get ugly."

He reached back into the pocket of his door, took out a sealed envelope, and handed it to me.

"What is it?"

"A subpoena," he replied. "Issued by Rockingham County Department of Child Services. An emergency action. You're required to appear in court on Monday. They're going to ask you about Spivey. The conditions out there. His health… His folks are pushing to have him forcefully brought home and placed in treatment."

"Can they do that?"

Whaley shrugged. "Not my area of expertise. I can tell you your father is behind it, pulling the strings. The judge who signed off on the order, Judge Schultz, I've seen him out golfing with your dad. I don't think this landing on his docket is an accident. A similar subpoena went to Marston's office this morning."

"For Spivey?"

He nodded.

"Anyone else?"

He plucked another envelope from the door and held it up. "Just me. They'll want to know about the parties out there. Maybe the business with Rory Moir… that's how these things usually play out. The attorney representing Spivey's parents is Donald Murdock. He's done work for your dad in the past, so I'm sure he brought him in. They'll paint the ugliest picture they can."

5

"WHY THE HELL won't they leave me alone?"

Spivey stomped across the living room. He looked like he might put his fist through the wall.

I was on the couch with Kira.

Matty and Izzie were on the floor. Alesia and Chloe were around somewhere, but they had wandered off.

After my impromptu meeting with Chief Whaley, I drove to Kira's house (she wasn't home), then I went to Rye Beach (she wasn't there either). At the marina, Matty's dad told me he took the day off. I was halfway back to my house when Kira finally texted and said she was on her way out to Wood Island and told me to meet her there. I hadn't had a chance to talk to her alone, and although we sat next to each other, there might as well have been a wall of ice between us. When I reached for her hand, she shied away. I'd glanced over at Matty several times, and every time our eyes met, he looked off in some other direction—anywhere but at me.

Spivey snatched the subpoena from the coffee table, crumpled the pages, then let them slip from his hand. "Fuck 'em. All of them." He glared at me. "You need to talk to your dad. Tell him to stay out of my business. He's pushing for all this."

That part stung. I didn't expect him to take things out on me. I was trying to help.

"It's all of them," Kira said before I could respond. "I overheard my mom talking to Mrs. Edgerton on the phone; she runs the property assessor's office down at town hall. She said she'd received more than a dozen requests for information on this house since your grandmother died."

Matty said, "My dad heard some of the local fishermen are thinking about getting a group together to file a claim with the Coast Guard against your great-grandfather's original purchase. They want to try and overturn it, or prove that it wasn't legitimate, or some other bullshit."

"Well, that won't work," Spivey muttered.

"How do you know?"

"Marston said they tried that years back when Grams inherited the property."

"What's he telling you to do?" I asked.

"He says this is all about the money. Every time the place changes hands, people come out of the woodwork and try to get a piece, but it always dies down. He told me to put an end to the parties and lay low, and this will pass."

"Do you want us to leave?" Izzie asked in a small voice.

"No. You guys are fine. We need to keep it small, though. For a while, anyway. Just us."

"What about Benny?" Matty asked.

I could see Benny through the window, shovel in hand. In addition to his security duties, Spivey had tasked him with digging up the island. He felt that if two bodies had been found out here at some point, there might be more. There didn't seem to be any rhyme or reason to where Benny dug. He'd start a hole, hit granite, then fill it back in and move off to some other spot. He hadn't stopped moving since I got here, not even for water. Dirt and sand and sweat caked his body.

"Benny's fine too," Spivey said. "But nobody else."

Alesia and Chloe appeared at the top of the basement stairs. "Okay, we're ready."

They were both dressed in black. Alesia in a blouse and skirt, Chloe in a sweatshirt and jeans. Both had dark eyeliner on and their hair pulled back. Apparently, Chloe had revived her goth look from last year and shared grooming tips with Alesia.

I caught Izzie frowning. I don't think she liked Chloe spending time alone with Alesia. I glanced back over at Matty, hoping to spot a pang of jealousy there too, but there was nothing. He was picking at a thread on his sock.

"Ready for what?" I asked.

With all the craziness of the day, nobody had brought me up to speed on Project Poltergeist, and frankly, I was looking forward to a distraction from all these real-world problems. I kept thinking about the note I'd left on my dad's desk and regretting it. I'd set myself up for a fight the moment I stepped through that door. Going home wasn't an option right now.

"There's something I want to do first," Spivey said before disappearing into the kitchen. He returned a moment later holding a steak knife and the coffee mug from Henry's. He set the mug down in the center of the coffee table between us. "We're going to make a pact."

"A pact?"

"Think of it as another rule, but this one is just for us." Spivey pressed the tip of the knife against his index finger and applied pressure until he broke the skin. A bead of blood appeared. He squeezed his fingertip over the mug until the drop fell inside. He then held the knife out toward Matty.

Matty chuffed. "I'm not doing that."

"You are if you want to stay."

He considered this for a moment, studying the other faces in the room. "What exactly is the pact?"

Spivey eyed each of our faces in turn. "From this moment forward, whatever happens in the house, stays in the house. No exceptions. Anybody talks and they're out."

I nodded toward the crumpled subpoena. "What about that?"

"We'll talk to Marston and figure something out. I'm not going to let those assholes take this place away from me, and you know where I'm at with the other thing. We'll get our story straight before Monday."

"What's the other thing?" Kira asked.

The purple blotch on Spivey's wrist had grown and gotten darker. She must have caught me looking at it, because she simply said, "Oh," and lowered her gaze to the coffee mug.

Spivey ignored both of us and held the knife out toward Matty. "Well?"

When Matty still didn't take it, Izzie rocked forward on her heels and held her hand out. "Wimp. I'll do it."

This drew another smile from Spivey, and he handed her the knife.

She didn't push hard enough at first, and her fingertip only grew red under the pressure, then she drew the blade forward and opened up a cut about a quarter-inch long and flinched.

Spivey managed to get the mug under her hand as blood trickled over her palm into the cup. When he told her he had enough, she pinched it off and put her finger in her mouth.

Unwilling to be overshadowed by his sister, Matty grabbed the knife and made quick work of his own index finger, adding to the small pool in the mug. Kira went next, then me, followed by Chloe and finally Alesia.

Using the blade, Spivey stirred the blood, then held up the mug. "By virtue of our blood, our very life force, the secrets we share within these walls will be bound by our silence. To speak of our confidences with anyone outside of those present in this moment shall be punishable by death, and—"

Matty balked "Seriously?"

Spivey didn't respond to that—the look he gave him was enough. And it wasn't just him. Alesia looked like she might kill him on the spot.

"Okay," Matty muttered. "Okay. Death to all who violate your sacred oath. Got it."

"Shit. Now I forgot the rest." Spivey sighed and looked over at Alesia and Chloe.

Alesia placed her hand on the mug. "The voices of souls past. The power of the dead unmatched. Should anyone speak of that they are to see, their betrayal will be their last."

The large floor lamp in the corner of the room, the only source of light, dimmed for several seconds, then burned so bright I thought the bulb might blow before it evened back out.

Kira let out a soft gasp.

"That was creepy," Chloe said.

"That," Spivey replied, "was the generator. The power fluctuates sometimes. Come on, everyone down in the basement. Nik nok."

As we got off the couch, I took Kira's hand and held her back. "Can we talk for a second?"

She twisted her fingers from mine. "Not now."

I stood there for a moment and watched her vanish down the stairs with the others, then I went after her.

6

CHIEF CLIFFORD WHALEY had no business standing in Lily Dwyer's bedroom—she lived in Portsmouth, outside his jurisdiction, and the FBI agent who had met him at her house and escorted him inside at this late hour knew it, but went through the motions anyway because she'd vanished a week ago and they had nothing. Her parents were both home, sitting in the living room like statues, eyes red, faces drawn from lack of sleep. Whaley was hardly the first law enforcement officer to traipse through their home, and at this point they were oblivious to it. On his way up the stairs, he caught sight of a loose stack of flyers on the kitchen table, along with tape and staple guns. A computer and printer whirred, spitting out more. Dozens of empty ink cartridges were discarded off to the side. That was their life now—print, hang, repeat—the cycle broken only by the occasional press conference and reporter's camera in their faces.

The stairs creaked as Whaley ascended, and he was grateful for the noise.

The FBI agent, a thirtyish woman with shoulder-length auburn hair and glasses, closed the door behind them and gestured around the room like some kind of tour guide who had given the same speech so many times she woke with the words rattling around in her head. She pointed at an empty desk. "The techs in Boston tore apart her laptop and didn't find anything useful. We still have that. She had several social media accounts, but looks like she only updated them for her parent s' benefit. Couple of photos and messages here and there, half of them pre-programmed to hit at specific dates and times. Typical kid stuff."

"Has," Whaley said flatly, looking around the room.

"Huh?"

"You said she *had* several accounts. Past tense. We don't know she's dead."

Whaley knew what she was thinking; he understood the odds. If you didn't find them in the first forty-eight hours, chances of a happy ending dropped significantly. That didn't mean she was dead, though, and he preferred not to go there.

The agent ignored him and went on. "Her cell phone data was clean. Pulled all that from the cloud. No messages with anyone named Brian. No messages with anyone who could have been Brian. Most likely she had some secondary burner phone and that hasn't turned up."

Although Whaley and his wife didn't have kids, he'd been in his share of teenage bedrooms. There was nothing that jumped out about this one. Several posters of bands and singers covered the walls—Lady Gaga, mostly. Lily's bed was made. Most likely the mother did that. Whaley had taken part in seven missing child cases over his career, and he'd noticed if the bed hadn't been made when the child vanished, the mother got in the room at some point and made it.

The closet door was open. Shoes lined up on a floor rack. Sweaters, shirts, and jackets all neatly hanging. "The mother straightened up?"

The agent tilted her head, a curious look on her face, then nodded. "Right after we went through it. She made the bed, cleaned the closet. Picked up some laundry from the floor. Straightened up her daughter's desk. Wasn't much there, just some homework and a few books. She put it all away. We found some ice skates under the bed. Her high school yearbooks. Things like that. She put all that away, too. They always…"

Whaley was nodding; he didn't hear the rest. He went over to the double bookshelf next to the girl's desk. There were a few framed photos on top. Lily with her parents, around ten years old. Lily with a dog, a few years later. Lily in a cheerleading outfit, in row three of a human pyramid. That one was more recent. "No notes or anything behind the pictures?" he asked the agent. "Hidden in the frames?"

She shook her head. "No, we looked for that. Checked behind all the posters. Nothing placed inside or written in her books either. We flipped the mattress. No hidden compartments or tears in the fabric. Checked all the HVAC vents. Behind outlet and switch covers. Light fixtures. This isn't our first rodeo, Chief. We know what to look for."

"I'm sure you do. I'm just thinking aloud."

When he crouched in front of the bookshelves, both his knees popped, clicked, and a tinge of pain shot up his left side. He brushed it off and leaned in close, read some of the titles out loud. "*Haunted Portsmouth, Rise of the Witch,* by Thad McAlister. *The Occult in Modern Society,*" (oddly dated 1841), "*Ghosts, Specters, and Witchcraft: New England's Cursed History, The Devil of Great Island.*" He pulled that last one from the shelf and flipped through the pages. "I've read this one before, back when I was a kid. Local guy wrote it. It's about a haunted tavern out on New Castle."

"Her mother said she had a"—she paused for a moment, caught herself—"… *has* a thing for the occult. Particularly local stuff. We checked that angle and didn't find anything that would make us think she was part of some group. It was an interest, nothing more."

Whaley was flipping through the pages. "I've got three cemeteries within a stone's throw of my front porch. Ghost stories generate a good portion of the tourist revenue around here."

She was watching him curiously. "Like I told you, we checked all her books. No notes. Nothing handwritten on the pages."

Whaley nodded. That wasn't what had caught his eye. He'd closed the book and was studying the tag on the spine. The one that said the book belonged to the New Castle Historical Society.

7

THE SMELL HIT me the moment I crossed the basement threshold. A damp, heady scent of dirt, must, and mold over something horribly sweet, like burnt sugar forgotten in a simmering pan. Thin wisps of smoke trailed up from below, illuminated by the flicker of candles. As I made my way down, I realized it was incense. Reeds were burning everywhere, planted among the mounds of dirt in the basement floor like a failed crop. Brown, leafless, and devoid of life.

I knew what each of those mounds represented, and there were so many now, the ground was riddled with them.

There were dead things here.

They'd taken dirt from the cemeteries. They'd buried numerous items pilfered from supposed haunted places. Items belonging to the dead had then followed, and when that didn't produce the desired effect, someone had suggested something dead.

That's what happened in the week I'd been gone.

That's what caused marbles to roll in impossible directions.

If the other world was behind some large door, a key had been found, and it was resting comfortably in the lock, just waiting for a twist. All these thoughts entered my mind as I stood frozen on the stairs looking down, and it was the smell that put them there, because there was no mistaking that scent. Death had a particular odor, one that always proved stronger than all others. My dad once told me our brains recognized that smell on an instinctual level, told us to flee from it because nothing good could ever come from discovering the source. That was what I wanted to do—turn and flee—and I almost did. I probably would have if I didn't catch Kira looking up at me. The girl I felt I was on the verge of losing. It was the soft bob of her head that caused me to take the rest of those steps and join her and the others.

"What is…" I said in a voice so low, only she could hear.

"A stray cat," she replied equally low. "Only a stray cat. Three days ago."

Found a dead cat? Killed a cat? Sacrificed… *a cat?*

All these questions rushed through my mind in a blur, but before I could ask her any of them, Kira stepped away from me toward the middle of the basement.

There was a large red circle in the center of the floor. In the dim light, I thought it was painted until I drew closer, then I realized it was made of crushed rose petals. Within the circle were several triangles intersecting at the middle, with thick white candles burning at the corners. I'd seen enough horror movies to recognize a pentagram, and while I told myself those things only held meaning within those horror movies, I couldn't deny there was an energy emanating from this one. Whether imagined or real, my mind told me it was there. The look in Alesia's eyes told me it wasn't imagined.

I'd never feared a girl before.

I know that's a silly thing to say. Men, women, boys, girls, we're all capable of the same atrocities, but I had never felt threatened by a member of the opposite sex until that very moment. Kira had told me this girl was the descendant of witches, and I hadn't believed her, not until now.

At the center of the pentagram, something was covered beneath a piece of black cloth. Satin, maybe. It shimmered under the light. I didn't want to know what was under there, and again I eyed the stairs. I think I would have left if Kira hadn't sat down beside Matty, then motioned for me to sit on her other side. I knew at that moment if I were to leave her alone with him, she would be lost to me. If our relationship was held together by a thread, I was standing on that thread, carefully balanced, and the wrong move would send me teetering over the side and falling into an abyss from which she and I would not recover.

I settled down beside her and firmly took her hand. I wasn't about to let her go so easily.

Across the circle from us, Alesia sat between Spivey and Chloe. Izzie sat next to me.

Candlelight danced across Alesia's face. "You've all heard me say the dead have energy, and I know you feel it now. It's all around us in this place, more concentrated than it was ever meant to be. There is only one energy stronger than that of the dead, and that is the energy of life. Emotion. Human emotion. Love. Hate. Lust. Revulsion. I'm going to ask each of you to do something, and you will do it without comment. Not a single word. That is the only way we can proceed. The only way we can truly awaken this house." She studied each of our faces slowly, methodically, with a gaze beyond intense. Her voice fell to but a whisper. "I want you to turn to one of the people on your side and kiss them. Kiss them with all your heart. Allow yourself to get lost in it."

With this, she faced Spivey, took his face in her hands, and pressed her lips to his. Izzie kissed Chloe too—a long, lingering kiss—and I saw both girls turn red, not with embarrassment but excitement. I turned to Kira and placed a finger under her chin, tilted her head toward mine. For a second, I thought she wouldn't do it, then her eyes closed and I felt the familiar warmth of her mouth against mine. I didn't want the moment to end, but it did. I tried to read the look on her face as we separated and couldn't.

A fleeting image of Alesia nearly naked on the stairs rushed through my thoughts. *Get a good look*, she had said. And I had. *And you want more, don't you?* With Kira's kiss fresh on my lips, it was Alesia I wanted. I didn't know why, and I hated myself for those thoughts. I felt myself grow hard, and with that came an overwhelming guilt.

When Kira pulled away, I tried to keep my gaze on her, lock my eyes with hers, but instead, I stole a glance at Alesia, and I'm certain Kira saw it. Her face filled with ice, and as she turned away from me, I caught Matty watching from the other side, an anger there too as he glared first at Kira and me, then at Spivey and Alesia, for he had kissed no one. Knowing he was in pain made me feel better, like I'd won some contest. Horrible, I know, but what Alesia said next changed everything.

"Now I want you to kiss the person on your other side with the same intensity of that first kiss."

And as if to demonstrate this, she faced Chloe, gently touched her face as she had with Spivey, and kissed her full on the mouth. Chloe hadn't expected this and her body stiffened for a moment, but quickly recovered. Her hand slipped to Alesia's bare knee as she returned the kiss. Beside her, Izzie's mouth fell open, and she turned an awful shade of red. When Alesia and Chloe parted, Izzie grabbed the back of my neck angrily and pulled me to her. I felt her tongue push into my mouth, nearly choking me. I pushed her away from me, not only because I didn't want to kiss her, but because I could see Kira kissing Matty from the corner of my eye. Anger and hatred coiled in my gut.

It only lasted a few seconds—by the time I got Izzie off me, Kira and Matty had separated too. I wanted nothing more than to grab the steak knife we'd used upstairs and bury it in Matty's neck. I glared at him, but he didn't look back; his eyes had fallen to the covered thing in the center of our circle.

"Love. Hate. Lust. Revulsion," Alesia repeated. "It's these emotions, heavy on all of us, we draw from now."

Alesia reached for the black cloth and gingerly revealed the items beneath.

A ceramic bowl covered in intricate carvings.

A glass jar filled with murky water.

A book.

All of these things were very old, there was no denying that. The edges of the bowl were uneven and chipped. Handcrafted, for sure. Even the jar, a mason jar meant for canning, was made of blown glass. Not mass-produced in a factory as it would be today, but made by an artisan through skills no doubt learned from those who came before them. The binding of the book was stitched leather, worn and frayed with tattered, uneven pages held loosely between.

"George Walton's Tavern may very well be one of the most haunted places on New Castle, but do any of you know why?"

Chloe perked up, ready to answer, but Alesia reached for her hand and quieted her before she could speak. This wasn't lost on Izzie, who slipped her own hand under Chloe's sweatshirt and rested it on the small of her back, silently staking a claim.

If Alesia noticed (or cared), there was no indication as she reached for the book. "This was written in 1684 by a prominent minister named Increase Mather. It's called *Illustrious Providences: An Account of Many Remarkable and Memorable Events*. He lived in Boston, but he made several trips out here to New Castle at the request of George Walton and documented them in this book. It didn't take Increase Mather very long to figure out the cause of the haunting. Trouble began on May 5, 1657. Alice Walton brought George's dinner to him out in the fields where he was working, leaving their eldest daughter to watch the other children. When she returned, she realized one of her youngest was missing, a daughter. After an extensive search, her body was found at the bottom of the family's well. That same well would later claim the lives of several family pets and livestock, yet George Walton refused to fence it in. According to Increase Mather, Walton placed blame for the death in two places." Alesia held up her index finger. "First and foremost, on his neighbor, Prudence Toliver, a woman he swore was a witch. And second, on God, for allowing the deaths to occur. He had been in a land dispute with Toliver, specifically over the well, and when he wouldn't relinquish his claim, he believed she cursed it. He'd often rant to anyone who would listen, these drunken rages at his tavern. He became so blatant in his blasphemy, he and his family were no longer welcome at their local church and became Quakers. Through all this, he asserted his claim— Prudence Toliver had cursed the well and his family." Alesia looked up at us, her eyes glinting in the dark. "As a descendant of Prudence Toliver, I can tell you, without a doubt, the curse *was* real—possibly one of the strongest ever cast. George Walton should have abandoned the well, but because it was his family's only source of water, they didn't. Every bucket they raised, every drop that passed their lips spread the curse, brought suffering, and ultimately destroyed his family." She paused for a moment. "I'm telling you this because it's important to understand the Walton haunting didn't start with death; it began with the curse. The deaths that followed only fed it, made it stronger. What happened there can all be traced back to that well, the water within it, Prudence Toliver's curse. As an element, water holds energy—both good and evil, like a battery that doesn't fade. And like a battery, that energy can be channeled and used for many things."

Alesia reached for the mason jar and held it up to the light. "This has been in my family for over three hundred years. It came directly from that well, bottled by Prudence Toliver herself."

She twisted the top and there was an audible pop as the seal broke. As Alesia lifted the lid and set it aside, the scent of that water filled the room—stagnant, stale, pungent. My eyes began to water, and it only grew worse as she emptied the jar into the ceramic bowl and set it aside. "Where's the mug?" she asked Spivey.

He reached to his right and produced the coffee mug from upstairs and handed it to her.

Alesia tipped the mug over the bowl, and our combined blood trickled over the mouth, thick and dark, found the water, and vanished in the bowl. With the tip of her finger, Alesia stirred the concoction until it went from murky yellow to dark pink. She then dipped the coffee mug into the bowl and filled it. "I call upon the curse of Prudence Toliver, my ancient sister. I call upon her strength and power and wisdom. I call upon the death and life captured for all time within this element, and I call upon all those we have brought here to this place in object and in spirit. Awaken from your slumber and find within this place, find within us a host, a channel, a vessel to know freedom, to know breath, to know your true potential. It is those of us who willingly volunteer who welcome you most."

Alesia brought the mug to her lips and drank, then passed the mug to Chloe, who also drank. When Izzie handed the mug to me, I considered pretending, but with everyone watching I knew I couldn't, so I allowed the liquid to pass my lips, enter my throat. I tried to swallow before the taste registered, but there was no escaping the acidic burn of it, like grains of jagged glass scraping the back of my throat, lingering there like thick syrup. I wanted something to wash the taste from my mouth, and I was grateful when Spivey produced a small bottle of Jack Daniels and passed that around too.

When the first rumble shook the house, I'm not sure any of us realized it for what it was. I quickly dismissed it as maybe thunder or some settling by the foundation, neither of which could be true, because there hadn't been a single cloud in the sky when I arrived and we were in the basement of the house—the foundation was around us, not beneath us. The human mind tends to grasp at logic long before it will accept the impossible, so that was where mine went first. There was no denying the second quiver, though—we all saw the ripples in the bowl between us.

"What's that?" Chloe said.

But she wasn't talking about the motion we had all just felt. She wasn't even looking down at the bowl. Her frightened eyes were fixed on the back corner of the basement, near the cistern, where the shadows were thickest.

8

"WHAT THE HELL?" Matty muttered.

Although I was still holding Kira's hand, our grip had been loose at best… until that moment. Her fingers tightened around mine to the point of pain.

The shadows were moving.

This wasn't just the flicker of the candlelight or the movement of dust or smoke from the incense, but instead a churning, as if the air had grown thick and stirred like dark fog trapped in the harbor, searching for a way out. It started at the ground in the dirt, there was no denying that, but it moved up the walls and over the rafters like endlessly long fingers exploring a world without sight, only touch. The rumble of the house returned, but became this steady thing, less like thunder and more like a large engine revving from idle to redline and back again, deep within the earth below us. A deep, throaty growl.

Kira pressed against me as the things crawling the walls drew closer.

"We need to keep going," Alesia said, her voice somehow still steady. "Tributes come next." She removed a ring from her right hand and studied it for a moment. Silver with a red ruby in the mount. "Rory gave me this last summer when we were dating. He told me it belonged to his grandmother."

She dropped the ring into the murky water of the bowl, then turned to Spivey. "Hurry, we only have a few moments for this to work."

He produced the crumpled subpoena from his back pocket and dropped that in the bowl. The pages floated for a moment, then grew dark as they absorbed the liquid and slowly sank until only a corner remained visible.

Spivey looked up at me. "We need something of your father's."

His voice sounded odd to me. Distant. As if he weren't a few feet across from me but on the opposite side of the room. My head felt heavy, like the weight of it had doubled and my neck was struggling to hold it up. I'd only had that one sip of whiskey, but I felt drunk, and I realized I was staring at him and all other eyes were on me.

"Anything of your father's," he said in that faraway voice. "Nik nok."

I produced my father's business card.

I didn't remember taking the card from my pocket or my wallet. I didn't even recall having it on me, but when I looked down at my hand it was there between fingers that felt as detached as Spivey's voice. I dropped it into the bowl and we all watched it sink.

From her pocket, Alesia took out a small cardboard matchbook. She didn't light one, only dropped it into the bowl with the other items, where it vanished in the murk.

We weren't alone anymore.

When I looked back up, I saw them.

I wouldn't describe them as people, not entirely. Collectively, they were more of a presence. Within the thick, churning shadows, I saw heads, shoulders, even some arms, as if a large crowd had gathered around us but was only visible in silhouette. There were whispered voices too, because they watched us with growing interest and couldn't help but chatter amongst themselves. They surrounded us, and while the candles all still burned bright, the light seemed to move around their loosely formed bodies rather than illuminate them, as if the light itself wasn't willing to touch whatever this was.

I wasn't alone in this drunk feeling—I could see it on everyone's face, the way our bodies swayed. Chloe's hand was on Alesia's knee, and she didn't seem to care who saw. Oddly, Izzie no longer looked mad. Her hand was still under Chloe's sweatshirt, gently caressing her bare skin, playing at the top of her jeans, dipping beneath the waistband. Kira's fingers twisted within mine, explored my palm, my fingertips. She moved my hand to her thigh and held it there under her own. She had done the same with Matty's on her other thigh, and before that thought could really register, Alesia spoke again.

"What you're feeling, what we're all feeling, is the emotion we generated earlier amplified by the energy within this room, everything buried here becoming one with us at the center. We have willingly drank of the water, and with permission, the energy within has entered us. We breathe of the air, and with permission, the energy within enters us. We sit upon the earth, and with our permission, allow it to surround us." She moved her palm over the top of the bowl, splayed her fingers out, and held it there. "But it is the fire that—"

"Wait—"

This came from Spivey. He was digging through his pockets, searching for something. He withdrew a silver locket, one I knew belonged to his mother. I'd seen her wear it countless times. He also took out a worn leather key chain bearing the initials *K.S.*, his father's keychain. He dropped both these things into the bowl, where they quickly sank and vanished.

Alesia eyed him. "You're sure?"

He nodded.

She ran her finger across the back of his hand, seemed to contemplate the meaning, then drew in a deep breath of thick basement air before returning her attention to the bowl, her hand again above it. "It is the fire that truly cleanses, devours one thing, and births another from the ash. It is fire we welcome most—"

The shadows around us. Those *things* around us leaned in close, hovered over our heads at our backs, and watched along with us as the liquid within the bowl first glowed luminescent pink, then burst into a flame of blue, purple, and white that leaped from the bowl, shot up, and licked at the rafters above. The shadows, smoke, and mist that had occupied that space didn't vanish but instead seemed to embrace the flame, twisting through the light, curling, kneading. While I knew I should be frightened, I was not. It was beautiful. There was a hunger in the way these things touched, and I realized my own hand was caressing Kira's thigh with the same ferocity. All of us touching each other with a longing, a desire to be closer, to become one entity, not these individual parts. Groping both above and beneath clothing with abandon, all of us caressing each other in ways we would normally never dare. I was kissing Izzie again, then Chloe and Alesia—I lost track of Kira, Matty, and Spivey, but they were there, too—all of us hungry mouths greedily searching these forbidden places without fear, tearing clothing aside in hopes of flesh, we all became a tangle of limbs.

None of this made sense, yet it all made sense. At that moment, it wasn't just our bodies that intertwined, but our souls, our very essences. We became one not only with each other, but with the house, the shadows, and the forces that inhabited that basement and all around us.

I don't know how long this went on, but when it was over, we were all spent.

With a collective gasp not only from us, but all those things, the flame vanished as quickly as it appeared, leaving not a single scorch on the wood above. The shadows rushed in from above, dropped down, and engulfed us, and all became black as pitch and so silent, I heard nothing but my own heartbeat until Alesia's whispered, exhausted voice broke the quiet.

"The tributes we've offered represent those attempting to keep us apart. Each belongs to someone who wants nothing more than to silence us, harm us, or take what does not belong to them. I call on the power we've summoned to protect us. Protect this place. Protect what we are trying to do. Because only our success guarantees your freedom from the realm in which you currently dwell."

Something else plopped into the water, and although I wouldn't understand the significance of it for several days, I later learned it was a rock taken from George Walton's property.

9

WHEN WE EMERGED from the basement, I realized more than three hours had gone by. The drunken feeling hadn't left me but only intensified, and I knew I wasn't alone in that. It lived within all of us. My head buzzed with sounds. I could hear everything from the waves crashing outside to the minute scrapes of a mouse's feet skittering through the walls somewhere in the house.

We had gathered up our clothing, and Kira went up the basement steps with me, leaning against my side for support as I leaned on her. In my ear, she whispered, "Take me to bed," as her lips brushed the side of my neck. Those words were more welcome than any I'd heard in weeks.

The others were somewhere behind us, their voices muffled and distant behind all those other sounds. They might have been a hundred miles away. As far as I was concerned, there was only Kira and me.

Together we ascended from the basement past the photographs on the first floor landing, beyond the second floor to the third. I hadn't been up here since our first visit. There was nothing but the small landing and the closed door of the closet Kira had attempted to claim as her own. I tried the doorknob and found it locked, as it had been that first day.

Do not lock the doors.

"So much for our private room," I told her, trying the knob again as if something might have changed in the past three seconds.

She tugged at my arm, pulled me toward the steep, ladder-like steps behind us, and simply said, "We're going up there," before vanishing through the open hatch.

I went up after her and found her standing in the tower, looking out at the dark water.

Across from the door leading out to the widow's walk, a sleeping bag and several pillows were on the floor. There were a couple candles too, but neither of us bothered to light them. Instead, Kira shed the rest of her clothing, lowered herself to the makeshift bed, and reached for me.

I dropped down beside her. "I'm sorry if I—"

She pressed a finger to my lips, then held my face in her palm. "No words. Not about any of that. Not now." With her other hand, she gripped the side of the wall, caressed the worn wainscoting. "You feel it, don't you? The house is alive. It's incredible. Just touching it... touching you."

I did feel it. The energy from the basement was all around us, but in that moment it was strongest where Kira held me, as if she were channeling it from the house, through her body, and passing it on to me. Every cell in my body was alive with it, and I wanted more. With her back against the wall, I made love to her. Lost myself in every inch of her. And I knew, somewhere else in the house, the others were doing the same—I felt them all. We weren't separated by the walls; we were united.

When Kira and I finally fell asleep, her naked body was draped over me, glistening with sweat. Both of us were far too hot to consider the sleeping bag. I didn't remember drifting off, nor did I remember dreaming. The sleep that found us was as deep as the waters beyond the tower and just as dark.

10

I AWOKE TO the sound of a ringing phone.

At some point, we had opened the windows, and a steady breeze came in from the sea. The tower had taken on an icy chill, and still above the covers, my skin crawled with gooseflesh.

Kira wasn't there. I had no idea where she'd gone.

I'd never noticed the phone in the tower before, but in all honesty, I hadn't really looked. It was mounted to the wall above my head, beige plastic with a long cord like the one down in the kitchen. Someone had written the number on a piece of tape and stuck it to the side. Although the ring sounded like actual bells rather than an electronic reproduction, the sound was muted, as if someone had opened the ancient phone and taped cloth over those bells to lessen the noise. I found myself staring up at it as the grogginess of deep sleep fell away, Spivey's rules bouncing around in my head.

I wouldn't have answered if it had stopped ringing on its own, but it didn't. I let it ring twenty or thirty times, then it fell silent and began again. I suppose I could have unplugged it, but I didn't see any of the wires. These old-school house phones pulled their power from the phone line, and if I remembered correctly, that line plugged into the back of the device. I'd need a screwdriver and motivation to complete that task, and in that particular moment, I had neither. I reached up with a tired hand and slapped the receiver from the base. It dropped to the ground with a thud a few inches from where my head rested on a pillow.

I heard a girl's voice, crying.

Gentle sobs between broken words.

I should have hung up the phone at that point, or just yanked it from the wall. Maybe thrown it through one of the open windows and let it sink into the waters below, but I did none of those things. Instead, I eased over to it and listened.

"Please don't..."

More sobs.

"Just let me go!"

I sat up with that one. I picked up the receiver and brought it to my ear. "Hello?"

"Oh, God! Oh, God! Please, you've gotta help me!"

"Who is this?"

"Who is this?"

"Billy," I whispered. "Billy Hasler."

"He's going to kill me. I know he is. He wouldn't have let me see his face otherwise. You've gotta get me out of here!"

"Whoa, slow down. Who?"

"I don't know his name. I've never seen him before. He drugged me with something. Put it over my mouth. And now I'm locked in... I just woke up... I think I'm in the trunk of his car. It feels like we're moving. Can you call the police?"

"Do you know where you are?"

More sobs.

"No."

"When did this happen?"

"I'm not sure. I don't know how long I've been out. Maybe an hour?"

"Do you know how long you've been driving?"

"No."

I was sitting up now, adrenaline coursing through my body. "Is there anything in the trunk with you? Anything you can use to maybe get it open and get out?"

She went quiet for a moment, then, "No, nothing. You've got to call the police."

I had my cell phone, but I already knew I had no signal out here and if I hung up, I'd lose her. I tried to think. "We need to figure out where you are. Where did this guy take you?"

"From the mall, Fox Run Mall. Oh, God, we stopped. He switched off the engine."

I felt my heart thud. "What's your name? You didn't tell me your name."

"Lily Dwyer."

There was a scream at that point, sharp and shrill, and it didn't come from the phone.

The line went dead.

Lily Dwyer's voice, gone.

But the scream remained, and I realized it was Kira.

I got to my feet—she was outside at the far edge of the widow's walk, leaning over the rickety railing. I dropped the phone and went to the door. At first I thought it was locked, but it was just stuck. I yanked the door open and the entire world swooned. It was the height. At least forty feet to the ground below. I wasn't sure I could go out there.

"Kira? What are you doing?"

I said this in the calmest voice I could pull together, which wasn't very calm. Each word wavered, and the last one caught on my breath as the sharp granite rocks below seemed to reach up toward us, beckoning us closer.

My voice cut off Kira's scream, though, and that was good. She stood at the far edge of the widow's walk on her toes, her back to me, her bare shoulders quivering under the brush of her hair caught in the night wind. "You need to come back inside."

"Okay," she said softly, but she didn't move toward me. Instead she pressed against the old railing and leaned over the other side. "After I fly. I think I can. I *know* I can."

There was a dreamlike smoothness to her voice, and I realized she must be sleepwalking.

I drew a deep breath and took a tentative step out onto the walk. "Just stay there. I'll come to you."

The wood creaked under my weight and I felt it buckle. Unlike the rest of the house, which had been kept in pristine condition, the boards of the widow's walk were splintered and cracked by years of exposure to New England's harsh weather. Several boards were gone entirely, and I could see right through to the ground. I gripped the railings on both sides and felt the wobble in them, as if a strong wind could take the entire thing down. I inched forward anyway as Kira stood statue-like on the opposite end. I told myself not to look down or off to the sides, focus only on her.

"You can fly with me, Billy. Won't that be fun?"

Unlike me, she wasn't holding anything. Her arms were at her sides, and she gently raised them until they were up over her head, then brought them back down again. I was only about two feet from her when she said, "Spivey's grandmother used to fly from here all the time. She'd ride the wind all the way to New Castle and back again."

With that, she tumbled forward in a quiet somer sault.

I jumped toward her.

My legs pistoned. I lunged for her with both hands, grasped at the air where she had been only a moment earlier, and felt nothing. The momentum carried me forward and I crashed down on the narrow walkway. My left knee went right through the aged boards and caught on the truss. I managed to grip one of the railing supports, felt it twist and give as my chest impacted with the wood, knocking the breath from me as I silently screamed out Kira's name.

I couldn't see where she'd landed. The tide was in, the waters were high, and there was nothing below me but swirling darkness.

"Billy? What are you doing out there!"

Hearing her voice made no sense, and that might be why I couldn't bring myself to look. When I did manage to swivel my head, I found Kira standing in the open doorway of the tower, her face ghostly white, a glass of water in her hand and my t-shirt hanging loose over her body.

"Billy, you all right?"

A shout from Benny.

He was standing near a wheelbarrow and a large hole a few feet from the shed containing the generator, the shovel in one hand and his fingers cupped around his mouth to help carry his words.

I took all this in as I lay there, sprawled out on the widow's walk, and realized I had been the one sleepwalking, not Kira. And I had nearly walked to my own death.

11

CHIEF CLIFFORD WHALEY sat behind the wheel of his personal SUV and stared at the small house across the street from where he'd parked. He'd pulled the address from Laura Dubin's DMV record, driven out after his shift ended, and parked.

That was nearly two hours ago.

He had no reason to be there.

He kept telling himself that, and it was the primary reason his butt hadn't left the seat, but he couldn't bring himself to leave either. His gut told him Laura Dubin was somehow involved in the disappearance of the Dwyer girl, but he had nothing to back that up. His mind was connecting dots that had no business connecting. There was zero reason to suspect this woman, yet here he was, unable to let it go.

Laura Dubin appeared to be home alone.

Whaley figured that much out simply by watching the lights switch on and off in the house, following the path of a single person. That meant her daughter was out somewhere, most likely on Wood Island with the other kids. He wondered if she had told her mother where she was going or fed her some other lie.

According to the files his predecessor had assembled, Laura Dubin had nearly two million dollars in the bank, yet she only earned $72,737 annually as the manager of the local Costco. When Whaley dug deeper, he learned the bulk of her money came from a life insurance settlement when her husband died of a brain aneurysm fourteen years earlier. A COD nearly identical to Geraldine Rote. And while that appeared to be a complete coincidence, the fact that Lockwood J. Marston, attorney-at-law, oversaw the dispersion of her husband's estate and signed as witness on the life insurance policy clearly was not.

That Marston fellow was a very busy man, and Laura Dubin stuck in Whaley's head like a bad itch.

The light downstairs in the house clicked off, and a moment later, a room lit up on the second floor. The dark silhouette of a woman appeared in the window and began to undress.

Whaley knew he shouldn't watch, and he didn't, not for very long.

He stopped when someone knocked on his passenger window.

An older man holding the business end of a leash. Whaley couldn't see the dog. He pressed the button in his armrest and rolled down the window. "Can I help you?"

The man appeared startled when he saw Whaley's uniform. "Oh, I'm sorry, Officer. I just saw you sitting out here for a while and figured I'd see what you were up to. Didn't realize you were a cop." He glanced up at Laura Dubin's house. "She do something I should know about? I run the local neighborhood watch. Me and Northop, here." He reached down and pet the dog Whaley still couldn't see.

Whaley gestured toward the file box sitting on his passenger seat. "I just stopped to review some material."

"Huh," the man said. "With your interior light off? That can't be good for the eyes."

A car door slammed, and when Whaley looked back over at Laura Dubin's house, her red Audi was backing out of the drive.

"Gotta go," Whaley said. He thumbed the button for the window before the man could reply, did a quick U-turn, and followed her down Summer toward Middle. Within five minutes they were on New Castle, and two minutes after that she made a left on Walbach. She pulled to the side of the street about halfway down. Whaley pulled into the Ingles' driveway and killed his lights. They weren't home, and it was the only move he had—there was no traffic. If Laura Dubin hadn't already figured out he was following her, she certainly would have if he pulled to the curb.

She didn't get out of her car. Best Whaley could tell, she didn't take her foot off the brake; her lights remained bright red.

The radio clipped to Whaley's shoulder chirped and Mundie's voice came through. *"Chief, you there?"*

Whaley thumbed the button. "What do you need, Mundie?"

"We just got a 911 call from Ralph Peck's house on Walbach. Any chance you're still close, or are you home?"

Whaley felt his heart thump. Ralph Peck's house was three doors down. Where Laura Dubin had stopped. When he looked up, her red Audi pulled away from the curb. She followed Walbach to the end and disappeared around the corner.

"I've got an ambulance incoming from Portsmouth. Ralph managed to dial, but he's unresponsive. Line's still open."

07/12/2010 - MONDAY

1

I'D BE LYING if I said I remembered the rest of that weekend. I remember shouting down to Benny that I was okay. I remember crawling back across the widow's walk and nearly diving through the door into Kira's arms (I hit her hard enough to knock the glass of water from her hand and hugged her for nearly a minute before I found myself able to back off). I also remember seeing the old telephone receiver on the floor next to our sleeping bag. Kira picked it up and placed it back on the base as I recounted my dream (more of a nightmare) with stunning clarity, wondering just how much I had imagined, because that phone didn't fall to the ground by itself. At some point, I'd written the number from the phone on my arm with black marker. I didn't remember doing that. I scrubbed it off, but not before those numbers were etched permanently in my memory.

I know we all talked about the two bodies mentioned in the news article I'd found in my dad's office. I know we talked about Lily Dwyer. And I know we went back down to that basement several times, but the specifics escaped me. It wasn't because we were drinking—we drank nothing but water for the rest of the weekend. The memories were just cloudy, and that started the moment I helped Kira down into *Merv* and motored us away from the island and back to New Castle. It was as if the memories decided to hang back, stay out there on the small island, and they dropped from my mind one by one as the distance increased. By the time I tied us off at the dock behind Piscataqua Café and the two of us got in my car, my only thoughts were of getting Kira home and what my parents would do to me when I walked back into ours. I hadn't seen them for three days. I was sure they'd found the note I'd left on my dad's desk, and I was due in court in less than an hour.

My mother wasn't home when I finally got there; she'd left for work. My dad was, though. I found him standing in the living room.

"Ralph Peck passed away last night," he said, buttoning the cuffs of his shirt. "Heart attack. Complained to Jolene Peterson just yesterday about chest pain."

I hadn't seen Peck since Geraldine Rote's funeral a few weeks ago. He seemed fine then, not that that meant anything.

"I put a suit out for you. Get showered and changed. We don't want to be late," my father instructed. "We'll talk in the car."

2

AFTER THREE ATTEMPTS, I managed to get a respectable knot in my tie, but I left the jacket on my bed. After the funeral, my regular suit had gone to the dry cleaners. I hadn't worn this one in nearly a year, and it was a little tight on me. I expected my dad to say something else about Ralph Peck when I climbed into his BMW, but he didn't. He only gave me a quick glance before pulling out of our driveway and heading toward Portsmouth.

We were halfway across the bridge to the mainland when he finally spoke. "I saw your note. Things have escalated far faster than I thought they would."

I wasn't sure what to make of that. "Is that supposed to be some kind of apology?"

He looked at me, his mouth opened slightly, then he seemed to reconsider whatever it was he planned to say and went back to watching the road for nearly another minute before continuing. "What do you know about Spivey's attorney? This guy, Marston?"

No apology then.

"Nothing."

Why would I tell him anything?

My father licked his lips and his grip on the wheel tightened. "I think you misunderstand. I'm not looking for dirt on the man. I'm asking you what you know about him."

I wasn't sure what he meant by that, so I didn't say anything. Instead, I looked out the window at the harbor, at the various boats bobbing around. The abandoned Portsmouth Naval Prison off in the distance like an old castle casting a wide shadow down over the water. A looming, quiet presence. At that moment, I wanted to be anywhere but in the car with my father.

"I had him checked out."

"I'm sure you did," I mumbled back.

His grip on the wheel tightened; he drew in a deep breath before going on. "I'm not trying to pick a fight with you. I just want to talk. Do you think we can do that? Without the snide remarks? I get that you're caught in the middle of all this. I'm not going to tell you I understand how difficult that probably is, because I don't, and I'm not trying to placate you." He slowed the car and let several people cross the street, then went on. "Your involvement in this has been fairly one-sided. That's skewed your perception. You're smart enough to understand there is more to it than that. I'm only asking you to hear me out."

When I didn't say anything, he went on.

"That firm of his dates back to the eighteen hundreds. One of the first law practices in Massachusetts. It's a family business, no outside partners. Only various Marstons at the helm—Theodore, Benjamin, Huxley, Amos, Chester, Clarence, Bernard, and the latest, Lockwood J. The *J* stands for Jonas, in case you were wondering."

I wasn't.

"They don't advertise," my father continued. "No signage on the office. He works out of an old brownstone off Beacon. Offices on the ground floor and a residence taking up the second and third. No employees, not even a secretary. Just a one-man shop. He bills himself as an expert in estate and financial matters. The building has never changed hands. Not a single real estate sale or filing. Taxes are paid through a shell corporation. It's valued at around six million; property taxes are around sixty thousand. Here's the thing—he doesn't seem to have any clients other than Spivey's grandmother. It's a sizable estate. I'm guessing Spivey has filled you in on all that by now, but still, tough to cover a nut that size off a single client. Seems a Marston has been representing the owner of Wood Island all the way back to the beginning. The note where Lester Rote bought it for one dollar—the witness was Huxley Marston."

"I'm not sure why any of that matters."

"Have you met him?"

I hadn't. Not really. The closest I got was at the funeral, an exchanged look, but I'd never spoken to him. None of that was my dad's business, so I said nothing.

"There's something… off… about that man."

"You don't like him, so I shouldn't either, is that it?"

I was getting angry. I didn't want to, but it seemed like every word he said was an attempt at manipulating me. I wasn't sure he even cared how I really felt about all this—I was just a piece on the chessboard he wanted to get in position for some move he was planning down the line. I didn't realize how tight I'd been holding the armrest until I looked down at my hand and realized my fingertips were white. I let go and tucked my hand under my leg.

He slowed for the stop sign at Marcy and made a right. Choosing his next words carefully. "You saw the story, right, the one about the two bodies found out on Wood Island back in the seventies?"

"You know I did."

He paused for a second, and I realized I wasn't the only one attempting to keep my emotions in check. "Beyond that news clipping, there's no record of that case. I had Mundie check the New Castle PD files—they don't have anything. There's nothing in Kittery either."

"Didn't the story say the feds took over the investigation?"

He nodded. "It did say that. So we filed a FOIA—Freedom of Information Act request—and guess what they turned up? Zilch. Not even a case number. Nothing with the Coast Guard either. Nobody knows who those bodies were or where they went after they were found."

"I suppose you're gonna tell me Marston covered it up?"

He went quiet for a moment, then nodded toward the glove box. "There's an envelope in there. Get it out. There's something I want you to see."

I opened the glove box and found the envelope. Inside, there was another printout of the news story and several black and white photographs.

My dad said, "I got those from the *Portsmouth Herald*. They had a photographer on scene with their reporter, but when they ran the story, they only went with text. I guess they figured none of those were worth printing."

There were three photographs in total. The first was a wide shot, probably taken from a boat because it captured most of the island. It didn't look much different. It actually didn't look any different. *Annabelle* was visible in the corner, tied off on the dock. A woman (most likely Geraldine Rote) was standing on the small porch, watching them approach. There were several other boats, too. Six people were clustered together on the southern tip of the island. The second photograph was a skull and part of an arm, both partially uncovered. The third photograph was of the men standing around the remains. Three of them were uniformed police officers. Another wore overalls, and the last two were in suits.

"The man on the left there is Peter Culley, with the attorney general's office out of Maine."

I wasn't looking at the man on the left. I was looking at the man standing next to him wearing a long black trench coat and hat, and resting one hand on a cane as he spoke to the first man.

I'd only seen Marston that one time, at the funeral, from a distance, but it was obvious this man was related. He was a dead ringer.

"My private investigator thinks that's Clarence Marston," my dad explained. "That would make him the grandfather of Spivey's attorney. If it's not Clarence, it's Chester. His great-grandfather. Either way, someone from Marston's camp was out there and this story vanished. So to answer your question—you've made me out to be the bad guy here, me and Spivey's parents. Believe what you want about us, but make sure you consider all the facts. The Marston clan has been leeching off that island for a very long time, and with Spivey being the only client of that particular firm, how far do you think the illustrious Lockwood Jonas Marston, Esquire, will go to protect his own interests?"

He pulled into a space in front of the courthouse, switched off the motor, and got out of the car without another word.

I sat there and studied the photographs for about another minute before reaching for the envelope, which had fallen to the floor.

If not for that, I may not have seen it, and to this day, I wish I hadn't, but I did.

On the floor, partially hidden under the seat, was a single strand of bright pink hair.

The same color as Lily Dwyer's.

3

"ARE YOU ALL right, son? You're sweating."

The question came from Chief Whaley, who was standing on the steps out front, watching me hobble toward the courthouse after my father, who was already inside. My heart was beating like a fist, and a buzz had filled my head like I'd stuffed it in a wasp nest.

"You look like you're going to pass out."

Whaley placed a hand on my shoulder to steady me, and I leaned against a mailbox on the sidewalk, trying my damnedest to not look back at my father's car while the Chief of Police was standing next to me.

"I'm… I'm just nervous."

I shouldn't have lied.

Lying was stupid.

But I did, and the moment those words came out of my mouth, there was no going back. I had to double down. "I didn't get much sleep. I don't want to be here."

He squeezed my shoulder. "Well, that makes two of us, but I can tell you from experience, it will be over before you know it. The waiting is far worse than the doing. Let's get inside. The others are already here."

He turned me around and guided me up the steps. I let him. Because even walking into the flaming pits of hell seemed like a better option than thinking about that strand of hair.

I expected a courtroom, but instead, he led me to a large conference room off the lobby. Spivey's parents were both sitting on the far side, and they watched me enter. My father had settled on Pam's left. An older man I didn't recognize sat on Keith's right. Most likely that was their attorney, Donald Murdock. He had that look about him—gold cufflinks, light blue dress shirt with a white collar and a matching dark tie. The man who had to be Judge Schultz was at the head of the table with a court reporter at his side. Sitting closest to the door, his back to me, was Marston. Spivey wasn't there.

Whaley pulled out the chair next to Marston for me (across from my father), and I wanted to sit anywhere but there, but fell into it anyway. I think I was still in shock. Whaley sat beside me. He reached for a pitcher of water in the center of the table and filled glasses for both me and him, then offered some to my dad and Spivey's parents, but they declined.

I hadn't seen Spivey's mother up close for at least a month. She'd lost weight, and her face might as well have been painted white, she was so pale. She was trembling, fidgeting, and when Keith tried to reach for her hand, she shied away from him and placed both in her lap under the table.

Marston cupped his hand over my ear. "At David's request, I'll be representing you in this matter."

His breath was warm and smelled heavily of peppermint, that sweet scent hiding something filthy beneath. A quiet voice in the back of my head spoke up, told me if something were rotting from the inside, it would smell a lot like that. If I were to dig up the things in Spivey's newfound basement, they would smell a lot like that too.

I wanted to pull away, but couldn't bring myself to move as he continued. "If you're unsure how to answer something, just pause and I'll weigh in. Aside from that, just be truthful. Nothing less. Understood?" His voice was thick with a New England accent, deep with a slight drawl to it.

I bobbed my head.

The judge cleared his throat. "If everyone is ready, I suggest we get started." He turned to Marston. "Will David Spivey be joining us?"

"No, sir. He has waived his right to appear in person. As counsel, I will answer any questions you may have on his behalf."

Murdock let out a sigh. "This is highly irregular, your honor. Mr. Spivey was subpoenaed."

"… And your subpoena was authorized by a New Hampshire court. Mr. Spivey is no longer a resident of New Hampshire; his domicile is in Maine."

"His residence is debatable. He was served at his parents' home. He is still a minor, is he not?"

Marston looked at the judge. "He wasn't served at all. The subpoena was *delivered* to his parents' home, handed to his father, not to him."

"Because he hasn't set foot off that island," Murdock shot back. "Do you expect someone to paddle out there to place it in his palm?"

Marston shrugged. "How you serve your subpoenas is totally up to you. I'm only concerned with your failure to properly serve, as is the case here."

"A copy was delivered to your office."

"And that is much appreciated, but that doesn't equate to delivery. Under case number—"

"Enough," the judge cut him off. "Let's not waste time with technicalities today." He looked over at Murdock. "He's not here, so ask your questions of his representative. If you feel the responses you receive are not adequate, I suggest you properly subpoena your witnesses the next time we get together."

The next time?

I didn't want to do this again, ever.

Judge Schultz took a drink of water and cleared his throat. "This is just a deposition, and I'd prefer to keep things light. Think of it as a conversation on the record. I think we can all agree our goal is to find a solution that is in the best interest of David Spivey, so bickering and infighting won't get us anywhere. As I understand it, we have a ticking clock due to health concerns. Arguing and delays will only complicate matters. If we need to go that route, we always can, but today, let's try to see past our differences and possibly come to an expedited solution."

Spivey's parents both nodded at this. My father was looking at me.

The judge took out a notepad and ran his finger over the first page, then turned to Murdock. "Why don't you kick this off?"

Murdock nodded, thumbed through the stack of pages he'd removed from his briefcase, and tapped the corner of the topmost sheet. "This is a copy of David Spivey's most recent blood work. His parents have authorized me to share it with you. His doctor was kind enough to review it with me and is available by phone should we need him, but the truth is, the report speaks for itself. Abnormalities are bolded and readily apparent. His lymphocyte count in his blood is highly elevated and his red blood cell count is dangerously low. Both his liver and spleen are enlarged and on the verge of failure. His doctor said these are all signs of late Stage 3, early Stage 4 leukemia. It's still within an acceptable range for treatment, but he's well beyond where they'd like him to be. To put this in perspective, treatment usually begins at Stage 2." He studied the faces at the table. "This blood draw was over a month ago. His current condition is unknown, but I've been told there is a high probability he is now in Stage 4 and quickly approaching the point of no return, if he hasn't already exceeded it."

I didn't understand half of what he'd just said, but I did know Spivey had never gone beyond Stage 2 before starting treatment in the past. He told me he wasn't that far along this time. He lied. Still, he didn't seem that sick to me. Aside from a couple of blotches on this skin, he didn't seem sick at all. The last time this happened, he'd been horribly fatigued, barely got out of bed. Didn't want to eat. I hadn't seen any of that, and if this was all true, wouldn't I?

"Mr. Hasler, is there something you'd like to say?"

My head snapped up at the mention of my name by the judge. Everyone was looking at me. I'd been mumbling aloud.

"He just… doesn't seem that sick to me. He seems fine."

Spivey's mother said, "He left all his medication behind. He's not taking anything and hasn't for at least two weeks." She glared at me. "How can he be fine?"

"He's fine because he's receiving treatment," Marston told everyone. "His illness hasn't progressed. In fact, it's improved."

Keith's leathery forehead creased. "What kind of treatment?"

"My client has not authorized me to discuss that. I can only tell you he's responded positively, and all signs are encouraging."

"Your client," Keith shot back, "is our son, a *minor*, and we haven't authorized any treatment. What are you giving him!?"

"*My client,*" Marston replied, "has completed all the necessary paperwork for emancipation. I have that with me today, and I've been instructed to file it should you continue to push this matter. His eighteenth birthday is only about two weeks away, so it seems like an unnecessary hassle, but if you'd like me to burden the court with it, I will."

"But he is receiving treatment for his illness?" the judge asked, ignoring the rest.

"He is. Like I said, I'm not permitted to provide specifics, but he is doing very well."

Pam's eyes were red and moist. "What are you doing to our boy? Is this my mother's doing? That goddamn place?!"

Marston rested both hands on the table and sighed. "Like I said, I'm not authorized—"

Spivey's mother lunged at him. "You can't have him! I told her that!" I'd never seen her move so fast.

Her chair cracked against the wall behind her. Her knee caught the edge of the table, spilling the waters. She would have gone up and over if Keith hadn't grabbed her around the waist and pulled her back.

The judge and court reporter were both on their feet, my father and the Spiveys' attorney, too. Marston hadn't moved, and I was frozen—I don't think I could have gotten up if I had to.

Keith wrestled her back into her seat and held her there, whispering into her ear, his face buried in her hair.

Pam looked over at Marston, a pleading look in her eyes. "He was only out there the one time. He was just a baby—I didn't know. It was my fault, I didn't know." Her hand reached out for him, but she came up short. "Take me instead. It was my fault, just take me!"

Through all this, Marston didn't move. He didn't say anything. He only watched her.

The judge's face was nearly as red as Pam's. "Mr. Murdock, if you can't control your client, I'll end this right now!"

There was a knock on the door, and when it opened, Deputy Sandy Lomax stuck her head in and took a quick look around the room before crossing over to Whaley, who had remained oddly quiet through all this. She knelt at his side and handed him a small slip of paper.

Whaley unfolded it, read the message, and looked my father dead in the eyes. "Ted, where were you last Friday?"

4

MY FATHER FROWNED. "Last Friday? Why?"

"It's a simple question," Whaley replied. "Last Friday, between the hours of three to ten."

Judge Schultz seemed to be at the end of his patience. "Is this related to today's proceedings, Chief?"

Whaley's eyes didn't leave my father. "I need an answer, Ted."

My father seemed to consider this for a moment, then told him, "My office until two. Out visiting properties from two until a little before five, then home."

"Were any of those properties near Fox Run Mall?"

Shit.

"The mall?" His frown deepened. "No. Why?"

"Gentlemen," Judge Schultz cut in. "Whatever this is, you either need to take it outside or wait for these proceedings to conclude. There is a time and place, and this is neither."

Marston cleared his throat. "Your Honor, if I may?"

Schultz nodded. "Please."

Marston said, "While I can appreciate the concerns expressed by my client's parents, he is receiving care that far exceeds their means and the treatments received throughout his childhood. For all intents and purposes, he is an adult capable of making his own decisions regarding his personal well-being. Interference at this point might actually jeopardize the care he's receiving, endanger his health rather than aid in his recovery. I don't think anyone at this table wants to do that." He reached into his suit jacket and took out a folded sheet of paper. He set it in front of the judge. "That is a copy of Mr. Spivey's *most recent* blood work. A sample taken just yesterday. While he doesn't wish to share it with his parents, he did authorize me to provide a copy to the court."

Judge Schultz unfolded the paper and studied the results. He then compared it to the report provided by Murdock. After about half a minute, he refolded the document and passed it over to the court reporter before resting his hands on the table and facing Spivey's parents. "I understand your need to protect your child—I have three boys of my own—but there comes a time when they are no longer ours to protect. Your son appears to be receiving adequate care. His mental capacity to care for himself has not been brought into question, and with legal adulthood so close, my hands are tied. I'm afraid he has left the nest, and as parents, you need to come to terms with that. You will witness him make many decisions in the years to come, both bad and good, but from this point forward, they are all his own to make."

This wasn't what I expected. Whaley had said the judge was a golfing buddy of my dad's. I figured he'd side with the Spiveys' attorney and roll right over anything Marston put out there. Instead, he appeared to be handling this objectively. None of them seemed too happy about that.

Pam's face was buried in Keith's shoulder, and she was crying deep sobs muffled by his shirt. His hand was wrapped around the back of her head, holding her close.

Murdock looked uncomfortably at the two of them, then told the judge, "Your honor, we'd like to have the boy evaluated for potential diminished capacity. I think it's important we determine if he's capable of making these decisions." He took a stack of documents from his briefcase and placed them on the table. "These are signed affidavits from a number of individuals who have been out on that island and witnessed Mr. Spivey drinking excessively and taking drugs. Both of those activities are counterproductive to any treatment he may be receiving and demonstrate he may not be of sound mind."

A look passed between them. The judge pulled the documents closer and leafed through them. He frowned at me. "Billy, have you witnessed this activity?"

That's when I understood.

My father. Murdock. The judge. They all knew Marston would win on Spivey's legal right to make his own decisions based on his age, so they let him. They gave him that win because they knew they had something better.

I paused, expecting Marston to object, but when he did nothing, I told the judge, "A little drinking, but no drugs."

"Not in your presence," Murdock chimed in.

"Not at all."

"You can't possibly know that. You haven't been out there 24/7."

The judge eyed me for a moment, then turned to Whaley. "Chief?"

Whaley hadn't taken his eyes off my father, and my dad was still staring back at him. He told the judge, "We responded to an incident out there ten days ago. There appeared to be a party going on. If David Spivey was drinking, I didn't see it."

Murdock jumped on that. "Do children readily show you their alcohol or illegal substances when you appear at these functions?"

Whaley shook his head. "They do not, no."

Judge Schultz reached for his pen and rolled it between his fingers, then nodded softly before turning to Marston. "I'm going to issue an order for an evaluation of Mr. Spivey by a court-approved professional. You're welcome to have a secondary evaluation conducted by a doctor of your choosing should you feel that one is necessary. Your client will have thirty days to comply. At that point, we will reconvene."

"He'll be over eighteen." The words came out of me before I could stop them.

The judge said, "If it's determined he's not of sound mind, his age will no longer be a relevant factor."

If any of this bothered Marston, he didn't show it. "Have your professional contact my office and we'll arrange transportation out to the island."

"I'll most likely bring in Harold Springton. His office is here in Portsmouth," the judge replied. "Why can't your client go there?"

"He shouldn't have to. This is an inconvenience, and considering he is recovering from a very debilitating ailment, I don't believe anyone should require him to travel. Particularly a court that technically isn't within the state my client domiciles."

Although this last bit wasn't technically a threat, everyone around that table caught the message—if the judge pushed, Marston would push back and force Spivey's parents to take all of this to a court in Maine. That probably meant starting over and certainly meant more time.

I caught a hint of anger in the judge's eye, but he knew a losing fight when he heard one. "That's a valid point, Mr. Marston. I imagine Harold will enjoy the boat ride. I'll ask him to get in touch."

He looked at the faces around the table. Pam was still crying. Keith looked like he wanted to throttle Marston. And my father and Whaley were still locked in some kind of staring contest. Judge Schultz said, "All right, with that we are adjourned. A copy of the transcript will be made available to both parties."

I expected him to produce a wooden mallet and hit the table like they do in the movies, but instead he leaned over and spoke softly to the court reporter.

Deputy Lomax was standing between Whaley's chair and the door we'd entered through, and when my father rose from his seat, Whaley said, "Let's talk outside, Ted."

5

WHEN I STARTED to get up, I felt Marston's hand on my shoulder. In a low rasp he said, "You served your friend well, Mr. Hasler."

Served?

From across the table, Pam said desperately, "You need to get him out of there, Billy! He'll listen to you. You don't understand the—"

Marston raised a bony finger, and that was enough to silence her.

The rules, Pam. Be mindful of the rules.

He might as well have spoken it aloud, and although he hadn't, I knew if he had, she would have understood exactly what that odd statement meant. It was all over her face. Not only did she understand, but it was something she had understood for a very long time.

Her eyes met mine for a brief second before Keith stepped between us and helped her from the chair. He was whispering to her again as he guided her toward the door. Pam shook her head defiantly. She might have been a hundred years old, she looked so frail.

Marston followed out behind them, and that only seemed to quicken their pace.

Whaley said, "Judge? A quick word?"

Schultz nodded and rose. He gestured toward a small anteroom off the conference space. The two of them disappeared inside for a moment.

My father took the opportunity to gather his things and start for the door, but Deputy Lomax blocked his path. "You'll need to hang back a minute, Mr. Hasler."

My father was about to argue when Whaley returned holding a sheet of paper. "Ted, this is a warrant to search your car. Authorized by this court."

"Search my car? For what?"

Whaley glanced over at me and seemed to weigh whether or not he wanted to have this conversation with me in the room. When he realized I wasn't going anywhere, he turned back to my dad. "We received a tip that places you at Fox Run Mall on Friday. A witness came forward and said she saw Lily Dwyer get into your vehicle and leave with you."

This only seemed to confuse my father more. "Who's Lily Dwyer?"

"A missing person. Teenage girl."

"The one on the news?"

Whaley nodded.

It took a moment for all this to register, then my dad looked over at Murdock, who had been packing up his things, preparing to leave. "Donald, can you do something here?"

Murdock pursed his lips, studied my dad for a moment. This was more than he'd signed up for today, but he had history with my father and couldn't just walk away. He reached for the paper in Whaley's hand. "May I see that?"

Whaley handed him the warrant.

Murdock scanned the text, then looked off in the direction where Schultz had disappeared before turning back to my dad. "It's signed by the judge. There's nothing I can do, Ted. You need to give them access to your car."

My father's face grew red. "And if I don't?"

"Then you'll be held in contempt," Whaley told him. "I'll tow the car back to our lot and have it searched anyway. Let us look now and you can be on your way as soon as we're done. If you didn't do anything, you've got nothing to hide, right?"

"This is bullshit," my father replied. "Who gave you that tip?"

"It was anonymous. They didn't leave a name."

"Of course not," he shot back. "Why would they?" He pointed at the door. "This is Marston. You get that, right? That asshole is trying to intimidate me, get me to back down. Well, I won't. None of us will."

From the look on his face, it was clear Chief Whaley had spent a career listening to people feed him excuses and try to reason their way out of whatever brought him into their lives, and while he let my father speak, nothing he could say would alter what was about to happen. "Is your car locked, Ted?"

My dad only glared at him.

"Are we doing this the easy way or the hard way?"

"Fuck you, Cliff. Fuck all of you." He gave Murdock another frustrated glance, then fished the keys from his pocket and threw them to Whaley. "Just be quick about it. I've got an appointment in less than an hour."

Whaley *was* quick.

It only took him about two minutes to find the hair.

6

"YOUR DAD?" KIRA'S voice was thin over the phone; she sounded so far away. "Are you serious?"

I was standing in the parking lot behind town hall, my back to the police station. The midday July sun beat down on me and the blacktop had an odd haze to it. I didn't care that I was sweating; I had to get out of that building. Henry's Market was right across the street, bustling with tourists.

"You can't tell anyone, not—" I cut myself off as a woman power-walked by me down the sidewalk in the general direction of the beach. When she was gone, I finished, "—not a soul."

Kira went quiet for a moment. "Do you think your dad... oh, wow... could he?"

"No way. My dad may be a lot of things, but some kind of kidnapper? Not a chance."

I had told myself this over and over again, and each time I said it, the words seemed to hold less weight. As I repeated it to Kira, I wasn't sure just who I was trying to convince—her or me. Probably both.

"This isn't kidnapping, Billy. Not anymore. That girl's been missing for ten days. Teenage girls don't go missing for ten days. She either ran away or she's..."

She's dead.

Kira didn't say it out loud and didn't have to. Even the tone in the press had shifted in that direction. Talk of rescue had gone to recovery, and a singular thought had wormed into every adult's mind—keep your daughters close, because whoever did this was still out there. There'd been several vigils; the mall's south entrance was covered in so many photographs, signs, and stuffed animals that the police had to rope off the makeshift memorial before it spilled into the parking lot.

"Does your mom know?"

I glanced back over my shoulder at the police station. "She's inside with Dad and that attorney, Murdock."

"Billy, how did her hair get in your father's car?"

"We don't know it's her hair," I shot back. I didn't mean for these words to come out as defensively as they did, but it was hard to hold back the frustration. "My dad's in real estate. He's constantly shuttling people around in his car. Some random hair could have come from anyone."

"Some random pink hair?" she said softly. "Do a lot of your dad's clients have pink hair?"

I kicked at a chunk of loose gravel.

"Do you think your dad would cheat on your mom?"

I opened my mouth to say no, then shut it, because I didn't know. I'd spent the last few hours thinking about that one too. He was barely home, and when he was, I rarely saw anything that would be considered affection pass between my parents. It wasn't that they didn't love each other—I knew they did—but they lived very separate lives. When my dad was home, he spent most of his time in his office, and my mom was constantly grading papers for her students. Even when they watched television together, they might be in the same room, but their heads were somewhere else. They rarely fought, so there was that. It didn't mean he wasn't cheating. If he was cheating, would he cheat with a high school girl? Lily Dwyer was only fifteen. That was statutory rape. That could land him in jail.

If he got caught.

If she told.

If he let her tell.

I tried to force those thoughts away too. I remembered what I'd dreamed Lily saying:

"He's going to kill me. I know he is. He wouldn't have let me see his face otherwise. You've gotta get me out of here!"

"I don't know his name. I've never seen him before. He drugged me with something. Put it over my mouth. And now I'm locked in… I just woke up… I think I'm in the trunk of his car. It feels like we're moving. Can you call the police?"

She didn't know her attacker.

Her attacker had put her in the trunk of his car, not the front seat.

But that had been a dream.

Fiction.

Bullshit.

I was seriously attempting to use a dream to create some kind of alibi for my dad because I had nothing else.

"At the courthouse, my dad tried to blame Marston. Said he planted it."

"You don't believe that, do you? I mean, why would he? How could he possibly know her?"

"How would my dad know her?"

There was another explanation, one neither of us had spoken of aloud. Alesia's curse. Although the events in Spivey's basement were fuzzy, I remembered that much.

Along with everything else, my father's business card had gone into that bowl of hers. A few weeks ago, I would have laughed that off, but I remembered snippets of what came after, and let's just say my beliefs had gotten muddy lately.

My phone vibrated with an incoming text.

My mother.

Where did you go? Get back in here!

"Shit. I gotta go," I told Kira. "Where are you? Can I see you when I get out of here? We need to talk. In person, not on the phone."

At this, she went quiet, then said, "I'm with Alesia."

I wanted to believe her, so why didn't I?

Another text—

Now, Billy!

"I'll text you when I get out," I told her. "I love you."

"You too, Billy," she said before disconnecting.

What the hell did that mean? *You too?*

7

THE NEW CASTLE police station wasn't very large. The lobby was little more than a hallway—a couple of chairs with a table between them on the right and a glass window on the left separating the duty officer's desk from whoever came inside. Deputy Lomax was standing at the far end of the room holding a door marked AUTHORIZED PERSONNEL ONLY, waiting on me. "Come on, I'll take you back."

She led me by several cramped offices, past some steps leading upstairs, then to a closed door. She knocked twice, then opened it. My father was sitting at a small table, Murdock on his right, my mother across from him. Her eyes were red and puffy; it was clear she'd been crying. When she saw me, she got up and wiped her cheeks. "I have to get back to the university. I want you at the house when I get home later. Enough of this running around doing whatever, you're grounded."

"Me? What did I do?"

She opened her mouth ready to answer, but Murdock cut her off with a look and a slight shake of his head.

She eyed him for a moment, then turned back on me. "*Home.* No excuses."

Deputy Lomax stepped aside and let her out. My mom might have trampled her if she hadn't. She shuffled quickly down the hallway, her heels clicking on the tile.

Murdock gestured toward the seat she'd vacated, waited for me to sit, then told Lomax, "Can you get the chief?"

Lomax nodded and disappeared down the hall, leaving the door open.

I looked at my father's hands. Part of me expected them to be in handcuffs, but they weren't. No orange jumpsuit either. Although he'd loosened his tie, he was still wearing his suit. He'd been drinking a cup of coffee. The paper cup was empty now, sitting in front of him. If he was the least bit worried, he didn't show it.

Murdock looked at his watch. "I'm supposed to be in court in an hour."

"You're not going anywhere," my father told him. "Not until we get this squared away."

Murdock lowered his voice. "I specialize in family law, Ted. You need a criminal attorney."

My dad's eyes narrowed. "You worked in the DA's office for six years before making the move to family law. Don't think for a second you can weasel out of this. You're here, you're staying. You and your firm collect a hefty retainer from my office. We can talk about bringing in someone more qualified if that becomes necessary, but for now, I expect you to do your damn job and protect your client."

I leaned forward. "Dad, I—"

"Shut up," he growled. "I don't want to hear another word out of you."

He'd never spoken to me like that before. The words stung like a slap to my face, and I fell back in the chair.

Chief Whaley appeared at the door, eyed all of us, then stepped inside the small room, pulling the door shut behind him. Rather than sit next to me, he moved the empty chair to the head of the table.

The room wasn't air-conditioned, there were no windows, and it was hot. Murdock was sweating and so was I. Not Whaley, though, and not my dad. It was like both men possessed a will strong enough to turn off that particular bodily function. Whaley rolled his fingers across the edge of the table, drummed them several times, then looked at me.

I did not expect what he said next.

"Billy, did you plant that hair in your father's car?"

My heart thumped. One solid beat against my ribs. My stomach seized up like someone stuck their hand down my throat and balled the lining in a fist. I expected Murdock to object, and when he didn't, I looked over at my father, who was watching me with the same cold stare he'd had back at the courthouse. All three of them waiting for me to answer.

What my dad said next didn't make me feel any better.

"Tell him the truth, Billy."

He looked me directly in the eyes as he said it. The words flippant, almost dismissive, as if he'd outright caught me in a blatant lie and he was allowing me the opportunity to come clean so I could clear my conscience and he could move on with his day.

"Of course not," I fired back. "Why would I? Where would I get her hair? I don't even know her!"

"You've never met Lily Dwyer?" Whaley asked. "Not once?"

"No! I told you that when you came out to the island the other night. This is crazy, why would I... ?"

Whaley raised both his hands above the table. "Calm down, Billy. We're just having a conversation here. No need to raise your voice."

No need to raise my voice. My father was accusing me of framing him for abducting and possibly killing someone, and there was no need to raise my voice? Fuck that.

"You were in your father's car this morning," Murdock jumped in, making it clear whose side he was on. "... And that hair magically appeared. How do you think it got there?"

"I have no idea! I saw it when we got to the courthouse, and I—"

"When you *got* to the courthouse?" Murdock interrupted. "So you knew it was there before today's proceedings even started?"

"Yeah, but not because I put it there!"

"Did you put it there?" my father asked.

I glared at him. "No!"

All three were staring at me.

Murdock went on. "Your dad's business interests with regard to the Spiveys' property don't align with your own. Nobody would fault you if this were some kind of retaliation. We just want the truth."

"The *Spiveys'* property? That island isn't the Spiveys' property, it's David Spivey's property. Maybe if all you stopped making grabs at it, none of this would be happening!"

Murdock sat back, a smug look on his face. He told Whaley, "The boy is obviously harboring ill will toward this entire situation. What makes more sense? An upstanding member of the community abducted a young girl and transported her in his own car, the front seat for that matter, or this boy—who had obvious access—planted a hair in an attempt to derail his father's activities?"

"I have never met Lily Dwyer," I said for what felt like the millionth time. "I didn't even know her name up until a few weeks ago. How exactly did I have access?"

"She was at the mall with your girlfriend, wasn't she? Not only Kira, but several of the other people who have been spending time out there on *the Spiveys' property*, if I have my facts straight. You *and* your friends clearly had access, *and* your anger toward your father and this situation gives you motive."

The blood left my face. I looked at my dad, and while he met my eyes again, he said nothing to defend me.

Whaley cleared his throat, interrupting before Murdock could take this further. "I'd like to speak to you without your father present. Are you willing to do that?"

Murdock snapped into defense. "You're not speaking to the boy without an attorney present."

"You're not my attorney," I told him.

Murdock opened his mouth to object to that, but Whaley cut him off. He looked back at me. "If you'd like an attorney present, someone else, I can have someone brought in."

I looked back over at my dad and Murdock. "I just want both of them out of here."

My father eyed Whaley. "You speak to him without an attorney present and it won't be admissible. I'll see to that. Regardless of how this shakes out, he's still a minor."

"I'm only looking for answers right now. Looking for a missing girl. As far as I'm concerned, we'll sort the rest of this dirt out in the wash." He tilted his head back and called over his shoulder, "Sandy, you still out there?"

The door opened and Deputy Lomax stuck her head in. "Yes, Chief?"

"Take Ted Hasler here and place him in one of our holding cells."

Murdock held his arm out across the table, between my father and Whaley. "You're holding him? On what charge?"

"No charge. Not yet," he replied. "I can keep him for forty-eight hours, you know that. The hair is on its way to the lab in Boston. Once we determine if it came from Lily Dwyer, we can discuss next steps. Until then, he can sit tight right here."

"A judge would grant bail, he's not a flight risk. You know that."

"No, I don't, actually. And in order for a judge to grant bail, I need to charge him. We need to hold an arraignment. That's a lot of public records. A lot of people talking. Press. You want to go that route, we can—I just assumed you'd prefer to keep this quiet for now. We should have a blood type by the end of the day, a few hours at most. If it turns out the hair is not a match, Ted walks out and nobody's the wiser. Your call. I'm fine either way."

"How about an ankle bracelet? Monitor him that way."

Whaley shook his head. "This isn't a negotiation."

My dad leaned closer to Murdock and whispered something into his ear.

"You sure?" Murdock frowned.

"As long as I can keep my phone. I've got a business to run."

"I'm okay with that," Whaley told him. "Sandy?"

Deputy Lomax gestured toward the hallway. "This way, Mr. Hasler."

My father stood, smoothing the creases in his pants, and paused at the door only long enough to tell me, "Give him the truth, Billy. We can get past this if you're honest. I'll forgive you."

Then he was gone; Murdock, too.

When the door closed, Whaley produced the envelope containing the photographs from my dad's car and set it in the center of the table. Spun it with his finger several times. What he said next, though, had nothing to do with the old pictures of Marston, or the bodies found on Wood Island, or my father.

"Did Kira and her friends hurt Lily Dwyer?"

8

"KIRA?"

"Yeah, Kira," Whaley replied. "Look, I don't think you did this.

And I don't think your father did either. He may be a lot of things, but he's not the sort to step out on his family with teenage girls. Consensual or otherwise. None of that feels right, and I've been doing this long enough to understand when my gut says it doesn't feel right, it's probably not. I think something happened at the mall, something involving all those girls, and all the rest of this is smoke and mirrors."

"Well, Kira would never hurt anyone either."

The chief studied me, scratched his nose, then pulled a folded piece of paper from his breast pocket. He smoothed it out on the table—it was a color printout from a computer, an image with a timestamp in the bottom right corner. His thick index finger landed on the page, pointing at a girl with bright pink hair wearing round John Lennon sunglasses. "That's Lily Dwyer. One of the last shots we have of her exiting the mall."

He turned the page so I could see it right side up. I recognized the south entrance—considering how often it had appeared on the news and in the papers lately, it would be impossible not to. But this wasn't the picture they were running in the press.

Whaley knew what I was thinking, so he explained, "The image they're running on television was taken after this one. They're both from the same camera footage, just about twenty seconds apart."

"I can barely make her out," I replied.

"Yeah, she's further from the camera and the quality isn't that good to begin with. You can't make out much of her face, but it's her. Clothing is a clear match to the other images we have of her. I'm more concerned with this." His finger moved to the top right corner of the image and pointed at something else.

His palm had been covering it up, so I hadn't seen it. I hadn't seen her. My heart thumped.

"That is Kira, right?"

I was smart enough to understand he already knew the answer. I was pretty sure his palm hadn't rested over that portion of the image by accident either. He let me see her when he wanted me to see her. But like Lily, her face wasn't very visible. The image was grainy and distant, distorted by what was probably some kind of wide-angle lens. It was her, though.

I nodded.

He pointed at two others. "And them?"

Holding hands. Standing several feet behind Kira. "That's Izzie and Chloe," I told him.

"Figured as much."

"I'm not sure what you're getting at," I said tentatively. "You know they were at the mall with Lily, they told you that. Even gave you a picture."

"They did, didn't they?" He settled back in his chair. "That happy group shot. All smiles. Looked like they were having fun."

Whaley took his phone from his pants pocket, swiped through several screens, and loaded up the picture. Not the one they'd been using on the news, cropped to show only Lily Dwyer, but the original shot. The one with Lily, Kira, Izzie, Chloe, and…

Something in my head clicked. I realized what he was getting at, but it wasn't exactly some smoking gun. Alesia Dubin was in the group shot, but not the surveillance image. I didn't say anything, but I didn't have to. He went on before I could speak.

"When I first saw this, I figured Alesia Dubin had gone to the bathroom, or maybe she was off shopping on her own. There are a million reasons for her to not be on this particular security camera at that moment. Hell, she might have been standing right off on the side somewhere, just off camera. There are blind spots all over the mall. And like you said, why does it even matter? We already know Lily was there with these girls." He settled back in the chair and clucked his tongue. "Something about this picture kept nagging at me, though. Like a loose thread on an old sweater. You ever get one of those? You can't help but tug on it even though you know it will probably do more damage than good." He looked down at the picture again. "What does it look like they're all doing to you?"

Again, I felt like he already knew the answer. At the very least, he'd come to some kind of conclusion he had yet to share. But I couldn't help myself. I looked back down at the picture and studied it for a moment. "Well, Lily's leaving. She's only a few feet from the exit, and I can't say for sure, but it looks like her arm is swinging forward, about to push through the glass doors there."

"That would be my guess," he agreed. "And what about Kira?"

"I don't know—she's just standing there," I said. "Watching her. Lily."

"Watching her leave." He tapped on Chloe and Izzie. "Them too, right?"

"Yeah. I still don't see why that matters."

Whaley's chair creaked under his weight as he shifted slightly, then he lined up the printout and his phone again, the image of all the girls still on the screen. "Take a close look at both. You'll see it. Just give it a second."

I wasn't sure what he was talking about, not at first. Then I was. Something so obvious, I wasn't sure how I missed it. "They're all wearing different clothes."

Lily's outfit was nearly the same—jean shorts and a white tank top in both images, but the tops were slightly different, the shoulder straps thin in the photo with the other girls and wider in the surveillance shot. Kira was wearing dark skirts in both, but her tee-shirt had text across the front in the group picture, a shirt I recognized. It said, *eyes up top, sailor!* In the surveillance image, her shirt was plain, no text. Chloe's clothing was similar too. Izzie's was completely different—shorts in one picture, jeans in the other.

Whaley said, "When we're asked to recognize people, we tend to look at the face. All else becomes white noise, blurry. We don't see because we're so focused."

"This doesn't make sense," I said softly.

"The photograph the girls gave me was taken on a different day.

One week before, according to the techs in Boston. They were able to pull the date from data embedded in the image."

"Metadata."

"Yeah, metadata. Date. Location. Make, model, and serial number of the phone snapping the shot, the camera... all that is captured in the image." He tapped the group shot with his finger. "We pulled all the video footage at the mall the day this was taken, and all the girls are together. Almost three hours, bouncing from store to store. Eating. Fending off boys, typical girl stuff. But none of that happened the day Lily vanished; it's all one week earlier. When we reviewed the footage for the date she disappeared, Lily runs into Kira once. They talk for less than a minute near the restrooms, but that's it. Aside from that, best we can tell, Kira, Izzie, and Chloe followed her from a distance, but didn't make contact."

"Okay, so where was Alesia? Was she even there?"

"Oh, she was there. She arrived with Kira and the other two, then broke off. We got her on video crossing the mall. Making a beeline for the west entrance."

"Why?"

"She went straight for this guy." Whaley flicked through a few photographs on his phone until he found the one he wanted. "She shows him something on her phone. They talk for about a minute— actually looks more like an argument or disagreement of some sort. There's no audio on the security system, but it's clear they're both agitated. He takes a second look at her phone, then stomps off. Heads back outside."

"That's Rory Moir."

"Yeah. Rory Moir. Her boyfriend."

Ex-boyfriend, but I wasn't about to tell Whaley that, because if I did, I'd also have to tell him where Alesia Dubin was resting her head lately, and Spivey had enough problems.

"If you look real close, you can see Rory's car parked at the curb outside."

"I still don't understand what you're getting at."

He studied me for a long moment. I could see the wheels turning behind his eyes. When he finally spoke, he said, "I don't think you do, and that's probably a good thing. For you, anyway. Not so sure about your friends."

When I only stared at him, he continued.

"I think Rory is our missing 'Brian,' or maybe there was never a 'Brian' to begin with. Either way, I'm pretty sure Lily left the mall in Rory's car. I think Alesia all but put her in that car with the help of Kira and the others. I don't know the *whys* of it all, haven't figured that part out yet, but to me, it looks like their first trip to that mall, the one with Lily, was some kind of trial run, like a scouting mission. And they pulled the trigger with the second trip. Lured her there, then followed her around to make sure she left with him. Maybe funneled her to him. They concocted some kind of story, fed it to me with that picture, to send me and the rest of law enforcement down a rabbit hole when Lily turned up missing."

As nervous as I was, I almost laughed.

Because that might have been one of the craziest theories I'd ever heard.

He must have understood how much of a leap that all was, because he was smiling, too. Grinning like he'd told me the greatest joke in the world and wanted to give the punchline a chance to sink in. Finally, he tilted his head and said, "Nutty, right? Just saying all that aloud makes me think maybe your dad really did grab her and that's the end of it. Some pervert impulse that probably ends with a body weighed down and dumped in the water somewhere. Simplest explanation is usually right— they teach us that in cop school." He spread his hands wide. "My theory, I'm jumping from A to C to X."

"It doesn't seem very plausible."

"Not in the slightest," he agreed. "Had it not been for last night, I would have never gone there."

My heart thumped. "What happened last night?"

The smile left Whaley's face. "Rory's dad got picked up in Exeter on a D&D, drunk and disorderly. Seems he'd been out celebrating. Apparently, he came into some money. Well, the way he told it at some shithole called Roosters, Rory came into some money and gave him a taste. But either way, he was out throwing cash around like he could print more. Buying rounds. Talking about getting his own boat, maybe a new truck. You'd think he won the lottery. But he didn't, not him at all— it was Rory. Here's the thing, though. In his drunken stupor, he said, 'Rory cashed in the pink cow.' That's where the money came from. His exact words. *The pink cow.*"

I'm not sure when he loaded it back up, but he had the group shot back on his phone, and his index finger lazily traced Lily Dwyer's hair.

"Like I said," Whaley told me. "I don't know the *whys*. Not the big one, anyway—why they would want her. But I think I've got the *how* and the *who*. Those girls paid Rory to snatch her up. Maybe she did something to them. Girls can get catty. Maybe they wanted to scare her, teach her a lesson, who knows. I think that part of the plan went sideways and now Lily is gone. I don't think they'd hurt her intentionally, not bad, but something might have went wrong. Even the best of plans can unravel. Field a curveball."

"If you believe all this, why don't you ask them? Why am I sitting here?"

"The truth?" He let out a sigh. "Because my theory has holes, and their folks would lawyer up before I got anything useful."

"And my parents won't, at least not to protect me, so you think it's okay to grill me instead?"

"I'm hardly grilling, Billy. I'm sharing. I think you know something even if you don't know you know it. You've got the missing pieces, but you haven't connected them. And for better or worse, that's because your friends have decided not to include you in this." He settled back in his chair, the wood groaning under his weight. "I think one of those girls planted the hair in your dad's car to throw us off, and that poor girl is out there on that island somewhere."

Thoughts of the basement flooded my head.

The smell.

Dead things.

Benny's hole.

I forced it out. They wouldn't go there. That was too far— they'd *never* go there.

"Why don't you just ask Rory? Nobody's spending money on a lawyer for him. Or his dad. I bet he'd roll on his son to get himself out of trouble."

"I would if we could find him," Whaley replied. "According to his dad, Rory hasn't been home for three days. Have you seen him?"

I shook my head.

He studied me for a moment. "Why are you so pale, Billy? You're sweating."

I looked around the room. The windowless walls were covered in so many layers of paint, they rippled with bumps. There was a ceiling fan, but it wasn't on. The air was as still as a tomb. "It's hot in here, that's all."

"Yeah, well, it is that," he agreed. "But you're also trembling." His voice fell low. "Here's the thing. It won't take long for the staties or the feds to make some of these same connections. They're looking for Lily Dwyer too. It may take a day, maybe two days, but someone else will see it, and when that happens, they'll come down hard on you, your friends, especially Spivey. They'll pounce on that island from every which way and tear up every inch. You heard Marston—he's two weeks shy of his eighteenth birthday. He'll learn the hard way what it means to be an adult. All of you will."

"She's not out there. I would have seen her."

The words came from me so weak, *I* didn't believe them.

"Take me out there," Whaley replied. "Just me. Talk to Spivey for me. Give me a chance to look around and confirm that. If she's not, I can tell everyone that when the question inevitably comes up. And if she is—"

"She's not."

"… And if she is. If you're the one who helped me find her, I'll do what I can to keep you out of trouble. I can see to it that you still have some kind of future." He licked his lips. "I want to be wrong here, I do. I hope to God I'm wrong. Help prove me wrong."

9

WE TOOK *MERV*.

Looking back on it, I suppose Whaley asked to take my boat rather than one from the police department because Spivey wouldn't bat an eye when he saw me approach. There was no easy way to sneak up on an island. Even at only a quarter-mile out, that bit of distance offered several minutes of advance warning.

Was this a betrayal?

Yes.

The knot growing in my stomach made that very clear.

There was a very good chance Spivey would never speak to me again after today.

Kira and the others, either.

But this was something I had to do. Not for Whaley. Not even for Lily's parents. *I* had to know. I totally understood how selfish that reasoning was, but that didn't make it any less true. When you're seventeen, the world may feel incredibly large, but it all revolves around one single point, and that point is you. I told myself this was the right thing to do, even if it felt completely wrong. In some twisted way, I convinced myself I was stopping things before they got worse, and the crazy thing was, even if Whaley and I found Lily out there—if we dug up Benny's hole and found Lily's lifeless body in the dirt—something in the back of my head told me this could still get worse. Her death was only the beginning of the bad to come. A catalyst. A spark. That's why I was doing this—I believed I could stop what came next.

I was an idiot.

Whaley sat up in the bow. One hand on the hull, the other attempting to hold his hair (and failing) as the warm wind whipped it about.

His eyes remained fixed on the tiny island, watching it grow as we drew close.

When I motored *Merv* around the rocks and to the dock, he stood and helped me tie off. *Annabelle* wasn't there. That meant Spivey wasn't either.

The world got very quiet when I shut down *Merv*'s motor.

Whaley climbed up on the dock and looked around. Standing behind him, I searched for Benny. He'd become a fixture out here, but if he was on the island, I didn't see him. No sign of his shovel or wheelbarrow either. The various holes he'd dug up around the house and beach were all filled in. He'd done such a good job, I didn't see them at all. Not an outline or fresh mound, nothing.

It didn't feel like anyone was there.

I expected Whaley to go to the door and knock. Shout out "Police!" At the time, I had no idea what the legalities of all this were, but I was pretty sure he couldn't poke around without permission.

Whaley didn't start with the house. He took several steps up the dock toward the door, then stopped and pointed at the shed off to the left. "What's in there? Any idea?"

"The generator. I think there's some batteries too. Not sure what else."

"Uh-huh." He followed the dock to the yard and made his way over to the shed, his head swiveling as he went, taking in everything. When he reached the door, he ran his hand along the frame. "Awfully quiet for a generator, don't you think?"

His left hand wrapped around the doorknob and his right settled on the butt of his gun. His finger twitched and snapped off the small piece of leather securing the weapon. "Anyone in there? New Castle, PD."

He said this just loud enough to be heard from the interior of the shed, but not loud enough to carry back to the house, and at first, I thought someone might answer, but nobody did. The only sound was the wind rustling the tall seagrass.

He twisted the knob, and when he realized it wasn't locked, his body tensed. He bobbed his head to the left, signaling me to step aside.

What did he expect? Spivey to come running out with guns blazing like some old Western?

Maybe not Spivey, but I could picture Benny doing that—eyes wide, swinging his shovel like David Ortiz ready to clear the bases and send one over the Green Monster. I opened my mouth to warn Whaley, but before I could, he yanked the door open with enough force to send it cracking against the wall and bouncing back. He blocked it with his right leg and fell to a crouch. His gun was out, arms outstretched and sweeping the interior left to right and back again. I'd never seen him move so fast and wouldn't have thought it possible. He was the man I'd grown up watching wearing a crossing guard vest in front of the elementary school every morning. The idea that he'd shoot someone seemed ridiculous, but I had no doubt he would.

Benny wasn't in the shed.

Nobody was.

And Whaley's gun was back in the holster as quickly as it had appeared.

I didn't see him put the weapon away; I was too busy staring inside the small building, trying to understand what I was looking at.

There was a generator sitting in the center of the space on a cracked concrete pad, but that generator was covered in cobwebs and flaked with so much rust and grime, it was clear it hadn't run in years. Two rubber hoses were visible, both rotted and cracked, filled with holes. What looked like a carburetor was in pieces off to the side, lying on top of an old gray length of cloth, frayed and chewed with time. There were a couple of gas cans too, piled in the corner of the shed, but those looked even older. Rusted and forgotten.

"There must be another generator somewhere," I mumbled.

And there had to be, because there was no chance this one was powering the house. The last time this one had run, Nixon was probably busy buying tape recorders.

"Maybe they're bringing power in from Kittery." A bare bulb hung from the center of the shed's ceiling. Whaley reached up and tugged the metal chain, but nothing happened. "Or not."

A wheelbarrow stood in the back corner of the shed, an old shovel and pickax lying inside. The wheel was flat, the rubber rotten, and this too was covered in webs. These couldn't be the tools I'd seen Benny using— they certainly looked like them, red-handled shovel and all, but the paint was faded and chipped. As old as everything else in the shed.

Whaley picked up a rusty screwdriver and wrench from the cloth near the disassembled carburetor, brushed the webs off, then dropped them to the ground before going back outside.

He stood there for a moment, his gaze sweeping over the large doors of the boathouse and the main building beyond, then he started across the overgrown yard toward the kitchen door.

10

THE BOARDS OF the small porch creaked under our weight, and in the harsh daylight, I realized the paint wasn't as fresh as I originally thought. Parts had peeled away, cracks and flakes riddling the railing. The lumber of the house itself was splintered and stained, and two panes of glass in the window off the kitchen were broken. Maybe Rory and his friends had made it back after all. Chucked a couple of rocks through the glass. I told myself that because it made sense, and I needed what I was looking at to make sense. It didn't explain the wood, though, or the paint. That might have been the result of a bad storm coming through, but we'd had no such storm, not in the handful of days since I'd last been out here. I supposed Marston might have hired someone to paint the house when Spivey took possession, and it was very possible that person used poor quality paint, but that didn't explain the wood.

Whaley opened the screen door and knocked several times , but there was no answer. He called out "Police!" again, much louder than back at the shed, and that brought no one, either. When he tried the doorknob, I wanted it to be locked.

Don't lock the doors

But it wasn't. It didn't turn easily, though; it turned like a knob that had forgotten how to turn. As if years of nonuse had driven the memory of that skill away.

The heavy door didn't want to move either. The swollen wood held it in place. I could see it around the frame—bulbous and cracked, tinged dark where the moisture had settled in and gone to mold like thin veins. The door on our storm cellar looked like that. The wood was soft, spongy. None of that was right, though. This door swung as if it were new the last time I was here. It *had been new*, recently installed; I remembered thinking that the first time we all came out here.

Whaley told me to step back and he came at the door again, leading with his shoulder. Wide receivers weren't known for their hits, but at some point between his ball-playing days and now, he'd perfected the move. With an audible crack, the door popped free and opened on the kitchen.

"Spivey, this is Chief Whaley… anyone here?"

His voice boomed through the empty room and the spaces behind not like he was shouting into a house, but standing at the mouth of a large tunnel.

"I don't think anyone's here," he said, stepping into the kitchen. When he realized I hadn't moved, he looked back at me. "You coming?"

I couldn't move.

My legs were frozen in place.

My head was buzzing with so many thoughts, I couldn't make sense of any of them. All I could do was stare into the kitchen.

What used to be the kitchen.

The stainless steel appliances were gone. Replaced with an ancient black stovetop and rusted white refrigerator… not even a refrigerator, an icebox—small with rounded edges and a mangled handle hanging on by one bolt, some relic from a time long gone. The walls were no longer pale yellow as I remembered them, but covered in tattered floral print wallpaper. Large sections were peeled away, the edges curled, caked with soot and grease from the stove. Several logs sat in an iron basket off to the side ready to feed that stove, but even those looked as if someone had brought them in a long time ago and forgotten them there.

The sign with Spivey's rules was still there, balanced precariously on the counter. Whaley was reading them as I finally found the will to step inside.

"This is all wrong," I heard myself say.

"It's not what I expected," Whaley agreed. "I don't see how anyone can live here. I'd heard talk a while back about condemning this place and tearing it down. I understand why."

"That's not what I mean. This isn't how it was. It's…"

"It's what?"

I could only shake my head. There was no explaining it. Not to him, not to anyone. I didn't understand it myself. Only those who had been out here might understand, and none of them were here. Nobody was.

Whaley had his phone out and was holding it up toward the ceiling, studying the screen. "No signal." He switched to the photo app and took several shots of the room. "I know he's your friend, but considering his illness, he shouldn't be living here. I'm not sure anyone should."

There were holes in the wood floor, and Whaley carefully maneuvered around them through the kitchen and to the living room. The furniture was gone. The stereo too. No large television on the wall. Nothing about the space was familiar to me— it was like walking through a dreamscape, and for a moment, I thought maybe I *was* dreaming. If I wasn't dreaming now, maybe I had dreamt my previous trips out here. Nothing else made sense.

A broom was propped up against the far wall, but if anyone had used it recently, there was no sign. The floor was covered in dirt and dust. The windows were caked with it, allowing only enough light to coat the room with gloom. The air smelled of mildew, and water stains lined the exterior wall around the window frame and up near the ceiling.

Whaley went to the center of the space, mindful of the damaged floor, and took a few more photographs. He didn't notice me walk by him to the stairs. I had probably been standing there for a minute before he came over.

"What is it?"

I was looking at the wall where the photographs had been, now empty. It was obvious something had hung there—the sun had faded the wallpaper around about a dozen squares where the pictures had been—but aside from that and bare nails, there was nothing. That wasn't the worst of it, though. I was looking at the stairs.

"Billy? You look like you've seen a ghost. Are you okay?"

At first, I could only point. Then I managed to say, "There were steps here leading down into the basement. They're... they're gone."

Whaley's face grew puzzled. "Basement?"

"Right here. " I traced the spot with a finger slowly through the dusty air. "There was an opening in the floor and steps leading down."

Whaley eyed me for a moment, then sunk to his knees. He switched on his phone's flashlight and brightly illuminated the area, tracing the floorboards, the wall. "Billy, there's no opening here. Look at the floor—these strips of wood are solid the full length of the room. I can't imagine you could even dig out here without hitting the waterline or stone.

"They blasted out the basement."

Whaley didn't reply to that, only looked at me. And when he couldn't face me anymore, he went back to studying the floor. When he finally stood, he said, "You've had a very hard day. Maybe I should get you home."

I wasn't going home.

Not yet.

I needed to see upstairs.

I pushed by him and took the steps two at a time. Even when one of them cracked under my foot, catching the heel of my shoe, I kept going.

11

I FOUND MORE of the same.

The room I remembered as the master bedroom was filled with clutter. Furniture and old Coast Guard equipment. Some covered in heavy cloths, others not, all of it coated in a thick layer of dust. There was no master bath. In that room (as well as the other closets), there were trunks with more clothing—boots, uniforms, rain gear. Old lamps and stacks of books. A government issue box of staples. No stapler, just staples, fifty thousand of them. Enough to last a lifetime plus twenty. There was even a bicycle, the rubber rotten and long gone from the rusted rims. An old phonograph, too. The kind with a crank on the side.

None of this had been here before.

Everything was different.

Like I was standing in a different house.

Whaley stepped around a pile of boxes and let out a soft whistle. "All these antiques are probably worth a small fortune."

A mouse skittered across the far end of the room. It paused for a moment, glaring at the two of us, the trespassers we were, then vanished through a small hole in the wall where the bed had been.

Whaley crossed the hallway to the bunkroom. "Is this where Spivey's been sleeping?"

In a half daze, I followed after him.

Of all the rooms, this one had changed the least. Although unmade, all the beds were still there. The metal footlockers, too. But unlike before, the paint was faded and the springs on three of the beds were broken. A sleeping bag was on the floor near the door, along with a camping lantern. Spivey's backpack was off to the side with half the clothes piled on top. His crate of CDs was there too. A few were out of their cases, but I didn't see any kind of player.

There was a bucket placed there to catch water from a leak in the stained ceiling.

Although some light slipped through the grimy windows, Whaley had his flashlight on again, pointing up. "Isn't there another level above this one?"

I turned and looked down the hallway, back toward the stairs, and realized that was all wrong, too.

There should be more steps leading up to the small landing, the one with the locked closet—regular steps, same as the others—but there were no more steps. Instead, there was only the steep ladder-like staircase that went to the tower and the widow's walk.

I approached the ladder tentatively, part of me expecting even this to vanish with a blink, but it didn't. My hand shook as I reached for it, touched it. I ran my fingers over several of the square-headed nubby nails holding it together. Felt the smoothness of the rungs, the wood worn to a stone-like finish from a lifetime worth of boots. When I looked up through the opening, I saw only the roofline of the tower.

An entire floor of the house had vanished.

There was no way I'd imagined it. There were conversations about it—the only locked door in the house. Kira had fixated on it, wanted to turn the closet into a small bedroom. Spivey had said the television came from that closet. The stereo, too.

None of those things were here.

Just thinking about all that made my head hurt. It was like those memories were hiding somewhere in my mind and didn't want to come out, fighting me when I tried to pull them into the light. If those things weren't real, if the house I remembered wasn't real, wouldn't I have memories of this house? The disrepair. The layout. The smells. All of it. I didn't, though. All of this was new to me, I was sure of that. As sure as I was about my memories.

Whaley was holding up an old Coast Guard hat. He'd taken it from one of the lockers and was studying the band inside. Whoever had owned it had written their name on the cloth with a black marker. The blocky letters were faded now, unreadable.

I could almost see it if I squinted my eyes and peered through the blur—a dozen sailors lining the hallway, shucking off their heavy rain gear and changing into more casual wear, returning from one call and preparing for the next. Laughter echoed all around. Heavy, brooding laughter. Not exactly real, but overcompensating for the horrors just seen at sea. A laughter meant to help forget rather than recall. Smells crept up from the kitchen below—vegetable broth, maybe chicken soup, hard to tell but real enough to make my mouth water.

From somewhere downstairs, a voice called out. *"Anyone see Emerson?"*

And from above, a phone began to ring.

12

THE VOICES VANISHED.

The smells, gone.

The hallway was empty again, only Whaley standing there, still holding the hat.

All of it gone as quickly as it appeared.

But the phone continued. A muted ring from up above. From the tower.

A tiny hammer clattering against bells wrapped in cloth.

Whaley's head tilted up, his face washed in confusion. Having grown up in a time before cell phones, the sound of a landline ringing was probably more familiar to him than it was to me, and so were the logistics necessary for such a thing to work. No doubt he was wondering how the phone company managed to run a line out to here. Across the harbor, over rocks and sand dredged a million times over the years in an attempt to maintain the shipping lanes. And if they were able to do that, had they also run power? If the answer to that second question was *yes*, then the current state of the generator could easily be explained. But he hadn't been here when Spivey told us the island was completely self-sufficient and not tethered to the mainland, and if that were true, then the phone above us had no business ringing.

I'd been told never to answer it, and I answered it that one time anyway. That might be why I shot up the ladder as quickly as I did—my conversation with Lily Dwyer had been abruptly cut off the last time that phone had rung, and she and I had unfinished business.

In the tower, I nearly tripped over the sleeping bag and pillows Kira had brought up for us. Just seeing those along with the candles we had failed to light brought some relief, because at least *that* was real. I desperately wanted something to be real, even if that raised as many questions as it did comforts.

The old beige phone rattled in its base up on the wall, and I stared at it for a moment before I managed to summon the courage to reach for it, to pluck it from that base and bring it to my ear, an image of the board in the kitchen flashing through my mind again—all those rules I so blatantly disregarded.

Don't answer the—

"Hello?"

It wasn't Lily's voice on the other end of the call, not this time. Unlike before, this was a voice I knew. One I recognized, even if it sounded muffled and far away.

"There was nothing you could have done. It wasn't your fault."

My breath caught in my throat, and in that moment, I couldn't have spoken if my life depended on it.

"What happened, all of it, those events were in motion long before you ever set foot out there. You need to take comfort in that, as difficult as that may be to accept."

Whaley's head appeared in the hatch. He stopped halfway up the ladder and mouthed the words, *Who is it?*

I didn't answer him. I couldn't.

"Think of it like a movie, one playing all around you. You can touch it, feel it, smell it… it's as real as anything else, but the beginning, middle, and end of the film… it's all in the can. The script is carved in stone, production has wrapped, and although you haven't seen the full picture yet, it's done. It's run its course. No budget left for edits."

"I don't understand."

"No. You wouldn't. You didn't. You couldn't. I told myself that before I dialed, but I had to do this as much as you need to do what comes next. It's in the script. It's in the movie. On some level, it's already happened. Hell, I'm still trying to understand it, and I've had far more time than you. At this point, I think I've taken solace in one simple thought. I'm smart enough to understand there are many things I don't understand."

"Is Lily... dead?"

At this, Whaley perked up. His brow lined with knots. *Who is it!?*

"Is she out here somewhere?"

"Nobody dies on that island, but that doesn't mean they don't come home. In the end, we all come home. In the end, that's all we can do."

Whaley came up the remaining rungs of the ladder and snatched the phone from my hand. "This is Chief Whaley with New Castle, PD. Who am I speaking with?"

I dropped down on the sleeping bag and pillows, and for one brief second, I smelled Kira's shampoo lofting up at me through the air. I watched the chief's face go from frustrated to confused, then to stark white as the blood drained away. I thought he might drop the phone but he managed to hold onto it, even if he was shaking. I couldn't hear what was said, and I suppose that didn't matter much. What was said wasn't nearly as important as who said it, and when the call ended, the chief had trouble finding his words. When he finally spoke, they came out as uncertain as my memories.

"That sounded like you," he managed. "Exactly like you."

"I think it was."

13

WE DIDN'T SPEAK on the ride home, not a single word. There were only looks and silent questions—a million silent questions for which neither of us had answers.

Merv practically maneuvered itself through the harbor and back to the dock behind the Piscataqua Café, and for that I was grateful, because a numbness had found its way deep into my bones, and the sound of my own voice did nothing to calm that.

I didn't trust my actions, my movements. My memories were suspect. I kept hoping I'd wake up, even though the only thing I was certain of was that this was not a dream.

It wasn't until *Merv* was tied off on the dock and I shut the motor down that Chief Whaley spoke. He was sitting on the bench seat near the bow, his face still an awful shade of white, and what he said didn't make sense. "I can still hear Patricia and William laughing, Chief, can you?"

He said this in a voice so low, it might have been the wind. If I hadn't been looking at him and seen his lips move, I might have assumed I'd imagined it.

I wasn't the only one shaking. Whaley folded his large hands into each other, kneaded his fingers together. He couldn't stop, though, no more than I could.

Whaley cleared his throat. "That's what the voice on the phone said to me. What *your voice* said to me."

The number for that phone was ingrained in my head. I'd tried to forget it, but couldn't. I'd never dialed it, though. I knew that wasn't me on the line. "Do you know who they are?" I managed to ask him. "Patricia and William?"

He reached into his pocket and took out the envelope from my dad's car, the one containing the photographs, and tossed it onto the seat between us. "The two bodies found out on Wood Island in '72. Took some doing back then, but they were ID'd as the Whidden children. Patricia and William. Fourteen and fifteen years old."

"My dad found an old article in the *Portsmouth Herald*, that's what the pictures are from. But it didn't mention their names."

"No, I'm sure it wouldn't."

"Because they were minors?"

Whaley scratched his head, then looked out over the water. "No, because they didn't die out there. They were only *found* out there. That was the real rub of it all."

Merv rocked gently as small waves found the hull. The motion should have been soothing, but it was anything but that. I got the impression the boat was rocking out of anticipation. Like it was bubbling over with a secret it could no longer hold.

Whaley went on even though it was clear he didn't want to. "They drowned. The both of them. But not out there." He paused for a moment before continuing, and when he did speak again, his confused eyes met mine. "They went missing in the summer of '51. Details are scarce; nobody knows what time or what exactly led up to it. Nobody realized they were even gone until their mother rang the supper bell and they didn't turn up. After a couple of hours, some of the townsfolk got together for an ad-hoc search of New Castle. They found their bodies a little after nine that night in the one place nobody wanted to look. They'd fallen into the well out behind George Walton's old place and drowned. The report says the well was covered up, boarded over. Old, though, rotten. They think one of them stepped on the boards, broke through, and fell inside. The other child fell in trying to save the first one. No witnesses or anything, so all that's complete speculation. There was no reason to suspect foul play, just the makings of a tragic accident. The bodies were recovered and buried out at Oceanside. The markers are still there, but you gotta hunt for them—east end, all the way in the back." He motioned with his hands and made a rough shape. "Only about six inches square or so. Hand cut granite."

"But they found them on Wood Island? Twenty years later? How?"

Whaley shrugged. "Nobody knows the answer to that one. They were friends with Geraldine. Played together as kids. They'd both been out to the island a few times, but they weren't on Wood Island the day they died, nowhere close. They died in the Walton well, bodies were pulled out of there in '51, that's for certain." He nodded at photographs. "Then some fisherman on a picnic out on Wood finds skeletons on the beach in '72. The responding ME, guy named Homer

Bueller, he could tell they were children. One male, one female. The male had a fracture in his tibia, lower leg, unhealed, so it occurred at the time of death. The female was wearing some kind of necklace. He recognized both. Old Homer was at the end of his career at this point, but he'd been new to the job when he got called out to the Walton well in '51, and you don't forget a thing like that. Said the boy broke his leg when he fell in. So when he saw those bodies in '72, *bodies he knew*, he had the Whidden graves dug up, found both to be empty. This wasn't some court-sanctioned exhumation— no judge would sign off on something like that. This was Homer and a few close friends in the middle of the night after drinking a bottle or two of liquid courage. When they found the graves empty, they put both those children back where they belonged and filled the graves back in. Put them to rest with their family. Swore to never speak another word of it." He looked at the envelope again. "For the most part, they kept it quiet. Like your dad probably figured out, the *Portsmouth Herald* never ran another word about it, and you can comb every law enforcement office from Maine to Boston, and you won't find a single report, local or federal. It's one of those things nobody can explain, so nobody talks about it except in hushed whispers. Probably only a handful of old-timers even remember at this point. The only reason I know about it is because the last chief told me the story on his way out. Kind of a rite of passage. Said it was one of those unsolved mysteries that kept him up at night. They either buried empty boxes or someone moved the bodies. Nobody's got an explanation for either of those things because there's no valid reason to do either. It'll drive you crazy just to think about it, so best to forget it."

"You know Lester Rote died a week after those bodies turned up, right?" I told him. "He got in his boat, motored out to sea, and vanished."

"You think he did that out of some sense of guilt?" Whaley replied. "Maybe he was the one who moved the bodies and didn't want to explain himself?"

I heard my own voice in my head, speaking to me from that telephone.

Nobody dies on that island, but that doesn't mean they don't come home. In the end, we all come home. In the end, that's all we can do.

"Maybe he knew how they got out there and couldn't live with it anymore."

Whaley's phone rang, and he fumbled it out of his pocket and answered.

I couldn't make out what was said, but I heard enough to know the voice on the other end spoke urgently. As Whaley listened, the little blood remaining in his face left him. By the time he hung up, I might have been looking at a corpse.

"What is it? What happened?"

A wobble filled his voice. "When was the last time you were out at Jaffrey Point?"

14

JAFFREY POINT JUTTED out from the southern tip of New Castle just beyond Fort Stark. A mix of rocks, brambles, and sand, it was difficult to reach by foot, and the shallow waters prevented most boat traffic unless the tide was in.

Chief Whaley didn't turn on his lights or siren, but he got us there quickly—it was less than a mile from the dock behind Piscataqua Café and there was very little traffic. He wouldn't tell me what happened, and I gave up asking.

Officer Mundie had parked his SUV in the middle of the gravel lot next to the fort, and Whaley pulled up beside him.

Like many of the historical elements of New Castle, the fort was one of those places my friends and I played at when we were kids, visited for the occasional late-night party as teenagers, and all but forgot as we went about our daily lives. Originally built back in the eighteen hundreds, it had been used as a stronghold during numerous wars and skirmishes, rebuilt and fortified as the times dictated, and left to crumble for the years between. The Navy had used it for training at some point back in the seventies, but for the most part, it was just one of those places tourists crawled over taking photos they'd probably never look at again.

Shifting into park, Whaley shut off the engine. "Stay behind me and don't touch anything. Don't go wandering off. You get in the way and you can wait this out in the back seat. Understand?"

He exited the car without giving me a chance to answer.

I waited a moment and climbed out too. My shoes crunched on the gravel as I rounded the SUV to where Whaley was talking to Officer Mundie.

Mundie wasn't much older than me. He'd graduated four years earlier and only recently joined the force after toiling around Boston for a few years doing who knows what. His gun belt hung loose on his lanky frame and he kept tugging it back up to his waist with his right hand, his left squeezing a thick roll of yellow crime scene tape. When he saw me, he stopped speaking.

Whaley looked off toward the water. "Down there?"

Mundie nodded.

"How many?"

Mundie licked his lips. "Three… I think."

"Put some barricades up and tape off a perimeter. Keep the locals off the rocks and out of the fort. They'll be here soon enough. Give Lieutenant Milchman a call too and see if he can place a Coast Guard boat or two offshore so the riff-raff can't get too close from the water. Tough now with the tide out, but the water will be back up in no time and someone will make a try at it. Press in particular."

"Yes, sir." He nodded at me. "Why's he here?"

"I want him to see this."

Whatever *this* was, it was bad. Nobody was moving fast, and that somehow made it worse.

Three.

That's what Mundie said.

Mundie frowned. "You sure that's a good idea, Chief? He's just a—"

"Get those barricades up. Call for backup from Portsmouth if you need it."

Whaley crossed the parking lot and started around the side of the fort's stone wall, down toward the water. "Stay close, Billy. Watch your step. Some of these rocks are slippery."

I'd gone down that way before. Spivey and I used to fish out there when we were younger. I'd fallen in my share of times, too. The rocks shifted and the path changed with nearly every tide. They were covered in algae, slime, and seaweed.

With one hand on the stone wall of the fort to help keep my balance, I followed after Whaley. I didn't see the boat—Rory's boat—until we rounded the far side of the fort. It was clear just by the way it was sitting in the water that something was very wrong.

The scent of low tide wafted through the warm air, a nasty mix of wet sulfur and iodine that made my eyes water. Spivey had once told me the smell came from sex pheromones produced by seaweed eggs meant to attract sperm. Like much of what Spivey told me when we were younger, this was information I'd rather not have in my head, but it didn't seem to want to leave once it got in there.

I saw then and wished I hadn't. "Holy shit."

We'd reached the boat and Whaley had stopped moving. "Yeah, holy shit."

Rory's small skiff was partially underwater. The stern was submerged with the bow sticking up in the air. It looked like a rocket on a ramp prepping for flight. I didn't see a hole in the stern, but it was barely visible, buried under rocks.

The smallest rock was no bigger than a pebble and the largest was about the size of my fist. It looked like a dump truck had backed up to his boat from above and emptied its load on top, partially burying the boat and spilling out to the surrounding water and the muck of the jagged shore.

I didn't see Rory, not at first, and when I did I wished I hadn't. Much like Spivey's various facts, the image of Rory's body carved into my mind with a blade so sharp and precise, I knew it would be there until the day I died.

He'd been behind the wheel when this happened, whatever *this* was. And maybe he tried to rise or maybe he didn't, but he was folded awkwardly at the waist, bent over the gunwale of the skiff. What was left of his right arm hung lazily over the side of the boat, his fingers in the water. Sand crabs—the kind we called bubblers—covered his flesh in numbers so great, they crawled over each other to get from the surf to the meatier parts up near his forearm and shoulder. There were ants, too. Who knew what else. Muscle, tendon, and skin swollen loose from the bone writhed with life that no longer belonged to Rory, but to the things that had taken possession of him.

I managed to turn my head before throwing up, but it still splashed over my shoes and the rocks at my side.

Chief Whaley glanced at me but said nothing. To this day I don't understand why he didn't get sick, and it made me wonder what other horrors he'd seen before this one, because something had dulled it for him.

I steadied myself on the rocks, one hand on the granite wall at my side, and didn't move. I couldn't.

Whaley crossed around the stern of the boat, his pants wet to the knees. He spotted something in the rocks and bent to get a closer look. "Zack Kirkley's over here. Someone else, too. I think it's that other kid who's always with them. Randy Booth's boy."

"Colin," I said softly.

He looked up at me. "Yeah, Colin."

The tide was coming in fast. The water rose even during the short time we'd been out there, and judging by the seaweed, sand, rocks, and water inside Rory's skiff, all of this would be submerged soon and had been several times. Whatever happened here happened a few days ago.

You know what happened here, my mind muttered. *You know exactly.*

I remembered Alesia removing the ring from her hand and dropping it in that bowl between us.

"Rory gave me this last summer, when we were dating. He told me it belonged to his grandmother."

A tribute.

Like my father's business card.

A number of things had gone into that bowl, including water from George Walton's old well. It was the rock, though, that came to mind as I looked at this—the rock from George Walton's property and the story I'd heard Chloe tell a million times.

The Stone-Throwing Devil—stones rained down on George Walton's tavern, and the devil had to be vanquished by some preacher out of Boston named Increase Mather back in 1682, around the same time the people of Salem, Massachusetts realized they had themselves a witch problem.

My parents even told that story when friends visited, pointed out the old Walton place. Tourists picked so many rocks out of the yard, the current owners were forced to replenish them. They kept bushels full in their shed.

Whaley was holding a large rock in his hand, his gaze moving from where he'd picked it up to the top of the bluff above us. I knew what he was thinking. If he'd been standing where I was, he'd see it even clearer. The rocks hadn't come from that bluff or the fort above. The angle was all wrong. The bulk of the rocks were in the boat and piled up along the port side, facing the water. If the rocks had come from the bluff, they wouldn't be there— they'd be on the starboard side, closest to the shore. Whaley's gaze moved from the bluff to the sky above. With his free hand, he shielded his eyes and looked straight up.

Rocks couldn't rain down from the heavens, but somehow these had.

Not only had they come from above, but they came down fast and hard and in numbers. Rory, Colin, and Zack hadn't had time to move. They were pinned down and buried.

Whether he believed it or not, I had no doubt Chief Whaley was thinking of the Stone-Throwing Devil too. He'd grown up hearing those stories, same as I had. He was thinking about that and everything else that had happened today.

My mind had raced ahead and I was trying to keep up.

A copy of the subpoena had gone into that bowl, and Spivey had avoided appearing. Some might say things played out in his favor. My father's business card had gone in, and Lily Dwyer's hair found its way into his car. Rory's ring, and now he was dead. His friends, too.

I wasn't thinking about the Stone-Throwing Devil because I was thinking about the other items that had gone into that bowl: a silver locket belonging to Spivey's mother and a worn leather key chain bearing the initials K.S.—Keith Spivey. Alesia's words:

The tributes we've offered represent those attempting to keep us apart. Each belongs to someone who wants nothing more than to silence us, harm us, or take what does not belong to them. I call on the power we've summoned to protect us. Protect this place. Protect what we are trying to do. Because only our success guarantees your freedom from the realm in which you currently dwell.

"Billy? You okay?" Whaley was watching me close, taking in my reaction. He wanted me to see all right— he was trying to determine if I knew what this was. The water was above the chief's knees now, lapping over the side of the boat with each gentle wave.

My legs were like thin threads beneath me, and my head swam with thoughts I didn't want. Impossible thoughts. When I opened my mouth to answer him, my stomach lurched again and I swallowed it back down.

"You need to tell me what you know, Billy. No more bullshit."

Crabs skittered up Rory's arm, disappeared under what was left of his shirt. Their tiny feet made a thin, papery sound. An urgent rustle as they carried claws full of—

"I'm gonna be sick again," I managed to get out. "I gotta sit down."

Whaley pulled a handkerchief from his back pocket. I thought he was going to offer it to me, but instead, he tied it over his nose and mouth. "Go back up and wait for me in the SUV. Tell Mundie to get someone down here with a camera. I want to get this on film before the tide comes back."

I forced a nod and turned away, started back up the hill. I was about to round the corner of the fort when Whaley added, "I want you to think about Lily. Don't forget about her in all this. She's still out there somewhere."

I hurried back up the hill.

Deputy Mundie was no longer alone in the parking lot. Nearly a dozen people were standing behind the barricades. Some I recognized, others I did not. There were two other patrol cars, both from Portsmouth PD, and an ambulance from Portsmouth Regional Hospital.

I told Mundie what the chief said, but he only half heard me—he had his hands full trying to tape off the far side of the parking lot.

I was halfway back to Whaley's SUV when I spotted Kira standing in the growing crowd.

15

SHE WAS STANDING behind Mr. Lowell, the man who ran our local post office. Who, at six-four and with the girth to support the height, towered over her. Our eyes only met for a brief second before she vanished behind him again, but I knew she saw me.

I looked at Mundie, who had his back to me, and at the several other officers standing around, none of whom seemed to know I was even there. Whaley was still down at the water, and I didn't expect he'd be back up anytime soon.

Before I could change my mind, I ducked under the tape, rounded the people from the outer edge of the parking lot, and came up behind her. When I tapped her on the shoulder, she nearly jumped out of her shoes.

Her eyes were filled with panic. "Billy, what's going on down there?"

I grabbed her arm, maybe a little harder than I should have. "We need to talk. Now."

"You're hurting me." She tried to shrug me off. "Let go or I'll scream."

"Kira, I—"

She glared at my hand. "Let go."

When I did, her eyes didn't leave mine, and I felt like I was staring at a stranger. Or maybe she was in shock. When she spoke again, her voice was cold, distant. She turned from me and looked out past the fort, toward the water. "Not here."

"I can't leave. I told Whaley—"

She turned and started toward the street. "Stay if you want—I'm going."

I almost grabbed her arm again, but something told me if I did that, I wouldn't get another word out of her. She'd walk off and I'd be alone in all this, and I couldn't be alone, not now.

With one last look at Deputy Mundie and the others, I followed her down the street to a red Toyota parked on the edge of Wild Rose Lane. "Why do you have Matty's car?"

She pulled the keys from the pocket of her jeans and opened the driver-side door. "Are you coming or not?"

When I didn't move, she frowned and shifted her weight to her left leg.

"I have Matty's car because I was with him and Chloe at the historical society when I got your text. He parked behind mine so it was easier to just take his."

"Text? I didn't text you?"

She frowned at me like I was some kind of crazy person, then showed me her phone. There it was, right on top:

Meet me at Jaffrey Point 3:45 PM 5/28/2021!

"Did you drop your phone or something? The time stamp is all screwy." She pointed at the screen. "This says you sent it like eleven years from now."

I took out my phone and scrolled through the messages. I didn't have anything going out to her since that morning. I'd sent her one right before we left for the deposition at the court house. Nothing after that. I held my phone next to her and stared at the two screens, as if expecting one or both to change. I was still staring at them when I noticed the message that had come in before mine on Kira's phone. Two words from Matty:

Hey you

That one had come in three hours ago.

She caught me looking at it, snatched her phone back, and let out a frustrated grunt. "You know, you really need to decide if you trust me. I don't see how we can move forward if you don't. A lot of guys hit on me—that doesn't mean I'm sleeping with them."

Kira dropped into the driver's seat and slammed the door.

The motor started.

A second ticked by.

Two.

I scrambled around the car and got in. We sat there in silence for a moment, both of us staring forward.

"A lot has happened recently," I finally said, unable to look at her.

"No kidding." She huffed. "And you think you're alone in that? We're all caught up in this—you, me, Chloe, Alesia, Spivey. If I can't talk to you, I need to talk to someone. And that's all it is: talk. You may not see it," she said, "but you've got a wall up. It's like you see me and the others as the bad guy, and we're not. No more than you are. We're all just trying to figure this out."

Kira turned toward me and her face softened. "My parents read every text that comes in on my phone. Every message on my computer. You know that. So we worked out a code. If Matty sends me a two-word text, doesn't matter what the two words are, it means *call me*. That's all that is. I called him. He told me he was meeting Chloe at the historical society building to do some research."

I wanted that to be true. I did. I told myself it made perfect sense because Kira and I had played that same game a million times when we didn't want her parents to know what we were doing. Hell, when she texted *I'm studying trig* it really meant she was ready to sneak out and she wanted me to pick her up.

This still didn't feel right. Fooling around with Matty. Not fooling around with Matty. That wasn't the only question I had on my mind.

I looked toward the flashing police lights in the parking lot off in the distance, considered whether or not I should ask, then figured to hell with it. "Did you and the others take Lily Dwyer?"

Rather than anger her further, this seemed to puzzle her. Her forehead crinkled and she tilted her head to the side, following my gaze toward Whaley's car. "What? No. Is that what the chief thinks?"

I told her what he said about the picture. What he found on the security videos.

When I finished, she said, "Billy, that's ridiculous."

"How do you explain it?"

"You know what the mall is like. You can't spend ten minutes there without running into someone you know. I'm there all the time. So are Alesia, Chloe, Izzie... probably Lily, and ninety-nine percent of the other kids around here. Does that mean there's some kind of crazy conspiracy going on?" She turned away from me and faced out the window. "Look, I didn't want to tell you this. I honestly wasn't sure how to tell you, or if you'd even believe me..."

"Tell me what?"

The rest of the anger left her. She reached over and took my hand. "The day Lily went missing, I saw your dad at the mall. First at the food court, then outside. When Lily told us she was meeting some guy named Brian, she said he was older. We told Chief Whaley we heard he went to Exeter High, but that part wasn't true. We were covering for *her*. She didn't tell us much about him, but he wasn't in high school. He wasn't even in college." She met my eyes. "Then I saw Lily get in the car with your dad. Izzie did too. I'm so sorry, Billy. When you called me earlier, I wanted to tell you, but I just couldn't. Instead, I hung up and ran through all the reasons for your dad to be there, for Lily to leave with him... tried to think of a valid excuse, but the truth is, there isn't one. Not a good one, anyway."

I sunk down into the seat.

No. No way.

My father did not

would not

take Lily.

"If he was inside the mall at the food court, why didn't they find him on the security footage?"

Kira took my face in her hand and forced me to look at her. "Billy, they just haven't found him *yet*. They will."

The lump in my gut grew to the size of a basketball. I felt like I was going to be sick again.

What Kira said next only drove her point home. "I think I know what he meant by 'pink cow,' too."

"What?"

She brushed a loose strand of her hair from her eyes and looked at her hands on the steering wheel. "You know Rory deals drugs, right?"

It wasn't exactly a secret. "I know he sells pot."

This pitiful smile briefly crossed her lips. One that told me I was either naive or blind or both. "Lately he's gotten into worse stuff. Pills, mostly. I don't know if it's true, but the rumor is his dad picks them up when he's out on the fishing boat. They meet up with another boat that comes down from Canada or someplace, then he brings back whatever. He gets the drugs to Rory, and Rory and his crew sell them at the local high schools and some of the clubs and bars downtown. A few months ago, he started dealing in something called U4. It's this light pink powder so some people call it pinky, or pink—"

"Or pink cow," I finished for her.

Kira nodded. "Alesia told me. It was one of the many reasons she broke up with him. She could overlook pot but not the harder stuff, and this one's bad. Rory's not just selling to kids, though. Fishermen. Business people. Adults. They're all buying it. Alesia said he called it his pink cash cow. Said it would make him rich."

Not anymore.

"Rory's dead," I said softly. "He's buried under a pile of rocks under the fort. Same with Zack and Colin."

I told her about Rory's boat. Then I told her what Whaley and I found out at the house on Wood Island.

"That's not possible," she said when I finished. I knew she believed me, though; I could tell by the way she was trembling. In her mind, she was running through the same things I had—the basement, Alesia's spell. What we saw. What we did. All of it.

Her fingers were still wrapped around mine, and as the seconds ticked by, I felt her grip grow tighter. Finally, she said, "Billy, what the hell is going on?"

A fist beat on my window, scared the hell out of both of us.

Matty was standing outside the car glaring at us. Kira's car was behind us, Chloe in the passenger seat. He looked nervously at the police cars near Jaffrey, then motioned for me to roll down the window.

Something about him seemed off. This wild look in his eyes. If we weren't blocked in, I might have told Kira to go. Looking back, I wish I had.

The moment the window was open, he leaned inside. "You talking to Whaley, Billy? What'd you tell him?"

"I didn't tell him anything."

"Bullshit. You took him out to the house. I saw you coming back." He waved a hand toward the flashing lights at Jaffrey. "You tell him about Alesia's spell? You tell him she cursed Rory? Put him under those rocks?" His voice grew louder with each word. More agitated. When he twisted, I saw the gun stuffed in the waistband of his jeans. I couldn't be sure, but it looked like the revolver Spivey had pulled the night Rory showed up. "What did you tell him, Billy?" he asked again.

He knew Rory was dead.

I hadn't told him. He already knew.

Matty pulled the gun, but he kept it out of sight, hidden behind the door. He looked at Kira. "I told you to pick him up and get him to my boat. Why the hell are you sitting out here? He trying to talk you into going to the sheriff?"

She quickly shook her head. "We were leaving when you—"

"Don't lie to me."

"I'm not," she insisted. "I wouldn't."

"Alesia was right—we can't trust either of you."

I tried not to think about the gun. Tried to keep my voice calm. "Matty, this is getting out of hand. Let's go back to my house, talk this out. Nobody's home. Maybe we tell Whaley, maybe we don't, but let's come up with some kind of plan. We don't want to do something—"

"Alesia said you'd do that too, try to talk us out of it. That's why we didn't tell you."

"Tell me what?"

Kira was squeezing the steering wheel so tight her fingers were white.

Matty shook his head. "I'm not gonna let you fuck this up, Hasler. No way."

He swung before I could react.

I caught a glimpse of the gun as it came through the window—he was holding it by the barrel, balled inside his fist. It cracked against my skull and the world went black.

16

WHEN MY EYES opened, I was lying on the stern of *Annabelle*, sprawled out under a gray quilt so riddled with dust I sneezed four times. A fifth tickle grew in my nose, but I managed to tamp it under control. All that caused my eyes to water and I almost wiped my face with the quilt (which would have started Sneezefest number two), but caught myself and used my sleeve instead.

An old man was at the helm, maneuvering *Annabelle* through the reach toward Wood Island. He heard me sneeze but didn't look back—too busy avoiding the rocks—only raised his left arm and called out, "Bless you!" over the noise of the motor.

It was dark and the temperature had dropped to an icy chill. Ugly clouds churned above, the start of a storm, and although I knew where I was, I wasn't certain on the when.

Sitting up, I tentatively touched the back of my head. I found a lump the size of a walnut, and it hurt like hell. "Where the hell is Matty?"

"Who?"

"Matty. Matty Fernandez. He hit me," I replied. "Knocked me out."

"I don't know no Matty." He eased up on the throttle. The whine of the motor dropped and *Annabelle* slowed. "Damn it all to hell," he muttered, smacking the steering wheel.

"What's wrong?"

"Night waits for no man, that's what's wrong." His left arm came up again, pointed at the angry sky, then toward Wood Island, ahead of us in the distance. All the windows of the house were dark. His finger was crooked, the joints swollen and purple with arthritis. "Thought I could get back before night settled, but nothing doin'. Looks like we're stuck out here until morning. Ain't no getting out to Wood in the dark." He reached for the key, switched off the motor, and turned toward me. "Make yourself useful and throw the anchor over the side, will ya?"

The left side of his face was gone.

Rotten.

Eaten.

I couldn't tell which.

His left eye socket was nothing but a dark hole, crusty and scabbed. A slick trail of yellow pus oozed out from deep inside and dripped down over what remained of his nose. His right eye was nearly white, thick with filmy cataracts. When he spoke again, I could see the muscles of his jaw clench and loosen over bone through the place where his cheek should have been. His voice was a deep drawl, heavy with a Down East accent typically found up in Maine. "Don't think we've been properly introduced." He held out his hand. "Lester Rote."

I tried to shuffle backward, but there was no place to go.

What remained of Lester's lips curled into a frown. "That Matty fellow must have done a number on you. You look like you're gonna yack." He took his hand back and jerked a thumb toward the front of the boat. "I got some whiskey stashed under the seat if you need a little something to take the edge off."

There was a loose rattle to his voice, and I realized that was because of the wide gash in his neck. Whenever he spoke, air slipped through the hole and the skin flapped. Dark saliva glistened there in the twilight. Other spots had dried to a brownish crust, causing the collar of his shirt to stick and peel away when he moved.

He caught me looking and wiped the spittle away with the palm of his hand, then raked his wiry hair back with moist fingers. "Not much of a talker, are you?"

"You're Lester Rote," I managed. "Geraldine's husband."

The man who died nearly forty years earlier.

His ruined face tilted to the side. "… And you are?"

"Billy. Billy Hasler."

He rose back up and stretched. A series of cracks and pops came from his bones. "Get the damn anchor, Billy Hasler. I ain't gonna ask you again."

As he moved back toward the bow of the boat, I reached to my left and hefted the anchor over the side. It broke the black surface with a plop and vanished, but not before I saw a large gray shape jerk quickly to the side to avoid it, then disappear under the boat. I fell back on my hands. "Holy shit!"

If a man with only half a face could grin, Lester did. "Nothing those bastards like more than grazing the rocks at sunset. Fuckers never stop eating, but post-dusk is when they're hungriest." His misshapen half grin twisted into something mischievous. "Wanna get a real eyeful?"

There was a wooden cooler built into the port side of the boat. He unfastened the two brass latches and opened the lid. A horde of swollen flies fluttered out, a living cloud of black. Lester cursed in a low voice and slapped at them with his arthritic hand until the last vanished, then reached down inside. His hand came back out a moment later, clutching a lump of glistening flesh about the size of a fist, and this time there was no holding back whatever was in my stomach.

I managed to get my head over the side of the boat and throw up in the water. I didn't realize the mistake in that until Lester pulled me back by the collar of my shirt. "Whoa! Careful there, son!"

A shark broke the surface and shot at least six feet into the air—came straight up and out—mouth gaping, right where I'd been. Its lifeless dark eyes met mine for an instant before it crashed back down and disappeared. A wave of saltwater slapped over us and it was gone.

Lester let out a loud hoot. "If I meant to feed them you, I wouldn't have brought this!"

He was still holding it.

A heart.

He didn't have to tell me it was human—I somehow knew. Don't ask me how; I just did.

I don't know if he twitched his fingers, squeezed, or whatever, but the damn thing beat, and black blood oozed out from one of the wide ventricles. He hefted it out over the water with a sideways toss and it splashed down about twenty feet from us. I counted no fewer than three fins slice the surface and rush toward it. The sharks clashed in a frenzied tussle, then they were gone. All of it over in only a few seconds.

Lester wiped his hand on the front of his flannel shirt. "Fucking monsters, but you gotta love 'em."

He reached back into the cooler and this time came out with a foot and part of an ankle bone, severed just below the calf, and threw it out into the water.

Something bumped the bottom of the boat, a thump that sent us rocking, then a missile of gray shot out toward the leg, beating the others.

I couldn't speak.

Couldn't breathe.

Lester rested his own foot on *Annabelle's* gunwale, leaned on his knee, and peered out. "We get blues and baskers out here. Makos too, but it's these whites that get me. I've seen 'em as big as ten to fourteen feet. Fast as hell and damn near silent. Only one thing on their minds—*munch, munch, munch.*"

He reached back into the cooler, produced what looked like an upper leg, and threw it overboard.

"How many are there?" I gulped.

"Oh, hell, I don't know." With a bloody finger, he pointed at his ruined face and head. "Only takes one. Good news is they move so quick—it's over before you know it. You'll see soon enough."

Reaching back into the cooler, he took out a slim arm and studied it under the thin moonlight. A gold-faced watch with a brown leather band was still fastened around the wrist. The first heavy raindrops smacked against it and rolled over the side, washing some of the blood away.

I knew that watch.

I'd bought it for Kira last year, gave it to her for her birthday.

She never took it off.

Lester's face contorted into that half grin again. "Heard she was a looker. Wouldn't mind breaking off a piece." His single eye glanced at the arm, then winked at me. "Or maybe I already did."

He threw the arm high into the air; it bounced off a jagged rock before hitting the water within feet of a gaggle of sharp fins.

Behind me, someone huffed. I turned and found my dad sitting at the back of the boat. Keith Spivey was there too, and Whaley. Geraldine Rote and Marston, the two of them huddled close, both clutching tea cups as they whispered in a low tone. Four other adults I didn't recognize. How they all fit in the boat, I wasn't sure. It was like *Annabelle* had grown to accommodate them.

Lester was digging around in the cooler again, and he dismissed the others with an aggravated wave of his bony, arthritic hand. "I never claimed to be much of a ferryman. Don't know why he keeps assigning more to my boat. *Annabelle* was never meant to hold this many. We don't shed some weight, we'll all end up in the drink." He lifted out the remains of a torso, nothing more than a chest wrapped in an old bloody shirt, and rolled it over the side. It hit the water with heavy plop and sunk. The sharks moved in a fast frenzy—one of them thumped hard against the bottom of the boat, causing *Annabelle* to list, nearly tip.

Lester howled, "Ooh! Now we've got a party! Who's ready for a swim!?"

My eyes snapped open.

I wasn't on *Annabelle* at all.

I was—

17

CHIEF WHALEY JAMMED the gearshift of his SUV into park and cursed.

He'd known Billy would bolt the first chance he got—Mundie was supposed to follow him to the others so they could round them all up. He'd failed miserably in that task. Luckily, New Castle was a small place, and three different people told him Kira Woodward, Matty Fernandez, and Chloe Kittle were holed up in the historical society building. The last one not thirty minutes ago. That meant Billy couldn't be far behind. Now none of them were there. So where the hell had they gone?

He picked up the microphone from his radio. "Mundie, you copy?"

"Yeah, Chief."

"They're gone. You still waiting on the staties out at Jaffrey?"

"Got here ten minutes ago. Two vans, half dozen people in rubber gloves and suits crawling over everything like ants."

"Anyone we know?"

"Walt Merton and Mitch Garrison out of Hampton. They drove up on their own."

Whaley knew Walt and Mitch well. They'd come up through the academy together, grew up in the area. He pressed the button on his mic. "Tell those two to keep an eye on things for you. I need you to drive by the Hasler house. If Billy's not there, get over to the dock behind Piscataqua Café. He's got an old rescue boat tied up out there—put a chain on it. Then head over to the docks off 1B South near Sagamore Creek and do the same with Matty's boat. If his dad's out there at the marina, tell him we need to talk to his boy. Matty shows up, he needs to bring him to us. I want all these kids down at the station house by nightfall."

He looked up at the darkening sky and knew that was a tall order. The sun was barely a speck on the horizon, and there was a storm coming in.

"Even if we manage to round them up, you know the parents won't let you talk to any of them."

"Let me worry about that. You find Billy Hasler. Cuff him if you have to. Put him in the back of the station with his dad."

"You got it, Chief."

He almost added, *and don't lose him this time,* but that was on him just as much as it was on Mundie. He should have kept him on a tighter leash out at Jaffrey Point. He clicked the mic again. "Mundie, one more thing—your boat gassed up?"

"Way ahead of you, Chief. Soon as I talk to Fernandez, I'll head out to Wood, see what's doing. My money's on that place."

"You okay going out in this weather? There's a nasty storm rolling in."

"Not my first rodeo. I'll be fine. Can be on the water in maybe an hour."

"Understood. Be safe. Over."

The line crackled, then, *"Hey, Chief?"*

"Yeah?"

There were several clicks. Mundie tapping the mic button on and off. He did that when he was nervous. *"Rory and those boys... you know what that looked like, right? Remember that old story about the stone-throwing dev—"*

Whaley cut him off. "Not on an open channel. We'll talk when we talk."

Mundie went quiet for a beat. *"Gotcha. I'll radio when I'm heading out to Wood. Out."*

Whaley sat there outside the historical society building for nearly another minute, drumming his fingers on the steering wheel. When he saw Rory and the others buried in the water out there, the first thing he'd thought of was that old story, too. The second thing he'd thought of was the book he'd found in Lily Dwyer's room—*The Devil of Great Island,* a book about that old story. A book she'd taken from here, the New Castle Historical Society. When you become a cop, the first thing they teach you is not to get shot. The second thing they teach you is there is no such thing as coincidences.

He eyed the old building, tried to pull it all together, but came up with nothing. If someone were handing him puzzle pieces, it felt like each one had come from a different box.

A fat raindrop struck his windshield, followed by another a few seconds later. Shaking his head, Whaley killed the motor and climbed out. He took the steps two at a time and pushed through the double doors into the small white-sided building. He hadn't been inside for over a year, but he remembered the smell. Not necessarily unpleasant—a musty scent, like stepping into the pages of an old book and pulling the cover down around you.

Before the door clicked shut behind him, Mrs. White had left her desk and was crossing the room, a frown on her face. "I'm sorry, Chief. I tried to keep them here. They were up and out the door the moment I called Sandy back. I didn't think they heard me but maybe they did."

Mrs. White was in her seventies, and while she would certainly qualify as a "young seventy-something," he couldn't expect her to keep up with three teenagers any more than he had. This was on him, not her. "Can you show me what they were looking at?"

"That's easy enough. They didn't put anything away." She nodded and indicated a table up near the front of the room covered with books and documents.

Whaley dropped into one of the empty chairs, wondering how many kids spent their summer break holed up in a place like this doing research. "What is all this?"

"They were digging into the history of Wood Island." Mrs. White settled into the chair across from him and drew closer to the table. "Are you familiar?"

Last month, no. Lately, I've been getting a crash course.

He didn't have time for a history lesson, not with Rory and the others dead out there under those rocks, not with a missing girl in play, but his gut told him Billy and the other kids knew exactly what was going on, and if they took the time to look at all this, it was important. "I know bits and pieces," he told her. "I know the Coast Guard used it years back and the island was sold to Geraldine Rote's family sometime in the 1940s."

She nodded. "And that boy owns it now."

"David Spivey."

"Yes, Keith and Pam's son. Seems someone digs all this material up every time that place changes hands. I remember looking at it when I was a girl. Ralph Peck and me playing detective after visiting Geraldine out there. Must be sixty years ago now. Gave me chills then, gave me chills again today to see it." She thumbed through the loose pages and settled on a brittle yellow piece of paper inside a protective sleeve and a leather-bound ledger of some sort. "Back in the eighteen hundreds , Wood Island served as a quarantine facility when yellow fever was running rampant. This is the passenger manifest and the captain's log for a ship called *Reina*. It was a refugee vessel that left Cuba at the start of the Spanish American War in 1898 and managed to slip by the conflict in the Caribbean in hopes of going north to Canada. They got about halfway up the U.S. Coast when yellow fever ravaged the ship. At first, the captain thought they could still make it, but within weeks his crew fell, and he was forced to make a decision: try and ride it out in the Atlantic with the shrinking number of skilled hands on board, or risk docking somewhere in American waters—enemy waters—and dealing with whatever came with that decision. Either way, he figured he'd lose his ship. Staying at sea most likely meant death, and if he docked, the Americans would take the vessel and use it against Spain in the war. He'd be disgraced as a traitor even if it meant saving the lives of his crew and passengers. When a large storm came in from the east, his hand was forced, and he directed his remaining crew to make way for landfall. They were further north than he originally thought—within sight of Maine, off our coast. U.S. ships intercepted them and escorted them to Wood Island, where they were forced to dock. The captain expected them to be boarded, but the U.S. Coast Guard had no intention of doing that, not with yellow fever burning through the crew and passengers. Instead, *Reina* was tied down to the rocks and the captain was told nobody would be permitted to exit the ship under any circumstance. This was May 1898."

Mrs. White tapped on the ledger, then indicated a ruffled old notepad, the topmost page filled with neat flowing handwriting. "This ledger is the original captain's log; it's in Spanish. I don't know who wrote up the translation, but this notepad has been in the archives for as long as I can remember. I'm hardly fluent, but I can hold my own, and I can tell you the translation is accurate. The first time I saw it as a girl, I questioned that. The translation starts clearly enough, but then it gets sloppy. I think the captain got sick, too. He went from coherent thoughts to ramblings as he got worse, then he stopped writing altogether. Here's an example:

> "May 8, 1898. Without access to shore, our food stores are both a blessing and curse. We left Cuba with supplies enough to reach the southern tip of Canada, but only if such essentials were disbursed with the utmost care and diligence. While my crew is familiar with the hungers of sea and willing to accept the accompanying pangs, our passengers are not. The wealthier of the lot refuse to ration. In the early days of our journey, they did anything but. They seemed more content to eat to the point of bursting as if consuming sustenance were just a means to pass the time. Many of our passengers (forty-three in total, twenty-two of which are children) came to us from an orphanage, and explaining limited supplies to children is no more fruitful than speaking to a rock. I've been forced to place guards at the food

stores in hopes of deterring the more aggressive. Had we continued on to Canada without delay, I have no doubt we would have run short. Our only saving grace in that regard has been the fever, which has substantially thinned our numbers. As of this writing, we have six dead and eleven ill, and I'm certain both of those numbers will increase in the coming days. The dead do not eat. The ill eat little, if at all. That has increased what remains for the rest of us. Ugly math, favorable for all the wrong reasons. Because we were expected to reach our destination by this time, now I fear our food is more likely to spoil and rot rather than meet consumption, and we will still be left to starve, for the Americans do not appear willing to replenish our stocks. While we are held here under the guise of a rescue, I believe their true goal is to wait us out. Wait for starvation and fever to clear our decks and holds so they can take possession of Reina without resistance. They watch from a distance as we bury our dead at sea, feeding the sharks of these waters, and they circle us from the shore just the same. Patiently waiting."

Listening to her, Whaley had to remind himself this was over a hundred years ago. "Was that common back then?" Whaley asked. "Let all those people die just so they can take the ship?"

Mrs. White pursed her lips, then nodded grimly. "Unfortunately. It happened with a few ships, not just *Reina* and not just here. By the time the crews and passengers figured out what was going on, they were too weak to fight. Even if they did, the military shot anyone who tried to disembark. They used the quarantine as an excuse. It was wartime. These people were the enemy and they were dead the moment they allowed themselves to be captured." Her gaze lingered on Whaley for a few more seconds, then she returned to the notepad and began flipping through the pages. "The entries for the next few weeks are extensive but fairly repetitive. Every day, more people got sick. More died. The captain confined everyone but crew to their quarters, but it didn't take long for his crew to thin out to the point where enforcement was impossible.

The children from the orphanage were all together down in the hold. That door was kept locked. At first, I thought he locked it to keep them in, but…" When she found what she was looking for, she smoothed the extra pages over the top of the notepad and circled several paragraphs with the tip of her finger. "Ah, here it is. This is where things go weird."

Then she read this entry:

> "May 21, 1898. The passenger in Cabin 9 made the offer to me again. Through the splintered wood of his closed door, he whispered his proposition to me, and God help me, this time—after hearing it four times prior—I listened. As he spoke, I couldn't help but wonder who else he had approached. Members of my crew? Other passengers? Against my orders, many still roam freely. Although this man has yet to leave his cabin under my gaze, others have no such qualms. Desperation is thick in the air, and as horrific as what he proposes may sound, it becomes increasingly tempting to anyone willing to listen. So much so I have taken to entering the hold no less than twice daily in order to count the children. It was this morning's count that I only found seventeen. We began the journey with twenty-two, and four have been lost to sickness. That leaves one unaccounted for—a girl of twelve named Amelia. If the other children are aware of when she was removed from the hold or who specifically removed her, they are unwilling to speak of it. The fear evident in their eyes at the question tells me all I need to know. She was taken, and the remainder were threatened to the point of silence. The hefty lock affixed to the hold door remains secure with no evidence of tampering. This makes her disappearance all the more perplexing as I hold the only key."

Whaley felt a growing lump in his gut. "What exactly did this man offer?"

Mrs. White flipped a few more pages and continued in a low voice.

> "May 23, 1898. Two more children are gone. Boys of fourteen and fifteen. Both were present at last night's count but missing this morn-

ing. With the lack of hands, a ship-wide search proved difficult and turned up nothing. I found myself glancing at the door to Cabin 9 at each pass, and it was only when I was certain those boys were nowhere else on the ship that I finally knocked. When no reply came, I shouted. And when that too went unanswered, I used my master key to open the door only to find the cabin empty. He wasn't on the decks or any of the common areas. Had this been anyone else, I would have assumed he was in the cabin of another passenger, but I somehow knew a door-to-door would not (and eventually did not) turn him up. He was not on the ship, as impossible as that may be. The air of the empty cabin was cold and still and held the musty odor of a sealed tomb. As I stepped inside, I found the deckhands who accompanied me were unwilling to do so. Both men spoke little Spanish—they were African muscle brought in from the docks at departure and their tongue was foreign to me—but I saw the same fear in their eyes that I had seen in the children below deck. I may have scoffed at this, but I felt it too—they were better men than me, willing to admit their fears to themselves while I still denied my own. There was no luggage in the cabin. No clothing. No books. No possessions of any kind. The room was as empty as it was in the weeks prior to us setting sail. The bed was made, but appeared unused. Again, he couldn't have left. Had he tried, the Americans would have shot him as they did the others who attempted to disembark. Lieutenant Commander Hertzog, the man in charge of this godforsaken rock, would have made it a point to tell me of his killing had that occurred. The death would have been presented as another warning to those who remained. Even if our passenger managed to sneak off the ship, there was no place to go, certainly not with luggage. The sharks prevented any escape by water. Yet this man was gone, and by all appearances, had never been here."

Mrs. White gave all this a moment to sink in, then turned the page of the notepad and went on.

"May 24, 1898. Three more adults dead, another child missing, bringing our numbers to fourteen children and fifteen adults, five of which are members of my crew. The man in Cabin 9 is back. I have no explanation. His cabin remained empty at last check minutes after midnight, then as I passed his door not an hour ago, I heard his whispering voice again through the wood. He presented the same offer he made to me and others so many times before—bring me a token of less than sixteen years, and I can guarantee you will live. It was then—"

"Hold up," Whaley cut her off. "Repeat that last part?"

Mrs. White looked up at him. "'Bring me a token of less than sixteen years, and I can guarantee you will live.'"

Whaley remembered some nonsense about tokens in Geraldine Rote's will:

Tokens of less than sixteen years of age will be considered property.

Mrs. White reached for another old book on a shelf next to the table. "The meaning of words sometimes changes with time. This dictionary is from 1850, so the definition should be close." She thumbed through to the *T*'s, located the entry, and read, "A token. One, a thing serving as a visible or tangible representation of a fact, quality, feeling. Two, a voucher that can be exchanged for goods or services, typically one given as a gift. Three, done for the sake of appearances or as a symbolic gesture."

The lump in Whaley's gut grew larger. "Am I misunderstanding, or is he asking for—"

"It's an offering," Mrs. White said quietly. "In this context, that's what he means. He's telling the captain if he gives him a child, he can somehow keep him alive. He made this offer to anyone willing to listen, and someone took him up on it. Multiple someones."

The color drained from Whaley's face. "What exactly did he want with the children? What did he do to them?"

If Mrs. White knew the answer, she didn't tell him. She only said, "Several kids were missing at this point, and it only got worse. Listen—

"May 28, 1898. Madness is swarming in my brain. Talk of witchcraft and mentions of dark arts have gone from hushed whispers to outright shouts among those left. Decorum be damned, even with the most refined of our passengers. We are a ship of nine children and eleven adults now, only two of which are crew, and of those two, only one I trust, a man by the name of Herberto, who has sailed with me for many years. The two of us stood guard outside the hold door last night, sleeping fitfully in shifts, and yet two more children vanished. The hold is secure. There is no way in or out other than the main door. The key is in my pocket, where it has remained the entirety of this godforsaken journey, and any chance at answers from the remaining children is gone, for they are nearly catatonic with fright, huddled together like lambs moments from slaughter. Cabin 9 was empty again at last check, although our passenger was there mumbling his demonic whispers behind the closed door only hours ago. Had I the manpower, I would task someone with sitting upon that man's bed until his inevitable return, but I'm not willing to spare Herberto, and none of the remaining adults are fit or trustworthy. I fear the ones who are not sick would be more than willing to wait on him, but not for my benefit. They would wait only so that they may agree to his offer and be spared death from fever. I've cataloged our remaining passengers into two camps—those who have accepted this man's offer and those who have not. It is not difficult to make that determination. One camp is fearful—isolating in cabins, venturing out only long enough to secure meals—while the others stroll the decks as if our nightmare trip were a leisure voyage. Laughing and joking and eyeing the rest of us like they are the holders of some secret, members of some club. While I may despise them, I have no reason to fear them. The ones who have already accepted the offer are no longer a threat; it is the others I must watch. Gauge their

desperation. If I am unable to protect the children, maybe I can stop whoever attempts to accept the offer next. Emerson must be fed? No, sir! Emerson will starve!"

Emerson?

Whaley recognized the name, but couldn't place it at first. Then it came back to him—the sign in the kitchen out at Wood. Something about "rules." It said: *Please feed Emerson.*

Mrs. White flipped the page and continued without looking up.

"May 30, 1898. Herberto is dead. He jumped from the ship last night and the Americans shot him. If there were indications of his intentions, I saw no sign. That leaves me with only Martinez as crew, and he is deep within the throes of fever, useless to me. I fell asleep upon the bed in an otherwise empty Cabin 9 only to wake in the hallway, my back up against the closed door, and the man's insidious whispers crawling to my ear. I know I will die if I do not accept. The Americans will see to that simply by keeping me aboard with the rest. The aches are upon me, and I pray those aches are only from sleeping on the floor and not illness. I do not know how many children are left, nor do I know how many adults who have not accepted the offer remain. Emerson, Emerson, Emerson. I am no longer willing to leave this spot. If I can't stop the children from vanishing from the hold, I will stop them here, before he can accept these tokens he so hungrily desires."

"I think that's where he got sick," Mrs. White said. "There's one more a few days later, but I'm not sure what to make of it."

"June 2, 1898. Why didn't I end him at the start? Soul be damned. I ache to the point of burning. Shiver under ice. The hold is open. Empty of children. Empty of all but my stench as I lie. Bile, piss, and shit surrounds me, and I welcome the vileness of it all, for as long as it makes me retch, I know I am still alive. We spoke, he and I, but I

do not recall the words. Others looked on, Herberto somehow among them. His hand on my head. His promise. The curse of it all. Damn the Americans and damned they will be—hunger is never satisfied for long. A man must always eat, and there is nothing to keep him aboard. This beast, this thing."

She let out a soft sigh and gestured toward the logbook. "That's the last entry. He had to be sick at that point, right? He's just rambling."

Whaley was thinking about the man from Cabin 9. "What did the captain do? Did he accept? Did he live? Or with all the children gone, was it too late?"

Even as he said it, the absurdity of that question wasn't lost on him; neither was the fact that a part of him believed every word of it. His rational mind told him it was all bullshit, but the other part of his brain reminded him what Billy had said out at that house—he said it had changed. He said the entire basement had vanished. And there had been more; it was written all over the kid's face as they worked through the house. He didn't recognize any of it. No different than a man and all his possessions vanishing from a ship's cabin.

Mrs. White pointed at a thick leather-bound book on the corner of the table. "That's an old Coast Guard ledger. There's a record of a ship called *Reina* being commandeered and commissioned in August 1898, but it only lists specs on the ship, nothing at all about where it came from or the previous passengers—healthy or sick. I'm guessing if they really did just let everyone die off, they wouldn't write that down anywhere. If they took them as prisoners of war, there might be a record somewhere, but there's nothing here about that." She gestured around the room. "What happened to those people is anyone's guess."

"What was the name of the man in Cabin 9?" Whaley asked, nodding toward the passenger ledger. "Is it in there?"

She nodded, pulled the ledger closer, and ran her finger down the text. "His name was Thybold," she said. "Thybold Marston."

18

WHEN I WOKE, I was in the bunkroom out on Wood, my throat as dry as sandpaper.

I'd been out for a while.

The sun was down, the room was dark. Not a single light burned.

Rain pattered on the roof.

Matty was nothing more than a shadow at first, and the moment I tried to focus on him, the spot on the side of my head where he hit me grew hot and throbbed. I went to reach for it and realized my hands were tied to the bunk bed frame behind my back.

"Before you say anything," Matty told me. "I want you to listen. Listen carefully. Can you do that? Or do you need more time to wake up? I can give you a few more minutes if you need them, but not much more. Nik nok, and all, like *he* always says…"

As he said this last part, he glanced over his shoulder, and I spotted Spivey sitting on one of the other bunks. He was hunched forward, gently rocking. He glanced over at me, but didn't say anything.

"Is he okay?"

Matty was holding the revolver. He tapped the barrel against his wrist. "We'll get to that in a minute. I want to be sure you understand what's happening, and you don't look like you're completely back yet. Your eyes keep rolling around." He raised a bottle of water to my lips. "Here, drink. You'll feel better."

I emptied the bottle Matty set it aside.

Although the bunkroom was dark, best I could tell, it had returned to the way I remembered it. No dust or cobwebs. The beds were all neatly made. The bucket was gone. The paint appeared fresh, no longer faded and peeling. There was no sleeping bag on the floor; Spivey's backpack and clothes were no longer scattered around. Out in the hallway, the steps leading up to the next level were back.

Thunder clapped. Angry and violent. White lightning momentarily crackled through the house, followed by another rumble. Beyond the window to my left, the sky was filled with livid dark clouds. Thick raindrops beat against the glass, and the wind gusted heavily enough to whistle through the boards of the old house.

"Benny's still out there digging, God bless that little shit," Matty said. "He can't seem to stop himself."

None of this made any more sense than it did earlier, and while I wanted to believe the hit to my head had something to do with it, I knew that wasn't true. What I was seeing now was just as real as what I saw earlier, and somehow, they both existed.

"Where's Kira?!"

"I'm here."

When lightning lit up the room again, I saw her standing in the doorway. Her arms were wrapped around her chest as if embracing herself. I'd like to say she looked worried, maybe concerned for me, but the truth was, I couldn't read her face. She watched the two of us from her place in the doorway. I was certain she saw the gun, but she made no move to free me. Didn't tell Matty to back off. Just stood there in the dark.

My throat was dry and it hurt to talk, but I did anyway. "Why are the lights off?"

"Something's wrong with the generator."

"Matty didn't mean to hit you so hard," Kira said softly. "Tell him you're sorry, Matty."

He chuckled. "Yeah, sorry. I clocked you pretty good. You were out almost an hour. My bad."

Matty reached for the side of my head, but I jerked away. "Fuck you," I spat out. "Fuck all of you." I tugged at the ropes on my wrists. "Get these off me!"

"You need to listen."

"I'm not listening to shit. Not while you've got me tied up with a gun on me!"

Matty looked down at the gun in his hand absentmindedly, like he forgot he was holding it, then turned to Kira. "Get him some more water or something."

Kira nodded, looked at me for a second. I swear she mouthed *I'm sorry*, then stepped across the hall into the bedroom, toward the bathroom that had no doubt returned too.

When she was gone, Matty pressed the barrel of the revolver against my cheek and slid it down the side of my face. "It's only a .22. One of the guys down at the marina told me if you shoot someone in the gut with a .22, it can take days for them to die. It's not the bullet that kills you, it's your own shit. It gets out through the hole and leaks into your body, causes infections, and rots you from the inside out. It's supposed to be horribly painful."

"Maybe if you read a fucking book every once in a while, you'd know that was called *sepsis*." I cocked my head toward Spivey. "Why are you letting him do this? Is this supposed to be some kind of game?"

Matty glared and raised the gun like he was going to hit me again.

"No game," Spivey said quietly as he rocked. "No game."

The detached way he said it might have frightened me more than the gun or the thought of getting hit again. I don't think Spivey was altogether with us.

Kira returned with the water. She knelt beside me and brought the glass to my lips. When I finished, she wiped the corner of my mouth and gently brushed my hair back behind my ear. "I'm so sorry, baby," she whispered.

"Back away from him," Matty told her. "I don't want you near those ropes."

"I'm not gonna untie him."

"I don't care. Get back."

Kira stroked the side of my face and stood. She went back over to the doorway.

I pulled at the ropes again, jerked them hard enough to rattle the bed frame, but they didn't come loose, only dug into my wrists.

"That's a hitch knot," Matty said. "My dad taught me. The more you pull, the tighter it'll get. So you might want to stop that. Or not, I don't really care. The bunk beds are bolted to the wall, ceiling, and floor. No way you can bust out of that. You'll just hurt yourself."

I looked past him to Kira. "You did take Lily, didn't you? Is she here?"

Kira said nothing, but there was a loud bang above us, like furniture flipping over, crashing against the floor. Spivey stopped rocking and looked up at the ceiling, his eyes wide.

A yelp followed the bang—like someone crying out and quickly silenced. The shortest, most horrifying scream I'd ever heard. Somehow, the quiet that followed was worse.

If the house was back to the way I remembered it, the locked closet was directly above us on the third floor. The only locked door in the house.

"You did take her," I managed to say. "Lily Dwyer. You've had her this entire time."

Kira and Matty were looking up too. Both their faces had gone white. Matty swallowed—honest-to-God gulped down air loud enough for the rest of us to hear, then he shook it off and looked back at me. "It might be best if you focus on your own situation and let the rest of us worry about that."

Alesia Dubin appeared in the doorway behind Kira. She paused there, one hand on her hip, and looked in at me. Her hair was pulled back away from her face, and she wore a white blouse and denim shorts. The top three buttons were open, enough for me to see that green amulet of hers resting against her pale chest. She licked her rose lips. "Everybody out but Spivey. We need to talk to him alone."

19

MATTY LOOKED OVER at Alesia, scratched his cheek with the barrel of the revolver, then stood and started for the door. On his way out, he took Kira by the arm with one hand and held the gun near the small of her back with the other, pushing her into the hall. "We'll be downstairs, Hasler. Don't try anything stupid."

He slipped his hand lower, to the curve of her butt, and Kira slapped it away.

"Whoa, I'm just playing." Matty laughed, waving the gun. "Gonna get yourself shot in the ass!"

"Don't touch her," Alesia said. "Not like that. Not unless I tell you to. Get her downstairs with Chloe and Izzie and wait for me."

How she had seen that, I didn't know. Alesia hadn't taken her eyes off me the entire time. Not so much as a glance back toward them.

Matty didn't seem to care. He let out a soft huff and the two of them disappeared down the hallway, gobbled up by the dark.

"Why don't you turn on a light?" I told her. "You're not scaring anyone with the theatrics."

Alesia pouted. "Oh, nobody's trying to scare you, Billy."

She snapped her long fingers and the bulbs above burst to life, flooding the room with light.

How the hell?!

My eyes had adjusted to the dark, and that sudden burst of light was painful. I pinched my eyes shut for a moment, then squinted at Spivey. He was still sitting on the bunk, near the switch, but if he had reached for it, I didn't see him do it. Aside from rocking back and forth, I didn't see him move at all.

Alesia's pout spread to a sly grin. "Not everything is what it seems, Billy."

I yanked at the ropes again, hard enough to shake the bed frame. "I think I've got a pretty good handle on what's going on. You've decided you'd rather go to prison than college. I may be willing to forget about all that if you untie me, but good luck explaining her." I looked up at the ceiling. "Half the state is looking for that girl."

Alesia leaned in closer. Her breath smelled like icy mint. "Like I said: not everything is what it seems." She stretched a hand toward Spivey and snapped her fingers again. "Letter."

At first, he didn't seem to hear her, then he reached into his back pocket and took out a crumpled sheet of paper, placed it in her hand. She set it on the floor between us, unfolded it, and gently smoothed out the creases, then held it in front of my face so I could read it.

It was a letter from Spivey's doctor.

I read it twice before the text really sunk in.

Words like *aggressive, spread, stage four* all jumped out at me, but it was the word *terminal* that felt like a punch.

I looked over at Spivey. "I don't understand. At the hearing today Marston said you were much better. He even had bloodwork to back that up. This says you're dying."

Spivey didn't answer, only continued to rock. This slow, rhythmic back and forth.

Alesia reached back and placed a hand on his knee.

He stopped, went completely still.

"It's okay," she said. "Tell him."

For the first time since I woke, he looked at me. I mean, really looked at me, like he understood what he was seeing and not just going through the motions. He licked his lips and sighed. "That letter is based on a blood draw back in June, about a week before Grams died and all this started."

"While we were still in school?"

He nodded. "Yeah. I thought I was still in remission. They tested me on the regular, every few months, but it had been so long since I had a problem and I felt okay, so I skipped the last couple. Stupid, I know, but nothing I can do about that now. The leukemia came back hard and fast. By the time I felt something, saw those patches on my arms, and went in for a test, it had progressed beyond the point of no return." He paused for a second. "Well, that's not completely true, there were still treatments available, but nothing that could put it back into remission, only buy me a little more time."

Now I was really confused. "So the paperwork Marston had at the deposition was fake?"

Spivey's gaze dropped from mine and he looked around the room before responding to me. "No, that was real too."

"They can't both be real."

Spivey swallowed. "I've gotten better since I came out here. It's like the leukemia is gone. I know it's not, it can't be, but I feel fine and all the tests say I'm fine."

To prove this to me, he held out his arms. His skin was clear—not a single bruise, blotch, or blemish.

"I'm fine as long as I stay out here on the island, in the house." He dropped his arms. "As soon as I leave, though, it comes back. I took *Annabelle* into town the other day. I was there maybe two hours and it hit me hard. I got so light-headed and dizzy, I barely made it back."

"He didn't make it back," Alesia said. "Well, he wouldn't have if he'd been alone. I wrestled him from the car into the boat, and even then I didn't get a cohesive sentence out of him until we'd been back out here for a few hours. I thought for sure I'd lost him."

Spivey swallowed again. "Something out here is keeping me alive."

Above us came the thump again, as loud as the first time. The crash of furniture followed by a thin yelp. Spivey's head jerked toward the ceiling and he slapped his hands over his ears, pinched his eyes shut. "Make it stop. Please, make it stop."

Alesia brushed her hand through his hair and leaned in close. "I'm working on it."

Spivey was trembling, and he wasn't alone.

"I think I'm gonna be sick," I told them both. "I need to use the bathroom."

20

"CHIEF?"

Whaley looked up, realized Mrs. White was staring at him from across the table. "Marston?" he said. "You're sure?"

She flipped the ledger around and placed her finger next to the name. There it was in a neat, flowing script next to the number nine. Thybold Marston.

Whaley's heart was racing and he felt a thin bead of sweat on his brow.

"Are you okay, Chief? You look like someone punched you in the stomach," Mrs. White said. "Would you like a glass of water?"

He forced his head to bob.

Mrs. White gave him a concerned smile, got up, and crossed the room to a small sink near the bathroom.

Whaley tried to make sense of all this, but his mind was swimming. He'd seen a lot of things over the years, much of which he wished he could unsee—traffic accidents, slip and falls, suicides—those faces never went away, they just learned to sit quietly in the dark spaces of your head, in a room near the back. Sometimes they leaned into the light, gave you a glimpse, a reminder, before settling again. Always with you, though. Always whispering amongst themselves. He could hear them now; they'd grown excited. One voice in particular louder than all the others—Billy Hasler on that phone call.

I can still hear Patricia and William laughing, Chief, can you?

Can you?

Two children who had no business mixed up in his head with the others, yet they popped up front and center—he'd never seen them, never investigated their death. Two children of less than sixteen years of age who had set foot out on that island and somehow found their way back after death.

Tokens.

Property.

Bring me a token of less than sixteen years, and I can guarantee you will live.

The detective in him drew lines, connected dots.

Judge Schultz at the deposition this morning—*But he is receiving treatment for his illness?*

He is, Marston had replied. *I'm not permitted to provide specifics, but he is doing very well.*

He thought of all the kids who had been out there in the past few weeks. How many were under sixteen?

Christ, Lily Dwyer.

None of the thoughts floating around his head could possibly be true.

They were the stuff of movies.

Ghost stories.

Not real life.

He didn't believe in that sort of thing, never had. All of this was connected, but there would be a logical explanation; he just needed to find it. He knew exactly where he'd start.

Fighting the tremble in his hand, Whaley reached for the microphone clipped to his shoulder and pressed the transmit button. "Sandy, you there?"

A moment later, *"Yeah, Chief. What's up?"*

He swallowed. "There's a subpoena on my desk from the deposition this morning. Can you get it? I need the address for the law firm that sent it."

"Sure. Stand by."

Mrs. White returned with a glass of water and handed it to him. He drank it in three quick gulps. Felt better.

"Got it, you ready?"

Whaley took out his own small notebook and unclipped the pen. "Go ahead."

Sandy Lomax rattled off an address in Boston and he scribbled it down. "Do me a favor. Reach out to Dennis Witt— he's a detective with Boston PD. Number's in my Rolodex. Ask him to take a drive by there and call me on my mobile when he's out front. Tell him I owe him. Then get on the computer and pull up everything you can for me on Lockwood Marston. His law practice. Family. Whatever you find. Print it and put it on my desk."

"Will do."

"Thanks, Sandy."

He wiped some water from the corner of his mouth and looked over at Mrs. White. "Do you know the name Lily Dwyer?"

"The missing girl from the news?"

He nodded. "She had a book in her room called *The Devil of Great Island*. It came from here."

Mrs. White gave that a moment of thought, then frowned. "She didn't take that book. Alesia Dubin walked off with it three months ago."

"Alesia Dubin? You're sure?"

She pointed at a clipboard in the corner of the table. "Hand me that?"

He slid it over to her and she flipped back through the pages. "We make a note here anytime we pull records from the archive, then check it off when it's returned, even if it doesn't leave the building. Ah, there she is." She tapped on the page and read off the date. April. Three months ago. "Come to think of it, that was a memorable visit. She pulled all this same material. Everything we had on Wood Island and that ship, *Reina*."

"Was she researching some kind of school project?"

She shook her head. "No. Nothing like that. I figured her mother put her up to it."

"Her mother? Why?"

Even though she and Whaley were alone, Mrs. White lowered her voice. "Her mother, Laura, has a thing for the occult and the paranormal, always has. Not uncommon for people around here, but it borders on obsession with her. Walton's haunted tavern and the well out back where those kids died, the old fort, Wood Island—every cemetery, ghost, and witch story from Salem to Bangor, she can quote them all." She gestured at everything on the table. "She's been through all this at least a dozen times over the years. Just a teenager herself the first time, I remember. That's why it struck me when I saw her daughter looking through all this stuff, reminded me so much of her. Then I saw those kids today and it was like a flash back in time, like Laura Dubin and her friends were here all over again. Like not a day had gone by."

Whaley's brow tightened up. "Who were Laura Dubin's friends?"

Mrs. White closed her eyes for a moment, sifting through the years. "There was Pam Rote, of course—Pam Spivey, now. Her future husband, Keith, and Teddy Hasler. Those four were inseparable back then from what I remember, at least for a little while. I think they had some kind of falling-out."

At the mention of those names, the hair on the back of Whaley's neck pricked up.

No coincidences.

Static crackled on his radio and he expected Mundie's voice, reporting on whatever he found on Wood Island. It wasn't, though. It was Sandy Lomax again.

"Chief, Mundie called in. Told me to tell you there's nobody at the Hasler house. Matty's not at the marina. His dad said he hasn't seen any of those kids all day, and Matty's boat's been gone. Might have docked it somewhere else. Mundie's got some kind of motor trouble on his own boat. He's working on it now, said he'd head out to Wood as soon as he gets it running."

Whaley stifled the urge to curse.

Sandy added, *"There's a woman here at the station named Laura Dubin. She wants to see Ted Hasler. Is it okay for me to let her go back?"*

He exchanged a look with Mrs. White.

No coincidences.

Whaley pressed the mic. "Keep her out front. I'll be right there."

He thanked Mrs. White and rushed to the door. Rain was coming down in thick sheets. He was pulling the collar of his coat up over his head when he spotted the car parked behind his SUV at the bottom of the hill. The antique black Jaguar shimmered ghost-like behind a vale of rain. The windows of the car were tinted dark, and even when the back door opened, he couldn't make out anything inside but the shadowed profile of a man deep on the bench seat. Whaley stepped out into the storm, and even though he was thirty feet from the car, all other sounds seemed to vanish as Marston called out.

"Probably best you and I spoke, don't you think? Some might say it's long overdue."

21

"I NEED TO use the bathroom," I said again, and that wasn't a lie. My stomach was twisted in a horrible knot, like someone reached into my gut and squeezed. The throb in my head where Matty had hit me ached, and I felt pressure behind my eyes. I'd never had a concussion before, but I was fairly certain I had one now, and all of that combined with an acidic bile creeping up my throat.

"Go in your pants," Alesia said flatly.

Spivey stopped rocking and looked down at the floor. "Let him use the bathroom. We're not fucking animals. Where's he gonna go?"

As he spoke, Alesia's eyes never left mine, that crazy green as bright at the amulet around her neck. Her breath felt cold against my face. "Matty's got the gun," she told me after a moment's consideration. "He's downstairs right now with Kira, Chloe, and his sister. Don't think for a second he won't shoot one of them if you try something stupid. If *anyone* tries something stupid, somebody is gonna die, understand?"

"Come on." Spivey groaned, finally turning toward her. "You don't have to do that. He's my—"

"Your friend, I know. But a dog will bite when it's backed into a corner, when it's frightened. Even one you've had all your life."

"Untie the ropes, Alesia. I'll watch him."

She stared at me for another moment, then sat beside me on the bunk, leaned around my back, and got to work on Matty's knot. I watched Spivey as she worked, but he wouldn't face me. When the rope fell away and I started to rise, she gripped my shoulder. "I'd hate to see something happen to Kira—she's sweet."

I shrugged her off and got to my feet. Maybe I rose too fast, or maybe it was the injury, but the entire room swooned, tilted, and my vision clouded. I reached out and grabbed the frame of the bunk and managed to steady myself. I remained still long enough for my vision to clear, then stumbled toward the hallway.

Alesia remained on the bunk while Spivey followed about two paces behind me. When I nearly fell again, he made no effort to help me. Instead, he actually shuffled back a step, startled, like he thought I might grab him for support and take him down with me.

I sucked in a breath, righted myself, and made my way across the bedroom to the bathroom on the far end. At the door, I stopped and turned to him. "Why didn't you tell me you were dying?"

He looked back toward the bunkroom, confirmed Alesia was no longer in earshot, and lowered his voice anyway. "Dude, I've been dying a long time now. I've just gotten better at it."

Another bang came from upstairs, followed by another pain-filled yelp silenced in a sharp second. Spivey's head jerked up. His skin looked as pale as the dead.

"If you're worried about Matty and the gun," I whispered, "I'll help you. We can take it from him, get Lily and the girls out of here. It's not too late for you to make things right. I'll tell Whaley you helped me. I'll tell him Matty and Alesia were behind all this, whatever, we'll figure something out... I know you don't want to do this."

The look on his face told me it wouldn't be that simple. If Whaley was right, and Kira and the others all helped take Lily Dwyer, then there was no easy way to unravel what they'd done. They'd brought her to his home and he'd let them. There was no getting out of that. "Things may look bad," I told him, "but they're only going to get worse unless you do something."

He bit his lower lip, and for one brief second, I thought I might have convinced him. Then this numbness washed over his face, and he glanced back in Alesia's direction before turning to me and raising his voice again. "Do you need to piss or not?" Reaching around the side of the door, he flicked on the light switch. "Nik nok."

I didn't know what else to say, so I said nothing at all.

I stepped into the bathroom, closed the door, and twisted the lock.

Don't lock the doors, my mind scolded me, and I ignored that too. The door was solid oak, and the lock wasn't one of those flimsy ones you could pick with a paper clip—it was a real lock requiring a key.

I went straight for the window behind the vanity on the far wall. I only had one shot at this, and I needed to move fast. There was no lock on the window, only a simple twist latch. I climbed up on the vanity, flicked the latch, and pushed the window open.

The storm roared in, and I was certain Spivey heard it. The wind whipped, and icy rain slapped against my skin, stung my eyes. It came into the bathroom with enough force to nearly knock me back to the floor. I grabbed at both sides of the window and hauled myself out onto the roof. Although the shingles were slick with rain and the roof was pitched, I found footing on a thin gutter running the length of the roofline. I had no idea if it could support my weight, so I only braced my feet on it and put the bulk of my weight on my backside as I eased down the slope toward the front of the house. By the time I reached the edge, my clothing was soaked, and I was so cold my entire body trembled. I didn't stop. I couldn't. If Spivey heard the window open, he was either working that lock or running downstairs to alert the others. Either way, I had very little time and not much of a plan.

When I reached the edge of the roof, about twelve feet from the ground, I didn't give myself a chance to hesitate. I rolled to my belly, let my legs dangle over the side, and slid down after them. I made a grab for the gutter and my fingers caught it, but only for a second, not enough to slow me down. I dropped those twelve feet and cracked against the muddy ground with enough force to nearly knock me out again. If not for the rain and mud, I might have broken a leg or even my back, but the storm offered its only saving grace in that the ground was soft. Not much of a cushion, but enough.

My body didn't want any part of this. My vision clouded and the urge to pass out came raging back. I sucked in more air, breathed long and deep, waited as long as I dared, then scrambled to my feet and ran toward the dock on pure adrenaline.

Both *Annabelle* and Matty's skiff were slamming against the dock, thrown by waves filled with ferocity and spite, some nearly as tall as me. Had I looked back over my shoulder, I would have seen lights tick on in the house, one by one. I would have seen each window come to life as if waking from slumber. Had I been looking where I was going instead of the angry water, I might have spotted one of Benny's holes before I stepped into it. I didn't, though—my foot caught the corner and I went flailing through the air. I landed face-first and skidded through the mud, stopping about five feet from where Benny stood.

"Well, ain't that something." He groaned, eyeing me curiously. His clothing was drenched through, a slick second skin hanging from his thin frame. Breathing hard, he'd paused the digging and rested his weight on the handle of the rusty shovel. He drew a filthy arm across his forehead, meant to brush his stringy hair from his face, but all he did was leave a black smear that dripped down his cheek with the relentless rain. "Mr. Spivey know you're out here?"

I got up far slower than I would have hoped. My legs both felt like rubber bands and my heart was beating like a jackhammer. I looked back toward the house; there was no sign of Spivey or the others. I said the only thing I could think of. "He sent me out here to check on the boats."

He looked over my shoulder toward the harbor, placed a hand above his eyes to block the rain, and squinted. "*Reina* was drifting a bit earlier, but the captain seemed to get her tied down. Couple of the other ones took a beating on the rocks. Not sure how they'll fare. Suppose we'll figure that out in the mornin'."

I had no idea what he was talking about. I turned and saw nothing out in the water, nothing but waves crashing against the jagged chunks of granite. Whitecaps jettisoning foam at least twenty feet into the air. I tried to see beyond all that, but the rain was coming down in thick sheets, visibility near zero offshore. I couldn't see the Coast Guard station, any of the houses along the shore—even the lighthouse at Fort Constitution was dark. When lightning flashed, I still couldn't see any of those things, and I told myself it was the storm because that was the only logical explanation. I told myself that even as my mind whispered another option to me, made a suggestion that couldn't possibly be true—

None of those things are actually there. Not now.

Lightning flashed again, illuminating the sky where the abandoned Portsmouth Prison building stood—

Should have stood.

My legs nearly did give out from beneath me because it was gone. In that brief instance of light, I saw the outcropping of rock at the edge of the shipyard where it should have stood, but there was nothing but trees. Several boats were tied up near the shoreline, but my glimpse had been so quick, I made none of them out. There had never been docks there, though—those waters were restricted. The Coast Guard only permitted vessels to tie down around the bend in the inlet. Everything I saw in that glimpse was wrong.

I didn't hear Matty come up behind me, and even if I had, I don't think I could have reacted. Something in my head snapped, gave up.

He didn't have the gun out. He didn't need it. He stepped between me and Benny and smacked the boy on the back of his shoulder. "How's that pilot light, Benny?"

Benny wiped the mud from his forehead with the back of his sleeve. "Burning tight and bright at last check, sir."

"Glad to hear it."

Benny shifted his weight on the shovel's handle and narrowed his eyes at me. "This one's looking a bit peaked. Probably best you get him out of the rain before he catches his death."

Matty gripped my arm above the elbow. "I was thinking the same thing. We had a rough trip out. The weather stirred things up good."

"Figured you spotted the sharks. They were kicking up some kind of frenzy out there just before the clouds broke."

"Seems like everything's getting worked up tonight, but we didn't see any sharks, did we, Billy?"

I didn't answer him. I wasn't sure I had the ability to make words.

Benny smirked. "Usually don't see 'em until they're picking chunks of you from between their teeth."

Lightning flashed again, followed by the deep rumble of thunder.

"Ain't that the truth," Matty told him, turning me back toward the house. "We'll let you get back to it."

"Thank you, sir. Lots to do," Benny replied, his voice muddled by the rain. That was followed by the blade of his shovel smacking the wet dirt.

Matty led me past several more holes and up the porch steps to the house.

Behind us, Benny started whistling. How he did that with all the rain, I'll never know. The song was one I recognized, but hadn't heard in a very long time. I might have been ten. My grandmother had a record of it and played it so often the needle would sometimes skip across the vinyl—"When My Baby Smiles at Me," by Ted Lewis and his orchestra.

I turned to look back at him and froze.

Standing on the porch, the added height gave me a far better view of the island, and with that better view, I saw not only the holes we just passed and the one Benny was currently digging, I saw all of them. At least a hundred, maybe more. The landscape was riddled with them— deep holes with mounds of dirt, sand, and rock piled between. It would take days for a dozen men digging 24/7 to replicate what I was looking at—none of these holes were here only a few hours earlier when I'd come out with Whaley.

Knee-deep in his latest, Benny was shoveling again, grunting as he went, dirt flying off to the side. My broken mind tried to do the math— thirty minutes per hole? Twenty? No. Even if he managed to knock one out every ten minutes, six per hour, that would only cover a fraction of what I was looking at.

"Benny's right," Matty joked. "You are looking a little peaked."

He pulled me into the house, into the kitchen, and closed the door behind us.

Had I turned back toward New Castle, took one last look with the next bout of lightning, I might have confirmed I was somehow looking into the past. I would have seen a shoreline that hadn't existed in over a hundred years.

I've often wondered what I would have done had I seen that. Hindsight is odd like that. It's supposed to be clear. It never has been for me, not when it comes to that night. Part of me is grateful for that. The memories of that night, the decisions we made leading up to it—some as a group, some not—what happened next…

Some things are better left murky—to see them clearly leads to nothing but madness.

22

SHIELDING HIMSELF FROM the rain as best he could, Whaley made his way down the steps and crossed a small plot of grass to the open back door of the car. Although Marston leaned toward him, the shadows seemed to move too, soupy dark oozing around the still air. His bony hand patted the empty seat between them with a rhythmic thump. "Join me, Chief, before you catch yourself a cold. You look like you could use a good sit."

Bad weather or not, Whaley considered telling the man to step out of the car. He considered reaching into the car, taking Marston by his scrawny little throat, and removing him from the car, but he did neither of those things. Instead, he eased inside and settled onto the back seat. The crushed velvet felt like it might swallow him whole, it was so plush. When he brought his feet up into the footwell, his right knee made an all-too familiar popping noise.

Marston tsked. "Ah, the hazards of aging. I hope you aren't in pain."

"I'm fine."

Someone sat up front in the driver's seat, but Whaley could make out nothing but the back of the person's head beneath a black cap.

"If it's not too much trouble, Chief, please close the door—this weather is dreadful."

Although the door was heavy, far heavier than modern vehicles, it moved effortlessly, as if the car had just rolled off the factory assembly line, freshly oiled and lubed.

Marston, wearing the same suit as earlier and not a single hair out of place, leaned forward slightly and spoke. "Driver, could you raise the partition? A little privacy might be in order."

"Yes, sir," came a voice that sounded much younger than Whaley expected. A voice he thought he recognized. He tried to get a look at the driver, but before he could, an opaque partition slid up between them, separating the front of the car from the back.

"Given your chosen profession, you most likely know this car as a police vehicle—that was its primary purpose back in the day. A 1958 Jaguar MK1 Saloon. They only made a handful of limousine models. I actually found this one in Germany and brought it here by cargo vessel more years ago than I care to remember. It's a bear when it comes to gas consumption, and I know I should purchase something more practical, but I can't bring myself to part with it." He gestured toward a silver tray on a small minibar built into the back of the driver's seat. "Would you care for some tea?"

"I don't think we have time for tea."

"Nonsense. If you don't make time for the finer things, what is the point?"

Marston slid an empty saucer and cup toward Whaley and placed a matching set in front of himself. Delicate white china with an intricate pattern on the various edges, no doubt etched by hand and probably far older than the car. He removed the lid from a matching kettle and steam wafted out. Whaley had no idea how the man had boiled water in his car and Marston offered no explanation, reaching for a small wooden box as if this was all perfectly normal. "I'm fond of a rather special blend of tea I purchase directly from a supplier in Mombasa. Drink far too much of it, I'm afraid, but we all have our vices, don't we, Chief?" With a round silver spoon, he dipped ground leaves from the wooden box, used a knife to slide the excess back in, and dumped what remained into the kettle. The scent of it immediately lofted through the confined space, this heavy, earthy aroma. Humid and hot. Marston repeated this four times before replacing the kettle's lid with a satisfied smile. "The amount of time tea is permitted to steep is key, I've found. Too soon and it's weak, a moment too long and it's bitter."

Whaley had no idea what he was talking about and didn't care. He was looking out the window, trying to make sense of what he saw. Something was very wrong. The street had changed. The buildings.

The historical society was perched up on Windmill Hill to Whaley's right, where it should be, but the sign that declared it the historical society was no longer there. Instead, a large plaque below the gable read Free Will Baptist Church, and that was wrong too because it normally read Public Library, and even though the Public Library sign was also incorrect, that's what *should* be there, that's what he'd seen every day for his entire life and now it was gone. He knew the history. It was drilled into the head of every local—in 1925, the town bought the old Baptist church and converted it to a library. In 1990, a new library was built out on the Commons and the historical society took over the building. The historical society left the library sign because, well, it was historical. He knew that was what had happened, but he was somehow looking at what came before all that. The clapboard siding was white but no longer held the luster of the Benjamin Moore enamel he and eight other volunteers had brushed on two summers before. Instead, the paint was dull. Chipped and peeling, several spots worn down to the bare wood. The trees to the left were different too—much smaller, younger, not as full as they should be. And the street? What had happened to the street? The blacktop was riddled with ruts and potholes. The yellow line down the center was gone, and the pavement didn't seem as wide as it should be.

Whaley's eyes narrowed and he brushed the glass of the car window with the tips of his fingers. "What is this?"

If Marston heard him, he gave no indication. When Whaley turned back to him, he noticed the man's lips were moving. Barely audible, Marston was mumbling, counting softly to himself. He reached some kind of target and his lips tightened over yellow teeth in a grin. "Ah, there we are." He retrieved the simmering kettle with his right hand while placing a small silver filter over the mouth of Whaley's cup with his other. "This method may be messier than traditional tea bags, but I think you'll find the superior flavor makes it all worthwhile."

He poured the tea slowly, giving the filter a chance to catch what remained of the ground leaves. After preparing his own, he set the filter aside on a cloth napkin and raised his cup in a small toast. "To enjoying the finer things among good company!"

Whaley jerked a thumb back toward the window, about to demand some kind of explanation, when he realized there was nothing to explain. The historical society sign was right where it should be, and so was the sign above the building's door. The paint was correct and so was the street. The only thing wrong was him—his head was buzzing, and there was a ringing in his ears. His balance felt off, as if he just stepped out of the car of a fast roller coaster and hadn't quite regained his footing.

Brigadoon gone as if it had never been.

"Drink, Chief. You'll feel better."

Whaley did. Not because he wanted to, but because his body somehow needed to and no longer required permission to act. His hands reached for the cup and brought it to his lips, and all he could do was watch. All he could do was part his lips and let the hot tea into his mouth, swallow. He took two more sips before setting the cup back down on the saucer.

Marston beamed, and for the first time, his smile appeared genuine. "Splendid, isn't it?"

Whaley thought it tasted like muddy water, but he didn't say that. Instead, he said, "Who is Thybold Marston to you? Who's Emerson?"

Marston's eyes narrowed for a moment, his long fingers resting on the edge of the silver tray. "Am I correct in assuming Mr. Spivey doesn't know you are here?"

"I don't answer to *Mr.* Spivey."

"No, I suppose you don't." He sighed. "I do, though. As Mr. Spivey's attorney, I'm bound by certain rules pertaining to confidentiality. Without his expressed permission, I'm afraid there is very little I can tell you when it comes to the house, the island, and all things associated." His tongue snaked out and rolled over his thin lips. "Rules are rules, Chief, and those rules extend to my predecessors."

"Rules are rules," Whaley repeated. "Tokens of less than sixteen years of age will be considered property. Those present at sunset must remain until sunrise unless permitted to leave by the Caretaker. The *entity* must never be sold… rules like that?"

"Precisely."

"None of it makes sense."

"It doesn't have to," he answered. "Not to you." He said this dismissively, like he was swatting away a fly.

Whaley wasn't about to be dismissed or intimidated. "I've got a missing child, and God knows what's happening out on that island. Multiple minors under my purview are caught up in some mess, and you seem to be pulling the strings. You can either tell me what's going on or I start making phone calls, getting subpoenas and warrants, and within an hour I'm down at your office in Boston picking through your file cabinets."

Marston's eyes grew wide and the fake smile returned. "Oh, Chief, are you seriously going to leverage a threat against me? Just when I thought we were becoming fast friends? Perhaps you should rethink that. I don't mind. Emotions can sometimes get the best of us, and emotions are certainly running high." He reached for the kettle. "Would you like some more tea?"

Whaley's cup was empty.

He didn't remember drinking it.

Had he been drugged?

He didn't see how. Marston was drinking the tea too. Maybe something in his cup before the tea was poured? Maybe Marston wasn't drinking his, only pretending. Maybe something in the air of the car? Maybe—

"Eyes front, Chief."

"Clifford," he replied, not exactly sure why. "Clifford Whaley."

"That you are. Chief Clifford Whaley, born right here on New Castle in 1969 to Elmore and Gerta Whaley. Two fine, outstanding citizens who passed away in a tragic car accident when you were only twenty-seven. You have no children, not for lack of wanting or trying, but you suspect fertility issues either in yourself or your wonderful wife, although neither of you has sought out a medical diagnosis. Instead, believing if it is meant to be, it will be, something I find simply charming."

Whaley opened his mouth to speak, but nothing came out. His heart was beating far faster than it should. An urgent rhythm. Each breath he took seemed to supply a little less air than he needed, and he fought the urge to gulp down a gasp. He didn't want to give this man the satisfaction. Half of what Marston said was public record and the other half could be nothing more than a calculated guess, but it still felt like a violation. Marston was attempting to throw him off balance, and it was working. Particularly with what he said next.

"How long has your dear Mary been coughing?"

Whaley's heart thumped. "How do you know about…"

His voice fell off. The look in Marston's eyes told him he not only knew about the cough, but much more. Mary had started coughing about two months ago, said there was a tickle in her throat and she couldn't quite reach it. She never smoked, and they'd let it go. Chalked it up to seasonal allergies. Last week, though, she'd gotten winded climbing the stairs to the second floor, had to sit down to catch her breath. She'd called Doc Lambrey, who gave her lungs a listen that afternoon, told her it was probably nothing, but he wanted her to see a friend of his, a specialist in Exeter, just to be sure. She had an appointment on the calendar for the day after tomorrow. "Probably nothing," Whaley muttered.

"And let us hope that's all it is." Marston nodded. "But if it is… something… hopefully you caught it early."

In Whaley's mind another sentence came, soft, whispered, as if heard through the door of any old ship's cabin: *Bring me a token of less than sixteen years of age, and I'll see that she lives. It doesn't have to be more than a tickle. In fact, it could be just that.*

Whaley nearly dropped the china cup, nearly shattered it on the silver tray. He wanted it out of his hands, away from his face. He wanted out of Marston's car. The cup was empty again, and again he had no recollection of drinking. With a shaky hand, he set the cup down on the tray and forced his breathing to steady.

Marston took a sip of his own tea and set his cup down on the tray next to Whaley's. He studied a drip slowly working down the side of the cup. Before it fell to the tray, he wiped it away with his thumb, changing the subject as quickly as one might change the channel. "The business with the missing girl is quite tragic. I assure you, I feel for both her and her family. I'm sure they are all grateful for your quick action this morning, apprehending Mr. Hasler. I understand he's a childhood friend of yours, so that must make this rather messy for you. You saw past all that, followed the evidence, and you have your man behind bars. For better or worse, I'm sure he'll tell you what he did with her. In time, these things tend to sort themselves out."

"We found one of her hairs in his car," Whaley told him. "That feels a little too convenient to me."

"Or your friend the real estate developer is not the criminal mastermind he had hoped he'd be. The careless tend to catch themselves with their own mistakes, or at least that's what I've picked up from the handful of mystery novels I've read. Give them rope and they're keen to hang themselves."

"Ted Hasler is no kidnapper," Whaley replied. "He was in your way, though, complicating life for you and your client. That's motive. He's pushing to get David Spivey off that island. Pushing to get him proper treatment. Pushing against whatever agenda you're working. That hair turning up in Ted's car, that absolutely was careless, you're right about that. If not for that, I would have never considered looking at you for Lily Dwyer."

At this, Marston only smiled. "Yet here I am, enjoying tea with the chief of police while your friend sits idly behind bars awaiting charges. Some might say you're wasting time, Chief. While you're doddering about, barking up random trees like a one-eyed coon dog, the Dwyer girl is still out there somewhere, perhaps alive, perhaps not, but if she is alive, how long do you think she'll remain that way without anyone to take care of her? Imagine if she's found a week from now on one of Mr. Hasler's construction sites, or maybe in his boat, tied up and dead of thirst. I read of such a case—not long ago in Chicago, I believe it was. Imagine if your superiors learned that instead of grilling Mr. Hasler and gaining her whereabouts from the moment you had him in custody, instead of chasing the simple clues in front of you, you were out accusing respected attorneys from Boston of wild conspiracy theories. Imagine what they would do to you. Some might also say that same attorney would have a strong defamation case against you, or maybe harassment." He waved a hand around. "Either of those things could bring your time in law enforcement to an abrupt end. The Dwyer family may even feel the need to sue you, rightfully so. All of it is messy, messy business. All because you didn't do what was expected of you."

Whaley wasn't about to let this man intimidate him. "If I'm already in so much trouble, maybe I should take you back to the station house and put you in the cell next to Ted. The three of us can hash this out together."

"Your tea is getting cold, Chief."

Marston had refilled the cup. He hadn't seen him do it.

Whaley raised it to his lips and drank. Didn't want to. Didn't realize he was doing it until he was returning the empty cup back to the saucer, and that scared him, it scared him a lot, but he wasn't about to back down. "I know you took her. If not you directly, someone acting on your behalf. Maybe those kids. I'll find her. Like you said, the careless tend to catch themselves."

Marston listened to this with mild amusement and the fake grin returned. "I'm afraid we've gotten off on the wrong foot. Perhaps we should focus. You and I are both in pursuit of the same thing: the well-being of Mr. Spivey and his friends. I assure you, that is my only intent. My sole purpose."

"Then why do I get the feeling you're using him along with everyone else?"

"That couldn't be further from the truth. I'm here only to serve. Perform my duties. Nothing more." He glanced at a clock built into the back of the driver's seat, above the small bar. "My, the hours have gotten away from me today, and there is still so much to do. Give me your hand, Chief."

"My hand?"

The words came out slightly slurred, and if Whaley hadn't been sure he'd been drugged before, he was certain now. As he said those two words, the world seemed to tilt slightly to the side, rest there, then wobble back.

"Yes, Chief, your hand."

Whaley held his hand out. He didn't want to, but he had no more control over that than he did when it came to drinking the tea.

Marston placed one of his hands under Whaley's, palm to palm, and placed his other on top. The man's skin was cold, clammy, not the touch of the living, but something else. He applied pressure, squeezed, and all things changed.

23

THE WORLD OUTSIDE the car had gone old again. Not just the historical society and the street itself, but every house and structure along Main Street. A carriage rolled by on their left, a large mare lazily tugging it along, hooves clopping loud enough on the pavement to reach them. Several people Whaley didn't recognize shuffled along behind the carriage: a man, a woman, and a boy of maybe nine or ten, all of them dressed in clothing reminiscent of a time long past. They didn't look at the car, and Whaley somehow knew they wouldn't see it even if they did—this was a one-way mirror, whatever *this* was.

"Where are we?" Whaley managed.

Marston's grip on him tightened, and when he spoke, his voice didn't come from any particular direction but wrapped around Whaley, engulfed him, rattled his bones. "I think we both know *where* is not as appropriate as *when,* and even that isn't truly accurate for a number of reasons I'll attempt to explain in the simplest of terms so you may understand." He turned from the window and faced Whaley again, his eyes dark pools. "Time is no more fixed in place than the waters of a fast-moving river. It's possible to step in the river from any location along the shore. It's even possible to step back out again. But here's the rub—riding the current downriver with the flow of the water and stepping out moments later, *following where the water is meant to go*, is far easier than swimming against the current and attempting to reach the place the water has been. It's not impossible, not for a skilled swimmer, but it's difficult—the current is strong. If you don't wish to fight it, there is one other option more akin to what we are doing now—you can step into the river. You don't have to go anywhere. You can stand perfectly still and simply look both up-current at what has been *and* you can look down-current at what is to come, where that water will go. The likes of you will never be capable of such a feat—it's only necessary for you to understand that I am. You need to understand in order to comprehend what I am about to show you. Do you follow?"

Whaley didn't follow any of this. He wanted to get out of the car, but he couldn't move. His body refused to obey him, and even when he blinked, when he closed his eyes for that short millisecond, the urge to open them again and stare into this man's gaze was overpowering. It was painful not to look.

Marston, still clasping Whaley's hand, pressed tighter. One of his fingers twitched, and Whaley felt the man's nail dig into his palm. This wasn't just a scratch; the tip of his finger burrowed in, twisted and churned through the skin to the meaty part below.

Whaley's vision went white, and when it cleared, he was no longer sitting in Marston's car. He was in a cluttered living room, one he recognized but couldn't quite place. The shades were drawn and the air was stagnant. It took a moment for his eyes to adjust, and when they did, he saw a woman sitting in a recliner facing a television that wasn't turned on. Although her eyes were open, she wasn't moving, and when he stepped closer, he saw the crusty spittle and vomit around her lips and chin, saw the vacant look in her eyes and the lack of movement in her chest, and he knew she was dead. He also knew who she was.

Pamela Spivey.

This wasn't some misplaced memory. He hadn't seen her like this when she overdosed two years ago. Not in the chair. The boy had found her, called 911, and by the time Whaley arrived, paramedics were wheeling her out. He recognized that recliner, though. Seeing it at the time had made him think of his own La-Z-Boy perched in front of his television. The one he fell into for the occasional Red Sox game, or when he needed a football fix and was willing to stomach the one-man show that was Tom Brady. His chair was a happy place, and hers was anything but. Both nearly identical, yet complete opposites. He hadn't seen her almost dead in her chair, not then, not ever, so this wasn't that. He was someplace downriver. Marston had pulled him into the water and was showing him where the water would go.

Whaley didn't see the bullet hole in her head, not at first, not until he stepped halfway around the chair, somehow able to move in whatever this was. The wound was from a small caliber gun, probably a .22. The barrel had been pressed tight against her forehead when the trigger was pulled, he could tell that much from the burn marks. He didn't see an exit wound. Unlikely a bullet of that size would get back out. It was still in her head somewhere after bouncing around like a pinball, chewing up her life as it went. The gun was on the floor next to her chair, inches from her outstretched fingers.

Whaley tried to jerk his hand away, and for one brief second, he was back in Marston's car sitting beside him. His knee came up and hit the table with the tea, spilling it everywhere. Marston didn't seem to care. He only leaned closer and whispered a single word: *See.*

There was a rush of air—walls shifting, closing, changing. The car was gone, and he found himself standing inside the New Castle Police station, not in the lobby but in the small glassed-off vestibule that separated his officers from the public in the waiting area.

Sandy Lomax was sitting next to the radio, and Whaley's own words to her in the moments before he walked out of the historical society came from the tinny speaker—

"Keep her out front, I'll be right there."

He watched as Sandy stood and went to the glass partition. "Take a seat, Ms. Dubin. The chief will be back shortly."

Whaley peered through the glass at the woman standing in the lobby. She was in her late thirties and wearing a tan blouse and dark jeans. A black raincoat was neatly folded and draped over her arm. Her auburn hair was wet, matted to her head. She looked back at Sandy with intense green eyes. "I'm really pressed for time. Can you at least confirm for me Teddy Hasler is here?"

Sandy nodded. "He's in back finishing up dinner."

The woman followed Sandy's gaze to the door at the back of the narrow lobby, and for a second Whaley thought Laura Dubin was going to try and open it. The door was locked, always locked, and was reinforced with steel. If she tried it, she'd be disappointed. She didn't, though. Instead, she smiled and set her raincoat on one of the empty chairs. "Well, I suppose that will have to do, then."

"Excuse me?"

Laura Dubin reached for the chair closest to the door leading into the back, and with a soft grunt, pulled it in front of the door, tilting it just enough so the back caught under the doorknob. She then kicked both legs with the heel of her shoe, jamming it in place.

At first, Whaley thought she was trying to break the knob, the lock, but that would never work. The chair wasn't strong enough; she'd never get the leverage. Then he realized that wasn't the case at all; she wanted to block the door, prevent Sandy (or anyone else, for that matter) from getting into the lobby. With that door blocked, Sandy would need to exit her booth, cut through the interior of the police station, go out the back, and round the building to the front door.

Sandy pressed against the glass to get a better look, her face growing fearful. "Ma'am, what are you doing?"

Laura Dubin took a step back from the barricaded door, admired her work, then began shuffling through her pockets. "It would have been nice to see Teddy, maybe catch up for a few minutes. He and I haven't talked for years. Haven't *really* talked since we were kids. Seems like only a week ago we were teenagers." She snapped her fingers. "Goes by like that." She looked through the glass at Sandy. "Do you have any children?"

Sandy shook her head.

The smile returned to Dubin's face. "I suppose that's good. They change everything about your life. Every thought goes from me, me, me to them, them, them. Don't get me wrong, that's not bad, just different. Someone once asked me if I'd jump in front of a moving car to save my daughter, and that was an unequivocal yes, no hesitation. Ask me the same of my ex-husband and I'd probably push him into traffic, given the chance. No way I'd be willing to die for him, not now, not even in the beginning when we were all gaga for each other. Kids, though? No question. We'll do anything for them." Still rummaging through her pockets, she stopped. "You sure I can't see Teddy? Just for a second?"

Again, Sandy shook her head.

The woman shrugged and tucked a loose strand of damp auburn hair behind her ear. Those green eyes picked up the light, shone with it. "I guess I'll see him soon enough. Pam, too. It's like we're getting the band back together again. Playing all the old hits." She hummed a couple bars of some song Whaley didn't recognize.

A bead of sweat had broken out along Sandy's brow. She'd inched along the glass and was near her door.

Laura Dubin, lost in her thoughts for a moment, blew out a frustrated breath. "Oh, well. Promise me something, then?"

Sandy stared at her.

"Promise you'll take me back out there… after?"

Sandy gulped. Honest-to-god gulped loud enough for Whaley to hear.

Laura Dubin pulled a matchbook from her pocket and struck a match. "It's important we go back, or it doesn't work."

Sandy pressed her palm against the glass. "Don't!"

"The things we do for our children," Laura Dubin replied smugly.

Her arm swung to the side and she tossed the match to the chair holding her coat. The flame caught and burst out with a fireball, and Whaley knew her coat wasn't just wet from the rain; she'd soaked it in something flammable.

Dubin stood perfectly still, the smile never leaving her face as Sandy let out a scream.

Whaley was there, in the room with her, yet he wasn't. He couldn't grab her, couldn't push her through the exit. He couldn't bust the glass and attempt to put out the fire— he was a spectator, nothing more. He was in the car with Marston, and to remind him of that fact, Marston twitched his finger and searing pain radiated out from Whaley's palm, up his arm, and into his shoulder. Whaley knew the man's finger was in there deep, scraping against bone and cartilage, worming between tendons and muscle. He tried to pull away and couldn't. "What the hell was that?!"

Marston didn't answer that particular question. The unreadable slackness of his face betrayed nothing. "It's time to wade out into the water, Chief. Try not to swallow too much—I'd hate to see you drown. You don't want to leave the lovely Mary to deal with that tickle in her throat all alone. We mustn't forget dear Mary in all this."

Marston's finger twitched again. The pain that followed was worse than any Whaley had ever known. Not only did his vision go white again, but he thought for sure he'd pass out, and maybe he did—when things cleared, he was no longer in Marston's car. Marston's car was gone. He was standing behind his SUV in the gravel along the edge of Main Street in the rain, the historical society at his back. He turned to look at the sign—he had to, for the sake of his sanity—and it was as it should be. His hand wasn't, though. There was a deep gash in the center of his palm. He stared down at it for a moment, watched the blood pool in that hole, watched it drip down his fingers to the white gravel and taint the puddled water at his feet, his mind racing. His good hand was shaking as he tugged a handkerchief from his pocket. He was wrapping the wound when he spotted the smoke. Thin coils of white and gray rising up toward the heavens just around the bend on Main Street, stirring violently with the winds and rain of a storm that had come out of nowhere. An alarm started to wail—one he recognized as the old copper bell hanging above the door at the police station.

24

I MAY HAVE fallen asleep, or maybe I didn't. I'd be lying if I said my memories were clear. I remember Matty leading me back into the house in a daze. I remember the quiet that came when he closed the kitchen door and sealed the rain outside. I most definitely remember the looks I received when we walked past the others in the living room and went back up the stairs to the bunkroom. Kira in particular, like I'd disappointed her somehow.

I dropped down into the bunk where I'd previously been tied and even held my hands still as Matty secured the ropes. All of that was clear—things only grew fuzzy after he left. When I was alone.

I don't know if they kept me there for minutes or hours.

I got thirsty, but nobody came with water.

My stomach grumbled, reminded me I hadn't eaten in a very long time.

Mostly, I just sat there, lost in my own head.

At first, I listened, then I didn't want to do that anymore.

I kept hearing those sounds upstairs—the crack of furniture against the floor. A sharp cry. Then nothing.

I pictured Lily Dwyer locked in that oversize closet beating against the door with something, but so weak after all this time she could only manage a single swing. Crying out at her own failure. Quiet again after that as she reset and prepared to repeat when she found the strength. She was like someone trapped under a collapsed building tapping a metal pipe, repeating the same motion until it became automatic.

They'd turned the lights off again, at least upstairs. The darkness closed in around me like a musty old quilt.

There were footsteps, and maybe that was the strangest of all because they seemed to move up and down the hallway just outside the bunkroom. Dozens of them. They came up the stairs, paused at the lockers, then grew louder as they made their way to the open door of the room where I was tied. Then they'd vanish. Just stop.

The first time it happened, I thought it was the others coming for me. The second time I figured it had to be in my head. But by the third (and every time after), I knew the sounds were real, at least on some level. When I accepted that, I started to hear the whispers, male voices I didn't know, just outside my door. Anxious, hushed conversations. I thought of the sailors who used to live here—it was impossible not to—

and the Coast Guard staffers who came later. Generations of Geraldine Rote's family after them.

When left alone, the mind can either be your biggest asset or worst enemy. When mine began rattling off the possibilities, it became the single voice I no longer wanted to hear.

If a soul occupies a place, do parts of it soak into the wood? Like sweat or exhaled breaths? Where do those things go? Do the living own a place or are they simply borrowing from the dead?

Nobody had ever died here, Spivey had told us, but many had lived. What kind of impression does that leave behind? How much of that could a place hold? How long before it spills over the edge?

I thought of the large splinter in my palm, the one I picked up going down into the basement. I thought of how it tore into my flesh and stuck there. Had I gotten it all out? If not, if this house somehow had a piece remaining inside me, was it spreading? Like an infection?

Had we created something with our stupid games, or had something been here all along and simply awoken? The latter made far more sense, and no amount of hoping it wasn't true could change that.

When I listened closely to those voices, there was talk of Emerson.

Pleasing Emerson.

Feeding Emerson.

Hopes of something from Emerson in return.

I couldn't make out much more than that and didn't want to.

Upstairs—the crack of furniture again.

A short scream.

Silence.

Nothing but the relentless rain outside.

When those sounds came, the whispering stopped. Hushed. As if whatever was whispering heard it too, and when those voices came back (and they always did), they seemed even more anxious.

The footsteps came again immediately after, those things climbing the stairs, and I waited for them to come to the door and vanish as they had before, but this time they didn't.

The footfalls grew louder and louder, came up the steps, down the hall, and walked to the door, but this time there was a shadow there, a person, and I damn near screamed. If Kira hadn't switched on a flashlight, revealed herself, I certainly would have.

She stood there for a moment, her face filled with pity at the sight of me, then she crossed the floor and knelt at my side. She leaned so close I could smell her hair, and that familiar scent brought me back from whatever dark place I'd gone to, if only for a little while.

Her warm breath washed across my ear. "They can hear us."

The words were so soft I thought maybe I willed them into existence. I wanted to hear something that proved she was still on my side, and those four words were what my brain conjured, but as she leaned back, her lips brushed against my cheek and she gave me the gentlest of kisses at the corner of my mouth, and I knew they'd been real. The harshness of what she said next only reinforced that.

"I don't want Matty to hurt anyone, but he will. He said if you try to escape again, he'll use the gun—not on you, on one of the others, maybe even me. So please, don't try anything. We'll get through this, I promise."

She leaned behind me and untied the ropes, then said, "There's something they want me to show you."

25

EARLY IN HIS career, back when he was with the highway patrol, Whaley had once arrived at a traffic accident on 95, a rollover—the front left tire on a minivan had blown out, the driver lost control, rolled the van. Somehow, he got tossed or managed to scramble out on his own—his wife and eight-year-old son did not. When Whaley got there, he found the man standing about thirty feet from the destroyed vehicle, broken arm dangling at his side, blood running down from his head and face, just staring at the wreckage. Stunned. Clearly in shock. Unable to move. When Whaley ran up, asked him what happened, the man took out his cell phone and began snapping pictures. "For the insurance company," he had muttered. "They'll want these."

The wife and son had been wearing their seat belts and only had superficial wounds when Whaley and the paramedics pulled them out. Both had run up to the man, and although they hugged him, he continued to stare at what was left of their car. It took three people to get him into the back of an ambulance.

Whaley had seen people in shock many times during his career; not once had he been one of them.

Not until now.

He watched the smoke rise. Stared at the growing black cloud in the night sky above what had to be the police station, and found himself unable to move. Unable to process. The gears of his brain had seized up. He didn't understand what had happened, didn't want to understand what *was* happening, because if he was looking at smoke (and he was), that meant the other thing was true, too.

Pam.

Don't forget what he said about Mary. He knew about her cough. He somehow knew far more than he was willing to share. Sometimes a tickle in the throat was only that, sometimes it was much more, but that bastard knew.

The storm raged all around him. A dark, angry summer downpour. Ugly clouds rode in and tangled with the smoke like some kind of morbid dance, feeding the fire rather than helping to extinguish it, reveling in the destruction. Each rumble of thunder was a disjointed laugh, and Whaley knew in his gut something had been set free, something that had no business outside its cage.

Marston had shown him this either before it happened or during, neither of which was possible, yet he knew it to be true.

If not for the throb in his hand, he might have stood there for an hour, his brain attempting to unravel a puzzle that was far too twisted to solve. There was a throb, though, as if Marston's prickly nail was still in there. It gave him another twitch.

Wade into the water, Chief.

The radio on his shoulder squawked. *"Chief!?"*

Sandy Lomax.

He grabbed for the microphone with his good hand and nearly crushed the transmit button. "Jesus, Sandy, it's good to hear your voice. Tell me you're okay."

"It... it was that woman, she..."

"I know. Did you get everyone out?"

And don't ask me how I know. I don't want to tell you that part. Saying it aloud might make it real.

"It all happened so fast. I would have stopped her if I could. Accelerant, I think. I don't know. Must have been... old building... so much wood... my God, she just stood there, I—"

"Sandy," Whaley interrupted. "Did you get everyone out? Ted Hasler's locked up in back, can't get out on his own!"

He released the transmit button, waited for her response. Nothing came.

"Sandy?"

When she finally spoke again, her voice was distant. Despondent. *"He's gone, Chief. The fire moved so fast. I tried to follow protocols. All those times you ran drills. Should have been second nature, but..."* She dropped out for a second. *"... I got out of the booth and made it down the hall... wow, the smoke... I got to his door and it was locked. Took me a few seconds to find the right key, but it still wouldn't open. I could see him in there through the observation window, just sitting there, staring down at the floor. I shouted, and he looked up at me and..."*

"And what, Sandy?"

Static. *"I swear he mouthed the word* go. *Then he looked back down at the floor. Chief, I think he barricaded the door, blocked it, like that woman did in the lobby. Did I tell you that part? She used a chair, she—"*

"It's okay, Sandy," Whaley told her. "It wasn't your fault." His eyes were glued to the black cloud. It had grown from a small speck to a monstrous blanket covering a good portion of the island, roiling and churning. Thick bands of smoke tethered it to the ground. New Castle's fire department was housed in a building directly behind the police station, but it was a volunteer fire department and, like everything else, thinly staffed. The only siren he heard was coming from somewhere behind him. Most likely trucks dispatched from Portsmouth. He knew he shouldn't ask this next question over an open radio channel, but he did anyway— he had to know. "Sandy, is Ted Hasler dead?"

She responded immediately. *"I'm sorry, Chief. I couldn't get his door open, and the smoke got so thick. I tried, but..."*

Whaley pinched his eyes shut and let out a slow breath. "This isn't your fault, Sandy. Where are you now?"

When Lomax continued, she sounded like she was on the verge of tears. *"Across the street at Henry's. Chief, there's something else—Jolene Peterson said she saw Keith Spivey run around the side of the building about the same time the fire started. She saw him get in his Ford and drive off."* She went quiet for a beat. *"She thinks he was trying to get into the station from the back door, but that one is always locked."*

Why the hell would Keith Spivey—

Whaley heard Mrs. White's voice in the back of his head.

Those four were inseparable back then. Laura Dubin, Pam Rote—Pam Spivey now—her future husband, Keith, and Teddy Hasler. Inseparable, at least for a little while. I think they had some kind of falling-out.

Two dead, maybe three. Did Keith own a .22? Did he kill Pam and come for Ted? Was he running?

Whaley ticked the mic again. "Did Jolene say where he went?"

"South on Main, toward the swing bridge near Blunt."

That was the opposite direction from his house. The Wentworth Hotel was down that way, the Wentworth Marina too. Keith didn't own a boat, but he knew plenty of people who did. "Are you okay to work? If you can't right now, I understand, but I need to know."

There was nothing for a few seconds, then, *"I'm okay, Chief. What do you need me to do?"*

Whaley cleared his throat. "Set up there at Henry's until we figure out something better. We need to bring Keith in. Call the harbormaster, ask him to lock down the marinas. Then get Mark Lemmy on the line, have him put up the bridge in case Keith's trying to run by road. Radio Mundie and have him set up a roadblock on 1B heading into Portsmouth—make sure he can't get out that way either. Lock it all down."

"I haven't been able to raise Mundie in nearly a half hour. Last he called in, he was working on his boat. Nothing after that."

"Then get Rye PD to put up roadblocks. If he gets off the island, we may not find him. Maybe have Portsmouth PD watch for his truck at 95. If he's driving, he'll probably go for the highway."

Christ, if he got off the island, he'd be in the wind. Whaley ran his fingers through his thinning hair. Who was he kidding? He might already be gone. "Just get a county-wide BOLO out. That'll be faster."

Whaley almost told her to send an ambulance out to the Spivey house to check on Pam, but it would have to come in from Portsmouth General, and he could get there faster. He clicked the transmit button again. "Is the fire department there? Do they have it under control?"

"I don't know about under control, but they're doing what they can. The building is all wood."

Whaley let out a sigh. This couldn't be happening. "If the police station is a loss, tell them to shift focus and keep it from spreading. Hopefully this rain will help. I'll get over there as soon as I can."

"Understood, Chief."

Whaley was glad somebody did, because he certainly did not. All he was sure of was that the fire was the least of their worries. Thunder cracked and he shivered. A dull ache burned in his knee, his shoulder too. All his old football injuries waking with the weather, coming out to play.

Cinching the handkerchief around his damaged hand, he ignored the pain and rounded his SUV, fired up the engine, and switched on the lights and sirens as he swung out on Main, nearly clipping a Subaru as he skidded through a U-turn. The wipers did what they could, but the rain fought back—the thunder sounded a lot like the rumbling laughter of a hungry beast.

26

I FOLLOWED KIRA and the beam of her flashlight down the steps. Either the batteries were low or the bulb was near death, but the little illumination the flashlight cast off seemed to dwindle with each step. I didn't know why the lights were off, and when I asked Kira she didn't answer me, only gripped my arm above the wrist and pulled me along.

We stopped at the landing, the weak beam playing over the framed photographs hanging there. "Have you ever looked at these? I mean, really studied them?"

Like the staircase (and the basement, for that matter), they'd been gone when I was out here earlier with Whaley, nothing but blank spots on the wall where they'd hung. All were back again, as if they'd never left, and just the sight of those frames was enough to dial up the pain in my head.

From the living room behind us, I heard a body shuffle, then Izzie's thin voice. "There's a reason we're all here. It was never an accident, the six of us coming together in this place."

I turned toward her voice, but saw nothing. The room was black as oil, as if the walls were somehow able to eat light.

"Show him," Alesia's disembodied voice muttered from the dark. "But be mindful of the time."

"Nik nok to the extreme," Chloe said softly. That was followed by the strum of Spivey's guitar, three untuned notes ringing out from the far corner of the room, near the fireplace.

My eyes fought to adjust, but every time a shape started to come into focus, the darkness seemed to fold in, double down. Spivey was nearly on top of us before I even realized he'd stepped forward, barely a ruffling shimmer in the gloom.

From somewhere in the blackness, Matty said, "Come sit with me on the couch, Kira."

I heard his hand pat the cushion. I couldn't see him, but I had no trouble picturing the smug grin on his face.

Kira shot a dirty look toward the dark, handed the flashlight to Spivey, and told me, "Let him explain. It's better that way. I'll be right over there with the others. If I stay, it might…"

"Might what?"

"Spivey will explain," she repeated. Then a little softer, "I love you, Billy, remember that. Always remember that I'd do anything… for you."

The skip in her voice jarred me, and part of me thought she was speaking in some kind of code, hoping I'd understand and the others would not. Maybe I was dense, or more likely, my brain had reached capacity for bewilderment and mindfuckery. Either way, I wasn't sure what she meant. Her hand fell from mine and I let her go. She crossed the room soundlessly, and I lost her to the dark.

When I turned back to Spivey, he didn't face me. Instead, he raised the beam of the dim flashlight to the photographs and played the light over the frames—they had changed again.

The one of Chloe and Izzie lying out on the dock in their bathing suits was still there. So were most of the ones of Spivey as a child, though some of those were different. I wanted to believe they had been replaced—taken down and these new ones put up—but I knew on some level that wasn't the case. *They had changed.* The photographs were like a window, a glimpse, a means for the house to… what? Communicate? No, that wasn't right. I knew the answer, I just didn't want to admit it. On some level, I may have known the first time I'd stood in this spot—the truth was, the photographs were no different than a hunter displaying his trophies up on a wall.

Spivey tapped the picture of Izzie and Chloe. "The second those two stepped off the boat, it had them. There was no taking it back, no do-overs. They became property. Tokens." He swallowed. "Food for Emerson." His voice dropped a little lower. "I told all of you I didn't want them to come out here, but nobody listened. Marston had explained the rules. I thought they were utter bullshit, but he had told me about them when we went over the will, and it seemed stupid to take a risk until I at least had a chance to figure things out. Then they insisted on coming, I realized how ridiculous what Marston said was, and I dropped it. But Marston *knew* they'd been out there. Brought it up the next time I talked to him. Here's the thing—when he told me about Izzie and Chloe, he almost made it seem like some kind of joke, like Grams had just been superstitious or something, even gave me this *I won't tell if you don't tell* kind of conspiratorial wink. Felt like a dare, so I pushed it. Why not more people under sixteen? See what happens. That's about when the parties started."

I knew what he was getting at, because the pictures told the entire story. Many of the new ones were images of our friends from school, other kids I'd seen out at the house. He didn't have to tell me they were all under sixteen any more than he had to tell me every person under sixteen who had set foot out here was up on the wall. I figured that much out when I spotted a small sepia image in the upper right corner that had to be Patricia and William Whidden. They were holding hands, standing on the rocks, some version of an ancient New Castle barely visible across the water behind them.

Tokens.

Property.

Food for Emerson.

"It didn't start with me. It's been going on for a long time. This one is my father," Spivey said, pointing to a shot of a boy a few years younger than the two of us. He was standing on a fishing boat next to another boy. A face I knew too well.

My breath caught. "That's… my dad."

Spivey nodded. "He was friends with my mom—they both were. Alesia's mother, too. The three of them used to sneak out here to see her. They kept it from Grams somehow; she never knew." He tapped the photograph with the flashlight. "Do you recognize the boat?"

He knew I did, it was impossible not to. "*Merv*."

"*Merv*," he repeated. "Here's the thing. *Merv* was Lester's boat, and after he died, Grams kept it locked up in the boathouse, wouldn't allow anyone to use it. When I let you take it out, that might have been the first time it was in water in more than thirty years. There's no way she would have let two kids take it out fishing. This moment—them posing like this—it never happened. The pictures don't seem to work that way. They're not *real* moments. They're facsimiles. Emerson claims them, then drops them into some image, whether it actually happened or not. We figured that out with this one."

He pointed at another picture—Matty standing waist-deep in the water, one hand up on a rock. It might have been the same rock I thought I saw him sitting on with Kira that first night out here.

"Matty said he's never been in the water, not out here, not like this picture—his dad used to take him fishing out here when he was younger, and they came ashore to eat and poke around a few times. Said he was around ten the last time. He's older in this picture. I guess this is how the house sees him." Spivey scratched his thigh with the flashlight. The beam went wild for a second, then he brought it back up and settled on another picture at the top left. "That little girl, that's Alesia. Her mom brought her out a bunch of times. She'd pack a lunch and they'd make a day out of it. Told her they were going on an adventure. She *wanted* her out here. Brought her out as often as she could." He went quiet for a moment, studying a few more. "There's Kira. She used to kayak out here with her dad. She doesn't remember ever getting out of the boat and stepping on the island, but she must have, or she wouldn't be up here. She figures she's twelve here in the picture. She remembers that flower bathing suit, but if her pic is anything like the others, that might not be right either; that's just how the house remembers her."

I remembered that bathing suit. Light blue with pink blossoms all over it. She wore it one summer for one of my birthday parties. My mom had set up the sprinkler in the yard and we took turns running through the water. Spivey and Matty had been there, maybe five others.

Spivey pointed the light at a small 4x10 black and white image off to the left. "That one there is Benny. The parties weren't his first time out; he'd been here before. He doesn't talk about it, though. I'm not sure he remembers."

In the photograph, he was wearing a light shirt with suspenders holding up his pants.

Britches.

In Benny's time, they were probably called britches.

Benny's time. I didn't know where the thought came from. Looking back, I think the house put it there.

I thought of him outside, digging, even as the rain and thunder intensified. He couldn't stop.

In the closet upstairs, there was the loud crack.

The pain-filled cry.

Spivey pinched his eyes shut until it was over.

27

WHALEY'S SIREN LET out a final chirp as he skidded to a stop in the Spivey driveway. The storm clouds had opened up and it was coming down hard. Heavy drops that sounded like fists beating down on the roof of his cruiser, smacking the glass and making it damn near impossible to see. Keith's truck wasn't there—he could make out that much—and he thought he caught movement in the curtain of one of the windows near the front of the house, but couldn't be sure. Might have been the wind, might have been his imagination wanting to see something, because if Pam was home and able to peek out the window, that meant she was okay.

Blindly slamming the driver-side door behind him, he rounded his SUV and ran up the porch steps to the front door—his uniform was drenched, and three minutes in the car did little to change that. He wiped the wet hair from his forehead and beat on the door with the back of his fist. "Pam!? Open up! I know you're in there!" When no response came, he hit the door again. It rattled in the frame. "Goddam-mit, Pam! Let me in! I need to talk to you!"

I need to know you're alive.

When she still didn't answer, Whaley tried the knob and found it unlocked. He gave it a hesitant twist and pushed. The hinges groaned as the door swung open on the living room. With all the curtains drawn and none of the lights on, the small space was gloomy, smothered in shadows.

Pamela Spivey sat in her battered recliner facing a dark television set. Her face was ashy, and a pill bottle sat on the table beside her. She had made no effort to hide what she'd done—the cap was off, the bottle empty. Drool seeped from the corner of her mouth, the collar of her blouse damp with it.

No sign of a gun, but her wrists were bloody. Not cut (that had been Whaley's first thought, and thank God he was wrong about that), they were rubbed raw. The skin was chafed, worried away, as if she'd itched at them until the blood came. Nowhere near enough blood to be fatal, but it probably hurt like hell.

Marston's vision—if that's what it was—had been wrong about that.

As Whaley stepped into the room, he choked back the phlegm in his throat and pressed the transmit button on the microphone clipped to his shoulder. "Sandy? I need an ambulance out at the Spivey house."

Pam's head turned toward him, slow and loose, her neck barely able to support the weight. "No need for that." She raised a hand toward him, palm out. "I only took four. All I had left." The words were slurred. As she said *four*, she tucked her thumb in and proudly showed him the remaining fingers. "Four. That's all."

Whaley took a step closer. "Four of what?"

"The pink ones."

Pink cow.

U4.

Whaley knew them well. Not much of a problem near the coast, but terrible deeper inland, particularly around the New Hampshire lakes and up in the mountains. A form of synthetic opioid, worse than fentanyl.

Pam eyed the empty pill bottle and let out a soft chuckle. "Seems I need to find a new doctor before I can get a refill. Mine got himself buried in the drink."

Christ, she'd gotten them from Rory.

"You heard what happened?"

"Rory stepped into a steaming pile of shit instead of going around, is what he did."

Sandy hadn't responded to his call. Whaley thumbed the mic again. "Sandy, you there?"

Nothing. Sandy had her hands full.

Pam rolled her eyes toward him and her head followed. "I'm fine, Chief. No need for all that. I normally take six, sometimes eight when I'm tucked in for the night. Four ain't nothing but an appetizer with the kind of practice I got under my belt. Figured I'd soften myself up before Emerson decides to make a meal out of me too."

Emerson again.

And she didn't sound fine. Each word she spoke folded into the last: *Immafinechief. Noneedforalluvdat.*

He went into the kitchen and dialed 911 on the landline and got the automated system. While the recording droned on, he set the receiver down on the counter. They'd trace it when someone eventually picked up. Dispatch when nobody responded. "How about some coffee, Pam?"

Someone had made some. The pot was still half full. Looked like it'd been sitting there a while, probably tasted like shit, but that was better than nothing.

"That would be lovely, Chief. Like teatime between friends."

She grinned, thrilled with her little joke, but all Whaley could think about was the back of Marston's car. He could still taste the bitter swill the man had served him. He fumbled through the cabinets until he found coffee mugs. "Where's Keith?"

Pam looked around the empty room, as if realizing where she was and not exactly sure how she got there. "Not here, obviously."

Obviuzolee.

Whaley returned with the coffee.

There was something clutched in her hand—an old photograph of Spivey as a little boy, maybe four or five. The edges were frayed and torn. White creases marred the image, but there he was, looking up at the camera with those big, goofy eyes of his, his teeth bared in a grin.

Before Whaley could ask her about it, she said, "How much"—the words came out slow, stuck in the thick molasses of the drugs—"do you know?"

Whaley didn't hold back, he rattled it all off—what Carol White had told him at the historical society. Rory. Everything Marston had said and done and showed him. He told her those things not because she had a right to know—

(He supposed on some level she did, but it was police business, and he tried not to lose sight of that)

—but because listening seemed to animate her, pull her back from the drug-haze, and also because he needed to say it all aloud. He needed to hear it, somehow make it real. He told her everything. Slow at first, to be sure she could keep up, then faster as everything poured out. She nodded along at some parts, only stared for others, but she didn't seem to get lost, not once. Whaley didn't tell her about the fire, that Laura Dubin and Ted Hasler were dead, but he finished with what he'd seen in Geraldine Rote's will—the rules—the same rules written out on a board in that house for all to see upon entering because as he spoke, as he worked this all out, on some level he realized how important they were.

Pam drank the coffee as he spoke, seemed fascinated by the steam rising from the mug. When he finished, she clumsily set her cup down on the table beside her, next to the empty pill bottle.

"It helps that you know about the rules," she said, her voice still garbled as if her tongue was swollen. "My dear ol' mom didn't bother to share those with me until the day I took her grandson out there to meet her, then it was too late. Until then, I thought we were dealing with nothing but foolish kid bullshit. Glorified ghost stories meant to scare the piss out of each other. I wouldn't have taken him. God knows I wouldn't."

Tokens of less than sixteen years of age will be considered property.

"You mentioned something about that this morning at the deposition."

Her head bobbed in a rough facsimile of a nod. Her eyes moved with it, but on a delay, as if her head moved faster than they could. "My dad, Lester, he died before I was born. It was just the two of us, and growing up out there, Geraldine never let me have friends visit. A couple snuck out over the years, but not many. She always said it was too dangerous—all the rocks, the current, fast-rising tide—and the damn sharks. Always with the sharks. She told me…" Her voice trailed off and her gaze drifted to the floor.

"Pam?"

When she didn't respond, Whaley tapped her lightly on the cheek. Her skin was clammy. She looked first at him, then the mug on the table. "Maybe a little more?"

The mug was still half full, but Whaley went and got the pot anyway, topped it off.

Pam picked up the coffee and brought it to her lips, tilted it just a little too much; some dripped out the side of her mouth and down her chin. She managed about a quarter of the cup before setting it back on the table. She continued, her voice a little stronger. "… She told me once the water was a little warmer out there and that brought in the fish, the sharks right behind them. Goddamn eating machines." She lost her train of thought for a moment, then grabbed it again like the end of a kite string fluttering away in the wind. "She told me nobody—and I mean nobody—could come out, ever. She didn't care 'bout how that made people talk behind our backs. Didn't give a damn what other people thought, and why should she? " Pam waved her hand around in a lazy circle. "She never left that rock. Didn't have to hear it. I did, though, every day. I heard it in school. I heard it in the park. I heard it at the library and at the store. She might have been happy being a widowed hermit with Marston's minions shuttling groceries and the like to us, but I wasn't, and I sure as shit didn't want to be some teenage outcast, but that's what she made me. I hated her for that. *Hated her.* Didn't matter how good I did in school; I was always the freaky girl who lived out on a rock, the girl everyone loved to talk about."

Whaley caught a glimpse of the photograph in her hand and realized it had changed. How the hell that was possible, he didn't know, but it had. It wasn't Spivey, not anymore, and he didn't recognize the face, not at first. He had to peel away the years, the leathered, sun-beaten skin, the abuse and stress. The hair was thicker because the boy in the picture was much younger than the man he knew, just a teenager, but he recognized the eyes—the photograph had changed from an image of Spivey to one of his father. He was standing on the bow of a boat proudly holding up a large striped bass. Another man was standing next to him. Younger too, but he hadn't changed as much. Whaley had no trouble identifying him.

Ted Hasler. About the same age Billy was now, maybe a little younger.

Did she know he was dead?

Pam's fist closed around the picture. "Teddy was nice to me. One of the only ones. He and I might have had something, but then he wised up and kept his distance. My mom turned me into social poison ivy. I begged her to move. *Pleaded.* Just sell it all and buy a house someplace normal. She wouldn't hear it, though. I didn't know that she couldn't—she wasn't "allowed." Pam made loose air quotes when she said *allowed.* "Goddamn rules." She turned to him, her eyes wide but not as dilated as before. "Would you believe I had a full boat to UNH? Can you imagine?"

Whaley had known that.

Ted Hasler has actually been the one to tell him.

More years ago than he cared to remember, Whaley had just finished a shift and stopped in the Thirsty Moose to catch the end of the

Red Sox game. He'd found Ted on one of the stools. He'd had some kind of argument with his wife, nothing serious from what Whaley could gather, but enough to keep him from going straight home after leaving his office. He was still in the smaller one down on South Street at that point.

"Saddle up," Ted had said, smacking the stool at his side.

And Whaley had.

An hour and a half later, it was the bottom of the eighth, the Sox were down bad, and that one beer had gone on to many. A mischievous drunken grin found its way across Ted's face and he leaned close. "Hey, do you remember what Pam Spivey looked like back in the day? Back in high school?"

The Moose was a locals bar, and the owner knew where the butter on his bread came from, so he kept a collection of old yearbooks from Portsmouth High on a shelf behind the bar—dozens of volumes dating back to the fifties. Ted reached over, plucked out 1988, and flipped to a photograph of Pam without much trouble. Whaley remembered thinking Ted Hasler knew exactly what page to go to. He didn't comb through alphabetically or check some kind of index; he turned to that page like someone who had been there many times before and remembered how to get back. When his thumb landed on her picture, there was a longing on his face, one he didn't bother to hide.

"She was quiet. Didn't run with any particular social circle other than a handful of us, but she had a smile that went on for days. And these legs..." He caught himself there, remembered who he was talking to, and dialed it back. "She could turn a head and give you whiplash is what I'm trying to say."

The smiling girl in that photo looked nothing like the woman Whaley knew. He'd never seen Pam Spivey smile, not a real one. Never heard her laugh. She looked forty years older than the girl in the yearbook, even though less than half that time had passed since the picture was taken.

Ted Hasler rolled his thumb over her black and white chin. "The years stack up behind your choices, Chief. One day you might find yourself at a crossroad. Take a minute and think hard about which way you go before that next step. Some streets are like rivers, only flow one way. There's no going back."

Whaley had known there'd been something between the two of them around junior or senior year. Until that moment, he'd chalked it up to some forgotten high school fling, but the look in Ted's eyes (drunk or not) made it clear he still held a torch for her.

"Water under the bridge," Ted had said, closing the yearbook.

Wade into the water, Chief.

The memory of Marston's voice brought Whaley back, and he found himself standing in the Spivey living room, Pam in her recliner. She looked like she was completing her own stroll down memory lane. She cleared her throat and her gaze fell to the empty pill bottle. "Full boat to UNH and Mom—Geraldine—didn't want to hear any part of it. She shot the idea down as soon as I dropped the envelope on the dinner table. Turned what I thought was one hell of an announcement into the argument to end all arguments. She said I couldn't go off to school. Said there was plenty of money and no reason. I wouldn't have to work. Didn't have to worry about none of that. She didn't get why I wanted to leave. Didn't understand how much I wanted to get away from the whispers behind my back and just start somewhere new. This wasn't about money or security. When I tried to tell her that, she shut me down. Even threatened to pull me from high school and make me finish up my last few years with a tutor on the island. I felt like a damn prisoner. On some level, I think I hoped Teddy would save me. Get me out of there. But he walked away instead. If Keith hadn't come around, I don't know what I would have done. He was a…" She drifted again, searching for the right words. "A knight in dented armor. He's always meant well, I suppose."

She turned the photograph back over and Whaley expected to see Keith, but it was Spivey again, same as before.

Had he imagined it?

No.

He saw what he saw.

"Why didn't you just leave?" Whaley asked, trying to shake it off. "Run away and go to college? You had a scholarship, so you didn't need your mom's money, right?"

Pam huffed. "Oh, I tried right after I finished high school. Geraldine and me had ourselves another scream-fest and I packed a bag, got in Keith's boat, and we motored off without looking back. Little good that did me. We got about halfway across the harbor when I felt the house pulling at me. It was downright painful when I stepped off the boat onto the dock. And when we got in Keith's car and drove off, we didn't even make it halfway across the bridge into Portsmouth before I was screaming for him to stop and turn back around. None of that had ever happened before—not when I went shopping or went off to school. Those times, the house knew I was coming back, so it let me go. Allowed me that time away. Running, though, that was different. Couldn't let that happen. Couldn't let me go. Anyone under sixteen who goes out there is considered property—that's in the rules—but when you're born out there, like I was, you're a different kind of token. You're his from the get-go."

28

SPIVEY RECOVERED, BUT he was visibly shaken, and he'd gotten worse each time we heard that sound upstairs. That was a good thing. It meant he wasn't altogether gone. If I made a play for the gun, there was a chance I could count on him to back me up. I wanted him to give me a sign, drop some word or phrase to confirm that was the case, but if he did, I didn't catch it. He pinched his eyes shut for a moment and did his best to shake it off. I could tell he couldn't, and then he went on, doing his best to mask the quiver in his voice.

"The pictures change," he said. "We think it has something to do with whoever is standing here. You might see something different if you were standing here alone, something else if Kira were with you instead of me… that sort of thing. The house seems to know I'm the current Caretaker, and it shows me the most, same with anyone standing here with me."

To prove his point, he stepped away, back toward the living room. My eyes followed him, if only for a second, but when I turned back to the wall, only about half the photographs of people were still the same. The others had somehow morphed into landscape shots. Another showed *Annabelle* from a distance climbing a tall gray wave surrounded by churning surf.

From behind me, somewhere in the gloom of the other room, Spivey spoke loud enough to be heard over the storm. "All of us had been out here at some point as children—tokens under sixteen. It's had us ever since, we just didn't know it. Some of our parents too, and thanks to those stupid parties, a bunch of our friends."

"The parties were necessary," Alesia broke in. "We needed more. *He* needed more."

"Food for Emerson," Chloe said. "Emerson had to be fed."

"*To save Spivey,*" Alesia corrected her. "This isn't all about Emerson."

"That's not all of it," Kira countered, and I wanted to see her, but couldn't. "If you're gonna tell him the truth, tell him *all* the truth."

Alesia said, "We give Emerson what he wants, and he gives us something in return. Something glorious."

"Glorious." Matty huffed. "Fuck that. We get rich, bro. Never want for money or anything else. Marston said we'd all be set for life, not just Spivey. And not a regular life, *a long-ass life*. Like we live on forever kinda life."

"And you believe him?"

"You don't? I knew you wouldn't." Matty shot back, then grunted. "That's why we kept you out of it. You're fucking clueless. Everything you've seen and you still don't get it." He paused for a second, and I could picture him shaking his head in the dark. "Our folks made a deal of their own when they were our age, not as sweet as ours, but they made one. Their folks before them. Someone else before them. Why do you think they've all done so well with their lives? Think their MFAs got it done? Smart business sense? Hell no. They all sat right here, in this house, and had themselves a good talking-to with Marston about Emerson and came to an agreement. A little give and take. We pulled one better, though. When our turn came, we brought in a ringer to negotiate on our behalf."

"A ringer?"

"Alesia's mom," Matty replied. "She'd been there, done that, understood where her little group had gone wrong, spent nearly her entire life going over all the details, then stepped up when it was time for her little girl and the rest of us to take a turn. She worked out a sweetheart deal. We finish this and we're all set, not just Spivey."

From somewhere in the dark came Izzie's voice, timid and thin. "We'll never be sick. Never grow old. We'll want for nothing."

"My mother spent a lifetime preparing," Alesia said. "She dedicated every spare second learning all there was to know about Emerson, this place, those who came before. She determined what was necessary to capture Emerson's gift. When she learned it was too late for her, she taught me. Gave me a roadmap, instructions."

"All of Project Poltergeist," Chloe chimed in. "All our preparation. Everything has led to tonight. What is to come."

"It's all ours for the taking," Alesia said. "Only one final step remains."

Upstairs came the thump again.

Lily's cry.

Then quiet, and I knew—

Lily Dwyer.

Fifteen years old.

Probably a virgin.

The token of all tokens.

Benny's hole in the basement.

They'd bury that poor girl down there with all the other dead things.

Matty said something else, but I couldn't hear him over the buzzing growing in my ears, the blood and adrenaline rushing through my body, my heart pounding to keep up. My brain was on overdrive and it spat out another thought, one even worse than the others.

Spivey had said they'd all been out to the island at some point when they were kids, under sixteen—that's how *they* became food for Emerson—and the house had pictures to back that up. They were all up on the wall—all but one.

There wasn't a single photograph of me.

I'd never been out to Wood Island. Not with my folks. Not with my friends. Not until Spivey inherited it.

What exactly did that make me?

What was I to Emerson?

Then something else clicked.

I remembered what Alesia had said in the basement when she'd mixed up everything in her bowl, when she'd cast that first spell—

It is those of us who willingly volunteer who welcome you most.

My dad had often told me the true meaning of a legal document wasn't necessarily in what was written—sometimes what wasn't written was equally important. Sometimes more. The implied. The words between the text. Geraldine's will said:

Tokens of less than sixteen years of age will be considered property.

It didn't specifically rule out those over sixteen, only claimed those under were property by default. What did that mean for people over sixteen who came out here? *Who came out here willingly?* That was what I had done, right? Maybe not this last time, but all the others. I wasn't forced. I'd come out because I was asked. Some might say I'd volunteered.

It is those of us who willingly volunteer who welcome you most.

If the others were all tokens, what exactly would Emerson give for something, *someone*, he could not take on his own?

From deep in the dark, from his spot on the couch next to Kira, I heard Matty click back the hammer on the gun. "Now he's getting it."

"It's time we go downstairs," Alesia whispered.

I tried to run.

I bolted past Spivey toward the door, but Matty was faster. How the hell he got off that couch and over to me so quickly, I'll never understand, but he did. He slammed into me with the full weight of his body. The air left my chest and my head cracked hard against the wall. If not for the previous hit, I might have recovered fast enough to fight back, but my head struck in nearly the same spot Matty had hit me with the gun—my vision clouded and the world tilted. I caught a glimpse of Matty raising a balled fist and Kira screaming out, "Don't hit him a—"

29

WHALEY COULD ONLY listen as Pam continued.

"Keith and I fully intended to run off to Boston that first night, further the next, maybe all the way to California, but we never made it off New Castle. We tried a bunch of times, but I got so sick I thought I'd die."

Outside, the storm raged. The Spivey house creaked against the wind. The wood frame rattled like old bones. The rain was hypnotic, and Whaley forced his mind to block it all out and focus on Pam's voice. She paused only long enough to string her next thought together, grab the words out from behind her drug-induced haze.

"I was eighteen at that point, absolutely hated my mother, and had no intention of talking to her again. As far as I was concerned, she was no longer my mother. I blamed her. I suppose if I had gone back, she might have told me what was happening—maybe thought me old enough to hear the truth—but I didn't go back and that conversation never happened. I just felt terribly sick all the time and didn't understand why. I knew it got worse the further away I went, but I didn't understand that either. I wanted to leave and I couldn't. I understood that much. Ultimately, I moved in here with Keith and most of the sickness faded. I suppose that place realized I was close and loosened its grip. I made it a habit to visit the Commons and look out at Wood

Island a few times a week, and that somehow made me feel better, too. I fell into that; like being close was some kind of treatment. Then life happened. I made no attempt to contact Geraldine, and she didn't contact me. She knew where to find me. I let it go at that. Days turned into weeks and months, then years."

Although Pam's hands trembled, she reached for the coffee mug on her own this time and drank. When she returned it to the table, her limbs still seemed weighted down, but she became slightly more animated as she spoke.

Her fingers played over the edges of the photograph.

Whaley wanted her to flip it over, wanted to see, but she didn't.

"David being born was a turning point for me," Pam continued. "I was young, only twenty. Maybe it was hormones, or just 'cause some time had gone by, but I wanted my mother to be part of things, to see her grandson. Two years had slipped away; I guess that softened the hate. Keith had been pushing me to try and patch things… So one Sunday, I bundled Baby David up, we got in Keith's boat, and motored across the harbor." Pam smiled and looked down at the back of the photograph, at her empty arms. "David was so small, but he was everything to me. I remember singing to him on the trip out, feeling like some horrible weight was coming off, lifting with each inch closer to that place—the sun was out, the weather was beautiful, the goddamn birds were singing like a fucking Disney movie. When we motored up to the dock and tied down, I just knew everything would be okay."

Pam fell silent. Her eyes went moist with tears, and she wiped them away on the sleeve of her sweater.

"We found Geraldine around the side of the house in her garden. When she first saw me, she was smiling too, then she saw the bundle in my arms, saw David's tiny hand and fingers poke out and reach for my face, and she went pale. She'd been holding a potato, just dug it out, and I remember her grip opening and that potato falling to the ground. Her mouth dropped with it. At first, nothing came out, then there was this scream. The most horrific, gut-wrenching, like someone just cut off her hand scream, and she pointed. She pointed at little David, my little Spivey. 'Go! Leave! No!' She shrieked it out, over and over. Chased us back to Keith's boat repeating those words. Kept screaming as we motored away. We were gone and halfway across the harbor back to New Castle, and I wasn't sure it happened at all. It couldn't have been real, but it was. Didn't see her again for eight years. She came here—no invite, no nothing—just showed up. And that's when she told us. Explained everything."

"Thanksgiving," Whaley muttered.

"David told you?"

He nodded. "The day Geraldine died and I went to get him at school."

Pam thumbed the edge of the photograph. Whaley only caught a glimpse, but it *had* changed again. No longer Spivey. No longer Keith. He only saw the fender of a car and part of a leg, someone sitting on the hood, before her hand covered it back up.

Whaley wanted to snatch the picture and turn it over, but the voice in the back of his head told him if he did that, the new image would be gone and only Spivey would be there. He cleared his throat. "What exactly is Emerson?"

Pam shrugged loosely. "Fuck if I know. Goddamn devil. Death. He infected that island a long time ago, the house… makes promises others have to keep. He's a disease on that place." Her eyes grew wide and her face filled with a mix of awe and fright. "That island, the house, that place, it will give you whatever you want, *whatever you want*—money, fame, love, friendship, health—but it also takes. It's not shy about carving out its pound of flesh in return. It's like there's a scale, and if Emerson gives you something, something of equal value must be given to him in return. But he's… he's hungry, he thrives on what you give him, wants to eat, has to eat, but can't… just eat. Do you understand? In order for him to eat, he has to give you something first; what he receives must be in return. Never the other way around. So he offers, he tempts, he takes…"

Emerson must not famish.

Whaley tried to wrap his head around this. "But Emerson is not Marston. Marston is not Emerson. They're not the same?"

She shook her head. "No. Emerson is a thing. An *it*. Marston is the asshole holding Emerson's leash, that's who he is. A leech. Best I've been able to figure out is his family latched on to whatever Emerson is generations ago and haven't let go. They keep one foot in the real world, the other on the back of whoever owns the island, and survive on the scraps."

The Caretaker.

That's what Geraldine's will called it.

With Marston as the Caretaker's Personal Representative.

This time when Pam reached over to the table, she didn't pick up the coffee mug, but instead wrapped her hand around the empty pill bottle and looked inside as if hoping she'd missed one or ten. When none magically appeared, she tossed the empty bottle across the room. It skittered over the hardwood floor and under the couch. Then she spotted one, a lone pink pill in the corner of the table. She scooped it up, popped it in her mouth, and swallowed before Whaley could stop her. The change in her was almost instant. Her entire body went limp, and the muscles of her face seemed to melt.

"Five minutes on that island was all it took; it laid claim to my son. Already had me and my mother. Took my dad and my grandparents and who knows how many others before, but that wasn't enough—had to have Spivey too. I didn't want to believe Geraldine when she told me that part. I even denied it when Spivey first got sick— told myself it was a coincidence. Then Marston started coming around and I knew." She looked up at me. "He gave Spivey a ride home from school once about two years ago, did he tell you that?"

Whaley shook my head.

"Two years ago, September. He usually rode with Billy Hasler, but Billy had the flu or something and stayed home sick. Marston's got this old Jag, black. I remember hearing it in the driveway, this low rumble, and I looked out the window. They sat there for about five minutes, then Spivey got out and Marston drove off. He wouldn't tell me what they talked about, but I knew. Emerson had cashed in his chip and Marston was there to deliver the news. That next night I... you know."

Pam OD'd.

Fentanyl with a Jack Daniels chaser.

But that didn't make sense. "Wait, two years ago? Spivey's known about all this for two years?"

"Oh, I think Spivey's known something from the first moment he got sick. He's no different than me when I tried to leave. The cancer's eating him from the inside out. He steps away, it gets worse. Out there, he's just fine. Why do you think Marston said they need to draw his blood while he's on the island? He's right as rain as long as he's in that goddamn house. That's the special treatment he mentioned this morning in court. Sooner or later, it will use him up like it does everyone else. Or maybe he'll just get fed up, wander into Henry's one day like Geraldine did, and drop dead when it all comes rushing back." Her eyes went wide and she glared at him. "You'll find him back out on that rock after that. I bet Geraldine's already out there. The two of them will keep a spot warm for me too."

Nobody dies on that island, but that doesn't mean they don't come home. In the end, we all come home. In the end, that's all we can do.

Pam's hand went back to the table, to the place where the pill bottle had been, and her fist closed on empty air. "This isn't right." Her body tensed.

"What isn't?"

That last pill hit her hard. Pushed her over some kind of edge. She looked around, a frantic gleam cracked into her eyes as if she just snapped awake. "This is all wrong. All of it. I don't want to be awake," she told him. "Not for what comes next."

"What comes next?"

She'd been lucid only a moment earlier, but now her eyes glazed over and her face went slack. Pam looked around the empty house again. Her finger twitched on the edge of the photograph. "They're all dead. As dead as me. He gave 'em a taste, and they'll want more. That's where it starts and how it ends. Always." Her head lolled toward Whaley. "It got its grip on you too. I can smell it on you. You saw it without its mask on, and now it wants you bad." She realized something and it jolted her awake, if only for a second. "It got Teddy, didn't it?"

There was no reason to lie to her. Whaley nodded.

Her eyes filled with tears and fell away from him.

Whaley gave her a moment, then told her what happened.

Pam's face grew tight at the mention of Laura Dubin, filled with harsh lines. As he spoke, her head slowly shook back and forth. "Greedy, selfish bitch... even when we were kids, when we started piecing things together, she never considered the consequences. I swear to this day, she knows more about what was happening out there than I did, and she played dumb. We all thought we were figuring things out as a group, but that wasn't the case at all. She was always one step ahead, steering the ship. The first time Teddy and Keith came out, it had been her idea. We were all fourteen. She knew what it meant, I'm sure of that, but she didn't tell anyone. Teddy and I talked about it once, years later. He said she was all nonchalant about it—'Let's go see Pam. We'll sneak by Geraldine, it'll be fun '—like some Friday night casual social call, but she knew. She condemned the three of them with that trip—on purpose. That was her snuggling up with Emerson like some girls flirt. Making good on a promise. Every time she came out, she was laying groundwork. The rest of us were clueless at the start, and by the time we figured out enough of it and I got the good sense to keep her away, it was too late. That Thanksgiving, when Geraldine and I had our little talk, I told her about Laura Dubin, Teddy, and Keith coming out, and I swear she nearly stopped breathing. She explained about the Caretaker, how only the Caretaker benefited from whatever Emerson had to offer, said what Laura Dubin was trying was pointless, would never work. So you know what Laura did?" Pam looked at Whaley with glassy eyes. "She got her daughter to get her nails dug in nice and deep in my boy.

She's collecting from Emerson by proxy. She's a bottom-feeder, just like her mother… Fire, you said? That's how she did it?"

Whaley nodded.

"She always fancied herself a witch. I'm surprised she didn't tie herself to a stake before dropping the match. God only knows what thoughts she's been whispering into her daughter's ear all these years."

Whaley kept thinking about his wife Mary at home, that cough of hers. The cough that was probably nothing but might be something. Marston hadn't brought it up just to rattle him; he'd been making an offer. You *stop* scratching my back, and I'll scratch yours. He couldn't make that offer though, could he? If what Pam had told him was true, Spivey would need to…

Stop. He couldn't let his mind go there. Couldn't let those thoughts creep into his head. Because if Mary was sick and this Emerson thing could change that, it would want something in return, and he couldn't live with that. He couldn't… Stop! Just stop, dammit. Whaley raked his hair and forced himself to keep focused.

"How do we stop all this?"

This brought on a sour laugh. "You don't stop it. You don't end it or even interrupt it. It just *is*. It *was* long before we all found it, and it *will be* long after we're all buried out there under the sand and dirt when it calls us home. Best you can hope for is it chokes on your soul when it eventually swallows."

Her words were slurred again. She was drifting off. Or maybe something worse.

I normally take six, sometimes eight when I'm tucked in for the night. Four ain't nothing but an appetizer with the kind of practice I got under my belt.

She had five, and maybe she lied about the rest. Her eyes rolled up into her head and went white.

Whaley gently smacked her cheek with the palm of his hand again. "Pam, where's Keith?"

"I don't want to be awake," she muttered, then repeated, "not for what comes next."

He slapped her again, a little harder. "Pam, I need to know where Keith is."

Her eyes opened lazily, thin slits. "Keith went to make a trade. Silly fuck thinks he can make some kind of switcheroo. Her for Spivey. It'll just take 'em both, though. Gobble 'em right up. Emerson don't care about her."

When Pam said *her*, her head bobbed toward the closed door of the back bedroom—an addition Keith had built on to the house years ago meant to be a guest room, but in reality, it had become a catch-all for random clutter.

Whaley quickly crossed the living room and opened the door. Watched it swing open into the room. His eyes locked on a twin bed surrounded by boxes.

The bed was empty.

Two ropes were tied to the headboard. Two more at the foot. A half-eaten sandwich was on a paper plate on the floor. There was a bucket too, and Whaley didn't have to look to know what was inside; he could tell from the smell.

Lily Dwyer had been in there.

In that very room.

"Where did he take her, Pam?"

When she didn't answer, he turned back around and asked her again—louder this time.

He had no idea where Pam had gotten the gun. He'd looked for it when he first got there, and she hadn't been holding it—he'd studied every inch of the room. It hadn't been there, but she had it now—Pam Spivey had a .22 pressed against her forehead, her fingers squeezing the grip tight enough to turn them white.

The word came out of her as nothing more than a garbled mess, but it was enough. Whaley understood.

"I'll see you out there, Chief. We all go home."

The shot was nothing more than a pop. The recoil sent her hand jumping back, the gun clattering to the floor. Her head dropped to the side. All of it over in under a second. Whaley hadn't moved, and he'd spend the rest of this short life wondering if he could have gotten to her if he'd tried. Four or five steps at the most, but he hadn't taken one. He'd froze. He remained frozen. Even in that moment, he couldn't bring himself to go to her. He'd caught a glimpse of the photograph as it slipped from her hand and fell to the floor, and that image had stopped him in his tracks.

The car was a '65 Mustang convertible. White with red trim. Chrome polished to a high glint under the sun. Sitting on the hood, a big shit-eating grin on his face, was a boy around twelve, maybe thirteen.

Whaley knew that car.

He knew that boy.

He also knew the picture couldn't possibly exist.

30

WHEN I CAME back around, we were in the basement.

The scent of rot was so thick I could taste it. The air was heavy and moist and so filled with death that I wouldn't have been surprised to open my eyes and find myself sealed in the Vaughn family tomb out at Point of Graves Cemetery, or in a pine box buried under a blanket of dirt with nothing but my own bloody scratch marks and stale breath as company.

The others were oily shadows as they moved around. Candles burned, but like upstairs, the flames were no match for the dark, just thin pricks of pale orange light fluttering on still, lifeless air heavy with slow-moving dust.

My chin was planted firmly against my chest, and when I finally willed my head to lift, my shirt stuck to my skin for a second before falling away. They'd propped me up in the chair next to the furnace and secured my hands and feet to the frame with duct tape. Another piece of tape covered my mouth, and when I tried to breathe, the globs of snot in my nose kept all but the thinnest trickle of air from getting through. I needed more. I sucked in, hard, and nearly choked on whatever caught in my throat.

"You need to take the tape off his mouth—he can barely breathe," Kira said from somewhere in the dark. "What if he throws up or something? That could kill him."

Matty's face appeared in the gloom, an inch from mine. He placed a hand under my chin and lifted my head so my eyes met his. "Tape stays on."

"Kira's right. It's not like anyone can hear us down here."

This came from Izzie. I couldn't see her, but she sounded close.

My eyes felt heavy, didn't want to stay open. They were nothing but slits when I caught a bright flash to my left. I forced them back open and glimpsed Alesia lighting another candle. "We don't need him shouting out random bullshit during the spell. Keep his mouth covered."

"Can I hit him again if he tries?" Matty beamed. "That was fun."

"You're a fucking Neanderthal," Kira muttered.

Matty's large shadow crossed in front of me. He flexed his arm. "You know it. That's why you love me."

"You wish."

"We don't want him dying yet, so no more hitting," Alesia interrupted, her voice flat. She'd moved off to the other side. I couldn't see her anymore. "Someone keep an eye on him. If he yaks, yank the tape off so he can spit it out, then put it back on."

"Eww." Chloe groaned. "Not it."

"Me either," Izzie echoed.

Their voices moved all around me. I had trouble getting a fix on any of them. I felt like I was wading through the thick muck of a dream.

"He's not going to throw up." Kira again. Right next to me now. "I'll watch him." She gently stroked my cheek with her palm. "Wake up, baby."

We don't want him dying yet.

That's what Alesia said. *Yet.*

My head lolled to the right—that's when I saw Benny's hole a few feet away.

The shovel was still there, along with several empty buckets, but the hole itself had been filled in. There was no mistaking where it had been—the packed mound next to the shovel made that very clear.

Lily. Poor Lily.

The furnace burned to my left. The door over the pilot light was partially open, the blue flame dancing, casting off a godawful heat far more intense than it should have been. A half-empty box of matches sat just below the pilot light's small door on a metal ledge. Discarded matches and several empty boxes littered the ground. The rest of the basement was dark. Candles were burning everywhere, but it was like the basement fed on the light. Gobbled it up before it could spread.

Matty reappeared in front of me, barely a shadow. He lowered the gun to his side and cleared his throat. "Before you say anything, I want you to hear me out. I know you. You're a moral Boy Scout, always have been, and every part of you is probably screaming right now, telling you we're doing something horrible, you've got to stop us, you need to end it, blah, blah, blah. Put all that aside and just listen. Can you do that?"

I only looked at him. I wouldn't give him the satisfaction of any kind of acknowledgment. Not while he had me taped to a goddamn chair. How could I say anything with my mouth sealed up?

Matty didn't seem to care; he leaned closer. "I can tell you, without a doubt, there is life after death. We've proven that. You don't have to believe me—you'll see soon enough. It's real. Project Poltergeist worked. Not only did we figure out how to open that door, we figured out how to close it, and…" He let that last word hang, he chewed on it a second. "We figured out how to move through it. We never would have cracked that nut without Alesia and her mom. *Especially her mom…* without her, we'd still be fumbling around in the dark. This place has always been powerful, but a battery is useless by itself. You need to attach it to something, harness that power. Alesia's mom taught us how to do that. She taught us that and so much more."

I turned away from him and glared down at Benny's hole. I could picture Lily down there, eyes wide, her face frozen in a terrified scream, mouth filled with dirt.

Matty reached for my chin again and turned my head back toward him. "I don't know what's going through your head, but you might want to rein it in. You're looking sick."

"He probably has a concussion." Kira stroked the side of my face. "Can I give him some more water? Or maybe some food?"

Behind him, Alesia came into focus. She was busy lighting candles around the pentagram in the middle of the basement floor. Whatever was at the center was covered with a black cloth. "He doesn't need anything. This will all be over soon enough."

A grin spread across Matty's face. "Show him what you showed me yesterday?"

Alesia paused. "What, this?"

She held her hand out a few inches from her chest, fingers splayed straight, then slowly lifted her hand higher.

The room grew brighter.

Either the gloom relented or the candle flames somehow burned more intensely, but the entire basement became brighter, like she had adjusted some invisible dimmer switch. The pentagram came into focus. Chloe and Izzie were both sitting where they had the last time I'd been down here. Matty crossed to the back of the room and leaned up against the concrete wall of the cistern.

I spotted Spivey sitting about halfway up the steps, cradling his guitar. His fingers slipped over the strings, but there was no sound.

"Not that," Matty replied, unimpressed. "The other thing."

Alesia dropped her hand, lit another candle, and sighed. "Seriously? Why do we need to prove anything to him?"

"I want him to see what he's missing, that's why. Real fast. It will just take a second."

She lit the final candle on the pentagram, shook out the match, and tossed it against the wall behind the furnace. "Okay, but only for a second."

Matty beamed at me. "Wait till you see—this shit is crazy."

Alesia kicked off her tennis shoes and dug her toes into the dirt, kneaded them until her bare feet were buried nearly to her ankles. Then she closed her eyes and drew in a deep breath. She began mumbling something, her voice so low I couldn't make out the words. I'm not sure it was even English.

An icy breeze slipped across my cheek, and the dust in the room stirred. The basement had no windows, so I knew the wind wasn't coming from outside, but even then, after all I'd seen, my mind searched for some logical explanation, at odds with the other half of my brain, which knew there wasn't one. The candle flames leaned, and at first, I thought it was the wind bending them, sending them nearly horizontal, but if that were the case, they'd all be leaning in the same direction. They were not. Instead, the tips of each flame bent toward Alesia, seemed to reach for her. And that's when the impossible happened.

At first, I thought Alesia had simply pulled her feet out from under the dirt, then I realized that wasn't the case at all. Her feet had risen out of the dirt along with the rest of her. Her entire body rose. In those first seconds, it was barely perceptible—she might have been pushing up off the floor, standing on her toes, some trick or weird angle making it appear she was rising—but then her feet weren't on the ground at all. There was half an inch between her toes and the dirt, then an inch, then two. I watched in awe as Alesia drifted gently higher, her lips still moving, her face marred in concentration. Six inches. Twelve. Two feet. Three. When it became clear her head was about to hit the rafters above, her body began to tilt—her head and upper torso rolled toward us, her feet away. She kept her arms pinned at her sides until she leveled off.

Alesia Dubin was floating.

"There's no wires," Matty whispered. "No mirrors, no bullshit hocus pocus. She's really doing that."

"And it's not easy," Alesia said, loud enough for us to hear. "So I'm coming back down. But I want to try something first."

Her face twisted in deep concentration and she drifted lower, came down about halfway, then she pulled her legs up, tucked her knees tight against her chest, and did a complete somersault like an astronaut in zero gravity. When she righted herself, she stretched her legs out straight and gently settled to the ground. Alesia eyed her shoes, must have decided she didn't need them, and kicked them off to the side.

"Oh, man! That was even better than last time!" Matty looked back at me. "Did you see that?! *Did you see that?*"

From their places on the ground, Chloe and Izzie both stared up at her in complete awe. Chloe's mouth fell open and she gripped Izzie's arm. Up on the steps, several notes floated out from Spivey's guitar.

"Wow," Kira said in a hushed tone. She was still standing beside me with one hand on my shoulder.

Alesia was smiling. She tilted her head, curtsied, and rolled her hand through the air. "Ta da."

"You need to teach me that," Matty said.

"Me too," Chloe added.

Alesia looked down at her wrist again, at the watch that wasn't there. "If we don't get moving, none of us will be doing anything. Who's got the rag?"

"I do." From the side pocket of her jeans, Chloe pulled out a stained rag. The rag I'd used to stem the bleeding from that big splinter a few weeks back. The one I caught on the railing coming down here.

Alesia took it from her and sniffed. "It should work, but it's not fresh. I'm not sure I want to take chances." She looked up at Spivey on the steps. "Is that steak knife still down here somewhere?"

31

WHALEY DIDN'T KNOW how long he stood there, unmoving, a thick lump growing in his throat that was unwilling to clear, even when he remembered to swallow. The house had grown inexplicably quiet following the gunshot—no steady tick of clocks, no hum from the refrigerator, no pop or gentle click as the wood frame settled in place, as old houses were wont to do. Whaley heard nothing but the wind outside and the rain beating down on the metal roof like fistfuls of gravel tossed from the heavens. He heard nothing but a gentle sigh as the last bit of air exited Pam Spivey's body and she slumped in that chair for the last time. Or maybe that sigh had come from him; he wasn't sure. He couldn't feel his fingers or toes or anything else. His body felt as foreign to him as the gun on the floor. The thin wisp of smoke rising up from the barrel filled the room with a metallic sulfur odor.

He hadn't moved, not because witnessing Pam's suicide had paralyzed him, as horrible as that was, but because his gaze was locked on the photograph, his mind struggling to make the least bit of sense from it.

The boy.

The car.

Whaley felt a pain in his chest, a tightening in his lungs, and he forced himself to breathe in deep. A long, full gasp of air in through his mouth. He held it for a moment, then let it out through his nose. Forced his body to relax even though it wanted to do anything but that. His body wanted to shut down, have no part in all this. He forced another breath, another after that, and when he felt able, he crossed the room on shaky legs.

He expected the photograph to change before he could reach it, *knew it would*, and that was why he didn't blink, didn't dare look away. Even when thunder struck outside, rumbled the entire house, caused his heart to skip, he didn't look away. As he edged closer, he stared even when his eyes began to burn. When his fingers gripped it by the frayed edge, lifted it from the floor, he didn't look away.

Couldn't.

He'd never seen the car, not in real life. His father had only told him about it. The '65 Mustang convertible he'd bought used from a dealer in Kennebunkport in '71, painfully restored, then had to sell when his wife (Whaley's mother) got pregnant with their first. Nor did he remember much about his brother. He'd died at ten of cystic fibrosis when Whaley was four. Whaley had known both of those things only in photographs and stories. Sometimes he'd catch his father looking at old Mustangs in magazines and lamenting. He'd slide his finger over the lines, trace the edges and curves. Sometimes minutes would slip away and he'd get lost in the memories. When he snapped back, it would always be with a hint of guilt in his glum expression, and he'd tell whoever was willing to listen they'd needed the money back then far more than they needed the car. He'd say he didn't regret selling it, not in the least, and it was painfully obvious the only person he could never fully convince was himself.

Photographs of Whaley's brother were all over their modest home. He'd been their first child, and his mother hadn't been shy with the camera. She'd settled down when Whaley came along—the photos of Whaley's brother probably outnumbered his at least three to one. Growing up, you couldn't turn around in their house without his smiling face looking back at you from the wall or the mantle or some tabletop. It was his brother's crooked front teeth Whaley remembered most. He'd see those pictures and a single thought would always surface—*I sure as shit hope my teeth don't do that.* And they didn't. If Whaley's brother had lived to become a teenager, he no doubt would have worn braces.

As Whaley lifted the photograph from the side of Pam's chair and brought it closer to his face, the tremble in his fingers grew until the paper fluttered enough to make noise.

He had no doubt the boy in the picture was his brother. He knew that wasn't possible because this boy was at least two or three years older than his brother had been when he died, but there was no mistaking his teeth. The eyes were the same too. His hair. Even the freckles across the bridge of his nose. He was sitting on the hood of his father's old car. The car that had been sold and gone before he'd been born. Those two things had never met, yet here they were. Not just that. Although blurry, Whaley could make out their old house on Campbells Lane in the background. His mother's rose bushes near the front door (roses she hadn't planted until at least five years after her firstborn had passed—she'd often referred to them as her remembrance garden).

Whaley didn't want to understand what he was looking at, but he was beginning to. He couldn't help but wonder if his dad had taken his brother out to Wood Island at some point. Maybe his mother too. Some family outing. His dad once told him Benny had loved to fish.

"Chief, you there?"

Sandy Lomax.

His eyes still glued to the photo, Whaley reached for the microphone clipped to his shoulder. "Go ahead."

"I got a call from Maurisa Bradley out on River Road. She reported a truck parked behind Piscataqua Café that's not supposed to be there. Red Ford pickup. Sounds like it might be Keith Spivey."

Shit, Billy's boat. He knew about Billy's boat.

"The Hasler kid's got an old rescue craft docked out back there. I asked Mundie to chain it up. Do you know if he did?"

"I have no clue, Chief. I've been a little busy. I haven't been able to raise Mundie. Fine time for him to vanish."

Sandy was one of the most even-tempered people he knew. It took a lot to rattle her. She was clearly rattled. Her voice trembled as much as his hand, and her tone was filled with frustration. *"Mundie, if you're in earshot, please respond."*

The two of them went quiet for a long moment, but there was nothing but the crackle of static.

When half a minute slipped by, Whaley pressed his transmit button again. "It's all right, Sandy, I'm not far. I'll go."

He eyed the back bedroom, then turned to Pam. He wanted to believe she was finally at rest, but her last words told him otherwise.

I'll see you out there, Chief. We all come home.

"I'm securing the Spivey house. We have a…" He almost said *suicide* and caught himself. He couldn't mention Pam's death specifically, not on an open channel. "We got a 10-56." Glancing back at the back bedroom, the ropes on the bed, the bucket, he added, "Something else, too. Not sure what to make of it."

He expected her to ask if it was Pam, but she didn't. On some level, she probably saw it coming. Anyone who knew Pam would have. *"Understood."*

"Call the staties. We're spread too thin. We need some help."

"Yes, sir." And there was relief in her voice at that one, if only a little.

Not for Whaley, though. Her words triggered another memory. The driver of Marston's car. The voice he recognized, if only vaguely. Who could blame him, he'd only been four the last time he'd heard that voice.

Breathing fast, not quite gasping, Whaley again looked at the picture, this time hoping it *would* change—change to anything else, but it did not. If anything, the lines grew slightly more defined. The blur came into its own, and the house he could barely make out a moment ago was now in focus. Benny's smiling face looked out at him from his perch on the car, and he'd be damned if brother's leg didn't move. Not much, just a twitch, but he saw it, he knew he did.

Whaley swallowed. "We'll get through this, Sandy… Hang in there."

He forgot to press transmit when he said that last part, and much like his father talking about the Mustang, those words were meant to soothe himself as much as they were meant to soothe her.

He stuffed the photograph of Benny in his pocket and bolted from the house into the storm, twisting the lock and yanking the door shut behind him.

32

AS WHALEY SKIDDED through the turn from Portsmouth Avenue to River Road, frothy waves crashed against the jagged shore on his right, sending spray up and over his SUV. The tide was in, abnormally high, and by the look of the night sky, things would only get worse. Engorged black storm clouds rolled with the wind, ugly and dark, twisting and shoving as if the sky wasn't large enough to hold them and the space would go to whoever came out strongest. Nature's version of a prison yard fight: scrappy, vengeful, and fueled by relentless rage.

He could only recall three times when River Road had washed out and flooded, and he was certain that tonight would be the fourth. The rain came at him sideways, and even with the wiper blades running on high, he could barely see where he was going. A frightened deer bolted out in front of him, and if he hadn't slowed when his right front wheel dropped in a flooded pothole a moment earlier, he certainly would have clipped it, and that might have been enough to send him over the edge into the water. A jolt of terror crawled through his body, but oddly it wasn't fear of losing his own life that rushed through his mind. It was thoughts of the photograph in his pocket—*would it survive those frigid waters?* Could he hold onto it or would it wash away? If he lived and it was lost, could he survive *that?*

Ridiculous. He knew that. But there it was.

That photograph wasn't just a picture, it was a link to his brother—not paper, but a living, breathing thing—and he had no intention of losing him again.

Twice while driving, he had hazarded a glance at the image, taking the picture from his pocket and pinching it against the steering wheel as he drove. Each time the picture had changed. Not much, but enough. The first time, the image had zoomed in on his brother's face, the car and house no longer visible, and his brother's smile had intensified. It was like he was happy to see him, knew they'd somehow be reunited soon, and his brother was bubbling over with the thought. Benny had looked younger in that one, closer to the age he'd been when he died, the way Whaley remembered him from all those other pictures. Whaley had quickly shoved the photograph back in his pocket, because he'd been excited too. The second time he'd taken the photo out, the picture had zoomed back out, and Benny wasn't alone with the car. Whaley's father was standing there next to him—one arm around Benny's small shoulders, the other hand holding up a large striped bass, the hook and line still hanging from its mouth. His father had been dead for twenty-three years now.

The photograph had gone back into his pocket, but both images were right there every time Whaley blinked. He wanted to take it out again, but didn't dare.

Whaley slowed as he passed Oliver Street and the Piscataqua Café came into view, illuminated only by the occasional strike of lightning and the red and blue flash of his strobes. The power had gone out at some point. He hadn't noticed exactly when, but all the houses and streetlights on River were dark.

Keith Spivey's red Ford was parked haphazardly at the corner of the building, the ass-end sticking into the street. The passenger door stood open, the interior no doubt soaked through. There was no sign of Keith, but he couldn't be far. The boat was still there, tied to the dock, slamming against the posts like a bucking mule trying to get out of the water. And if the water continued to rise, it just might. With each wave, the dock vanished, lost beneath the whitecaps. Several of the boards had come loose. At least two were gone altogether, leaving gaping holes like bad teeth gone to rot.

Keith went to make a trade, Pam had said. *Silly fuck thinks he can make some kind of switcheroo. Her for Spivey. It'll just take 'em both, though. Gobble 'em right up.*

He might be inside. The Piscataqua Café had been shuttered years back. Whaley had chased his share of kids out of there over the years (several adults too). Maybe this trade was taking place inside.

No. Not inside. Any trade would take place out on the island. Some animals are best left in their cages for feeding time. If they were inside, Keith would head out soon enough.

Whaley shook the thought away, not sure where it came from, and parked directly behind the Ford, blocked it in. He was under no illusion he'd snuck up on Keith. He may not have run with the siren, no need around here, but his lights were on and they lit up half the block—Keith would have seen that, inside or out.

Whaley thumbed his microphone. "Sandy, I'm at Piscataqua Café. It's definitely Keith's truck. I'm gonna take a look around. You don't hear back from me in ten, send backup. Copy?"

No reply came.

He repeated the message.

Still nothing.

Either Sandy was occupied or the storm was interfering with the radios— maybe both.

When Whaley released the microphone, his hand went to the pocket holding the photograph and rested there a moment.

You know this can't wait, right? Best to get to it. Nik nok, and all.

Nik nok? Where the hell had he heard that?

The world lit up bright white with lightning. Thunder cracked, shook the SUV. Rain slapped against his windows.

This couldn't wait. Not if Keith had that girl.

If she was still alive, by some miracle, this couldn't wait another second.

Whaley figured it best to leave the strobes on rather than go dark, so he flicked the switch from running mode to flashers and climbed out of the SUV into the storm. His right hand automatically went to the butt of his service pistol, and he thumbed away the leather safety strap more out of habit than anything else.

His clothing was soaked, cold, water squishing around in his boots. He thought of the photograph again—it was in his shirt pocket, probably wet, too. He considered leaving it in the car (maybe locking it in the glove box), but no, that was a bad idea. He wanted it close. The photograph felt warm. He knew that had to be his imagination because photographs didn't give off heat (no more than they changed), so if this one felt like it was, surely that was in his head. But if it was giving off heat, maybe that was Benny's way of telling him he was right there with him. They'd finish this night together. That's what big brothers were for, right?

Whaley darted across the pavement, splashed through the puddles, and saddled up under the overhang on the side of the building. All the windows on the first floor were boarded up, and he didn't see any evidence of tampering. He doubted Keith got in through one of them. The back door had an old padlock on it. That lock had been hit so many times over the years, it only took a good yank to open it. If he'd entered the old building anywhere, it was there.

He rounded the first corner, moved fast along the wall, and was about to round the next when he spotted something out on the dock, perched precariously near the edge, hanging over the boat. He couldn't be sure from this distance, but it looked like a rolled-up rug strapped tight with duct tape.

Christ, that's Lily Dwyer. Got to be.

Keith killed the poor girl.

The photograph in Whaley's pocket grew hot, nearly burned his skin—that *wasn't* his imagination. His hand left his gun, went into his pocket, and he felt the edges of the picture with his fingertips. It wasn't wet, didn't even feel damp. The heat flashed and vanished as quickly as it began.

Whaley heard a soft *click* behind his head and felt something press against his skull behind his right ear.

"Don't move, Chief," Keith said. "I don't want to hurt you, but I will."

There was another flash of warmth from the photograph.

Had it tricked him?

Distracted him into releasing his gun?

With his free hand, Keith tugged Whaley's pistol from his holster. He looked down at the gun for a second, then heaved it into the water with a sideways throw.

A wave rolled up and over the dock, soaked the rug, nearly pulled it down into the water before it petered out and settled. The rug rocked, then went still.

"Is that the Dwyer girl?"

Keith looked toward the dock. When he spoke, the scent of stale rum drifted from his mouth. "You shouldn't have come out here, Chief. None of this concerns you."

It did, though. The photograph told him so.

"I'll do what I can to help you, but you need to tell me what happened." Whaley lowered his voice. "A lot of people are looking for you. They know I'm here. This is over. Let me take you in before someone else gets hurt."

Keith let out a soft, liquor-tinged groan. He gripped Whaley's shoulder and nudged him toward the dock. "Head over to the boat. Don't try anything stupid. I don't want to hurt you."

"You don't want to do this. It won't end well for you."

Keith grunted. "It was never meant to."

33

"A KNIFE?" KIRA stepped between me and Alesia. "Why do you need a knife?"

Alesia shifted her weight to her left leg and cocked her hip. "Why do you think? Don't worry, I won't cut him bad."

"You didn't say anything about cutting him."

Alesia's face twisted with frustration. "My mother sacrificed herself for us, *for this*, and you're worried about your boyfriend getting a little cut? Grow up, Kira. Where is the knife?"

When she didn't answer, Matty pulled a black buck from the back pocket of his jeans. "Here, use mine."

It was the same pocket knife he'd carried since we were kids. Glossy black handle with a three-inch stainless steel blade.

"I sharpened it last week," he told Alesia, handing her the knife. "It won't hurt."

The hell it wouldn't.

I tugged at the duct tape, tried to stand up, but I did nothing more than rock my chair.

The blade was spring-loaded and Alesia had clearly handled it before—she popped it open with a quick flick of her index finger and stepped toward us. Kira didn't budge. Alesia raised the blade and brought it within an inch of Kira's eye. "If you plan to continue to get in the way, we can bring in another chair. We have plenty of tape left. As far as spells go, two is always better than one."

When Kira still didn't move, I grunted from behind the tape on my mouth—shouted—told her to get out of the way. Me getting cut was one thing, but it was obvious Alesia had no qualms about going through her to get to me, and I didn't want to see her get hurt. Not to buy a few seconds. I shouted again.

Kira's eyes welled up; she nodded softly at me and took several steps back. She was rattled, not watching where she was going, and her left foot caught on the mound of dirt over Benny's hole. She managed to catch herself before she fell, but only after several awkward hopping steps and a grab for the wall.

Alesia thought this was all funny and let out a soft laugh as she approached me with the knife. I barely noticed her—my gaze was fixed on the mound of dirt. Although whoever filled it in had packed it tight, Kira's heel took out a sizable chunk. A divot nearly a foot in diameter. Sticking up through the dirt were two fingers—an index finger and middle, an outstretched hand reaching up from the makeshift grave. I'd never seen skin that white, as if every drop of blood was gone. There was a slight yellow tinge at the joint and the first knuckle was black. The nails were long, once painted bright pink but now chipped and cracked. Faded and caked with dirt.

Oh, God—had Lily still been alive when they buried her?

Was this her reaching? Her final attempt to escape her own grave?

My heart was pounding like a jackhammer.

I realized Alesia wasn't laughing at Kira; she was looking down at those fingers. As she stepped up to me, she kicked the dirt back in place and stomped it down with her bare foot. She shook her head. "Gotta love Benny. He digs a six-foot-deep hole and still manages to flub the burial. The kid's got heart, but not a lick of common sense."

"Does it matter?" Matty asked from behind her. "For all this to work, I mean. We can have him redo it."

"I don't think so." Alesia brought the tip of the knife to my neck, pressed, and jerked it down. One quick movement.

I felt the warmth of the blood seeping out before the pain of the actual cut found me.

"Ooh." Alesia tossed the knife aside and quickly pressed the rag against the wound. "Got you a little deeper than I planned. I don't think I cut anything important. Guess we'll see." She looked over at Kira. "I'll need this rag. Do you have something else you could use to plug this up?"

Kira's eyes were glued to that mound of dirt. She looked up when she realized Alesia was talking to her, nodded, and tore off a strip of her t-shirt. When Alesia took the rag away, Kira came back over to me, wrapped the cloth around my neck, and cinched it tight. She leaned close to me. "It's not as bad as she said. This should stop the bleeding."

The cut throbbed and my neck felt hot. The pain radiated up the side of my head. I wanted to believe her, but I could feel the cloth soaking with my blood, some trickling down my neck. I was already woozy from the hits to my head, most likely had a concussion; this only made things worse. My eyes wanted to close, but I didn't let them. Instead, I jerked my head to the side and looked down at Matty's knife, willed Kira to understand.

She did, but instead of getting the knife for me, instead of sneaking it into my hand so I could cut myself out of the tape, she stepped on it and ground it deeper into the dirt. She took away what was probably my last chance to get out of this.

Alesia looked down at her empty wrist again, her nonexistent watch. "I need everyone to take their places in the circle."

Matty dropped down next to Izzie and Chloe in the dirt and eyed Spivey up on the steps. "You too."

Spivey remained still for a moment, then set his guitar aside and came down into the basement. He seemed to make a conscious effort not to look at me as he stepped by and took his place in the dirt.

Alesia raised her free hand, twisted it in the air, then slowly lowered it. The light emanating from the candles dropped with her movement, fell nearly to full dark, transforming all of them to shadows again. Only the candles of the pentagram burned bright, somehow brighter than the rest.

Like Spivey, Kira didn't look at me before taking her place in the circle.

When Alesia sat, she tugged the black cloth from over the items in the center of the pentagram and tossed it aside.

I strained to make out what was there, barely visible in the gloom. I saw Alesia's bowl and several bottles of water. There was a small plastic packet, some kind of white powder inside. She placed the rag with my blood in the bowl, then looked up at Matty and held out her hand. "Gun?"

When he handed it to her, she set the revolver to the right of the bowl, near the water bottles.

Heavy thunder rattled the house hard enough to send dust down from the ceiling in slow-moving flakes. Black snow falling through the candlelight.

Alesia looked at her wrist again and cleared her throat. "Okay, it's time. Everyone join hands."

34

WHEN WHALEY DIDN'T move, Keith gave him another push near the small of his back. Harder this time, enough to force him to stumble forward. "Boat—now," Keith said. "Or I swear to God, I'll shoot you right here before I'll let you slow me down." The heavy rain did little to stifle the sharp alcohol on his breath.

Whaley did as he was told and walked toward the boat. The muddy earth sucked at his shoes. He used that to buy time, kept his pace sluggish. "You've been drinking, Keith. I need you to think hard on what you're doing. We may be friends, but to everyone else, you're pointing a gun at a law enforcement officer. Maybe slowing down a spell is the best thing for you. Give your head a chance to clear."

Keith grunted again. "I think my head is about as clear as I want it to be for this, but thank you."

He'd been drinking, no doubt about that, but he didn't seem drunk. That made this far more frightening. When alcohol was running the show, you could count on people to do stupid things. Someone taking a drink or two to take the edge off, calm their nerves, was a whole other matter. That suggested a plan, one they weren't willing to commit without a little liquid encouragement. Keith's speech wasn't slurred. He wasn't stumbling. In fact, Whaley couldn't remember the last time he'd seen the man so focused. That scared him more than anything.

When they reached the dock, Keith nudged Whaley forward, forced him to step over the missing deck planks toward the boat, pushed him until he was standing at the edge of the dock next to the bundled rug. There was a body in there, no mistaking it from this close. Even through the rain, Whaley could smell it. The shape of it, the bulges—shoulders and hips. Poor girl. Nobody deserved to end up like that.

Keith gave him another push. Water sloshed over their feet, the waves and rising tide making a grab for both of them. "Get in the boat, pull the rug down behind you, then take a seat on that bench up front so I can keep an eye on you."

Whaley didn't move. "We're staying right here and waiting for backup. You're going to set the gun down on the dock so nobody shoots you by accident, then we'll take a ride down to the..."

He almost said *station*, then remembered the building probably wasn't there anymore. The glow in the sky was gone, but the damage was done.

"I didn't start that fire, Chief," Keith said as if reading his mind, stepping into view. His eyes were red and the hand holding the gun was shaking. "I went down there to bust Teddy out and the fire was already going."

"I know you didn't. It was Laura Dubin."

"Laura Dubin?"

Whaley nodded. "Dropped a match in the lobby. Sandy got out, Teddy Hasler didn't."

His bloodshot eyes grew wide. "Teddy's... dead?"

Again, Whaley nodded.

Keith took a moment to process that, then grunted, stale rum wafting through the air. "It was no more Dubin than it was me. It was that place, the thing that lives out there. It laid claim to Teddy and Laura, called in its marker. It's coming for Pam and me next, just like it did her folks and the others, I know it is. I gotta end it first. Make good on a promise, that's the only way."

Whaley couldn't tell him about Pam, not now. Keith was already teetering on the edge. He did what he could to keep his voice calm, but it cracked nonetheless. "How 'bout we go back to your house, check in on Pam, and sort all this out? I'll send someone out to Wood Island to look in on your boy and the others, too. Make sure everyone's safe. How about that?"

The photograph grew red hot for a moment, then cooled again—either excited or angry, Whaley couldn't be sure.

Keith only half heard him. His face tightened. He looked out over the water, peered through the rain, then down at his watch. "Oh, Jesus, it's late." He leveled the gun at Whaley's face. "Get in the boat."

"You going to shoot me, Keith? You gonna kill a cop? A friend?"

"Get in the fucking boat!"

Whaley looked down at the rug. "I can't help you with this. I can't be part of it. That poor girl deserves better. I think you still get that. Think of her parents, what they're going through. They need her back. You need to give them closure."

Keith's face filled with confusion. His free hand reached around to a flask in his back pocket. He started to take it out, thought better of it. "That ain't the girl."

"Then who is it?"

"It ain't her," Keith repeated. "You'll see Lily Dwyer soon enough."

Whaley was about to object again when Keith shoved him. A palm, hard and fast to his chest. Whaley's feet went out from under him and he stumbled over the side of the dock, fell into the boat. His back smacked against one of the bench seats and he rolled off to the floor. White pain filled his vision as he looked up at the dock, and for a moment, he thought he'd broken something. He wiggled his fingers, his toes in his boots, slowly rolled his head. Everything still worked, but every inch hurt like hell.

Keith moved fast. He shoved the gun under his belt at his back and went to work tugging the ropes free of their cleats. Mundie had chained the boat like he'd asked, but Keith had cut the lock off before Whaley got out there—both lock and chain were up on the dock, cast off to the side.

With the last rope still in hand, Keith jumped down into the boat. Drunk or not, his sea legs worked just fine. He grabbed the edge of the rug and pulled that down too. It thumped over the same bench Whaley had hit and settled next to him on the floor. Whaley forced himself into a crouch, was about to push back up to the dock when Keith yanked the gun back out and waved it toward the bench seat at the front of the boat. "Get up there and don't move. You do anything else and I'll put a bullet in your head. You ain't slowing me down no more. Move!"

Whaley did, every inch of his body aching. He gripped the edge of the hull, worked his way to the seat up front, and fell in.

Still pointing the gun, Keith settled behind the wheel. He twisted the key and fired up the motor. It screamed as he pushed the throttle forward and pointed them toward Wood Island, fighting the waves.

The photograph in Whaley's pocket went hot again, pulsed this time, excited with heat. It wanted him to go. Just the thought of it made it warmer. Whaley tried to ignore the heat, forced himself to focus on that rug, the one Keith just told him did not hold Lily's body.

35

BOUND TO THE chair, I could only watch them. Watch and listen. Whether the candles burned brighter again or my eyes simply adjusted to the darkness, I will never know, but I saw them clear enough in the flickering light—Spivey, Matty, Kira, Alesia, Izzie, and Chloe all joined hands. They closed the circle as if I had never been a part of it, their hands reaching over the place I once sat, and Alesia began to speak in that low, controlled voice of hers.

"It is often said the living only borrow from the dead. Life is a thin veil stretched over the eternal world of all that which has come before. That which is most ancient is buried deepest. Buried beneath the layers of everything that arrived after. The most recent is right here, so close, yet just out of grasp, as lost and unobtainable as a second that has just passed. This... this barrier stands between and separates both worlds, a wall between the living and the dead. It's the most solid wall ever built, yet invisible to most. As high as eternity and deep as origin, there is no way over or under, there is only *through*, and that way through is only known and understood by few. Those of us within this circle have seen the door. We have been blessed with the key, and we ask that those charged with protecting that boundary consider us worthy of trespass as we welcome those from the other side to join us here."

I knew a storm raged outside—wind and rain battering the house—but I heard none of that. The outside world went as quiet as a sealed vault. It was as if the basement sunk deeper into the earth, distanced itself from all else. The shadows were back, deep and dark, crawling over the walls and corners, oily black with anxious fingers grasping for the six of them, but unable to reach. The sounds of the storm had been replaced by papery whispers coming from those shadows, hurried and hushed. They might have been people at one time, but not anymore.

Was this what happened to people…? After…? Maybe with the passage of time? Is this what we became? Or were they something else? Something summoned from some place I didn't know or want to understand?

Unlike before, they had come so quickly. Brought here with so little effort compared to the last time. Was this because they now knew the way? Or had Alesia simply grown stronger? Gotten better? Maybe some combination of both.

I eyed the spot in the dirt where Matty's knife had been buried, only a few feet away, but impossibly far. I yanked both my arms up, tried to kick my legs out, but the tape didn't give at all. The whispers were everywhere—excited, hungry. I tried not to look at the mound of dirt to my side, Lily Dwyer's hasty grave, but I found myself drawn to it. I expected her fingers to reappear, twitching and grabbing at the air above, attempting to claw her way out.

Alesia went on, her voice steady. "We've all drunk from the well of George Walton. The water cursed, then collected by my long-lost sister, Prudence Toliver, has spent weeks coursing our veins, mixing with our blood, and becoming a part of each of us. That water not only joins us together but binds us to this place, the spot where it all started. Provides us with the key to the door. And we"—she looked around the faces—"are not the first."

There was a loud bang from somewhere above. Not thunder, not deep enough for that. This sounded more like a tree falling on the house, but I knew that couldn't be right either—there were no trees on Wood Island. Something dropping from the wall? Benny maybe, slamming a door? Finally coming inside. Although I doubted that too. I somehow knew that Benny had business of his own tonight. If Benny belonged anywhere, it was in the storm.

If the others heard the bang, they didn't flinch. Their eyes were fixed on Alesia, hypnotized by her every word.

She reached for the bloody rag in the bowl between them and stirred it gently with the tip of her finger. With each swirl, the wind grew, circled the basement, following her movement. Flecks of dirt and dust caught in the air and brushed over my skin like sandpaper. Those in the circle closed their eyes, but I could not. I forced mine to stay open enough to see what she was doing.

Alesia's voice rose. "Blood of blood, ash of ash, drawn today but born of the past. With a fire's kiss, you come to life, I beckon you against all strife. Bring to us the gift of sight, and show those who doubt our taken right!"

A bright red and orange flame shot up from the center of the bowl and nearly kissed the rafters before dropping back down into the bowl like liquid fire poured down from above. The rag with my blood was gone in an instant, enveloped and eaten. It went from cloth to ash, became nothing but soot. The wind circling the basement picked it up, carried it, scattered it across the dirt, then blew with a harsh fierceness that whipped over me with enough force to nearly topple my chair. Grit caught in my eyes and I couldn't keep them from closing as Alesia screamed out, "I command you, Billy Hasler, the doubter among us—I command you to see!"

The wind vanished.

All went quiet.

Absolutely silent.

I opened my eyes and through tears filled with grime and filth, I looked out over the basement at faces I didn't recognize.

36

THEY SAT IN a circle around a pentagram, candles burning bright between them, but they were not my friends. There were five, but their clothing was all wrong. The two girls wore dresses. One wore a bonnet, and the other had several blue ribbons twisted through her long, blond hair. Two of the boys wore dark slacks, white button-down shirts, and suspenders. One of them handed a mason jar across to the third, who was dressed in faded overalls. "It's got kick, Ralph. Lightweight, like you; careful you don't lose hold of your senses!"

The boy he called Ralph smirked and clearly took this as some kind of challenge. He brought the jar to his lips and took a long swig. Made a show of it, then set the jar down at his side. He grimaced, pinched his eyes shut, and cleared his throat. When he spoke, there was a gruffness to his voice. "You don't know from kick, Les. You need to taste my granddaddy's shine. He makes it from peaches so ripe you can run a plow off it."

Les—Lester Rote?

Ralph Peck?

They were only kids.

How was I seeing this?

That wasn't right. I wasn't *seeing this*. I was living it. This wasn't some vision; I was sitting in the exact same spot of the basement, and—wait, it *was* different. The furnace was gone. There was only the old wood-burning stove. The metal door was closed, but a fire glowed inside.

For a second, I thought I'd passed out again, but it was all too real. The heat of the fire. Their voices. I could smell sweat and dirt on the boys, and I knew they'd spent the day working fields. The basement smelled different too, and I realized all the dirt from the cemeteries was gone. Lily. Benny's hole. The items buried. Instead, the floor was covered in wide wooden planks.

"No kick? Then why's your eyes waterin'?" The girl in the bonnet asked with a nervous giggle. She reached for the jar, but Ralph snatched it away.

"Not a chance. Not with your momma right upstairs," Ralph said. "She'll tell your pa and he'll beat me senseless." He nodded across at the other boys. "The three of us."

"I haven't slept in three days and you're worried about my folks smelling something on my breath?" The girl (Geraldine?) grabbed the jar away from him and gulped down a mouthful, another after that. She didn't stop until the coughing started, and when that happened, she nearly spilled what was left before Ralph got ahold of the jar and took it away.

"Jesus, Ger," he said softly.

Geraldine coughed for nearly a full minute. When she finally stopped, she wiped her mouth with the side of her hand. "Momma don't even know we're down here, and Pa's fishing. Can't hear us no ways."

In a timid voice, the other girl said, "I want to try."

Ralph and Lester exchanged a look, then turned to Geraldine. "Will that even work?"

She looked across at the other girl and shrugged. "I don't know. Let her try. I wanna see."

"Has it been long enough?" he asked.

Geraldine shrugged again. "Told ya, I don't know. Give it to her— we'll find out soon enough."

Lester snatched the jar away. "That's all I got and I don't want her spillin' it. Try something else first."

"Oh, I swear," Geraldine muttered, looking around at the dirt near their hands, then she reached for one of the ribbons in her hair and pulled it free. She held it out across the circle toward the other girl.

The girl in the bonnet eyed the ribbon nervously for a moment, then reached for it. Her fingers froze in the air about an inch from the length of cloth, then she pulled her hand back. "I don't know."

"*I don't know* what, Patricia?" Geraldine replied. "You don't know that you can, or you don't know you wanna try?"

Patricia Whidden, I realized. That meant the other boy was probably her brother, William.

I didn't know what year this was, but Whaley said they died in 1951.

"I'm just a little nervous is all," Patricia replied softly. She turned toward Ralph Peck. "You got what you wanted, right? We know that part worked just fine?"

Ralph said, "It worked. My pa's boat has brought in nothing but big catch after big catch since you done it. Says he ain't seen nothing like it. He came back empty for nearly a month, now he ain't got enough room."

"So that part worked?" she asked again.

He nodded. "That part worked. Praise Emerson."

"Praise Emerson," the others repeated together.

William nodded at his sister. "Try it. What have you got to lose?"

Patricia seemed to consider all this, then reached for the blue cloth, twisted her fingers around it, and lifted the thin material from Geraldine's outstretched hand.

Geraldine gasped.

Lester gawked as the girl rolled the material around her wrist. With shaky hands, he brought the mason jar to his lips and took a long swig.

"Praise Emerson," William said again in barely a whisper. With dirt-stained fingers, he reached for the jar. "My turn. Gimme that."

They all seemed equally amazed when he took it and drank.

"My stars," Patricia said softly. "Yesterday I couldn't touch nothing. Now it feels the same as… as before."

William set the jar down and wiped his mouth triumphantly. "It does have a kick to it, no doubt 'bout that. Oh, and look at this—" He stretched his leg out straight, flexed it several times at the knee. "It don't even hurt no more. Like it never been broke. I ain't ever felt this good. This strong."

"I wanna go next," Geraldine told them, her face filled with awe.

"No way," Lester Rote shot back. "We agreed I'd go next."

Ralph Peck reached for the jar, brought it close, but didn't drink. Instead, he turned it between his fingers. "I don't think anyone should go until things calm down. Half the town is still crawling around the Walton well, calling to board it up, fill it in. Church was all buzzing with talk about blessing it." He glared at Patricia and William. "The two of you couldn't come up with something a little less attention drawin'? Shoulda hung yourselves in the woods like we talked 'bout."

They looked back at him, but said nothing.

When nearly a minute ticked by, he reached into the center pocket on his overalls and took out a small revolver. He placed it between them and gave it a gentle spin. "Next time it's got to be fast. And someplace where they won't find the body. Maybe leave a note."

"Like a runaway?" Geraldine asked.

"Exactly." Ralph Peck nodded. "Ain't nobody look for a runaway."

37

HIGH WINDS FORCED the rain sideways; the cold drops sliced across Whaley's skin like shards of glass as the boat rolled up and over the white-capped waves toward Wood Island. *Merv's* motor groaned and fought, but refused to quit. The closer they got, the louder it seemed, like an excited pet heading home. Whaley kept his head down, one hand gripping the bench, the other over the pocket holding the photograph. The pain in his back had eased from screaming to a dull cry. Keith half stood, half sat behind the wheel. With the rain, the windshield was useless—he stood just high enough to see over. Whaley knew how treacherous these waters were on a good day—even with the tide in, granite stuck up everywhere like cracked teeth. Add the wind, rain, and waves, and there was a good chance they'd die long before they made the quarter-mile run out to Wood. The water was sixty degrees on a hot summer day, and he knew the sharks would be out. Weather like this churned the water, stirred up the fish. A frenzy would be an understatement. They were feasting down there.

Shielding his eyes from the rain and salt spray, Whaley stared at Keith—his eyes were darting about like a madman. The man's lips were moving fast, mumbling words and phrases only he could hear. Whaley was no expert lip-reader, but he'd swear to his dying day the man was saying, *The entity must never be sold all items found on or within the entity are considered property of the entity and may not be sold only borrowed loaned and returned under pre-established terms tokens of less than sixteen years of age will be considered property don't answer the phone watch the pilot light it's been known to go out anyone here at sunset must stay until sunrise never lock the door Emerson must be fed don't answer the phone...* Repeated, again and again.

"Keith, you need to calm down!" Whaley shouted out over the

roar of the motor and storm. "Let's get help! We'll all go out there together!" He said this because he didn't know what else to say. Keith didn't look like a man willing to turn back. Keith didn't look like a man who planned to *ever* go back.

Keith's head jerked up and he glared —like he'd forgotten Whaley was on the boat. The mumbling stopped and he seemed to make one last grab at sanity. "I used to think we started this!" he yelled. "Back when we were kids. Fucking naïve, but when you're that age, the entire world revolves around you. Used to sneak out here—Ted, Laura, and me. Pam would get us in the house and we'd hide down in the basement. Scare the shit out of each other with ghost stories. Back then, I figured we stirred up Emerson the first time we broke out a Ouija board, but that was bullshit—he was already there, just waiting. Laura knew that, damn sure of that, even then. I think it was the fifth trip out when Laura told us about the Whidden kids back in '51. You know about them, right?"

Whaley nodded, because engaging Keith was good. Getting him talking meant he was also listening. But he was also talking about a basement that did not exist. Whaley knew that, too. He'd seen it himself. He kept telling himself that because he couldn't get roped into this delusion. His mind threw back a counterargument, one he didn't want to consider—what if *not seeing* the basement was the delusion?

Keith chewed the inside of his cheek and peered back at him. "Course you know about the Whidden kids. That story might be the worst-kept secret in New England. I remember hearing about it when I was a kid—them finding the two bodies out on Wood, nobody knowing how they got out there. Big fucking mystery back then. Lester Rote taking off right after, looking guilty as hell. Heard lots of stories about how those kids died, too. How they fell in that well out back of the Walton place. Same place George Walton's daughter died three hundred-some years earlier. Someone filled that hole in right quick after the Whidden kids. Don't know why they didn't do it the first go-round. Here's the real kicker though: Pam told us they didn't fall. *She said they jumped*. Said she got that from her mother, Geraldine. Laura lit up like a Christmas tree when she heard that, so many lightbulbs went off in her head. She'd suspected it, but was never sure."

Jerking the wheel hard to the left, Keith missed a ten-foot block of granite sticking up out of the water by no more than three feet. Whaley's grip on the hull slid, but he managed to stay in the boat. The rug rolled and smacked against his leg. He braced it with his foot as best he could as Keith cut back to the left and turned into a wave. Water shot over the side, they listed, nearly rolled, then righted again.

"We got to go back!" Whaley yelled. "We'll sink in this!"

Keith shoved the throttle forward, the motor cried out, and they cut through the next wave head-on. Went up and over. Whaley's stomach lurched.

"Here's the kicker!" Keith shouted out over the motor, ignoring him, waving the gun around. "When Pam said they jumped, I figured she was full of shit until she started sharing details she had no business knowing—told us how William pried the boards up. The two of them held hands when they did it. William snapped his leg when they hit the bottom. Both of 'em drowning when they couldn't stay afloat no more. She knew the play-by-play down to what they'd been wearing. Pam's mom, Geraldine, she let it all slip one night, unloaded it on Pam. You don't believe me, ask Ralph Peck. Geraldine said he was there, watched 'em do it."

"Ralph Peck?"

"He was part of *their* circle—Ralph Peck, Geraldine, Lester Rote, and the two Whidden kids." Keith rose up over the windshield, steered around another cropping of rocks, then settled back down. "That's what I'm getting at—I thought Pam, Teddy, Laura, and me were first, then we heard about Geraldine and those other kids before us. This keeps repeating, every generation. This thing… Emerson… it lays claim to any children who set foot out there, tempts 'em with promises, whatever they want, but in the end, ain't nothing comes free. It owns 'em. Emerson collects. All us… tokens. If it can't get you out there, it sics its lapdog Marston on you like it did with me and Pam until you cave. One way or another, it collects."

"I don't understand," Whaley had to ask. "Why would the Whidden children kill themselves? Why take it that far?"

"Death ain't always the end, Chief. Emerson gets your ear, and it'll convince you of that, too. Make you think what comes next is far better than what we got now. Puts you in a hurry to get there. If those kids ain't dead yet, they will be soon enough. He did his damnedest to tempt us back then, but we didn't give in. Once we figured out what was going on, the four of us made a pact. We agreed to starve it until it gets weak and dies. None of us would sacrifice ourselves no matter how hard things got. Emerson fought back, gave us plenty of reasons, but we held firm. At least Pam and me did." His voice trailed off, went quiet for a moment, then he looked back at Whaley. "Turns out, Laura Dubin fucked us. Teddy too. You ever ask yourself why he did so well in life? Why things always seemed to go easy for him?"

A heavy wave crashed over the side of *Merv*, nearly capsized them. Keith jerked the wheel hard in the opposite direction and Whaley gripped at the bench, somehow managed to keep from going over the side. The rug, bogged down with water, barely moved.

Keith righted their course and shouted, "Laura got Teddy back out there, right before his sixteenth birthday, and the two of them worked out a deal of their own." He fell quiet for a second. "Teddy thought she was joking. He didn't believe any of it back then, just went along. The years since that may have changed his mind, but there was no taking it back."

"Taking what back?" Whaley shouted out.

"She got him to offer up his firstborn to Emerson. He told me that a couple weeks ago, right after Geraldine died. 'Bout the same time he grew a conscience and tried to buy the island. When he offered to help." Keith smirked. "He actually thought he could outsmart it. Find some loophole in the will, the rules, something. He wanted to save his own skin and his boy." Keith's head dropped. "You can't reason with it. It don't work that way. Emerson just takes. Took him. Took Laura…"

Took Pam, Whaley thought. He found himself looking down at the rug, the bundled body at his feet. "If you can't reason with it, then why—"

"Hold on!" Another large wave smacked into them. Keith jammed the throttle forward, steered hard left, and managed to get over it. The motor sputtered, nearly died, then caught again.

Whaley jerked around on the bench again, and for one brief instant, he caught a glimpse of Wood Island, the house. Lights burned bright behind every window, unnaturally so. He thought of the wreck of a generator he'd seen earlier in the day when he went out there with Billy Hasler.

He knew that house had no power.

The sight of it jarred Keith again, slapped him back. He resumed muttering:

The entity must never be sold all items found on or within the entity are considered property of the entity and may not be sold only borrowed loaned and returned under pre-established terms tokens of less than sixteen years of age will be considered property don't answer the phone watch the pilot light it's been known to go out anyone here at sunset must stay until sunrise never lock the door Emerson must be fed…

Just off the jagged rocks of the shoreline, someone was walking in the rain. No, not walking, *digging*. Nothing more than a silhouette.

In Whaley's pocket, the photograph burned again, hotter than ever.

38

I SNAPPED BACK.

It felt like someone grabbed me by the back of my shirt collar and jerked me across the room. The chair rocked as I slammed against the frame, and the only thing that kept me from toppling over was dumb luck—the leg of the chair caught on something buried in the dirt, something hard. I had no idea what that *something* was and didn't want to know. "What the hell was that?!" I shouted, but with the tape over my mouth, the others heard nothing but a muffled cry.

From the circle on the floor, Alesia looked out at the others. "Praise Emerson."

"Praise Emerson," they replied—even Kira, although her voice seemed to come on a slight delay.

The flames in Alesia's bowl died as quickly as they appeared. Within seconds, the bright orange became a dull red, then it was gone altogether. If it was hot, Alesia gave no indication as she reached down inside and removed what was left of the rag. She set it off to the side of the bowl, smoothed it flat, then reached back in to retrieve something else. She repeated this until six items were sitting there, lined up in a neat row:

The rag.

The silver locket belonging to Spivey's mother.

Half of my father's business card.

The remains of the matchbook.

Keith Spivey's keychain.

Blackened pages that had once been Spivey's subpoena.

All of these things were burnt until barely recognizable, all but Keith's keychain. It appeared untouched. Alesia cocked her head as she looked down at it, considered what that meant, then wrapped her fingers around the keychain and dragged it close, leaving a thin trail in the dirt. "Previous tokens have all been returned home to you, my dear Emerson, all but one—Keith Spivey. I ask you to be patient with us— you will have him soon enough." Her eyes pinched shut for a moment, and when she opened them again, she added, "He comes to you of his own free will. Of that, I am certain. And that," she said, "leaves only the one." Alesia turned to me, the candlelight flickering against her pale skin. "The token gifted by his father. Yours, forevermore."

A lump the size of a fist grew in my throat.

"And Emerson welcomes him," the others droned.

I jerked around in the chair, but there was no escaping. The tape around my wrists and ankles only seemed to cinch tighter.

The darkness drew closer, filled the outer walls until they were no longer visible. The air turned to ice. The only heat came from the furnace at my side, emanating from the open pilot light door.

Alesia's voice fell low, yet I could still hear her perfectly over all else. "As those who have come before and as all those who will come after, we offer all that we are. Mind, body, and soul. We are blessed to be among the taken, and we are blessed to be among those who receive. We give all that we have willingly and take only what you are willing to bequeath. Our gift for yours, your gift for ours. Praise Emerson."

"Praise Emerson," the others repeated.

Those papery whispers from the basement's corners rose to a crescendo, an audience of the damned. Dark shapes pushing and shoving, clambering for a better view but not willing to get too close. Were William and Patricia Whidden among them? Lester Rote? Ralph Peck, Geraldine? I couldn't see any of them, but I knew they were. Somehow I knew they were all there, all who had come before.

Alesia went quiet for nearly a minute, her body swaying with those voices, listening. Then she was muttering, urgently replying in some language I didn't understand. Listening. Muttering. Listening. Arguing. This heated conversation between her and the unknown. Finally, she went silent and nodded. When she opened her eyes again, they glowed with a green bright enough to light half the room. She turned to Izzie and Chloe. "It's been decided. The two of you are next."

I expected them to object, but neither did. There was a moment of shock on both their faces, then hasty nods.

Matty reached across the circle and patted his sister's leg. "It's all right, I'll be right behind you. I promise."

Chloe inched closer to Izzie, pressed so tight against her their bodies looked like one in the dim light. Her wide-eyed gaze met Alesia's. "I'll be able to do what you can do?"

Alesia's face softened with a reassuring smile. "And so much more."

She looked around the circle at the others. "All of you. This isn't an end, it's a beginning. You will want for nothing. You will never get sick, you will never grow old, you will never know death. Your strength and power will be immeasurable. What I've shown you is only a taste."

Izzie swallowed. "And we won't have to stay out here? On the island?"

"Only at first," Alesia assured her. "Only long enough to grow accustomed to what you'll become. I won't lie to you—I never have. You will need to adjust, learn to exist in the physical world as your reborn self, but in time you will. And we'll have all the time… Those who have come before us have proven that. In time, you'll become so strong, so complete, you'll be able to rejoin your loved ones, and they will be none the wiser. Those who have come before us have proven that, too. We will become gods among mortals."

Izzie inched closer to Chloe and rested her head on the other girl's shoulder. Chloe raised Izzie's hand to her lips and kissed her fingertips. The two of them held each other for nearly a minute, and Alesia let them. She watched until both girls finally looked back at her. "We're ready," Chloe said. "We both want this." And again, Izzie nodded.

Alesia reached over the revolver, which was still sitting near the bowl, and retrieved one of the water bottles. She twisted off the cap, dropped it, then picked up the small plastic packet of white powder. With her thumb and forefinger, she got it open and dumped the contents in the bottle, placed her thumb on the mouth, and gave it a good shake. When she finished, the water was slightly cloudy. She handed the bottle to Chloe. "It's called pentobarbital; they use it to euthanize animals. It's not painful in any way. You'll just feel like you're falling asleep. It will all be over in a few minutes, then… you know."

With a trembling hand, Chloe raised the bottle to her nose and sniffed. "I don't smell anything."

"You won't. It's just like going to sleep," Alesia assured her.

Chloe gave the bottle another sniff anyway, then turned to Izzie and gently stroked the girl's cheek with her free hand. "I love you more than anything. You know that, right?"

Izzie's head quickly bobbed up and down. Her eyes were damp with tears. "I love you, too."

"This means we'll be together forever. Nobody can take that from us."

"You'll never age," Alesia said softly. "You'll never get sick. You'll be capable of performing the most incredible things…"

"We'll be like superheroes," Izzie whispered. "Always together."

Chloe nodded, leaned closer, and gave Izzie a gentle kiss on her forehead. Her lips lingered there for a moment, then brushed away. "Together forever."

She raised the bottle and drank.

She didn't stop until half was gone.

She didn't stop until Izzie took the bottle from her and drank the rest.

39

THE STORM MIGHT have been the worst Whaley had ever witnessed. It was certainly the worst he'd ever been out in, and to be out on the water was nothing short of suicide. He swiveled in the bench seat only long enough to look back out over the reach toward New Castle—the water was unrecognizable, something out of a nightmare. Although less than a quarter-mile away, he couldn't see the shore. There was nothing in that direction but a wall of cascading rain beating down on the rocks, meeting the waves, which seemed to climb ungodly high.

Kittery was lost, too. Portsmouth, for that matter. No visible lights or other boats. Even the lighthouses at the Coast Guard station and Whaleback were both dark, and that *never* happened. Between gennies and batteries, Whaley couldn't remember a single night either had been dark, let alone both. They might have been in the middle of the Atlantic, days from civilization, if not for the house on Wood. Every window there was lit up like a warm and welcome beacon, drawing them closer, guiding them.

Whaley had lost Keith again. Although he continued to handle the boat with expert skill, his mind was someplace else. His gaze remained fixed on Wood Island, but there was a blankness to his stare. As if merely looking at it was enough to mesmerize him. His lips moved in that soundless epitaph—

The entity must never be sold all items found on or within the entity are considered property of the entity and may not be sold only borrowed loaned and returned under pre-established terms tokens of less than sixteen years of age will be considered property don't answer the phone watch the pilot light it's been known to go out anyone here at sunset must stay until sunrise never lock the door Emerson must be fed...

—and when he stopped, the boat would jerk hard to the left or right, like Keith had been drifting off to sleep and managed to yank himself back. He'd steer them around the rocks, get them moving in the right direction again, and the muttering would return as if the words, not just his skill, were guiding them. He added something to the mess of words, something Whaley hadn't caught in the repeated mess—

Let Merv come home.

Or

Welcome Merv home.

Or

Allow Merv to come home.

Something like that. The words barely audible and only said once.

Whaley thumbed the microphone clipped to his shoulder and got nothing. If Keith noticed between his mind-numbing jabber, he didn't care. It didn't matter—the radio was either fried or unable to transmit through the weather. Whaley didn't get so much as a crackle of static, and the tiny green bulb that normally lit up when he was transmitting had decided to sit this one out.

As they neared the dock, he caught glimpses of whoever was outside. A boy, he thought, although it was impossible to tell for sure. Not very large. And as crazy as it was, he *was* digging. He was digging like a damn machine—no regard for the weather, the shovel moving with unperturbed rhythm, tossing mud, dirt, and sand to the sides as he stood knee-deep in a hole. No sign of tiring. No sign of stopping. And that wasn't the craziest part—the hole the kid was working on was only one of dozens, maybe over a hundred. Every time a wave lifted up their boat and threw them through the air, Whaley got another look at the island from up high, and every inch of land looked like Swiss cheese. None of those holes had been there earlier in the day. The boy had to be the last man standing in some kind of digging army.

They were about fifty feet from the dock, closing on an open space behind *Annabelle*—Geraldine Rote's boat, which meant Spivey was probably out here—when Keith finally broke from his reverie and said loud enough to be heard over the storm, "Chief, there's something you need to know—something I'm not proud of."

No shit, Whaley thought, trying to look Keith in the eye rather than down at the body wrapped in a rug at his feet. "Yeah? What's that?"

Keith twisted the wheel hard right into another wave, then spun them back around on the other side of it. "I was worried—been worried—Pam might do something stupid. Not to someone else, she'd never hurt anybody, but to herself. She hasn't been right these past few weeks, not with all this. So I…" He paused, wiped the wet hair from his eyes. "I've been keeping her tied up in the back bedroom. I know how that sounds, but it was for her own good. She's there right now. I don't get out of this, I need you to go to my place and set her loose."

Whaley felt a pang in his chest. He remembered Pam's wrists when he'd first gotten to the house—bloody, chafed raw. The bloody ropes on the bed. It hadn't been Lily Dwyer tied up on that bed, it was Pam.

He looked down at the wrapped body.

Keith went to make a trade. Silly fuck thinks he can make some kind of switcheroo. Her for Spivey. It'll just take 'em both, though. Gobble 'em right up.

If not Lily, then… "Keith, who do you have here in the rug?"

If Keith answered him, Whaley didn't hear, because right after he asked the question, they came up along the side of the dock, cracked against the old tires attached there, and someone tossed a rope down to them.

Whaley looked up to find the boy who had been digging standing there—the sight of him was enough to wipe all other thoughts from his head. Although the cold rain had numbed his skin, he still felt the blood leave his face. His heart thumped so hard in his chest it felt like it might tear right through, and if it did, it would bump right up against that photograph in his breast pocket. The photograph that now burned hot enough to nearly catch fire.

"Benny!" Keith yelled out. "Get a line on the stern before these waves take us back out!"

The boy quickly nodded. "Sir, yes, sir!"

Whaley was unable to move.

He didn't breathe.

He could only watch as his long-dead brother helped tie down the boat.

40

NOTHING HAPPENED.

Not at first.

When Izzie finished the bottle, she set it in the dirt and gripped both Chloe's hands in her own. The two of them faced each other, their eyes wide and filled with fear, false smiles on their lips as seconds ticked by loud enough to rattle my bones.

Chloe coughed.

That's how it started.

She was sitting there, perfectly still, and her body jerked. A cough came from deep, shot up her throat, and erupted out from behind her smile even as she tried to pinch her mouth shut to stop it. This wasn't a tickle in her throat— every inch of her being was part of it. The smile vanished from her face, slapped away by fear, and it only became worse when Izzie started to cough too. They went from holding hands to desperate grabs, lashing out, first at their own throats and bellies, then each other—unable to stop it, unable to slow it, only searching for the comfort found in the touch of another between spasms.

I'm not sure who started foaming at the mouth first. The rest happened so fast.

Thick white spittle dripped, then poured, soaked the fronts of their shirts. At some point, that white became tinged with red. Izzie's back went ramrod straight like someone grabbed her by the hair and yanked up while somehow forcing her to remain seated, then she fell back, her legs kicked out, arms wild. Chloe collapsed on top of her and they both began to convulse.

All of this took maybe thirty seconds, a minute at most.

The only thing worse than the sounds they made was the silence that came after—when neither moved and would never move again.

I was frozen in my chair.

Kira's mouth fell open. I thought for sure she would scream, but nothing came out. When she tried to stand, tried to go to them, Matty pulled her back down and forced her to remain in the circle at his side.

The candle flames grew tall, first reached for the rafters, then bent toward the lifeless bodies of both girls, grabbing but unable to touch.

"Praise Emerson," Alesia said quietly, her voice steady.

"Praise Emerson," Matty repeated.

Spivey said nothing. Through all of this, he hadn't uttered a sound. He sat there next to Alesia, but his mind had gone elsewhere.

Kira blinked away tears and seemed unable to look away from Izzie and Chloe. I shouted her name from behind the tape on my mouth, but it was just a muffled grunt and didn't break her from the spelled silence. Matty, who'd been holding her by the arm, reached up and rubbed her back—the bastard actually grinned at me as he did it. His sister was lying dead three feet away and the bastard was still hitting on my girlfriend.

The rustle of whispers had gone quiet, but they began again. Maybe discussing what they'd just seen or possibly deliberating what came next, their volume came roaring back with lustful excitement.

Spivey buried his face in his folded arms, drew his knees to his chest, and began to rock slowly back and forth. Something in him had broken.

Alesia ignored him. She gave Kira a quick glance, then splayed her fingers over the rounded butt of the revolver, her mind on fire with a million thoughts behind those green eyes. She locked eyes with Matty. "I have another packet of pentobarbital or you can use the gun, your call." She produced another small package of white powder from her pocket and dropped it to the dirt between them.

Matty eyed the powder, then shook his head as he glanced over at me. "He'd never drink it. Let me see the gun."

I shook the chair with as much force as I could pull together and only grew angrier when it barely moved. Shouting was pointless, but I did anyway. There wasn't anything else I could do.

Alesia slid the revolver over to him. Matty picked it up, popped the cylinder, and frowned toward Spivey. "Do you have more ammo? There's only two rounds."

Spivey stopped rocking but kept his face buried as he replied in a muffled voice, "That's how I found it."

Matty considered this, waved the gun toward me. "I cap him, use the other shot on myself. Then you've got enough of the pentobarbital left for…" His words trailed off as he looked from Alesia to Spivey, then Kira and back again.

Alesia nodded. "It'll be enough. More than enough." She looked over at me, tilted her head. "But the gift must be voluntary, not taken," she said. "He must end his own life, as must you. Taking his life against his will would nullify the agreement my mother forged for us."

"All these goddamn rules." Matty groaned. With his thumb, he snapped the cylinder back in place. "I guess we're doing this the hard way." He twisted to his right and pressed the barrel against Kira's temple. "We don't need her to finish this, Hasler. You're going to drink

Alesia's special cocktail or I'm spreading your girlfriend's brain across the basement wall."

Oh, the shadows liked that. They liked that a lot. The sound they made was nothing short of glee.

41

IT WAS HIM.

Bennett "Benny" Whaley.

The brother who had died of cystic fibrosis at ten years old when Whaley was only four. The brother whose grave was in the northwest corner of the Pleasant Street Cemetery under a sprawling oak. The brother who had screamed at him for accidentally leaving a LEGO brick in the carpet near the ladder of their bunkbed—the LEGO brick Benny stepped on at three in the morning, shouting loud enough to wake the house.

His brother Benny.

Soaked and covered in dirt, his dead brother Benny was standing right there on the dock, fumbling in the rain with a tangled rope, somehow looking fifteen or sixteen. It *was* him. Whaley had no doubt about that—the crooked front teeth were a dead giveaway, but he knew the boy's face too; he knew that face as well as he knew his own. It wasn't just the physical attributes Whaley recognized; it was the way he stood. The way he walked. The sound of his voice. He recognized all that as easily as he'd recognize himself.

Blood.

Kin.

Family.

His brother, Benny.

"Catch!" the boy called out.

Whaley didn't catch. The rain-drenched rope slapped him in the chest and fell at his feet. Whaley still couldn't move.

Keith shuffled over, grabbed it, and twisted it around one of the cleats, then used his foot as leverage against the side of the boat to pull it tight. "You still with me, Chief? We got work to do."

He was no longer holding the gun. Keith hadn't set it down (at least, Whaley hadn't seen him set it down). There was a bulge in the back of his shirt near his waistband—he might have tucked it there. Whaley could tackle him, overpower him, and—

"Chief!" Keith called out, staring at him.

When Whaley still didn't move, Keith cursed under his breath, pushed by him, and picked up one end of the bundled rug. He tugged it forward and lifted it toward the dock. "Grab this, Benny. Help me get it out of the boat."

Benny had fallen still too. His head was cocked slightly, his eyes narrowed, looking down at Whaley.

Whaley wanted to believe Benny recognized him, but that didn't seem altogether accurate. Benny recognized *something*, but it was like he couldn't put his finger on it. And how could he? Whaley had been four the last time he saw him.

And Benny hadn't lived to see his teen years, yet here he stood. So how was that possible?

Benny snapped out of it, reached down, and gripped the rug.

Keith gave it a three-count, then he pushed from below, Benny tugged from above, and between the two of them, they wrestled the rug to the dock.

The photograph burned so hot in Whaley's pocket, he was certain the next time he took off his shirt, he'd find a scorch mark on his chest.

Benny heaved one end of the rug up on his shoulder and began carrying it down the length of the dock, past *Annabelle*, toward shore. It weighed at least a hundred pounds, probably closer to a hundred and thirty, but he lifted it as if it were nothing.

Whaley's head was buzzing so loud, he hadn't noticed Keith come up beside him.

"He's not who you think he is. Not exactly," Keith said.

"He's my…"

"I know. But he also isn't. I know all about your brother. Laura kept detailed notes of everything she learned, shared some with me, shared more with Ted. At some point, your brother was out here before he died. That made him a token. When he died, Emerson called him back. Anyone less than sixteen who visits the island becomes property of Emerson, Chief. That's how it works. They become fuel for his fire. When they die, he calls them back. Doesn't matter if they die of natural causes or some accident a thousand miles away, whatever. That makes no more difference than *when* they die. Could be young, might be in their eighties. Time means nothing to him or this place. One way or another, all Emerson's tokens come home. Ain't no rest for them unless they do."

"How is that *rest?*"

Keith shrugged. "Call it peace, then. All I know is it's better than *not* coming back. I've been told trying to stay away is nothing short of hell, dead or alive. Pam'll attest to that."

"But he was ten when he…" Whaley couldn't bring himself to say it, not aloud.

"Some keep aging, just not as fast. Others go back to an earlier age. When Geraldine came out and talked to Pam and me, she said she thinks they return to the age when they were happiest. I don't know if that's true, but it helped her sleep to think that. Maybe your brother wanted to grow up; maybe that was all he thought about toward the end. Emerson gave him that much."

Whaley's hand had closed over the pocket with the picture. He pressed it through his shirt, felt the warmth on his palm. His brother sitting on his dad's car. None of what Keith said should make sense, yet it all did. He'd be willing to bet Benny thought of nothing but the years he wouldn't have when he was lying there in that bed at the end—years with him, years with his parents. He had a lifetime ahead of him, and that disease snatched it all away.

He had to talk to him.

At that moment, nothing else mattered.

Whaley gripped the edge of the dock, ready to haul himself up, but Keith grabbed the back of his shirt. "Chief, there's one other thing you need to know."

Whaley shrugged him off. "What?"

Keith reached behind his back again and for a second, Whaley thought he was going for the gun. He didn't; he patted the flask in his pocket, confirmed it was still there, then said, "The holes he's digging… He's been at that for a very long time."

"What's he looking for?"

Keith pursed his lips. "His own body. He's been trying to find it since he first came back out here. Never has, so he just keeps digging."

Benny's body was buried at Pleasant Street, right where it'd always been.

Nobody dies on that island, but that doesn't mean they don't come home. In the end, we all come home. In the end, that's all we can do.

Oh, Christ, Benny.

Whaley damn near jumped out of the boat.

He almost slipped running down the dock.

Benny had made it about halfway back to the house. He'd stopped next to one of the many holes he'd dug and set the rug down near the edge. He looked like he was about to climb down inside.

"Benny, wait!"

The words came out of Whaley's mouth, but to his own ears, the voice didn't sound like the grown man he was— it was his four-year-old self.

Benny froze at the sound of it, halfway in the hole, his brow creased in confusion. He dropped the rest of the way, both his hands resting on the muddy lip of the makeshift grave, water oozing over the edge. His mouth hung open slightly and his gaze fixed on Whaley.

When Whaley stopped about a foot from the hole's edge and crouched down next to the bundled rug, a single word escaped his brother's lips.

"Cliffy?"

That was too much. Whaley's eyes welled up; his breath hitched in his throat. Every ounce of strength washed from his body and drained away with the rain.

Whaley nodded weakly; that was all he could do.

What little color Benny had was gone. "My God, Cliffy, can that really be you?"

42

KIRA TRIED TO get up, but Alesia grabbed her like a vise and held her still. "Matty's right. We can do this without you, but if you still want to participate, you can. You just have to go after Billy, that's all."

I'd given up trying to tear my way out of the tape; there was no way I'd get out on my own. Shouting seemed pointless too, but I screamed anyway. I yelled out Kira's name, jerked my head back and forth. I rolled every inch of my body to try and bust out of that chair.

Matty looked like he was enjoying all this. The corner of his lip twisted up in a smirk. "Take the tape off his mouth. I wanna hear him beg."

Alesia glanced over at me, pointed, and the tape peeled from my mouth and dropped down into my lap. Although I knew she hadn't actually touched me, I felt her fingertips, her nail under the corner of the tape.

My mouth was filled with a disgusting mix of snot and gritty saliva. I spat it all out in the dirt and glared at Matty. "Your sister's dead, you ignorant shit. Chloe too. Even if all this is true, how do you know Alesia's not playing you? Maybe she's got some deal all her own! All of us in exchange for whatever? You saw what she did—floating like that—*what do you think she'd get for all of us?* All of us, including you? She doesn't give a shit about anyone but herself, you know that!" I jerked my chin toward Izzie and Chloe's lifeless bodies. "Look at them! You did that!"

Matty didn't look. Not at them. Instead, he pressed the gun harder against Kira's temple. "They did that to themselves," he replied flatly. "I watched, same as you. You make me kill Kira here, that's another story, that's murder. I get it. But I'm okay with a little blood on my hands if it gets us over the finish line. Got my eye on the prize and all. You fuck this up and I'll shoot you anyway. Two bullets—one for her, one for you. That's how this will end." He nodded at the powder. "I'll chug that after I do the two of you and they'll find me right here with Izzie. Maybe I'll even leave a quick note, tell everyone you made us do it. Ain't none of us walking out of here."

"Nik nok," Alesia said softly.

"Mix it up," Matty told her without taking his eyes off me.

Alesia opened another water bottle, poured in the powder, and shook it until it dissolved. When she was satisfied, she held the bottle out toward Matty. He didn't take it. Instead, he cocked the hammer on the revolver back with his thumb. "What's it gonna be, Hasler?"

"We shouldn't do this," Spivey said. His face was still buried and his voice was muffled. "I don't want to do it anymore."

"Shut up," Matty shot back. "Keep your goddamn mouth shut."

Spivey went quiet again.

Kira's eyes had filled with tears.

I couldn't watch her die.

If none of us were meant to leave this basement, I couldn't watch her die. Despite everything, I still loved her.

I didn't have to say it, not out loud. Kira knew.

"No." Kira groaned. She frantically began shaking her head. She shook her head so hard and fast I thought for sure the gun would go off. Matty must have too—

He jerked the revolver back and took his finger off the trigger. He kept the gun pointing at her as he took the water bottle from Alesia and pressed it into Kira's hand. "Take it over to him. I want to see him drink at least half."

Kira's fingers closed over the bottle, but it was more of an instinctual move than an intended one. She seemed surprised to see it there, and if Matty hadn't clasped his free hand around hers, she surely would have dropped it.

When she didn't move, Matty pressed the gun against her head with enough force to nearly shove her over. "Now, Kira."

I met her watery eyes and tuned out everyone but her. "It's okay," I said softly. "Everything's going to be okay. Bring it over to me."

Nearly another minute passed before she found the will. Clenching the bottle, the gun against the side of her temple, Kira rose on wobbly legs. Matty stayed so close it was like they were one person. I don't know what he expected her to do, what he thought she might try, but he wasn't about to give her any leeway. She crossed the few paces between us with a slow shuffle, then dropped to her knees between me and the furnace. Matty remained standing and pointed the gun at the top of her head.

"Praise Emerson," Alesia said from her spot between Spivey and the two dead girls.

"Praise Emerson," Matty repeated.

The shadows said nothing, as if too captivated to utter a sound. They managed to draw closer though, and the candle flames bowed in their presence, dimmed to nearly nothing.

"Bring the bottle to his mouth," Matty told Kira. "Careful not to spill. He needs to drink half, no more than that."

Kira pursed her lips, tried to stop them from quivering, but it did little good.

She raised the bottle, held it about an inch from my mouth.

"I love you, Billy," she whispered.

And for the first time since we began dating, I knew she meant it. It was there in her eyes, her tone, the warmth emanating from every pore of her body. Matty must have felt something too. His grip on the gun loosened and he blinked. It was gone as quickly as it came; he straightened back up and narrowed his eyes at me. "Drink."

I looked at Kira, I looked at nothing else, I *forgot* all else, and forced a smile. "I love you, too."

If I was going to die, I wanted her image to be the last thing I saw.

I leaned forward, pressed my lips against the rim of the bottle, and when she raised it, I drank. Hesitantly at first, then in deeper gulps. The water tasted chalky, but not unpleasant.

"No more than half," Alesia reiterated, leaning forward to get a better look, her eyes as bright as emeralds.

I felt a thousand eyes on me.

All watching.

All waiting.

Even Spivey. He'd stopped rocking and had turned, his mouth gaped.

They all watched me so closely, nobody noticed when Kira leaned over toward the furnace.

Not even Matty moved fast enough to stop her as she blew and the pilot light blinked out.

43

BENNY VANISHED.

There was no flash of light. No audible pop. No nothing.

One instant he was there, looking up at Whaley from the hole, then he wasn't.

The hole was gone, too.

His brother's shovel.

The wheelbarrow.

Everything—gone.

Crouching in the muddy earth, Whaley fell to his knees. The ground threatened to swallow him, and the heavy raindrops beating down from above only forced him lower.

His head jerked around as if operating independently from the rest of his body. His heart seized with an influx of adrenaline, and for one brief second, he thought that was it—the moment he would die. He lurched, forced himself to inhale, flood his lungs, then coughed. His body sputtered back to life much like the motor of *Merv* did back at the dock, and that particular thought popped into his head because he realized *Merv* was gone, too. So was *Annabelle*.

The dock was empty.

There was no sign of Keith.

When he turned back, he realized *all* of the holes were gone, not just the one Benny had been standing in. Every single hole. They hadn't been filled in (not that they could have been in that blink of an eye); the ground looked as if they had never been there. The rocky shore and yard were overgrown with tall, untamed weeds.

It had grown darker, too. It took a moment for Whaley to understand why, and when the thought clicked in his mind, he willed himself *not* to turn back around, *not* to look at the house. He knew what he'd see if he did. He knew he'd find every window dark. Every light extinguished. He knew that because he could no longer hear the whine of the generator coming from the shed on the opposite side of the house. The steady hum of the generator had been present behind the wilds of the storm, and now it wasn't. He knew that if he went to the shed, he'd find nothing inside but the mangled ruins of the machine that had once powered this island, the mess of a generator he had seen earlier with Billy. A generator that couldn't possibly have been running five minutes ago, one that hadn't run for decades.

Thunder clapped, and Whaley jerked so hard he nearly tumbled over. One hand slipped in the mud and he grabbed at the rug with the other, managed to steady himself.

The rug was still there.

On some level, that was comforting. That meant he hadn't imagined all the things he'd seen.

Not all *of them.*

No. He hadn't imagined any of it, because if he had, that meant Benny wasn't real.

And how could he be?

How exactly could your dead brother be real?

Whaley nearly tore his shirt getting the photograph out. The button broke clean off and landed about four feet away with a splash. He fumbled with the picture, yanked at it, and when the corner caught—

Christ, don't tear it!

—he slipped his thumb under the edge and managed to get it out, and rain be damned, he held it a few inches from his face so he could make it out in the dark.

His gut tightened into a knot.

The edges were frayed and torn. White creases marred the image. And looking up at the camera with those big, goofy eyes of his was David Spivey, maybe five or six years old. No car. No Benny.

"No! No! No!" Whaley shouted, shaking the picture like it was one of those old Polaroids that developed in your hand, like the motion would somehow change it back. But it didn't matter how many times he shook it. The photograph was no longer hot either. Not even warm. It was cold, lifeless.

It was a fucking photograph and nothing more.

"No…" Whaley groaned. He leaned forward, kept leaning until his forehead was resting on the rug, and for the first time in nearly thirty years, he cried.

He might have stayed like that all night if not for the smell coming from within the rug. It snapped him back after only a minute or two, and he lurched up into a sitting position and looked down at the rug. He didn't remember putting the photograph back in his pocket any more than he remembered tearing at that first piece of tape. He hadn't blacked out—it was more like his brain hit the reset button in order to get him moving again, but when he did realize what he was doing, he'd torn away about half the bindings holding that rug together and he was working on another piece at the opposite end from where he started. He had to use his teeth on that one, but he got it loose and peeled it away. He gave the rug a gentle push, just enough to get it rolling. The odor was terrible, one he knew all too well as a cop, one he'd smelled out at Jaffrey Point not that long ago. Death had seeped into the rug, soaked into the fibers, and he tried not to breathe it in as the rug unspooled.

When he reached that final roll, he slowed, unwilling to disrespect the dead even now, even after all else. He peeled away the last bit with a shaky hand.

Geraldine Rote's lifeless body looked up at him from behind closed eyes, the tiniest bit of glue visible in the corners. Her skin was a sickly pink with makeup caked on by the mortician, now flaking and cracked. Her lips were parted slightly, and Whaley could see the clear stitches preventing her mouth from opening further.

Keith had dug her up.

Keith was bringing her home.

Whaley didn't hear the approach of footsteps. Between the rain and shallow gusts, he couldn't hear much of anything. It wasn't until Keith spoke that he realized the man was standing there at all. He was clutching a ratty black duffel.

"Chief, we gotta get her in the ground."

44

THE BASEMENT WENT dark.

Not only because the pilot light went out, but because *all* the lights went out. When Kira blew out the pilot light, I could only see the candles from the corner of my eye.

They didn't blow out. They didn't extinguish.

They just... *weren't.*

They were gone.

The light dancing from their wicks vanished as if it had never existed. There was no leftover scent of sulfur; there was just nothing.

The whispers were gone, too. And—

I realized I was no longer taped to the chair, like the tape had never been there. I tried to wrap my head around that when my gut lurched. I felt a sharp pain deep within my stomach like someone was trying to cut their way out.

Alesia's poison.

How much had I drunk?

Oh, Christ, I—

Before that thought finished, fingers pried open my mouth. A hand scraped against my teeth, shoved inside. More fingers pushed over my tongue, reached for the back of my throat, found the—

I gagged.

My stomach squeezed, convulsed, and all that was inside came rushing out. The hand pulled out as wet vile heat spewed out of my mouth and shot out into the darkness, every inch of my body working to expel it. I jerked forward, fell out of the chair, and someone caught me—I couldn't see who; it was too dark—and slowed my fall to the dirt.

I felt fingers brushing through my hair a moment before I heard Kira's voice, inches from my ear. "It's okay, let it all out. Get it all out. It's okay. It's okay…"

She cradled my head against her chest until the last of the convulsions stopped, until nothing but air was left in my stomach. The last couple of heaves felt like shards of glass, then it finally stopped.

"It's okay," she said again.

I still couldn't see her, but I felt her fumbling around. Her right arm stretched out and frantically searched the dirt for something. She found what she wanted, and it wasn't until she struck a flame that I realized she'd scooped up the matchbox Spivey kept near the furnace.

The match wasn't very bright, but it was enough for me to see her, see myself. I could make out the dirt where the others had been sitting around the pentagram, but none of that was there. The floor was bare. Izzie and Chloe's bodies were still there, but Spivey, Alesia, and Matty had vanished.

I jerked around, looked behind me—where the hell?

Kira held the match up high, tried to get a better view of the basement. "Do you see Matty?"

"I… don't see any…"

The stairs were gone.

The match petered out and Kira quickly lit another.

I could make out the faint outline of the wall where the stairs had been, but even that was nearly indiscernible. It was like I was looking at the idea of a wall rather than an actual wall. The matchlight didn't reach the rafters of the ceiling, and for that, I was partially grateful. A good part of me was certain they were no longer there. Neither was the door at the top of the stairs.

My mind flashed back to my trip to the island earlier with Chief Whaley—the missing basement.

Somehow, I was in that missing basement.

"I don't understand," I muttered in a voice that might have come from a frightened child. "Where is everything?" I jerked my head to where Alesia had been sitting. "Where are they?"

Kira spun around with the match. Urgent, fearful. "Where's Matty? DO YOU SEE HIM ANYWHERE?!"

She sounded terrified.

I'd never heard her so scared.

I shook my head. "No."

They'd gone out with the furnace. With the pilot light.

I don't know where that thought came from, but there it was, and I knew it was true.

"Can you move?" Kira quickly lit another match. "Did you get it all out?"

I wiped my mouth. "I… I think so."

"There's something you need to see."

She tugged me across the dirt, toward Benny's hole, and *that* was still there. This grave in the middle of the basement floor.

Kira handed me the burning match along with the box. "Keep the light going. I need to see what I'm doing."

She started scraping away the dirt. With her bare hands, she started digging.

I grabbed her wrist. "We can't."

She pulled away from me and kept going. "You *need* to see this."

Kira yanked away the divot from earlier, revealing the fingers. She hesitated, but for only a second, then brushed the fingers clean of dirt and kept digging. She uncovered the wrist, part of the arm. There was a watch on the wrist—I didn't recognize it at first, then I did—and that wasn't possible, because—

Kira kept digging.

A shoulder.

Dark hair.

She uncovered only enough of the girl's pale chest to reveal the green amulet caked to the side of her breast with moist dirt.

Kira started on the head. I wanted her to stop. I didn't want to see this, but there was no stopping her, not until we could see the face, and only then did she quit and fall back on her heels, gasping.

The smell was horrible, but I was beyond throwing up. I think I was deep in the throes of shock.

I'd forgotten about the match, and the flame burned my fingertips. I quickly shook it out, fumbled with the box, and lit another.

I brought the flickering light down near the body.

The girl buried in Benny's hole wasn't Lily Dwyer; it was Alesia Dubin.

And Alesia Dubin had been dead for some time. Several days. Maybe a week.

From deep in the dark, near the basement's far corner, a throat cleared.

45

WHALEY LOOKED DOWN at the body of Geraldine Rote. The rain made quick work of the mortician's makeup—most had washed away, revealing wrinkled alabaster skin puffy and lined with dark veins. "It's not the girl," he managed to say. "Not Lily Dwyer."

Keith set the black bag down in the mud and dropped to a knee beside him. "I told you it wasn't. Told you the girl was safe."

"Safe where?"

Unlike Whaley, Keith *did* look up at the house. He gave the place a hard stare before turning back to him. "She called me, couple weeks back. Right after Geraldine here turned up over at Henry's. I didn't know her, never talked to her before, but she seemed to know all about me, Pam, about this place. Said she was friends with Laura Dubin's kid, so that explained that. Laura filled her daughter's head over the years with everything she dug up, everything she pieced together, not only on this place and Emerson since he crawled off that ship years back, but things he done before he ever set foot on Wood. She traced him hundreds of years, maybe as much as a thousand, to places all around the world where he left his mark. Damned places. Cursed places. Places of death. I always figured Laura might be the only one who knew what Emerson was, but when I listened to this girl, I realized Laura's daughter might actually know more." Keith looked up at Whaley with sallow eyes. "Laura was a witch. Spent her life on it. *Did you know that?* An honest-to-God, full-on black magic witch, and she taught her kid everything."

"Alesia," Whaley said softly. "Her daughter's name is Alesia."

"Yeah, Alesia. That's it." Keith nodded. "Laura had herself a copy of Orlan Walton's will. That was Geraldine's father. It had been written up by Clarence Marston, Lockwood Marston's grandaddy, I think. Those bastards have always been close to all this. Don't know how she got ahold of it, but it had the rules, same as Geraldine's, spelled out nearly word-for-word but for one difference. Geraldine's will listed only two ways ownership of the island could change hands—donation to the township of Kittery or bequeath to a blood relative." He paused for a second, licked his lips. "Orlan Walton's will had a third, four words—*joined through sacramental coitus.*"

Keith struggled with the pronunciation, and Whaley wasn't sure he heard him right. He hadn't cracked a Latin book since college, but, "Doesn't that mean—"

"It means"—Keith cut him off—"marriage. A union. Today's world may require a piece of paper to make marriage legal, but for thousands of years prior, it was sex that made two people one. Laura believed if her daughter slept with my boy, they'd somehow be bound, and that tie would be enough for her to take ownership, or at least make a claim to it in the eyes of Emerson. Lily told me the two of them were already sleeping together, so there was nothing I could do about that. That wasn't the worst of it. Ownership of this place might get you health, money, some kind of status, but that's only the half of it, and it's not the half Laura Dubin ever cared about, and certainly wasn't what her kid wanted. They wanted the *power* of it. Geraldine told Pam and me Emerson was thousands of years old, maybe as old as time. Older than heaven and hell. Maybe as old as everything." Keith's head swiveled back toward the house. "Him being here, in this place, all that dark energy trapped in one spot. It's like a battery, one that grows stronger— it feeds off the souls it's claimed, the 'tokens.' Laura's kid wants *that*. Lily said she's willing to give Emerson whatever he wants to get it. She tried to get Lily to come out here with the rest of them, but Lily knew better. She's only fifteen and figured Alesia only wanted her to help feed the fire. Figured right."

"Where is Lily now?"

"After I talked to her, I called Teddy. We knew Lily was in danger, so he made arrangements to pick her up from the mall. He stashed her in an empty house up in York—guess he was in the middle of flipping it and said nobody would look there."

"And she's still there now?"

Keith shook his head. "We think some of the kids may have been following her, saw her get into Teddy's car, so he moved her around a few times. Other houses he owned. I'm not sure where she is now, but he kept her safe. I'm sure she is now."

Whaley recalled the surveillance footage at the mall. Kira Woodward, Chloe Kittle, Izzie Fernandez, and Alesia Dubin only a few steps behind Lily Dwyer.

Lightning cracked across the sky, and from the corner of his eye, he caught a glimpse of the house—dark, decaying—some dead thing left to rot on the shore.

Whaley didn't realize how bad he was shaking until he tried to stand. His legs were noodles. If not for the sucking sound his shoes made in the mud as he steadied himself, he might not have known he was actually standing. But something in that sound seemed *real*. More real than the rain and the wind and the house. A house he wasn't sure was actually there any more than he was sure he heard the generator sputtering along not more than ten minutes ago. If he walked up to that house—his shoes making that suckity-suck sound the whole way—if he walked up and placed a hand on the white siding, would it be solid or would his hand pass right through? He turned and peered toward the empty dock, shielding his eyes from the rain.

"The house is cycling right now," Keith explained. "The boats belong to the island, to Emerson. They cycled out with it."

"Cycling?"

"It's like two worlds existing in the same place—the living and the dead. They can't both be here at the same time, so it cycles from one to the other."

And Benny wasn't in this one.

"Brigadoon..." Whaley muttered.

"Huh?"

When Whaley didn't respond, Keith looked back at the house. "We need to get inside before they're all dead, *but not before it cycles back.* We go too soon and we'll get caught on the wrong side."

He said all this as if it made perfect sense.

Perfect crazy sense.

Goddamn Brigadoon.

Whaley's hand had gone back to his pocket, the one holding the photograph, hoping for a warmth that wasn't there.

Keith reached for a corner of the rug, folded it over Geraldine Rote's face. "When it cycles back, we gotta get her in the ground. That world, not this one."

"Why?"

The word slipped out and Whaley regretted it the moment it did, because he didn't want that answer. He wasn't sure he could handle much more.

Keith told him anyway.

"For those claimed by Emerson, death isn't the end. It's only the start of something else. For her to have any chance at peace, we need to bury her. Bury her *there*."

"I thought you brought her here to trade?"

"Huh?"

"You told Pam you were gonna make some kind of trade." He looked down at Geraldine. "*Her* for your boy. That's what Pam said."

Keith pursed his lips, confused at first, then he got it. "No, not Geraldine. *I'm gonna give him Laura's kid.* She wants it anyway. She can have it. Fuck her, fuck her mother, they both deserve to burn." Then something clicked and his face grew pale, his brow tightened, and his words caught in his throat. "Chief, when did you talk to Pam?"

Whaley didn't answer that; he didn't have to. Keith somehow pieced it together.

The little life in the man's eyes drained away. "She's gone… isn't she?"

Several seconds ticked by before Whaley nodded solemnly.

When Keith finally spoke again, his voice was as broken as he appeared to be. "This thing has taken everything from me. I'm done giving. I'm done." He placed his palm on the rug holding Geraldine Rote. "We bury her, then we bury *it*."

He nodded at the black duffel.

The rusty zipper was only partially closed, and when lightning lit up the sky again, Whaley caught a glimpse of what was inside—dynamite. A half dozen sticks, maybe more. Some kind of timer and a bundle of wires.

46

KIRA HEARD THE sound too. A throat clearing. She pressed against me, grabbed the match from my hand, and held it high above our heads, toward the sound. "Matty? Is that you?"

The flickering flame did its best, but if the dark basement was oily black before, it had somehow managed to grow darker— like the ceiling, like the wall where the stairs had been. I got the distinct impression the outer walls of the basement were no longer there, nor the cistern. Because the basement no longer existed. We were in that other house, the one that didn't have a basement. If Kira were to tell me the small plot of dirt where we sat floated in some spaceless void, I would have believed her.

Kira didn't say that; she pressed tighter against me, her breathing hard. "Do you see him? *Do you SEE HIM!?*"

Matty clucked his tongue, and while such a thing should have made finding him that much easier, it didn't. The sound didn't come from any particular direction, but from all around us. It echoed off the nothingness of the dark, circled the room like it was trying to find a way out.

He spoke with a slow, hypnotic drone. "You should cover Alesia back up. I don't like her like that. I don't think she'd want us to think of her that way. She's so much more now. Unearthing that shell feels... disrespectful. I'd hate for her to be angry when she comes back." He blew out a breath in a slow whistle. "You know how she gets... got... whatever."

Alesia's lifeless eyes stared up at me, cloudy with cataracts. Her mouth frozen in a scream. Long-dried white spittle colored the corner of her mouth, ran down her cheek and neck, crusted her shirt. She looked no different than Chloe and Izzie—Alesia had drunk the poison too. She'd been the first to die. Yet she'd been in the room with us; she had been *right here* with us only moments ago. I didn't blink because I knew if I did, her fingers might twitch, might reach up and take hold of me, pull me down under her blanket of dirt.

"You should see your face, Hasler. You look like you saw a ghost."

Kira reached back toward the chair, started clawing at the dirt. "Help me find the knife."

Matty's knife.

The one she'd buried after Alesia cut me.

I dropped down next to her and started scraping away the dirt.

Matty let out a soft laugh. "I saw you bury it earlier, Kira. What makes you think it's still there? Maybe it cycled out with everything else. I'll give you a second to find it. I think this next part will be far more fun if you've got a knife. If you think you can actually get away."

Was he closer?

He sounded closer.

The ground shook.

Rumbled.

Flecks of dirt rained down from above like black snow.

Kira's head shot up, tilted toward the place the ceiling should have been.

"What was that?" I whispered.

"Just keep digging," she replied quickly, going back to the dirt.

"You're not gonna tell him, Kira? You should probably tell him."

"Fuck you."

"You wish." He laughed.

"Tell me what?"

She didn't answer, only kept digging.

"We're not supposed to be here," Matty said. "The dead don't like it. They want us out. It's a double standard, if you ask me. We let them roam around our world, why can't we hang out in theirs?"

The ground rumbled again.

Not only the ground, *everything*. The air, the dark. I sucked in another breath and realized it was getting hard to breathe.

"You feel that, right?" Matty said. "Everything closing in on us. Alesia told me the longest she sat in this realm was three minutes. We've been here for over five. How long do you think we got until it all collapses in on us? Can we die here? I'd be willing to bet we can. If we do, do we get to haunt the dead like they haunt us?"

He *was* closer. No doubt about that.

I still couldn't see him; I couldn't see much of anything.

"Keep digging!" Kira groaned as she lit another match.

The darkness had closed in so tight, I could no longer see Izzie and Chloe's bodies off to our side. Alesia's vacant eyes were flickering pinpricks, watching us with a blank stare.

"It's not there," Matty said. "You know it's not. I suppose the real question you should be asking yourself is if the *gun* is still here. Unlike the knife, I was holding the gun when you blew out the light. Maybe I still am."

Kira muttered something I couldn't make out.

"What did you say?" I pulled in another breath. The air had grown so thin my lungs gasped, sucked in more. I was getting light-headed. Was the oxygen going? *Were we running out of air?*

Kira spoke quickly, like a rambling mantra. "He doesn't have the gun. He doesn't have the gun. The gun vanished just like the tape that had been holding you to the chair. You were touching the tape and it's gone, so he doesn't have the gun."

When Matty spoke again, I had no doubt he was closer. He sounded like he was right on top of us.

"I'm okay dying here, Kira. Are you? You okay with killing Billy? If not, you better fire up that pilot light while you still can. Suffocation is a weird thing. It sneaks up on you. You get all lightheaded, then you start seeing stuff, crazy things that couldn't possibly be real. If you're lucky, you black out before you die. Not everyone is lucky though. Most are wide awake. I hear it's like breathing after a solid hit to the gut."

By the time I saw him, it was too late.

Matty's fist came out of nowhere—he landed a knuckle punch to my right kidney, and when I twisted around, he hit me again in the center of my abdomen. The air rushed from my lungs, and before I could suck in more, he hit me again.

My vision went white, but not before I caught a glimpse of Kira diving toward the furnace, furiously striking matches as she went. She caught the pilot light and it burst to life, blindingly bright.

47

EVERYTHING SHIFTED.

Whaley felt it this time, the change, the world around him *cycling*. It happened insanely fast, a millisecond, not even a blink, but he *did* feel it. His balance was gone, then it wasn't, like the ground tilted and jerked itself back. In that instant, the holes were back. If Whaley hadn't shuffled a step to the right, he surely would have fallen into the one nearest him, the hole Benny had been digging when he vanished.

The generator hummed in the distance. Light burned bright from every window of the house. Unnaturally bright for an instant, then settling, as if the generator kicked out a few extra anxious volts.

Both boats were strapped to the dock, rocking violently in the tall waves, smacking loudly against the rubber bumpers.

The holes were back, but Benny was not.

The photograph burned at Whaley's chest as if someone had set a match to it. He pulled it from his pocket and looked down at the image.

Benny sitting on the fender of the car, beaming up at the camera again. But there was something else, something different. On the far right of the image, cast across the driveway in front of the car, was the shadow of a much younger child. He didn't need anyone to tell him it was a four-year-old boy. Him.

Still crouching near his bag, Keith glared at him. "Did you get that from Pam?"

Whaley nodded.

"The photographs lie. You shouldn't look at it. You should destroy it."

Whaley moved as fast as a child scooping up his favorite toy and crammed the tattered picture back in his pocket before Keith tried to take it from him. *Nobody* would take it from him. "I'm keeping it," he said, and even that came out embarrassingly fast.

Keith huffed and got to his feet. He wiped his wet hair back and grabbed one side of the rug holding Geraldine Rote. "Help me get her down in that hole before the house cycles again."

Whaley looked down into the hole. It was at least five feet deep, and there was a good five or six inches of water sitting in the bottom. Putting Geraldine Rote's desecrated body down there seemed horribly disrespectful.

Keith cursed under his breath. "You gonna make me pull the gun on you again or you gonna do what's right?"

What's right.

Nothing was right about any of this, but Whaley gave a defeated shrug and went to the edge of the hole, started to climb down.

"Whoa!" Keith shouted. "Stay up top. You don't want to get caught down there if the house cycles back. We'll use the rug to lower her. Just watch the edges—all that mud's loose. You don't want to fall, neither."

Whaley pinched his eyes shut for a moment, told all the voices in his head shouting for him to stop to shut the hell up, then grabbed the rug by the corners, opposite Keith. Together they wrestled it to the side of the hole, as close to the edge as they dared. Keith gave them a three-count, and with several grunts, they pulled the rug over the opening and carefully lowered her down.

Benny's shovel was planted in the pile of dirt behind the hole. Keith grabbed it and tossed it to Whaley. "Help me fill it in."

Before Whaley could object, Keith dropped to his knees and began clawing the dirt into the hole with his bare hands, moving with a frantic pace, fistful after fistful.

Had Whaley looked up, had he peered through the rain at the shore, he would have seen the bodies rising from the many other holes. All those who were not Benny. He would have seen all those eyes watching him and Keith with curiosity.

48

I SAW KIRA ignite the pilot light. Matty didn't, and the sudden shift took him by surprise. He froze for one brief second, and when he did, I brought my knee up into his ribs and heard the snap of bone. He let out a sharp yelp and rolled off me to his side, clutching his belly. My arms were tangled in something, and when I got a closer look, I realized it was the remains of the duct tape still clinging to my wrists—somehow it came back, loosely wrapped without the chair. I tore it away, brushed it off quickly like I'd gotten caught in a spiderweb.

From behind me came a scream.

A scream bridled with gut-wrenching terror, and for a brief second, I thought it was Kira. It wasn't, though. I turned to find Alesia standing over her own body. "Why is that uncovered? WHY IS *THAT* UNCOVERED?!" She shrieked.

She had one hand over her mouth, the fingers splayed across her cheeks, and she was standing there, pointing with her free hand—and every bit of that was impossible, yet there she was. The glow I'd seen in her eyes earlier shone as bright as the pilot light at my side—so bright it lit up wherever she looked. When she turned on me, that light crawled over my skin like a million ants. She hovered about an inch off the ground, her bare feet dangling.

I skittered backward through the dirt, shuffled on my hands, and cracked against Matty. He grabbed for my shoulder, but I spun away and off to the right before he could grip me. That was good, because if he somehow managed to hold me still long enough for my brain to catch up with what I was seeing, I certainly would have lost it.

Along the outer walls, at least twenty people were in the basement with us, their bodies motionless, as still as statues, save for their dry, cracked lips, which moved ungodly fast in muttered whispers. Words I didn't understand, then I did and wished I could unhear.

Emerson welcomes you, Billy Hasler. Emerson has waited. You are your father's son, your father's gift. Give yourself and you will know joy. Give yourself and you will know life eternal. Give yourself so he may feast upon your soul. Emerson deserves to be hungry no more. Praise Emerson.

I didn't recognize the faces, not at first, certainly not all of them, but Lester Rote was there. Patricia and William Whidden. And so many others. People frozen in a time that wasn't mine—their clothing told me that much. There were boys not much older than me dressed in Coast Guard uniforms, others dressed in the drab grays and whites of Puritans, others still in the tattered ruins of clothing worn far too long at sea. Women and children too, all of them whispering from expressionless faces.

All of them drifted closer, maddeningly slow, *floating*, Alesia nearest of all. Inches now from the bodies of Izzie and Chloe.

From somewhere in that crowd came Matty's voice. "I think you busted one of my ribs, Hasler. I'm gonna fuck your shit up—ah, there's that damn gun."

My fingers scraped at the dirt, dug, as if I could somehow burrow and hide in there. When they brushed against something hard and metal, I didn't realize what it was at first. When I did, I scooped up the knife, popped the blade, and held it out, my hand shaking so bad I thought for sure I'd drop it.

The stairs had come back along with everything else, and Spivey called down from near the top. "Billy! This way, come on!"

Someone grabbed me from behind, wrapped their arms under mine, and lifted, and I nearly stabbed them with the knife before I realized it was Kira, trying to get me to my feet. "Hurry!"

I scrambled up, shuffled toward the steps with her, unwilling to turn my back on Alesia and the others. I didn't see Matty raise the gun, but I heard the shot. The bullet whizzed by my head close enough to flutter my hair.

Alesia's head twisted around angrily, twisted nearly halfway around. "You can't kill him! He needs to kill himself!"

"When I'm done with him, he'll tear his own throat out to end what

I've got planned," Matty told her, then raised his voice. "You wanna play, Hasler? Let's play!"

Alesia faced forward again. Her eyes grew wide and her mouth fell open in a gaping smile. She looked around slowly—at the walls, the steps, up toward the ceiling. Her fists tightened into knots. "Oh, he's here. I can feel him everywhere. It's glorious! I'm for you, Emerson! All of us are for you!"

When I gripped the railing, I felt him too, an energy pulsing through the wood, hot and throbbing. Not an inanimate object but a living, breathing thing. It came from the walls, the wood at our feet. The air was alive with it, with *him*.

A voice flooded the air, low and pure, maybe the most beautiful voice I'd ever heard. If someone told me it belonged to an angel, I would have believed them. He spoke in an even tone that seemed to radiate out from no particular place but everywhere, *everything*, and I knew it was Emerson. His words reached down through my flesh and pinched my bones.

"I accept your offering, but it is incomplete."

"He's yours!" Alesia shouted back. "We all are!"

"The remaining tokens must offer themselves willingly."

"They do! They will!"

"For I am all, and they are mine."

"Yes!"

"Perhaps a taste of what you shall receive? Perhaps with that you will see a path to bring me what is mine?"

Floating several inches off the ground now, Alesia's body stiffened, her back arched, and her mouth dropped open. The glow in her eyes and the amulet around her neck became so bright I could barely look, yet I couldn't turn away—the tips of her fingers, the tips of her toes, they glistened with green light. Her hair became a living thing, fluttering wildly in a wind that seemed to come from everywhere and nowhere.

"Oh…"

The single word fell from her lips. Her face contorted and became nothing short of orgasmic delight as the green light played across every inch of her body.

"It's all yours if you bring me them. If they offer themselves willingly."

Alesia's glow lit up the room, and I spotted Matty in the far corner of the basement, bracing himself on the cistern wall and pulling himself up with one hand, clutching the gun with the other.

Matty said, "Oh, he'll give himself to you, don't you worry about that. He'll beg for it by the time I finish with him. I'll show him what his girlfriend looks like on the inside. I'll gut her with my bare hands. I'll force him to watch until he's screaming to end himself. Then I want what's mine, too."

"Yes."

Matty shuffled toward us, toward the stairs, holding his ribs. "That's what I'm talking about!" he beamed, waving the gun.

Kira had her hand on my back, pushing, a fear-drenched sound coming from her—a thin, gut-wrenching wail I knew I'd hear anytime I was alone from that moment until the second I died.

Spivey appeared in the doorway up top, stood at the landing, watching *them*, not us, and there was no way I'd turn around and look—if I did, I knew I'd never make it up those last few steps.

Alesia's voice rattled through the air below, and this time it wasn't altogether hers. It was a mix of her voice and Emerson's. "Run if you want, Billy, but there's nowhere to go that isn't his. Praise Emerson."

"Praise Emerson," all the voices of those in the basement said in unison.

49

WHALEY FELT THE eyes on him long before he saw them. When the hair stood on the back of his neck, when the gooseflesh pricked up on his arms, he didn't look up. He fought every instinct in his body and forced his head to stay down, to keep digging. This was the cop in him. If someone were watching them bury Geraldine Rote, that someone might have a gun, a knife, or a goddamn rocket launcher for all he knew, and the only thing Whaley had going for him was the element of surprise. He plunged the tip of the shovel in the mud, folded his arm over the top, did his best to look like he was resting, then quietly told Keith, "Somebody's out there."

Keith's hands were raw and scratched. If he kept at it, they'd be bloody pulp by the time they finished, but he hadn't stopped once. Not until that moment. "They've been out there."

"Gimme the gun."

"Gun won't do you no good."

Whaley still hadn't looked up—he kept his eyes on Keith and tightened the grip on the shovel. "Gimme the damn gun."

"Can't kill what's dead."

Whaley's heart thumped. With those four words, he no longer wanted to look up but understood he didn't have a choice. He swallowed the lump in his throat and cautiously raised his head.

At least a dozen people stood near the southwest corner of the house, a few feet from the small porch off the kitchen. The wind stirred their hair, fluttered their clothing, but *they* didn't move, their bodies remaining perfectly still. All of them faced Whaley and Keith, expressionless, faces frozen, some mouths slightly agape, others pinched shut, but all watching. Whaley didn't recognize any of them, and thank God for that. He wasn't sure if his mind was on the verge of snapping or had cracked twenty minutes earlier, but seeing a familiar face among them might have been enough to seal the deal and drive him full-on crazy. All of them were wet, soaked as through and through as he was, and that didn't make sense if they were—

"They don't look dead."

"They wouldn't. Not here."

"What's that supposed to mean?"

"It means what it means. In this place, they're not altogether dead any more than they're still alive. They're somewhere between. They're—"

"... property," Whaley muttered.

"Tokens. Emerson's." Keith looked down at his bloody hands, then at Geraldine Rote's half-filled grave. "If someone Emerson laid claim to dies away from here, their soul is called back, called... home. Without their body, they're caught in limbo. That's what they are... caught. Body's got to be buried out here too, *buried properly*, that's how you stop it, give them peace." He reached into his pocket and took out the small flask—Whaley had thought he dropped it—but instead of drinking, he poured some on Geraldine Rote, then crossed himself. "Holy water from the church in town," he said without looking up.

"So she won't come back," Whaley said. "Not like them."

"Shouldn't."

"That's why those men brought the bodies of the Whidden children back out here and buried them on the beach all those years ago? To give them peace?"

Keith nodded. "And some idiot dug 'em up and took 'em away again in '72. 'Cause of that, I'd be willing to bet they're wandering around out here somewhere right now. Stuck. Caught again."

Oh, Christ, Benny.

His body was buried out at Pleasant Street Cemetery.

Whaley's head shot back up.

He meant to look for his brother among the faces, but realized—

"They're closer. All of them."

He hadn't seen them move, not so much as a twitch, but somehow they'd all drawn several feet closer. There were more, too—standing behind him and Keith, others near the house, more still out on the shore around the rocks. More than he could (or wanted to) count.

A shudder passed through him, and although he was certainly terrified, that's not what this was. He sucked in a shallow gasp.

Keith's eyes widened. "You felt that too, didn't you?"

Whaley nodded.

"It's Emerson. I think he's here."

"You best let me finish that," a voice said not more than a few inches from Whaley's side. He swung around, wielding the shovel, and managed to pull the blow back a moment before the blade would have cracked against Benny's head.

Benny didn't flinch; he only stood there as still as the others, rain rolling down the sides of his pale face.

To anyone watching, Whaley might have been one of them, he was so still. He stood so close to his brother he could smell him, a scent as familiar as his own. He brought the palm of his hand within an inch of Benny's face—wanted to feel the warmth of him—but he didn't dare draw closer. If there was no heat, no sign of life, he wouldn't be able to bear that. It was better to believe.

"Something bad's about to happen," Benny told him, his eyes darting toward the house, then back to meet Whaley's. "Something terrible. I'd rather be out here in the storm. The rain makes me feel…"

Whaley didn't hear how his brother finished that sentence; his own mind ended it for him with the one word he desperately did not want to hear aloud.

Alive.

Benny took the shovel, and Whaley let him.

Keith rose to his feet and reached behind his back. He tugged out the gun, looked down at it for a long moment, and held it out toward Whaley. "Take it if it will make you feel better."

Whaley did.

It didn't make him feel better.

Not one bit.

50

BY THE TIME Kira and I reached the top of the basement steps, Spivey was halfway to the second floor. "Hurry up!" He paused only long enough to make sure we were behind him, then disappeared around the bend.

Somewhere near the top of those steps (I think it was Matty's threat that did it), Kira had shut down— not completely, but enough to slow her down. Like part of her mind retreated inward and found a good place to hide. I'd grabbed her by the arm and pulled her along behind me, doing my best to hide the terror chewing at my insides like ravenous worms trying to get out.

As we passed the photographs hanging on the landing, I made a conscious effort *not* to look at them. Instead, I turned toward the living room, and that may have been worse.

Eight or nine others stood in that room, all of them facing toward us. Faces from the past I didn't know and didn't want to. They stood perfectly still, like those in the basement, muttering that same chant over and over.

Emerson welcomes you, Billy Hasler. Emerson has waited. You are your father's son, your father's gift. Give yourself and you will know joy. Give yourself and you will know life eternal. Give yourself so he may feast upon your soul. Emerson deserves to be hungry no more. Praise Emerson.

It was the two sitting on the couch that caused me to freeze right where I stood. My heart pounded so hard it threatened to explode in my chest.

Izzie and Chloe sat on the couch.

I knew they were dead in the basement—Kira and I had nearly tripped over their bodies fleeing—yet there they were, just sitting there. They were holding hands, a look of listless bewilderment in their eyes, their bodies almost as motionless as all the others in that room save for Chloe—she was reaching for a can of Diet Pepsi someone had left on the coffee table, trying to grab it and failing. Izzie stared at her outstretched hand; her fingers wrapped around the can, but were unable to grip it. When she squeezed, they passed through as if the can weren't really there. But that wasn't the case at all—*they* weren't really there, or if they were, they were no longer…

My mind flashed back to the odd scene of Lester Rote, Geraldine, Ralph Peck, and the two Whidden children. How William Whidden had held that jar and the amazement of the others as he did. Patricia and that ribbon.

Kira gasped at the sight of Chloe and Izzie. Her head jerked around and looked down the steps toward the basement, then twisted back again in a moment of realization all her own.

I pulled her toward the kitchen, toward the back door, then froze—there were more—

Oh, Christ. How many? What were they?

—people, ghosts, spirits, apparitions, wraiths—shoulder-to-shoulder, blocking the way, their lips moving in unison with the others, that horrific chant.

Were they solid? If we tried to force our way through them to the door, could they stop us? Would *we* pass right through *them?*

Could they stop us?!

I didn't want to touch them.

Didn't want them to touch me.

Like they carried an infection and their touch would—

"Come on, dammit!" Spivey called out from above. "Before they block this way too!"

The last thing I wanted to do was go up, risk getting trapped deeper in the house, but we had no choice. Matty was right behind us, grunting his way up the steps, his monstrous shadow lit by Alesia at his back. She hadn't bothered with the stairs; she simply rose, drifted up through the air as effortlessly as a fleck of dust caught in a breeze. Her hands were outstretched and she was clenching her fists—clenching and unclenching—every inch of her glowing, burning with energy, and I got the feeling if she didn't use it, she might explode. She certainly wanted to use it.

I started up the steps, tugging Kira behind me, and when she dug in her heels, when her cries morphed into shouts of *NO! NO! NO!* I pulled her, half carried her up the steps. I had no choice, because she didn't see Matty come around the corner and level the gun at her head. She didn't see the fucked-up grin on his face, and she certainly didn't see his finger squeeze the trigger.

51

LIGHTNING STREAKED THE sky and thunder cracked with a harsh whip-snap as loud as a gunshot. The rain twisted on the wind and came at them sideways. Whaley paused for a second, then chased after Keith. With the bag hefted on his shoulder, the other man was halfway to the small porch off the back door of the house before Whaley took his first step. Whaley didn't look back at Benny—oh, he wanted to, but he didn't. He didn't want to let his brother out of his sight again, but he knew he was descending into some kind of hell—the fact that every hair on his body was standing up told him so—and he couldn't let himself get distracted. Distracted would get him killed. As they drew closer to the house, he kept his eyes front and held to the sounds of Benny filling in the grave, the smack of the shovel against wet earth—he listened to it through the rain. As long as he could hear that, he knew Benny was back there. That had to be enough.

Keith and Whaley weaved through all those standing between them and the house. They made no effort to stop them, but they didn't get out of the way either. Whaley got the impression they were only observers in all this, curious to see how it would turn out, nothing more. That was until he looked back and realized they had closed ranks behind them. By the time they stepped up on the porch, those lost souls (and that was how Whaley thought of them) had drawn so close, stood so near one another, they had formed a wall.

They're corralling you.

That's what they're doing.

Corralling you.

Keith grabbed Whaley by the shirt and tugged him up the steps. "It's best to ignore them."

"Can they hurt us?"

Keith chewed the inside of his cheek, but didn't answer.

Whaley shirked his arm out and pointed at the ground. "If they're dead, why are they leaving footprints?"

Keith didn't look at the ground, the trampled mud; he kept his gaze fixed on Whaley. "Not all of 'em, only the ones who have been here for a while. Takes 'em a little time to learn how to do that."

Like the business with the house cycling, Keith said this as if it made perfect sense, and to him, maybe it did. He didn't bother to clarify further; he only shifted the bag from his right shoulder to his left and reached for the door.

Whaley grabbed him. "Let me go first."

Keith seemed amused by this. He stepped to the side and gave Whaley room. "Be my guest."

Whaley eased up to the door and pressed the microphone button clipped to his shoulder. "Mundie, if you can hear this, I'm out at Wood. I'm going in the house. We need backup out here."

When he released the button, no reply came. The LED on the radio was still off. Most likely it hadn't transmitted at all, but it felt good to go through the motion, fall back into cop rhythm. He banged on the door with the back of his fist. "Spivey? This is the police. We're coming in!"

He didn't expect an answer, and there wasn't one.

Gripping the gun, he reached for the doorknob and twisted it.

Frowned.

The knob turned, but the door wouldn't open.

"He must have a dead bolt on it. Got it locked from the inside," Whaley said.

Keith shook his head. "That's not it at all."

"Then what?"

"Emerson's waiting for me, not you."

Keith gave the knob a gentle twist and the door eased open.

There were more ghosts in the kitchen.

Four men dressed in ancient Coast Guard uniforms leaning back on the countertops, allowing Whaley and Keith just enough room to pass. Their faces were awash in emerald green light coming from the next room.

Whaley trained the gun on them as they stepped by, but they

ignored him—the sailors' eyes were all locked on Keith. Together they muttered in the faintest whisper:

He has come of his own free will. Returned home. He is yours. He is ours. Praise Emerson.

"Fuck Emerson," Keith shot back under his breath.

Behind them, the door slapped shut with an angry *crack!* and Whaley didn't have to try the knob to know it wouldn't open again.

Not until it was ready.

He shook that thought away.

Everything about the house looked different, like he was standing in another house altogether. Unlike before, all the kitchen cabinets, countertops, and appliances were new. Same with the flooring. Fresh paint. The cracks in the plaster ceiling were gone.

Whaley forced himself to ignore all that. He didn't care if the house was *cycling*, like Keith said. He didn't care if it turned into a pumpkin at midnight. All he cared about were the kids. Getting them out and away from whatever this was.

Keith stopped at the doorway to the next room, Whaley behind him, when the four sailors said something else.

A cough is just a cough, right, Chief? Mary is just fine. No need to worry about her. Until you do. Right? Praise Emerson.

Whaley snapped around, glared at the four of them, but they looked past him. Looked through him, as if he weren't even there.

"Ignore them, Chief," Keith told him. "Don't let them in your head."

As he said that, he stared through the open doorway, squinted, his face filled with bright green light.

The light vanished the moment he stepped through, and for a second, Whaley thought Keith vanished with it. He didn't, though. Whaley found him standing in the living room, and, oh God, they were there too.

52

THE BULLET MISSED Kira by maybe an inch and vanished into the wall with a *crack!*

That was Matty's last shot, and as he stood there looking at the smoking barrel of the revolver in one hand, clutching his busted ribs with the other, I knew I could take him, and I was about to try when one of those things stepped up beside him.

He wasn't much older than me, might have even been younger, I couldn't tell. His pale skin was dotted with freckles and he wore a Coast Guard cap cocked at an angle. He shoved his hand down the pocket of his pants—pants that looked to be at least two sizes too big—and came out with a fistful of bullets. With a sly grin, he held them out toward Matty. The words *Praise Emerson* rolled silently off his lips.

If Kira was frozen before, she was even worse now. The shot, the brightening glow of Alesia somewhere behind Matty, backlighting him and the entire first floor as he snapped open the revolver and reloaded—Kira was gone. I grabbed her around the waist, hefted her up, and carried her up those stairs, the word *no* coming from her like a metronome—*no... no... no...*

I paused at the second floor only long enough to get a look down the hallway—there must have been fifty of them there, crammed tight around the lockers lining the walls, spilling out from the bunkroom and Spivey's bedroom across the hall. Sailors dressed in ancient Coast Guard whites. Others, older still, dressed in tattered rags held together by nothing more than salt and sweat, grimy boots crawling with muck and things better left to the sea.

I thought of the bathroom window where I'd gotten out before, but there was no way to reach it. Not without going through them, and if one of them could hand bullets to Matty—*solid bullets*—that meant they were probably solid too. Solid enough to stop us if—

"Goddammit, Billy, come on!"

Spivey again.

Third floor.

Even half-carrying Kira, I took those stairs two at a time, chasing his voice.

When we reached the landing, we found Spivey standing at the locked closet door, only it wasn't locked anymore. He twisted the knob and inched it open. The darkness on the other side was so thick, it threatened to ooze out. "Hurry! Lock the door behind you. He won't look in here!"

A million thoughts raced through my mind—I didn't want to be in a trapped room, but we couldn't keep running either. Kira was moving too slow. I twisted the knife in my hand. I'd been gripping it so tight my fingers were numb.

Matty was already hurt.

If I could surprise him…

Take him…

I quickly shot up the ladder to the trap door leading to the tower, snapped the latch back, and shoved it open. Wind and rain gushed down, screamed through the opening. I just needed Matty to think we went that way, only for a second.

Spivey nodded up at me and disappeared into the closet.

I dropped back down, shoved Kira through the opening behind him, and yanked the door closed.

The darkness folded around us like a wet blanket festering with mold.

I heard something then that I hadn't heard in several hours.

The slam of furniture overturning, smacking against the floor.

A sharp yelp, followed quickly by a sharper crack.

Then quiet.

And those sounds came from directly behind us in the closet.

53

I HAVE NO idea how Kira managed to hold onto the matches, but somehow she had, and even knowing that, I wouldn't have believed she was capable of actually striking one, but she did that, too. Her voice had dropped to a whimper, and I caught a glimpse of her quivering lips as she held the match up and slowly turned toward the sound.

An old wooden chair was on the ground, overturned, and hanging from the ceiling—

Oh, God—hanging from the ceiling—

Kira screamed.

The air left my lungs in a rushed gasp, and I backed up until I smacked against the door.

Hanging from the ceiling by a knotted rope was David Spivey.

His bloodshot eyes bulged from his head. His mouth lolled open, tongue drooping from the corner. His skin was pasty gray, oily, the fluids within him seeping out, his clothing stained with them. One of his shoes had fallen off and was lying in a puddle of—

"Do I smell?"

Somehow Spivey was also standing there between Kira and me, looking up at the body. *His body.*

I jerked back again, hard against the door. My fingers pawed at the knob but refused to work, only slipped over the metal and thumped back down against my thigh.

"Sorry if I do. I wet my pants when my neck broke. Or maybe it was right before. I'm not exactly sure."

The loud crack of the chair overturning again.

Spivey's short, pain-filled yelp.

The snap of his neck.

Silence.

Spivey pinched his eyes shut at the sound of it all, slapped his hands over his ears. "Why does it keep doing that? Make it stop, Billy! Make it stop!"

We'd heard the sounds, but the chair hadn't moved, and neither had Spivey's body. It was like a soundtrack out of sync with the film.

A note was pinned to his shirt. Three words scrawled in Spivey's shaky handwriting:

Fuck you, cancer!

When we heard the sounds a third time, my mind flashed back to that first night (was that really only three weeks ago?) and Chloe's story about the ghost at the John Paul Jones house, how he comes out from the attic dressed in old-fashioned clothes and walks into a room and vanishes, over and over again, like a video stuck on repeat.

Spivey shook his head. "Please make it stop, please…"

Kira was pressed deep into the corner, shaking so bad she had to hold the match with both hands. Her gaze kept jerking back and forth between the dead body hanging from the ceiling and the other Spivey, the one standing between us. She had known about Alesia; it was clear she hadn't known about Spivey.

He was breathing, the one standing next to me. Blinking. His eyes brimmed with tears.

He was alive, yet…

Before I realized what I was doing, I tentatively reached out and placed my hand on his shoulder.

He was warm, solid, as real as Kira and I.

I looked from him to his body hanging from the ceiling, then back again. "How?"

"I don't know exactly," he replied. "Emerson brings us back… after. I feel… alive. More alive every hour. Alesia said we'd have to stay here for a little while, out on the island, but with time we'd get even stronger. We'd be able to go back to the mainland. Short trips at first, then longer." His eyes lit up. "The cancer doesn't hurt anymore, Billy. It's gone. There's so much more. So much I wish I could tell you, but I can't. Not until you join us. You will, right? I don't want to do this alone. Chloe has Izzie. I think Alesia is with Matty now. You have Kira. I have… nobody. I need you here." He looked over at Kira. "Both of you. All of us, together."

The loud crack of the chair overturning again.

Spivey's short, pain-filled yelp.

The snap of his neck.

Silence.

Spivey flinched. "You can help me find a way to stop that. Everything will be okay if we just stop that sound. I know it." He looked down at the knife in my hand. "Use that. First you, then Kira, can go. None of us needs to be alone. It'll only hurt for a second. Nik nok—I promise."

Kira let out a soft whimper.

The floorboards creaked—not inside the closet, but just outside the door.

Matty.

54

LIT ONLY IN the soft glow of candles burning around the room, Izzie Fernandez and Chloe Kittle both sat on the couch. Huddled close together, hands intertwined, they watched Keith and Whaley enter the room with wide, frightened eyes, but said nothing.

Alesia Dubin was there too. The sight of her stopped Keith in his tracks, stopped them both.

Her skin had taken on a soft pallor, almost luminescent. Something akin to the radiance of a pregnant woman, but different. Whaley couldn't put his finger on it and wasn't sure he wanted to. It wasn't natural, he could tell that much. She was dressed all in black—heeled boots, short skirt, and a blouse partially unbuttoned to reveal an emerald hanging from a chain around her neck. Her dark hair hung in loose curls over her shoulders. The fact that the emerald was the same color as the light they'd seen from the kitchen wasn't lost on him, nor was the fact that it perfectly matched her eyes.

A coy smile edged the corner of her mouth and she brought the tip of her finger to it, covered it, like she had some scandalous little secret and that finger was the only thing holding it back. She glanced at Whaley, but it was the other man who drew her attention.

"Hello, Keith," she purred. "I've missed you."

With those five words, Whaley knew they weren't talking to Alesia Dubin, not exactly. This was someone—some *thing*—different. He'd only spoken to the girl once, when he came here to collect her and her friends after Lily Dwyer went missing, and he remembered her voice. The timbre of it. The voice he remembered was there, but it wasn't alone—there was another voice behind it; older, deeper. Another behind that one, deeper still. Multiple people speaking in unison when that girl opened her mouth.

Whaley motioned at Izzie and Chloe on the couch, a clumsy *come here* gesture, waving behind his back with his free hand, the gun loosely pointed toward the floor near Alesia in the other. "Both of you come over here now—get behind me. Step around her."

Neither girl moved, only stared at him glassy-eyed, and Whaley had an odd thought. *This is what it would be like to be on the inside of a television looking out.* They were observing him. Watching. They weren't altogether in his world any more than he was altogether in theirs.

Alesia cocked her hip and shifted her weight from her right foot to her left. "Teddy should be here soon too. And Pam. It's like we're getting the band back together. Playing all the old hits. Isn't it, Keith?"

The sense of déjà vu slammed into Whaley even before she started humming. Unlike when he heard those exact words in the vision back in Marston's car, this time he did recognize the song—"What a Difference a Day Makes" by Esther Phillips.

> "*My yesterday was blue, dear*
> *Today I'm part of you, dear*
> *My lonely nights are through, dear*
> *(Since you said you were mine)*
> *What a diff'rence a day makes*"

This wasn't Alesia Dubin, this was—

"Laura," Keith said softly.

She reached for the emerald dangling around her neck and curled her fingers around it. "Emerson made good on his promise to me. Got a little worried there in the final seconds, but he snatched me right out of the fire, just like he said he would. Praise Emerson."

"Praise Emerson," the two girls on the couch repeated with a conviction Whaley found unnerving.

Keith swallowed. "What does that mean for your daughter?"

She tilted her head and pouted. "Oh, Alesia's in here too. So's Emerson. It's wonderful. It's like… like having three minds all working together. Only that's not exactly right either, because Emerson is so… many. So *much* more. Oh, the things he'll teach me! It's been a long journey, but I'm home now. I'm right where I was always meant to be. Now with you here, having come here *willingly*, all us tokens are home. You must feel it, right? The energy of that? God, the air is electric with it. This place, the power, it would have been wasted on your boy, but now…" She held her hand out toward him, long fingers beckoning. "Take the final step and it can be ours to share together." When she said this last bit, her gaze drifted to the gun in Whaley's hand, then back again. "You know the rules, though. You need to do it yourself."

"I won't do that."

"Yes, you will," she replied with a careless shrug. "And it's not polite to keep a girl waiting." Her finger twitched and the gun ripped from Whaley's hand, rolled through the air, and landed at Keith's feet. "I suppose the only real question is who will feed Emerson next?"

55

I RAISED MY finger to my mouth, silently hushed both Spivey and Kira, and pressed my ear against the door. I heard nothing over the wind whipping through the open hatch above, but I did catch a shadow moving across the gap beneath the door.

Kira saw it too. She pointed down, but nothing else moved.

Was he standing out there?

On the other side of the door?

Then I had another thought. *Was Matty alive or dead?*

I couldn't tell with Alesia.

Even with Spivey standing next to me, I couldn't tell.

But Matty? He had to be alive. I'd hurt him. Broke at least one of his ribs.

You can't hurt the dead, can you?

"Billy, Billy, Billy," Matty muttered from the other side of the door. "Always a pain in the ass, Billy."

I couldn't tell if he was facing the closet door or looking up at the open hatch leading to the landing, but he was close.

He was *right there.*

"I'm gonna shoot you in both kneecaps. Then your left elbow. I won't fuck up your right arm—you'll need that for the knife. But after the left elbow, I'll put one in your gut, maybe two. I've heard that's the most painful way to die, and it can take hours, days even. When you're lying there trying to keep your insides from spilling out, I'll help you get a good grip on the knife, maybe even help you get the point to the right spot on your neck, but when the time comes, you'll do the cutting. You'll want nothing more than to end yourself. 'Cause after I help you out, get you all lined up, I'll go to work on Kira. I'll do her right next to you so you can watch, and oh, man, are we gonna have fun… That little prick-tease of yours and I are gonna have ourselves a party. An all-nighter, maybe! How long is totally up to you. I've got Alesia's magic poison cocktail with me. I'll set it across from her, just out of reach. I don't care if she begs for it, I won't let her drink until you're dead. Until Emerson has what he wants. That's when she'll get her relief. Not a second sooner. That's a gift *you* can give her."

The closet knob rattled.

Gentle at first, Matty giving it a cautious twist. Then he turned it with more force.

Locked.

I hadn't locked it. Neither had Spivey or Kira, but it was.

Locked, as it always was. The only locked door in the house.

Matty went quiet for a second. When he spoke again, he sounded further away. Not much, maybe a foot or two, but—

"You up there, Billy?" he called out. "You hoping to stick me when I poke my head through?"

That's when I moved.

I flicked the lock with my thumb and twisted the knob in one fluid motion, then slammed into the door, shoved it open with all my weight. It swung out over the landing. Matty *was* facing away, looking up at the hatch, and the door cracked hard against his back. He bounced forward, off-balance, and smacked hard against the right corner of the ladder. He didn't drop the gun, but it went off, sounding much like thunder in the small space.

56

THE SHOT CAME from upstairs.

Whaley jerked his head toward the ceiling. Muffled by the distance, but definitely upstairs.

He turned and started for the steps, then several things happened at once.

The room behind him erupted in emerald green, a light so bright his eyes involuntarily pinched shut.

Something slammed into his lower back with the force of a linebacker from his high school football glory days. The blow caught him in the kidneys, wrecked his balance, and sent him flailing forward. He landed with a hard grunt at the base of the staircase, and that was when he realized the stairs were different—when he'd been out here with Billy Hasler, they only went up. Now, there was another staircase, this one leading down from the landing into a dark basement. His brain registered that thought in a fraction of a second, in the instant before another blow came at him from behind, this one shoving him through the basement doorway and tumbling down those steps.

Had he been thirty years younger, he might have taken such a fall with only a few bruises to show for it, but he was far from being a kid. His collarbone cracked when it caught the corner of step number five, and his right leg broke in at least two places when he twisted at the midway part—when his own bulk forced the leg to bend in a direction God had never intended. He rolled the rest of the way down and landed in a semiconscious heap at the bottom. That might have been the death of him if not for the loosely packed dirt floor. Inertia carried him a little further, and for that saving grace he was thankful, because Keith came down right behind him, thumping even louder because of the heavy bag still strapped to his person. Through all the pain, through all the noise, a single thought kept repeating in Whaley's head with each of those bangs: there's a fucking bomb in that bag, and it's gonna blow.

Keith hit the last step much harder than Whaley had, bounced over Whaley, and slammed into the dirt floor. He rolled several more feet and finally stopped when he got tangled up in an old metal folding chair on the ground next to the furnace.

That's when Whaley saw the bodies.

The only illumination in the basement came from the furnace. Someone had left the door meant to protect the pilot light open—a bluish-white glow inched out, barely enough to scratch at the harsh shadows, and for that he was grateful, because what he saw belonged in the shadows. If he saw what he saw in full light, he'd surely go mad (or perhaps he already was), because those bodies couldn't be there any more than the basement could be there, yet he was only a few feet from them—Chloe and Izzie, the same girls he'd just seen on the couch upstairs, both clearly dead.

When Keith groaned, Whaley turned his head in that direction and saw Alesia, half-buried, and that made even less sense because he'd just *talked* to her.

"How bad you hurt?" Keith rolled tentatively, got his arms out from under him. He pulled his bag closer and used it to rise to his knees.

Whaley pinched his eyes shut. He had to—there was no way he could speak while also looking at Alesia Dubin's dead hand sticking up from the ground, her face buzzing with flies, already starting to decompose. The basement stunk of death, fluids from those bodies seeping out, moistening the dirt with—

"Goddammit, Whaley—snap out of it!"

Whaley did.

And the pain that had hit the pause button while his mind wrestled with the impossible came flooding back. "Collarbone," he managed to spit out. "Right leg, busted up bad."

"Fuck, ain't that the way?" Keith grumbled.

Whaley wasn't sure what he meant by that and was about to ask him when he heard the whispers coming from the far corner of the basement, somewhere beyond the reach of the thin light. "There's someone else down here. Where's the gun?"

"Forget the goddamn gun." Keith tugged open the zipper on the bag, reached inside, and began removing the contents. Lining everything up nice and neat—six sticks of dynamite, blasting caps, a bundle of wire, lantern battery, and a small white timer. "Oh, hell." He squinted and held the timer toward the thin light. "The timer busted. Fuck!" Keith chucked it against the far wall. It clattered when it hit the stone and vanished in the dark.

Whaley was perfectly fine with a broken bomb. He was more concerned with the people stepping out of the dark, walking toward them.

57

MATTY'S SHOT DIDN'T hit anyone, but that didn't mean the next one wouldn't, and his gun hand was coming up even as Kira scrambled up the ladder to the landing above. He squeezed off another round in Kira's general direction as he tumbled back, but it went wide and high, disappeared somewhere in the ceiling.

If the space had been larger, he would have gone down, but Matty met the far wall before his legs had a chance to come out from under him.

I followed the momentum of the door, dug my heels in, and leveled my right shoulder toward his chest. I'd hoped to get his ribs again, but rain coming in from the hatch above slicked the floor—I slipped, twisted slightly, and caught the corner of his pelvic bone instead. With a grunt, he rolled to the side, managed to get his footing, and I found myself down on one knee, looking up at him.

Matty licked his lip and pulled back the hammer on the gun. "Elbow or knee? Where do you want the first one?"

I was still holding the knife, and when I tightened my grip on the handle, he let out a soft laugh and took a step back.

"Think you can stick me before I can get a bullet in you?"

He was cradling his belly with his free hand again, pushing back on his ribs. His skin was pasty white and coated with a sheen of sweat. Clearly in pain.

"Spivey's dead," I told him.

"No shit. Who do you think helped him tie the rope?"

I cleared my throat. "And he's standing right behind you."

"So?"

Spivey *was* right behind him. He'd stepped out of the closet at some point and I waited for him to do something, but he didn't. He only stood there.

"He can't hurt me," Matty said. "Emerson won't let him."

From behind Spivey, in the closet, came the *crack*, the agonized yelp, the *snap*.

Spivey pinched his eyes shut, jerked his head back and forth, fighting some invisible demon.

Kira's leg came down from the hatch above.

She'd braced herself somehow and brought her foot down on the top of Matty's head with a sickening *thud*.

I shot forward, sliced upward with the knife, and caught him in the belly below his hand before he managed to stumble back and out of reach. His body crumpled, but not before the gun went off again. The bullet struck me in the shoulder like a fist. I lost my hold on the knife, spun away, and fell into the opposite corner, gripping the wound.

Matty was already getting back on his feet, clutching at his stomach now rather than just applying pressure to his ribs. Thick, black blood oozed out from between his fingers, and I realized I'd cut him deeper than I thought. He didn't seem to care. He raised his other hand again, got it level with me before he realized the gun was no longer there. It had skittered across the floor, behind him, behind Spivey, who had become as still as the apparitions I saw in the basement.

Kira kicked Matty again. She'd dropped down about halfway on the ladder and her shoe connected below Matty's chin. His head snapped hard to the side and he fell back to his knees, a stunned look on his face.

"Billy!"

She held her hand toward me, fingers outstretched, and I managed to get to my feet.

Pain radiated from my shoulder. I peeled my bloody hand away only long enough to realize the bullet hadn't gone in, just sliced through the skin, fat, and muscle, leaving a bloody trough. I looked around frantically, spotted the gun against the wall on the opposite side of the room.

"Leave it!"

Kira grabbed my arm and pulled me toward the ladder. Matty was already stirring, trying to get back to his feet, fumbling toward the gun.

Spivey was gone.

In the second I looked away, he'd vanished.

Kira gave me a hard yank, nearly pulled me up the first two rungs of the ladder, tapping strength I didn't know she had. She scrambled up through the hatch above, then laid on the floor and reached back down for me. Gripping the collar of my shirt, she pulled.

White-hot pain ebbed out from my shoulder with each tug and I hobbled up behind her, maneuvering the ladder as best I could with my one good arm.

When I reached the top, Matty was at the first rung, blood pooling at his feet.

Grinning again.

The bastard was still coming.

58

WHALEY TRIED TO sit up and push away from the shadowy wraiths closing on him—a harsh wave of heat rolled up his arm and exploded in his shoulder with a stabbing pain unlike any he'd ever felt. The only thing worse was the pain that followed when he dropped back down to the dirt. It felt like a dozen butcher knives slicing up from his elbow and twisting when they reached the top. Although his shirt was soaked from the rain, a new moisture pooled out from the base of his neck, hot and wet, and he didn't dare try to touch it because he was fairly certain his collarbone was sticking out.

There was a pentagram on the floor to the left of the dead girls. The candles placed at the various points ignited all on their own, and that extra light was enough for Whaley to see the rest of the basement, see who else was there. There were many.

Men, women, children—too many to count. They'd stopped moving and were standing so still and silent, they might have been statues—a historical display representing humanity's last five hundred years.

"You don't belong here," one of them said. And when Whaley followed the voice, he realized it was Teddy Hasler, wearing the same clothing he'd been wearing earlier that day. Geraldine Rote was standing to his left, and next to her was—

"Oh, God… Pam. " Keith went deathly pale at the sight of her. His mouth dropped open and every inch of the man trembled. "Oh, why did you…" A defeated look crossed his face. He glanced up at the ceiling. "Our son's already gone, isn't he?"

If Pam heard him, there was no indication. She stood as still as all the others. Not so much as a blink. Her gaze was fixed on the pentagram on the floor.

When Keith spoke again, his voice was rushed, irrational. He wasn't looking at his wife anymore, seemed like he couldn't. Like if he looked back at her, he'd forget all else. "Chief, I need you to listen to me, listen carefully. We don't have much time." He had the six sticks of dynamite bundled together, and with fumbling fingers went back to attaching the blasting caps. "I'm going to need your help with this. Without the timer, I'll have to detonate manually. That means this is now a two-man job."

"I'm not going to help you set off a—"

Keith cut him off. "I'll handle the bomb. I need you to do something else."

What he told Whaley next made no sense.

"Keith, that's—"

Insane.

That's what he was going to say, but he clipped it off. Saying it aloud would do neither of them any favors, and it might be just enough to push Keith over whatever edge he was teetering on.

Whaley had to get the hell out.

He eased his good arm under his torso and tried to push up, managed about four inches before he dropped back down. He caught a glimpse of his broken leg and realized the foot was facing the wrong direction, everything below the knee twisted and bent.

"Neither of us is leaving here," Keith rushed out. "I'm sorry for that. It was only supposed to be me, but it is what it is, and there ain't nothing we can do about that now. I need you to do what I said when I tell you to do it. Not a second earlier, not a second later. You get that? You understand?" He finished with the blasting caps and started attaching the wires. His hands were shaking so badly that when he tried to thread the wire through the cap-screws, he kept missing. With a slew of curses, he tried again and again until he got one, then moved on to the next, adding in a low mutter, "We're gonna end this fucking thing."

"Pam said you can't."

Keith almost looked back at her, caught himself, fumbled with the next wire. "Yeah, well, Pam wasn't always—"

"Oh, you poor little man," a voice whispered at Whaley's ear, cutting Keith off. So close, hot breath washed down his cheek. "That must hurt something fierce."

Alesia Dubin was crouching next to him, her eyes filled with that green light, so bright he couldn't look at her. She hadn't come down the stairs; he would have seen that. She was simply there—mere feet from her own dead body. The tip of the girl's finger brushed through his hair, down the side of his face, and flicked the sharp splinter of his collarbone protruding from his shoulder.

The shriek that came out of Whaley sounded like a wounded animal on the side of the road after an unfortunate run-in with a vehicle. Something that needed to be put down.

You don't belong here.

You don't belong here.

A thousand voices all chanted in unison.

Alesia raised her hand, silenced them, then licked the blood from her fingertip.

His blood.

"They're right, you know," she told him in that voice made of many. "But I'm willing to make an exception. A trade."

Praise Emerson.

They all said together.

Praise Emerson.

She was holding the photograph. How she'd gotten it from his pocket without him knowing, he didn't know, but there it was, pinched between her thumb and index finger, and it looked so wet and tattered—frail, like it might disintegrate if it suffered another moment of this night, not much different from Whaley himself. She gave the picture a hard shake, then studied the image, her face filled with concern.

Whaley wanted to draw closer, but couldn't bring himself to move. "Let me see."

She tilted her head. "Are you sure you want to?"

He managed the feeblest of nods.

When she turned the photograph around, he swallowed.

His father's car.

Benny sitting on the fender, Whaley standing next to him. Both older now—Benny in his teens, as he was outside, and Whaley as he appeared now, right down to his wet and bloody uniform. His broken leg was cocked at an odd angle as he balanced against the old Mustang. The sun glistened off the bone protruding from his neck. As bad as that was, it was the sight of Mary sitting behind the wheel of the convertible that got him most. Most of her hair was gone, nothing but patches left. She'd lost a lot of weight, barely recognizable. Her eyes were sunk deep into her skull, dark and yellow.

"It's the chemo," Alesia said in that strange, multiplied voice. "It can be as cruel as the cancer, sometimes worse. She'll hang on for a little while, she'll do that for you, but in the end, the time is only borrowed. Her slow death started the day that tickle in her throat began."

She shook the photograph again, and this time Mary was in a hospital bed, alone in the room, and in that picture, her lips were moving.

"Make it stop," Alesia whispered. "That's what she's saying..."

"Don't..."

Alesia cocked her head. "Don't what? End your wife's suffering or show you more?"

Whaley didn't answer that. He couldn't.

"But this is your fault," Alesia told him. "Don't you see that? This is what happens if you leave. If you manage to crawl up those stairs and leave us. It's true, you don't belong, but I'm understanding. Compassionate even. I don't want to see her suffer any more than I want to see you in pain."

Alesia eased her hand down Whaley's chest, past his waist to his destroyed leg. "This doesn't have to hurt either, not anymore."

And for one brief second, it didn't.

"I'll help you if you help me. You stay with us and I'll see to your wife. I'll make sure her cough is nothing more than a cough. I'll give her the years you're sacrificing, and when her time is over, she can come here too. The years will pass in a blink—I can guarantee that. And then you'll be together forever."

"Chief, remember what I said," Keith muttered. "Remember what I told you you need to do."

Alesia's head spun around at an impossible angle. She took in what he was doing.

Keith had the blasting caps all wired together. One wire was attached to the battery; he was stripping the other with his teeth. If that wire came in contact with the battery, the bomb would detonate.

Alesia smiled playfully. "Oh, Keith. Always the prankster!"

She pointed at him and flicked her finger.

Keith shot up off the floor, cracked against the ceiling joists, then dropped back down, landing in a motionless heap next to the furnace.

"Praise Emerson!" the chorus of voices cried out.

And Alesia rose.

She dropped the photograph near Whaley's head, rose, and went to them.

59

KIRA AND I weren't alone in the tower.

I noticed the young girl huddled in the corner the moment after I slammed down the hatch and engaged the heavy bolt. She wore a filthy white dress that seemed several sizes too small; it barely fell halfway down her thighs. Her naked feet were caked in mud. More was on her face, caught up in her stringy blond hair. When she opened her mouth, a deep singsong voice came out like wet gravel from between rancid, yellow teeth.

> *"My yesterday was blue, dear*
> *Today I'm part of you, dear*
> *My lonely nights are through, dear…"*

"What the fuck," Kira muttered, shuffling back from her on her hands and knees. "What the actual fuck."

This was George Walton's daughter—the first girl to drown in that well in 1657. It had to be.

From below, Matty slammed into the bottom of the hatch. It jerked up, but the dead bolt held. "Hey, Billy, Billy… thought you didn't like heights? How 'bout you come down from there? Better yet, let me up—I'll help you, buddy."

He slammed against the hatch with ungodly strength, hard enough to rattle the entire floor.

Kira grabbed my blood-soaked arm and pulled me toward her. Fresh pain radiated out from the bullet wound, hot, thumping with my heart. I let out a sharp hiss.

"Sorry," she breathed out, but didn't let go. "Let me see how bad…"

"It's okay," I told her, although I knew it wasn't.

Our sleeping bags were still there, bunched up in the corner and forgotten in some other lifetime.

The phone rang.

I'd forgotten about the phone. Its bells clattered in a dull shrill, went silent, and rang again.

The girl in the white dress leaned back on her heels. "Oh, don't answer the phone. The phone lies. The phone loves to lie."

Matty slammed into the hatch again—

How was he able to hit it so hard?

—and the screws holding down the dead bolt shrieked. A few more hits like that and he'd get through.

I snatched up the receiver. "What?!"

The voice on the other end of the call was so distant, between the shrieking wind and rain beating down on the small room from all sides, I couldn't make out the words. The voice faded in and out as if riding the roiling waves of the churning tide down below. The first time he spoke, I only heard one word—*Bell.*

"I can't hear you!" I shouted back.

The young girl rocked back and forth on her muddy heels, the harsh singsong voice back again. "Operator, operator—I can't hear you! I can't hear you! I… can't… hear… you… please… speak… up! Please speak up!"

A muffled grunt from Matty.

The hatch jerked up again, and I heard the sound of metal twisting in a way it was never meant to, a sharp, short squeal.

The voice on the phone said, "… to the bell. Get to *Annabelle…*"

With that last word, lightning streaked the sky. There was a pop on the line and the call was dead.

It was me.

My own voice.

Get to Annabelle.

Kira hadn't heard. She couldn't possibly have heard, but even as I dropped the phone, she was looking out the door toward the rickety widow's walk on the other side.

60

ALESIA WENT TO the center of the pentagram.

She left no footprints in the loosely packed dirt, and Whaley realized although her legs and feet moved as if she were walking, the girl wasn't touching the ground. She hovered about an inch above it. When she reached the center, she closed her eyes. "*Ego hic quod mea.* I am here for what is mine."

"Praise Emerson!"

Whaley didn't know how many were in the basement, far too many to count, and when they spoke in unison, the volume was loud enough to rattle the foundation walls, shake the rafters above. There might have been a hundred down there. A thousand. Ten thousand. Some impossible number, and Whaley suddenly realized whatever this was, it went much further back in history than when *Reina* docked out here in 1898, well before that passenger made his ill-gotten promise to the captain. This was something as old as the Earth. This was something evil.

Alesia raised her hands, and the candle flames rose from the wicks to a height several feet above her head, no longer orange and yellow, but a bright emerald green. Her eyes and the pendant all glowed with it, and the basement air came alive, swooshing excitedly through the room. "I have given you what you want. I have fulfilled your every desire and need. *Venio quod mea.* I come for what is mine. *Adsum ad colligunt.* I am here to collect. The time is now. You are me and I am you. I am Emerson, for we are many!"

Only she didn't say *Emerson*, not that time, she said *Legion*, and with the mention of that name, Whaley remembered a story he hadn't heard since he was a child. A biblical story about a demon cast out of a man into a herd of pigs, pigs that then jumped from a cliff and took their own lives. As Whaley looked around the basement, at the dead girls near his feet, the apparitions born of the dark, he realized he was witnessing the opposite of that biblical story—he was watching the dead become one, feeding…

I am Legion, for we are many.

Pam was first to move. She stepped from the many, went to the edge of the symbol on the ground, and stepped inside. She walked right up to Alesia, then somehow *walked into Alesia.* For one brief instant, the two of them seemed to occupy the same space, then Pam was gone. Teddy came next, his face blank, trancelike, his motion that of a sleep-walker. He followed in Pam's footsteps and vanished too. One at a time, they stepped to the center, became part of her—five, ten, twenty, fifty—impossible to count, and with each, the green light grew brighter. Alesia pinched her eyes shut, her face filled with ecstasy. Her body twitched, hovered there, took them all in and—

"Chief…"

The voice was weak, barely a whisper. It was a miracle Whaley heard it at all.

Keith was still on the ground where he had dropped, but his eyes were open. He tried to sit up and failed miserably. Instead, he dragged himself toward the battery. "Chief, we need to do this… now!"

61

I YANKED THE phone cord. It broke from the base and snapped across the small room. "Get the sleeping bags!" I told Kira.

She eyed the cord. "What are you doing?"

"What are you doing," the girl mimicked, shuffling a little closer. She smelled like something left behind on the beach by the receding tide.

Matty cracked against the hatch again, and this time, one of the screws *did* come out. The hatch bounced up enough for me to glimpse him for a quick instant before it slammed back down.

The girl saw him too, and she seemed to like that—she crawled over to the hatch and lowered her cheek to the floor at the edge of the trap door. When Matty hit it again, she let out a playful giggle.

"The bags, Kira. Hurry!"

I scooped up the phone receiver and went to the door at the catwalk. The padlock was back, locked, but it broke away after only three hits with the phone.

When I yanked open the door, the raging storm reached in and snatched at all three of us—icy rain whipping around the room, exploring every inch with a hungry fascination. Salty air stung my face, my eyes. My shoulder burned, but none of that compared to the jolt of fear that enveloped me as I looked out over that widow's walk—the rotten boards slick with rain, the railing that wasn't much of a railing at all, just some old 2x4s nailed precariously in place. The height of it, three stories from the rocky ground.

I sucked in a breath, then another. I stood at the edge of that walkway and tried to slow the relentless slamming of my heart, but all of it grew worse. I wasn't breathing; I was hyperventilating. I'd lost some blood, and my limbs quivered like an engine running on fumes. My knees started to buckle, and I would have fallen if not for Kira. She got one arm around me, the other clutching the two sleeping bags. "I've got you," she said softly. "Take it one step at a time."

I looked back at her and wished I hadn't—the girl in the white dress was busy working on the slide bolt for the hatch. I couldn't see her face, but I imagined she was frustrated. Her fingers passed through the metal the first two times she tried, then seemed to grip it, if only for a second. Frustrated or not, she was patient, and with each attempt that bolt slipped closer to disengaging even as Matty banged from below.

Kira shuffled forward, pulling me with her. She maneuvered around the missing and broken boards, and I followed in her steps. "Keep your stance wide," she told me. "The boards will be strongest at the sides."

Between the height and the pain in my shoulder, I was breathing in short gasps. Each time the wind gusted, I grabbed at the railing, dug my fingers in. Each time, Kira nudged me along, forced me forward.

I didn't see *Annabelle* until we reached the end of the walk. It wasn't tied to the dock. Between the high tide and the storm, the water blanketed a large portion of the island, and *Annabelle* was directly below us, cracking against the foundation of the house. For a quick second, I thought Lester Rote was at the helm; then I realized it wasn't Lester, it was Spivey. He was facing away, hands on the controls, his body stiff, statue-like, as if he had been built there when the craft was assembled, his gaze lost on some distant thing out there in the raging waters.

I twisted the phone receiver around the base of the railing and knotted it with the cord, then dropped the cord over the side. It was long, but not long enough. It was about eight feet short.

"Use the sleeping bag to grip the cord so you don't burn your hands. Squeeze as hard as you can and slide down. Try to land on your back, on the bag," I told Kira, realizing just how crazy that sounded as I said it aloud.

She was looking at my shoulder. My shirt was soaked in blood. "How are you going to hold on?"

Behind us, the hatch banged open with a crash.

Matty's head came up through the hole, the sickening grin on his face widening as he spotted us.

"Go!" I shouted at Kira.

Matty's arm appeared, the gun in his hand. Using his elbow as leverage on the floor, he worked his way up.

The girl in the white dress watched him for a moment, then turned toward Kira and me. Her face twisted with wild excitement. She started skittering toward us like a crab—through the door, down the widow's walk.

Kira went over the side, pinched the cord like I told her, and slid.

Slid far too fast.

I watched as she picked up speed, reached the end of the cord, and dropped down to the deck of *Annabelle*, half on the hard wood, half on the sleeping bag. When she didn't move, I thought for sure she was dead, then she looked up at me and rolled to the side.

I couldn't do it.

Not with the height.

And I wouldn't have been able to if the girl in white hadn't slammed into me.

She hit me with a sickening crunch, as if her bones were nothing but rotten twigs held together by a loose bag of flesh, and I went over the side with her latched against me. Somehow I managed to grab the cord with my good hand and wished I hadn't—the plastic sliced my palm like a hot knife. I squeezed anyway because anything else surely meant death, and when I hit the deck of the boat, it cracked beneath me—not completely, but enough. The boards buckled, cratered, gave just enough to spare me. Maybe a second ticked by, long enough for me to register I was alive, hear Kira screaming my name, then the pain came, a hellish roll of electric heat starting at the center of my back near my tailbone and working out. With a mind all its own, my good arm flailed, swatted at the girl in the white dress, but she was no longer there—she'd vanished.

Matty jumped.

He went over the edge of the widow's walk and tumbled toward me.

62

WHALEY CRAWLED TOWARD Keith.

The pain, the fear—he used it. With each inch, he used it like fuel. He used his one good arm to pull himself closer, his broken body dragging through the dirt. When he dropped down the stairs, he hadn't landed far from the furnace, only a few feet, but it might have been a mile.

Whaley's heart was beating to the point of bursting—blood throbbed behind his eyes, his temples; it screamed through his veins. The breath he sucked in felt like half of what his body needed, and he knew he was at his breaking point, *beyond* his breaking point. Every second he existed now was borrowed.

He didn't so much as glance back at Alesia. If he did, he wasn't sure he'd be able to turn away. If he could block out the sound of it, he would do that too—he heard each of them enter her, heard her somehow absorb each of those souls, and with each, the green light flashed bright. He didn't have to look back to know it was happening faster. The many becoming one, the many becoming Legion. He—

Whaley blacked out, only for a second, but when he tried to move again, pain radiated out from his broken collarbone like a sharp slice of electricity. It followed the length of his back, down his leg, and when it met the broken bones down there, his vision flooded with white, he drowned in it, and there was nothing else.

"Chief!"

Although Keith shouted, his voice was distant. It came to him down a long tunnel. The man yelled again and sounded even further away. The third time, he could barely hear him at all.

Whaley didn't feel the arms around him, not at first. For a second, he thought he was floating like Alesia, then his eyes were open again and saw Benny kneeling beside him, *pulling him toward Keith*. "I've got you," his brother said. "Almost there."

And then Whaley was.

He nearly collapsed again when he reached Keith at the furnace, but Benny held him up.

"I've got you," Benny said again.

I know you do.

The photograph had fluttered across the basement floor; it was right there.

Keith had one wire attached to the battery, the other wire in his hand less than an inch from the exposed terminal. His eyes met Whaley's, and there was a strange calm there. "On three," he instructed. "One…"

63

KIRA PULLED ME out of the way and Matty slammed into the deck, partially standing. His right leg took the brunt of it—shattered and buckled like a meaty accordion—then swept out from under him as Spivey gunned the engine and forced *Annabelle* up and over the nearest wave in the direction of New Castle. Matty staggered toward the stern of the boat and fell in a heap.

He stopped moving, but I knew he wasn't dead.

I caught a glimpse of Wood Island behind us—the house, all the lights burning bright, nothing more than a blur behind the storm.

Kira's arms were wrapped around my chest; I was partially in her lap. I tried to sit up, couldn't.

From the corner of my eye, I saw Spivey shove the throttle nearly all the way forward—the motor screamed and the boat climbed over another wave, then dropped into the trough on the other side with a salty splash.

Spivey tried to pull the throttle back, but his fingers passed right through it. Frustrated, he grabbed at it again—this time, not only did his hand pass through the throttle, but the console too. He realized his other hand was no longer able to grip the wheel—we were too far from the island. I could see through him. He was—

Kira screamed.

As broken as he was, Matty had rolled, managed to get the gun up. Squeezed the trigger and—

64

THE PHOTOGRAPH WAS upside down; Whaley couldn't see the image on the other side. What he saw existed only in his mind's eye, but he saw it as clearly as if he had taken the picture himself—he saw the face he wanted to see, the face of his wife. Mary on a summer day many years earlier, the first time he'd ever laid eyes on her. The sunlight at her back and a smile that could melt the world. He saw perfection.

Keith closed his eyes and let out a soft breath. "Two—"

Whaley felt Benny's arms tighten around him, and together, they leaned toward the furnace and the small pilot light. And blew.

65

SILENCE.

Water.

We were in the water.

Sinking.

Kira still had her arms around me, and she either managed to push off something or kick, but we broke the surface, both of us coughing out saltwater. We managed to grab a quick breath before a large wave rolled over us and sent us back down.

When we came back up, *Annabelle* was gone, vanished right out from under us. Spivey was gone too.

Simply blinked out as if neither had ever been there.

We were bobbing in the water.

"Where's Matty?!" Kira managed to get out before coughing again. Frantically twisting around, searching the water.

When I turned my head, it felt like it was attached to my neck with knife blades. The slightest movement sliced through the muscle and scratched at the bone.

"Try not to move," she told me. "I think you broke your back when you hit the deck."

"My…"

The world swooned and went black for a second, enveloped me in a cloud of nothing.

Kira slapped me. "You've lost a lot of blood. Just stay with me!"

My legs were kicking, helping us stay afloat—muscle memory, involuntary movement; I didn't much care how—and I wouldn't be able to kick if I broke my back. This was good, even if it hurt like hell.

Another wave slammed into us, picked us up, and dropped us at least ten feet from where we started. I managed to catch a glimpse of Wood Island before we came back down.

The house was dark.

Even through the storm, I knew it had changed.

Reverted back to—

"The house cycled," Kira said, her lips near my ear. "That's what Alesia called it. Something must have happened."

Maybe it cycled out with everything else.

That's what Matty had said about the knife when Kira…

Oh, God. *Annabelle.* Spivey.

That's where it all went.

Gone.

The water around my shoulder was warm. I realized that was from the blood.

"Help!" Matty's voice echoed in the distance. "Help me!"

Garbled the first time. Louder the second.

I spotted him first. Maybe thirty feet from us. He disappeared beneath the water, then clawed his way back up. Screamed this time. "Shark! It's right—"

Then he was gone.

It happened that fast.

He sliced sideways through the water, as if someone in a speedboat had tied a rope around him and gunned the motor, then he dropped below the surface—

Didn't drop, he was pulled.

—and he didn't come back up.

Kira let out a soft gasp. She froze. Stopped kicking. I didn't, couldn't—I was keeping us both afloat. I quickly looked back at Wood Island, then (pain be damned) I managed to turn my head in the opposite direction, toward the beach at New Castle.

"We'll never—make it," Kira shouted, her voice broken by another wave crashing over our heads. "We're too far from shore!"

She was right.

Annabelle had only gotten us about halfway across the reach. We were at least an eighth of a mile from the narrow beach at the Commons.

I pulled Kira tighter against me, held her as close as I dared while still pumping my legs to keep us afloat. My muscles didn't want to work anymore. The burn and pain I'd felt only moments earlier had been replaced by pins and needles and numbness creeping through my limbs. The icy water sapping the strength from me. I couldn't stop, though. I didn't want to die. "Do you see it? Where did it go? Where the hell did it go!?"

Kira didn't answer, only buried her face deeper into my shoulder and sobbed.

"I need you to swim, Kira! You gotta swim!"

Her head bobbed in a quick nod, then she started kicking too.

The shark would smell my shoulder.

It would come for me.

If it found me, it would take her.

"You should go," I told her. "You're faster than me." A deep pain shot from the small of my back. "I'm not sure I can swim at all."

And if the shark is busy with me, you might make it.

She shook her head and gripped me tighter. "Maybe we should both try to get back."

We were too far, though; we wouldn't make it.

We sank beneath the surface for a second—my mouth filled with saltwater. I coughed it back out. I had stopped kicking, only for a second. Didn't want to, just did. I couldn't keep this up. I couldn't swim for both of us, and Kira was barely paddling if at all. "We gotta move. Gotta—"

"Oh, God, there!" Her body went stiff as she pointed to our left.

I followed her finger, but only caught a glimpse of the fin before it vanished beneath the surface about twenty feet away.

My feet brushed against something—granite, one of the large rocks sticking up in the reach—I caught it with the toe of my shoe, managed to inch us closer. Then Kira grabbed at a corner, pulled us partially onto the slick surface.

"Stop kicking," she whispered. "Hug the rock. Get as close as you can. Try not to move."

The next time we saw it, the shark was less than ten feet away, circling our rock.

I no longer felt any pain.

The cold water. The loss of blood. Shock. Probably all those things.

"I love you," I managed before my vision clouded again.

"I love you, too," Kira whispered, her warm breath the only thing I could feel. "Don't move. I've got you."

And that was good, because I blacked out.

66

I'M NOT SURE how long I was out, but when I woke again, the storm had ended. It was still dark, but I got the sense that would change soon. The tide had receded and only my foot was in the water; the rest of me was draped over the rock.

Kira was gone.

I shouted out her name until my throat was hoarse, kept shouting even then.

I screamed until the blackness returned.

This time, I let it.

07/14/2010 - WEDNESDAY

1

"BILLY?"

A gentle touch on my cheek.

"Get the doctor! He's coming around!" someone shouted. "Billy, can you hear me?"

My mother.

It was my mother's voice.

A door opening.

Shuffle of footsteps.

Fingers pinched my eye open and a bright white light burned down, drowned out all else.

"Can you follow the light for me?"

Male voice.

The halo around the light shrunk just enough for me to see a gray-haired man dressed in white hovering over me, moving a penlight slowly right, then left, and back again. Wanting to squint but unable with him holding my eye open, I did as he asked.

I could move my eyes, but not my head.

"Good." He switched off the light and stepped back. "That's real good."

The tag clipped to his lapel said Dr. Alfred Rainer.

He made several notes on a clipboard near the foot of my bed, replaced it on some kind of hook, and looked over at my mother. "I can give you a few minutes, then we'll need to take him to run some tests."

She nodded.

He placed his hand on my chest.

I saw him do it, but I couldn't feel his hand there.

"Good to have you back, Mr. Hasler." He rolled his fingers, thumped them, and I didn't feel that either.

Then he was gone.

"Am I paralyzed?"

My voice sounded nothing like me. Weak, deeper, rough. My throat felt like sandpaper.

My mother turned away from me, retrieved a plastic sippy cup from the bedside table, the kind I had when I was a kid, and brought the straw to my lips. I think I drank half before she pulled it away. "Don't drink too much, it might make you sick."

The panic welled in my gut. "I can't move, Mom…"

She licked her lips. "You shattered your pelvis and cracked two vertebrae in your lower back. The doctors had to fuse them. They think your spinal cord is intact, but they won't know if you sustained permanent injuries until they're able to get you out of this bed. Your neck's in a brace. Whiplash. Not as serious as your back, but they don't want you moving it right now. The wound in your shoulder was superficial. They cleaned it and closed it up. Thirty-six stitches. There will be a scar."

She tapped my chest. I still didn't feel it, but I heard the dull thump.

"They've got your lower body in a cast to restrict movement."

Her eyes were bloodshot, the skin under them dark and puffy either from crying, lack of sleep… probably both.

I swallowed. "Where am I?"

"Portsmouth General." When she caught me glancing at the sunlight squeezing between the blinds on the window, she added, "Two days now."

Two days.

I swallowed. "Is Kira here?"

Someone knocked on the door, stuck their head in, and cleared their throat.

Officer Mundie.

I heard the scuff of his shoes on the floor as he stepped into the room and approached my bed, came into view. He looked like he hadn't shaved in a while. His uniform was wrinkled and his hair was a mess. Without taking his eyes off me, he told my mother, "Ma'am. I need to speak to him."

She shook her head. "Not until his attorney gets here. I just texted him."

"You're well aware of the urgency, Mrs. Hasler. This isn't only about your son."

When she didn't reply, he went on. "You're welcome to stay. I ask him anything that makes you feel uncomfortable, I'll back off. I promise. Your attorney can sit in when the staties arrive. They're on their way too." He paused for a moment. "We owe a lot of people some answers."

"It's okay, Mom."

I wanted to tell him what happened.

Needed to tell him. Someone.

Mundie took out his phone and tapped several buttons. "I'm going to record this."

"No." My mother frowned. "You're not. Whatever he tells you is off the record. You want to question him officially, you wait."

He bit his lower lip and put the phone back in his pocket. "Fine."

My mother nodded at the IV bag. "He's heavily medicated. Nothing he tells you right now should be considered admissible."

A look passed between them, but she said nothing else.

Mundie moved a chair from the corner of the room and sat beside me. "Tell me what you remember. Take your time. Everything that happened from the moment you left Chief Whaley and me at Jaffrey Point. Can you do that?"

I nodded.

And I did.

I didn't leave anything out.

I knew how crazy it all sounded, and I didn't care.

It took nearly two hours.

I expected the doctor to come back, and when he didn't, I got the feeling someone stopped him in the hall. Told him he needed to wait. At one point, I thought I heard him arguing out there.

I kept talking because I needed to get it out. I only paused long enough to drink more water, which my mother diligently refilled from the bathroom sink.

When I finished, the room fell oddly quiet. There was only the sound of machines and muffled voices out in the hall.

Mundie had a notepad out. He tapped his pen on the corner and seemed to think carefully about what he said next. Then he leaned closer. "Billy, I really need you to tell me where your friends are—Izzie and Matt Fernandez, David Spivey, Alesia Dubin. I need the truth now. Their families are very worried."

"I… I did tell you."

He leaned back in the chair, closed his eyes, and pinched the bridge of his nose, like he had a bad headache coming on. Then he leaned toward me again. "You said Izzie, Chloe, and Alesia died in the basement. There is no basement in the house out at Wood. There's barely a crawlspace. I know, I went there after I got my boat going. Less than an hour behind Chief Whaley. I was out there about the same time the Coast Guard pulled you off a rock out in the reach. We've been over every inch of that place. There's no closet where you said David Spivey hanged himself. His body's not in the house. Neither are the girls."

"Because the house cycled. They're there. Just not…"

"Billy. I need the truth. Their families are worried sick. It's been two days."

I felt a pang in my chest. "You didn't say Kira."

Mundie went quiet. Pursed his lips.

"You named all of them but Kira." My heart was racing. "Did she swim to shore? Did she make it?"

Mundie looked up at my mother. She turned from him and faced out the window.

"I need to see her!" I tried to sit up, couldn't. "You found her, didn't you?"

Mundie's voice dropped low and his eyes went to the foot of the bed. "We found Kira Woodward's body on the second floor—the storage room across from the room with all the bunk beds. She'd been dead for some time. A few days at least. The poison she drank… the empty cup was still in her hand. Pentobarbital, according to the medical examiner." He paused for a moment, scratched at his scruffy cheek. "They found the same medication in your tox screen here in the ER, but much less." He met my eyes. "Was this some kind of suicide pact between the two of you?"

She'd been dead for some time.

That couldn't be true. She wasn't like them. She was solid, able to touch me. I felt her warmth. Her breathing. She couldn't have been dead.

I violently shook my head. It hurt like hell in the brace and I didn't care. "No. No. Kira didn't kill herself—*Chloe and Izzie drank the poison.* I think Alesia did, too. I threw it up. Kira helped me throw it up, she…"

Mundie's gaze dropped to the floor.

It was clear he didn't believe me.

"Kira helped me throw it up," I repeated. "She helped me get away from Matty. Got out of the house—"

"To a boat driven by the ghost of your friend," Mundie interrupted, shaking his own head. "I can't go to their folks with that. I need the truth, and you're not helping yourself with—"

The door to my room opened and Marston stepped in. He wore a black suit, identical to the one he wore the last time I saw him. He gave my mother a quick nod and frowned at Mundie. "That's enough, Officer. I'd like to be alone with my client."

2

RED-FACED, MUNDIE GAVE Marston a frustrated glance, looked like he wanted nothing more than to unleash a tirade, then thought better of it. He pointed at me instead. "You need to tell this kid to stop with the bullshit. We've got five missing kids, one dead girl, and he was the last person to see *any* of them. The state police are on their way; you can bet the FBI won't be far behind them. Not to mention the press camped outside. He gets charged as an adult in all this and you can guarantee he won't set foot outside a prison until he's old enough to collect social security."

"You have yet to prove my client even committed a crime, Deputy." Marston's thin lips drew back in a placating grin that looked anything but genuine. "Perhaps you should divert some of your resources toward locating your missing sheriff rather than throwing around baseless accusations. You sound as if you desperately need the help. He picked a fine time to vanish on you. My sources tell me he was last seen with Keith Spivey—also missing, I might add. Both men are fond of fishing. Maybe they took a trip to Lake Winnipesaukee. Have you considered David Spivey might be with his father? With the both of them? Considering the Fernandez boy, Matty, was also a fisherman, it's not a stretch to assume he's there too. Maybe they're *all* together—his sister, her girlfriend, that Alesia Dubin girl—I bet they're all holed up in a cabin somewhere on some outing and will come waltzing back into your little town none-the-wiser of the trouble they've caused. Kids will be kids, Deputy. And sometimes, adults can be absent-minded. Given time, the truth will present itself. For now, my client requires an opportunity to heal. He's obviously been through a terrible ordeal, and your needling is only making matters worse."

Mundie looked like he might explode. His hand dropped to the leather case on his belt housing his handcuffs. "Get the truth out of him or he'll be recuperating up at State Correctional—you can count on that."

He pushed past Marston and slammed the door on his way out.

When he was gone, Marston faced my mother. "I'd prefer to speak to your son alone, ma'am."

"He's a minor."

"Not for much longer, and I'm afraid that deputy was correct about one thing—if charges are filed, they will pursue your son as an adult. Aside from that, he may feel he's able to speak more freely if it's only the two of us." The grin returned. "I'm sure you understand."

She didn't look like she understood.

She looked like she was tired of fighting and had done a lot of it in recent days.

My mother walked out without a single word to me or Marston. She was gone before I had the chance to tell her not to leave me alone with that man.

When the door closed behind her, Marston eyed the chair Mundie had vacated near my bed, then went over to the window instead.

The brace around my neck offered little play, and I could only see him from the corner of my eye. I didn't know what kind of pain medications they had in my IV, but they were what Spivey would have called "the good stuff," because the little bit of motion I did manage seemed to come on a two-second delay after I sent the instructions to my brain.

"Mr. Spivey asked me to represent you should something happen," Marston said in a low tone, the light from the window turning him into a dark silhouette. "Of course, I'm referring to your friend, David Spivey, not his father. Your mother was hesitant at first, but when the man representing your father, Donald Murdock, backed out, she was left with little choice. I suppose she sees me as second fiddle. I can only imagine what you must think of me."

I swallowed the lump in my throat. "Is Kira dead?"

I had no doubts about what happened to the others. It didn't matter if Mundie didn't believe me. I remembered every second out on that island, and I certainly remembered what came next. If I closed my eyes, I could still feel Kira holding me on that rock. We both got out. And yes, I *did* pass out, but Kira was a strong swimmer, and I was sure—

Marston raked the blinds with his bony finger. "Do you accept me as your personal representative in this matter? I'm afraid I can't speak to you in confidence unless you do."

"Yes, dammit! Is she dead?"

The silence that came next was nearly overwhelming. If I hadn't been immobile in that bed, I might have jumped up and strangled the truth out of him.

"She doesn't have to be," he finally said. "Not for you. I think you know that. In fact, I'm certain of it. Perhaps you should ask the question that is really on your mind."

I pinched my eyes shut, blinked away the tears, and forced the words out. "*When...* did she die? "

"Ah," he breathed, pleased with himself. "There it is."

"Tell me."

"Two nights ago, not long after sunset, Ms. Woodward sat upon the bed in the master bedroom out at Wood Island, got herself situated, and drank the poison provided to her by Ms. Dubin. She did this about twenty minutes before Mr. Spivey hanged himself in the closet. Ms. Woodward chose that particular room of the house because she knew they planned to put you in the bunkroom when you returned. She wanted to remain close to you, which I found rather charming. That was her only request. I can assure you her death was fast and painless."

In my mind's eye, I saw Chloe and Izzie convulsing on the basement floor, white foam dripping from their mouths.

Fast and painless.

"Of your friends," he went on, "Alesia Dubin was first to offer herself. Ms. Woodward next. Followed by Mr. Spivey, Izzie Fernandez, and Chloe Kittle, whom you witnessed. Although Matthew Fernandez died out in the reach, he came home shortly after, as is the way with all tokens. Emerson was very pleased." He stepped back over to my bed and ran his tongue over his yellow teeth. "That is the truth, *your* truth. Of course, with the house being what it is, only the body of Ms. Woodward was, or will ever be, found."

"Because the house cycled," I muttered.

The closet where Spivey died doesn't exist in this—World? Reality? Time? Space?

I didn't know the word for it, and the pain medication kept me from closing on it. Finding the right word was like trying to grip a ball made of water.

The closet didn't exist.

The basement where Alesia was buried, where Izzie and Chloe died…

I breathed, "Everything Kira did… helping me…"

She did after she died.

"She loved you… very much," Marston said.

And I loved her.

"That is *your* truth," Marston told me again. "One nobody outside this room will ever understand or believe, and to share it will certainly commit you to a life of persecution. More importantly, sharing it—no matter how many people you tell—will not bring back your friends. There is no way to do that." He licked his lip. "No way for anyone but you. No way… but one."

He reached out with his long fingers and placed his hand on my chest. "Offer yourself to Emerson and you will be reunited. Give yourself to him, and you will know the love and embrace of Ms. Woodward from that moment until the end of time. Of that, I can assure you."

I was so grateful for the thick cast beneath that man's hand, the only thing that kept me from feeling his touch.

My mother came back into the room and found us like that, Marston hovering over me with his hand on my chest, his final words to me hanging heavy and thick in the air.

She cleared her throat, some awkward announcement of her presence. "Mr. Marston, can you wait for me out in the hall? The doctors would like to run some tests on Billy, and there's something I need to tell him first. Something that can't wait."

He left without another word to me, at least that particular day.

My mother sat on the edge of my bed and wiped the tears from my face. "It's about your father…"

05/28/2021 - FRIDAY

1

THAT WAS ELEVEN years ago.

I suppose you and I have come full circle, right back to where we started this exchange, if it could be called that.

I don't expect you to believe me.

I wouldn't believe me.

Dig up an old copy of the *Portsmouth Herald*; you'll want June 8, 1972. The day the bodies of the Whidden children were found out on Wood. Or Lester Rote's obituary eleven days later. It's easy enough to track down information on that ship, *Reina*. Search 2010, and you'll stumble into a slew of stories about the teenagers who vanished or the girl found dead out in the house or blurry pictures of me. We were all minors, so none of us were named back then, but that didn't stop the press from following me, or talking about them, or making things up about all of us and quoting their "unnamed sources" to cover their collective asses. The last story they wrote about me appeared in the *Seacoast* on May 28, 2013. If you want to verify any of what I told you, it's not too hard to track down information.

Or don't; I don't care.

This isn't about you. This is—

Sorry.

This is one of the reasons I've never talked about it. It all makes me angry.

The truth is, I miss them. I'm sure it's hard for you to understand that, considering what they did, but they were my friends. I grew up with them. I loved them. Kira, most of all. I've spent the last eleven years trying to forget that handful of weeks and doing my best to remember all the good times that came before, and I've failed miserably at both of those things. Why is it the bad things stick with such clarity while the rest fades away? I'd give anything to remember the warmth of Kira pressed against me, but instead, my mind serves up our last moments on that rock—cold granite digging into my busted back and her muffled sobs. I try to conjure images of my dad and me playing catch when I was a kid, but all I get is our last fight in his car.

Worst of all is Marston, what he said to me in that hospital room.

Most nights, I wake screaming, but it's the nights I wake thinking of him I scream loudest.

Offer yourself to Emerson and you will be reunited.

Goddamn Marston for putting *that* thought in my head.

To his credit, he did what he said he would. He kept me out of jail. There was plenty of talk of charges, but Kira's death was clearly a suicide, and while they wanted to hold me accountable, me being in the house wasn't enough to be considered criminal. Her folks filed a civil suit against me claiming I convinced their daughter to do it, and my mother settled that one out of court. She agreed to write a large check to a suicide prevention non profit in Kira's name in hopes of making it all go away. A messy handshake at best, one negotiated by Lockwood J. Marston, Esquire. Because Chief Whaley vanished along with Spivey's dad the same day as Izzie, Chloe, Alesia, and Matty, he spun that, too. I suppose a good lawyer is a lot like a magician—watch my right hand while my left does the real work. Without bodies, it didn't take long to shift the narrative. Several people came forward and said they saw Whaley and Keith take *Merv* out toward Wood Island the night of the big storm, but nobody saw them come back. *Merv* was found drifting through the reach three days later, empty but for about six inches of water. The prevailing theory was they managed to pick us all up, but everyone went overboard on the trip back. High wind, rain, turbulent waters, whatever—somehow I managed to get to that rock and live, while the rest of them did not. The fact that I remembered none of that only added kindling to the idea, because, of course, how could I be expected to remember something so traumatic? Some thought I'd been drugged— that rumor spread too. Kids who had been out to the parties claimed maybe there was something in the water, something that made them see things, something that maybe affected my memory…

Bullshit, all of it, and I hate myself for allowing it to stick.

At first, I only went with it because I was scared. Then I clung to that story because I wanted it to be true. Alesia could have slipped something in my water, right? Hell, we all drank from that mug. In many ways, that particular outcome was a tidier bow. Easier to stomach over what I remembered, *my truth*.

Chief Whaley and Keith Spivey went down publicly as heroes, and I didn't learn what really happened to them until months later when Marston finally told me. He told me about Whaley and Keith the same night he told me Wood Island had officially become the property of Kittery township. With Spivey gone, there was no next of kin or blood relative to take possession, and even if there had been, it wouldn't have gone to them. The moment Keith set foot on Wood Island, ownership transferred to Kittery as per Geraldine Rote's last will and testament. The paperwork was finalized that morning. There's been talk of turning it into a museum; I'm not sure how I feel about that. I asked him what that meant for Emerson, for the souls out there, for everything that vanished the last time the house cycled, but he gave me no answer. Three years later, I went to his office in Boston with duct tape, a gun, and a fifth of Jack Daniels *planning to get an answer*, and I found nothing but an empty brownstone that hadn't been lived in for a very long time. The irony of that wasn't lost on me, because I found the same thing when

I eventually found the courage to return to the house on Wood Island three years after my friends died—May 28, 2013, to be exact.

I've been back many times since.

We'll get to that in a moment.

We need to discuss Lily Dwyer first.

If you're reading this, you probably already know she walked into the Portsmouth Police Department the morning after the big storm. In fact, she stepped through their door about the same time I was coming out of surgery for my pelvis and lower back. Her hair was no longer pink. She'd dyed it brown, and because of that it took the desk sergeant a moment to recognize her. Turns out my dad moved her around several times, some shell game between his various properties to keep her away from Alesia and the others—she knew they planned to kill her, and she wasn't ready to die. She didn't think her parents would understand any of it, so she went to Keith—she knew Spivey's dad would understand *all of it*. The last house they stashed her in had been a small Victorian that my dad had recently renovated off South Street, not more than three miles from New Castle. I know she gave a statement, but not until her attorney was present, and I think you can guess who that was. I'm sure he was responsible for the large payment that found its way into Lily Dwyer's college fund, too. I have no idea what her statement said, but I can tell you what was printed in the paper—she'd had a fight with her mother and ran off, broke into the empty house, and stayed there because that would "teach her." The press never picked up on the hair found in my dad's car, but Mundie once told me the hair was written off as potential transference—Lily was squatting in a property owned by my dad. He most likely picked up the hair there and transferred it to his own car totally by coincidence. In other words, more bullshit. No way to prove otherwise, and with my dad dead, no reason to chase it.

Early on, I tried to contact Lily, but she didn't return my calls.

Six months later, I cornered her coming out of Starbucks, and before she could get in her car, I told her who I was. If she recognized my name, she gave no indication. I told her who my father was, and even that brought nothing but a blank stare. I asked her about the phone call I answered up in the tower that one night. Told her I knew it was her on the line. Told her what she said. And while this drained the color from her face, she told me it wasn't her. She said she never spoke to me. Was never in the trunk of a car.

Never, ever. None of it. Nope, nope, nope.

I took the hint and let her be after that.

The phone lies. The phone loves to lie.

That's what George Walton's long-dead daughter had told me in the tower on that final night, and I believed her because I had heard my own voice come from that phone too, and I knew I never placed those calls. Or (playing devil's advocate here) if I did make them, I had no memory of it.

On May 28, 2013, at 1:18 p.m., *I did* send a text to Kira's old number, one that said:

Meet me at Jaffrey Point 3:45 PM 7/12/2010!

I'm not exactly sure why. Superstition, maybe? I didn't know what would happen. Kira had been gone for three years. I imagine her parents had switched off her phone long ago , but the message didn't bounce back, didn't say *undelivered*, it just went. I was standing out on Jaffrey Point when I sent it, out on the rocks not far from where Rory Moir, Zack Kirkley, and Colin Booth had died. Prior to that, I had spent a few hours at Fort Stark, sitting up top next to one of the deep ammunition shafts, looking out at Wood Island between pages of a Dan Brown novel. Much like Spivey once had his favorite place to sit and think out on the beach, that had become mine. It was quiet, something I desperately needed, and I could watch the house from there, from a distance—something else I desperately needed.

I thought about Spivey and Kira a lot. Sometimes Chloe and Izzie. Not so much Alesia or Matty. What those two did was born of greed. A lust for something they were never meant to have, fed by Alesia's mother, who had a drive worse than them both. They weren't worth my thoughts. They deserved to be forgotten. But the others…

Spivey only wanted to get well.

Chloe and Izzie only wanted to be accepted.

And Kira… I tell myself she went along to protect me. While that may not be completely true, it helps me sleep on the few nights I'm able. It helps me accept.

Spivey once said nobody died out there. Until that particular night, that may have been true. Aside from everything I shared here, I've never found a record of anyone else. Not before and not after. Unlike me, the house had no trouble sleeping.

It sat still and quiet.

Dark.

Empty.

From a quarter- mile away on the shores of New Castle, it appeared as alone as I felt.

But was it?

Was anything out there?

As I stared at that house over days, nights, years, two thoughts chewed at me and refused to let go.

Do the dead know they're dead?

And Marston.

Offer yourself to Emerson and you will be reunited.

The first a question, the second a suggestion, and both of those things fueled the thought that came next.

What if I relit that pilot light?

Years of that before I could take no more.

On May 28, 2013, shortly after I sent that text to Kira, I stashed my red backpack along with a few other things at the bottom of the ammunition shaft at Fort Stark, and I rowed out to Wood Island for the first time in three years.

Setting foot on shore, seeing the house up close, I realized it had not only been alone all that time, but had fallen into complete neglect. Many of the windows were cracked or missing. There was a large hole in one portion of the roof, and it was sagging terribly in another. The widow's walk, once perched at the top of the peak, was now lying in a ruined pile near the crumbling foundation. There were several beer bottles scattered around, and I couldn't help but wonder if whoever left those behind had been younger than sixteen. Was Emerson still collecting tokens or had he moved on?

I found a rusty shovel in what was left of the storage shed. I hadn't brought one, which was silly considering what I had in mind. I suppose part of me knew the house would provide.

In the kitchen, the sign that once contained Spivey's rules was no longer there. None of the appliances remained (old or new), and judging by the damaged cabinets and scuffed floor, it was clear someone had come through and taken anything that might hold value. The living room was no different. No television or stereo, nothing like that. There was an old couch mashed up against the wall, but the window behind it was missing, and Mother Nature had reached in over the years and done a number on it. The cushions were wet and rotten with holes. When I stopped moving, I could hear the rats living inside for a quick second, then they went quiet too, waited for me to move along before they returned to whatever it was rats did.

Although my back and pelvis had healed up as best they could, I sometimes felt a twang of pain when I walked. Cold weather brought it on, sometimes rain. When I grew anxious, agitated, or stressed, it came on worst of all, and when I turned to face the staircase, my lower back was on fire. I used the shovel as a cane to take the handful of steps over to the landing, the blade biting into the rotten wood of the floor. And when I arrived at the base of the stairs, I was so thankful for that shovel—if I didn't have it to lean on, I certainly would have collapsed.

Cracked glass, the frames layered with dust, the wall was still covered in photographs.

Spivey was there.

Kira, too.

Chloe and Izzie standing on the beach looking out over the water.

There were none of Matty. None of Alesia, although I could still feel her around me. Like if I turned fast enough, I'd catch her coming down the stairs behind me like she once did a lifetime ago.

One of the largest photographs was a family portrait—Keith, Pam, and Spivey. The three of them with their arms around each other, smiling for the camera. They looked genuinely happy, and that made me happy for them.

There was a picture of my father. Younger than I remembered him, somewhere in his twenties. He was wearing a blue button-down shirt, khaki shorts, and grinning from the stern of what had to be *Annabelle*. The sky was bright, the sea was blue, and there wasn't a speck of land in sight. Made me wonder if Lester Rote was on the boat with him. Unlike *Merv*, *Annabelle* had vanished after the big storm and had yet to return. I had no doubt it would.

The photograph of Chief Whaley and his wife was smaller, only about four inches square. Unlike the others, there was no dust. This picture seemed newer than the rest.

I vaguely remembered Whaley's wife had a cancer scare a few years back, but it turned out to be nothing too serious, just a cyst in her throat. She checked in to Portsmouth General at eight in the morning and walked out at two in the afternoon. I saw her about a week ago at the annual New Castle plant sale. She looked well.

I suppose the picture of me should have frightened me, but it didn't. I expected it. Not finding it might have been worse, but there I was, hanging slightly crooked next to Kira's photo. Me about an hour earlier out at Fort Stark standing next to the ammunition shaft. I was holding the rope in that one, playing it out down the hole, the top of the noose slightly visible. Still trying to decide if I could go through with it. Marston's words rattled around in my head.

Offer yourself to Emerson and you will be reunited.

If you're reading this—my final note, my truth—you know I eventually did. I would have burned it all otherwise.

Do the dead know they're dead?

The answer to that is yes, although maybe not at first. Time moves differently... after.

The thought of holding Kira again filled me with a warmth I hadn't known in more than a decade, and I found myself looking up the steps, toward the hallway above.

I'd see Spivey again... the thought of that was nice, too.

Like returning home after a long trip away.

I didn't go upstairs, no need for that. I was here to go down.

With the blade of the shovel, I pried up the floorboards above the place I knew the basement stairs to be. That only took me a few minutes. The digging though, that went on for a while. I'm honestly not sure how long. It might have been days, maybe even weeks. Once I started, the motions became mechanical, fevered. I lost all track of time, and there was only the digging—deeper, deeper. Particularly after I uncovered what was left of the rotted steps under all that dirt. That's when I really started to move. They gave me direction, renewed purpose.

I didn't have to dig out the entire basement (although I would have), only a path down, a path to the furnace, and when the blade of my shovel finally clinked against the metal, I stopped only long enough to cry. From there, I used my hands. I found the small door securing the pilot light, pried it open.

"I'll be with you soon, my love," I said, surprised by how loud my voice sounded echoing off the dirt.

My hands were shaking so bad, it took me several tries to get a match lit, but I did. As I brought it toward the ignitor, I felt Kira's fingers around my hand, holding my wrist, guiding me.

Together, we relit the pilot light.

Together, from that moment forward.

Nik nok.

AUTHOR'S NOTE

Seven.

That is the number of times I changed the name of the town in this story from New Castle to something else. There was Millbrook Harbor, Coldwater Cove, Foxhollow, Ravensbrook, Thornbury, Ashford Mills, Misty Haven… I liked that last one—Misty Haven. New Castle nearly became Misty Haven on several occasions. None of those names felt right, though. New Castle isn't a fictitious town. It's a real place, a sleepy little town on a real island off the coast of New England. My family and I moved to New Castle in the summer of 2019, about a year before the world ran a practice drill for the apocalypse. We bought a beautiful house from a loving family, renovated it from top to bottom, and made it our own. New Castle is the location of our "forever home."

You see my dilemma, right?

This is a book of fiction.

(It is, right?)

You can't use the name of a real place in a book like this.

(Of course not. I would never do such a thing.)

But… hypothetically… if I did, how would that go?

In Authorland, this is how that sort of thing plays out.

I sent the book to my agent. While I've made several attempts to hide from her over the years, she knows where I live. The town name jumped out at her, and she quickly shot me an email.

"You know you have to change that, right?"

I told her I would.

(I think that time it became Foxhollow.)

Then I quickly changed it back.

When submitting the book to my publisher, there's this form you have to fill out listing any real people or places mentioned in the book. I penciled in New Castle and sent the form off. I waited for an email from some lawyer in New York to appear in my inbox. It would come, I was sure of that.

I could live with Misty Haven, right?

I didn't want to change it, though.

I can throw a stone from my front porch and hit a house built in the 1600s. Paul Revere rode through here. Wars were fought here (two forts are still standing as a reminder of those, and the active Coast Guard station at the corner of the island is a hint at what could come).

When you move to a place as old as New Castle, you hear your share of stories. New Castle has a history. New Castle has ghosts.

Wood Island sits right off the coast of New Castle, visible from our beach. Every night, the lights burn bright from inside the white clapboard house with the red roof. And if you watch closely, you'll see people moving around in there. Knowing what I do for a living, the locals were quick to share the stories they'd heard about that place as children. The same stories kids whisper to each other today. One in particular stood out to me.

In 1972, two bodies were found on Wood Island. Skeletons buried on the beach.

(Go ahead and Google it, I'll wait.)

Local police (presumably from Kittery, Maine, or Portsmouth, New Hampshire) took the initial report. The state police came in shortly after. A state's attorney told reporters it was a federal matter. The case went to the Boston office of the FBI...

Sounds big, right?

That's what I thought too.

I contacted the FBI and was told they have no record. I reached out to the state's attorney mentioned in the story—still alive and practicing—and he told me he had no recollection of the events. Kittery PD, Portsmouth PD—nothing. New Castle PD had no file either. Bodies were found (a real-life event) and vanished.

The newspaper article Billy Hasler discovered on his father's desk a few hundred pages back is real.

In a previous book, I told you about the *what if* gene. The little thing every writer has that starts to itch when we learn this sort of thing. I went down a research rabbit hole and learned all I could about Wood Island, both fact and lore. New Castle and Portsmouth, too. Cemeteries. Haunted houses. A body found hanging in one of the local forts.

A picture started to form.

Pieces of a puzzle came together.

A story.

Billy's story.

Much of what you just read is fiction, but there are equal parts of fact mixed in to add a little flavor. I'll leave it to you to decide which parts are what. If you do a little research of your own, I think you'll be surprised by just how much of Billy's story is real.

That takes us back to the name of the town, New Castle.

To date, the lawyers at my publisher haven't asked me to change it. If you're reading this, they never did (or they hit send on their email after someone hit the *GO* button on the printing press). Either way, the name stuck, and I'm grateful for that. Changing the town name would have been like tugging at a loose string on a sweater. If I changed the town, I'd have to change Wood Island, Henry's Market, Piscataqua Cafe, the Wentworth Hotel… all these other places that were (and still are) real.

Names shouldn't be changed, not when they are part of history.

History shouldn't be changed either.

Not even the scary parts.

Especially not the scary parts.

If you happen to find yourself in Portsmouth, New Hampshire, there are boats that will take you out to Wood Island. I promise you, it's worth the trip. *Merv* is on display. Walk the beach. Take in the light-house. Explore the house with the white clapboard siding and red roof. It's all shiny and new again. Be sure to say hello to Emerson for me. He's never far. If you happen to brave the steep steps to the widow's walk, see if you can spot *Annabelle* out there on the water and give Lester Rote a wave. Be sure to leave by sunset, though. Bad things have been known to happen after dark.

Until next time,

jd

New Castle, NH

August 1, 2024